Praise for *Hari – A Hero for Hire*

'Hari Majestic is a worthy addition to the ranks of hardboiled gumshoes in great crime fiction. But it's his creator Zac O'Yeah who is truly the criminal mastermind. *Hari – A Hero for Hire* lives up to its name as a majestic tour de force of world crime literature. The attention to detail, the pitch-perfect style, the intimate knowledge of Bengaluru life are all used to perfection. This is not just another terrifically entertaining read, it's one of the best crime novels set in India written by anyone'

– Ashok Banker

Hari – A Hero for Hire
A Detective Novel

Zac O'Yeah is the author of the popular comic thriller *Once Upon a Time in Scandinavistan* and *Mr Majestic! The Tour of Bengaluru* which is the first of the Hari Majestic crime and detective series. He has written twelve other books which have been translated into several languages. Previously, he worked in the theatre and music business in Sweden until he retired early, at age twenty-five, to come to India. His books range from bestselling detective fiction to history and travelogue, and he has also translated Indian literature into Swedish. A veteran travel writer, he is a frequent contributor to *National Geographic Traveller* magazine, a columnist with *The Hindu Business Line* newspaper and is also an influential literary critic. *Hari – A Hero for Hire* is the second book in the Hari Majestic series. Follow Zac and Hari Majestic at www.zacoyeah.com

Other titles in the Hari Majestic series

Mr Majestic! The Tout of Bengaluru

Hari – A Hero for Hire

A Detective Novel

ZAC O'YEAH

PAN

First published in India 2015 by Pan
an imprint of Pan Macmillan India,
a division of Macmillan Publishers India Private Limited
Pan Macmillan India, 707, Kailash Building
26 KG Marg, New Delhi – 110 001
www.panmacmillan.co.in

Pan Macmillan, 20 New Wharf Road, London N1 9RR
Basingstoke and Oxford
Associated companies throughout the world
www.panmacmillan.com

ISBN 978-93-82616-65-8

This is a work of fiction. All characters, locations and events are fictitious. Any resemblance to actual events or locales or persons, living or dead, is entirely coincidental.

1 3 5 7 9 8 6 4 2

Typeset by Manmohan Kumar
Printed and bound in India by
Manipal Technologies Ltd, Manipal

To Anjum,
without whom
nothing.
To Bengaluru,
for everything.

I wouldn't be surprised if my grandmother didn't have an affair with a Labrador. Now that I look at my muzzle, I see there's a white patch on it. I wonder how it got there.

The Heart of a Dog, Mikhail Bulgakov

Don't take tension, brother.

Munnabhai MBBS

Health is wealth.

An old saying heard someplace

Prologue

Hari Majestic felt like an unadulterated hero. He heard deafening explosions and smelt acrid smoke. He was ready to save the world, if it should turn out to be necessary.

The festival season was peaking and Bengaluru was, as usual, being blown into bits. The good thing with the racket was that nobody paid much attention to two men on an abandoned rooftop. Hari and Triplex too had bought crackers that they threw down to create a smokescreen. They were pros.

The October air was cool but Triplex, Hari's second-in-command, was sweating. Given that his normal attention span never exceeded three seconds, he had been remarkably focused for a change.

'Damn hot,' said Triplex.

'What's hot?' asked Hari, pretending to mend a cable hanging limply from a coconut palm.

Triplex aimed a small camera at the squat pink hut across the lane. Using the digital zoom he framed a close-up of the woman taking down laundry. It was possible to make out details as fine as her eyelashes. 'Majestic, you've got to see this!'

'What?' It was afternoon and Hari was suffering from a bad headache, which made him irritable, but in another couple of hours the sun would mercifully slip down the horizon. It had been a painful day. It wasn't always easy to be a hero.

'The item, of course.'

'Don't get ideas,' said Hari. 'We're professionals and she's off limits.'

'Chill out, Majestic. I was just making an observation for the report. This is a romantic-jealousy case and so it follows that our job is to peep at her.'

Hari kept his cool. 'Good, try to think like a detective.'

Triplex's appreciation of female beauty was his main drawback as a detective. Three seconds after the woman had gone inside with the washing and there was nothing else to zoom in on he said:

'So what do we do next, Majestic?'

A propensity to be easily bored was his second greatest drawback.

'Wait and see.'

'What if nothing happens?'

'That would be the best thing that could happen.'

Triplex lit a cigarette and started watching a song-and-dance clip on his phone. Hari Majestic scanned the muddy lane below for layabouts, lechers and louts – not necessarily in alphabetical order, of course. Just the other day, he too had been an unemployed drifter, struggling to find a job, but now, all of a sudden, he was a professional full-time hero and the director of a detective agency.

Here on the rooftop of an old brick shed in a slum, spending the afternoon spying on a beautiful woman, he had plenty of time to think things through. It had all started a week ago and his thoughts meandered back to that momentous day when everything changed.

1

How to Get a Hero's Job

Buildings were like people. Sometimes a modest exterior concealed the scariest things and vice versa. 'Take this one for example,' Mr Majestic said to himself.

From across the busy street it looked like a humble and homely building. The three-storey box of monsoon-worn concrete could have belonged to any middle class part of town, but for the record it stood a short motorbike ride west of Bengaluru City railway station in Rajaji Nagar – a vast area of shops, random offices and small-scale industries, a sprinkling of temples to improve your life, hospitals that claimed to cure anything, including death if that was what you suffered from, and a public crematorium if you didn't survive despite taking every precaution.

Hari Majestic scanned the office building's facade again but it bore no signs of imminent threat. One just couldn't tell. He was used to weird things and creepy places. But entering police stations and related establishments made him queasy without fail, since he never knew if he was going to come out a free man.

The motorcycle's engine cooled and he slid off after padlocking his military style helmet to the handle bar. The late monsoon wasn't really happening and therefore the city was experiencing drought. Small clouds of dust mushroomed from underneath his rubber sandals.

As for a getaway plan, he had parked his bike so that it faced away. The motorcycle manufacturer's motto appealed to him: 'Made like a Gun, Goes like a Bullet'. It dated back to the days when armies bought Enfield Bullets in bulk. In case he must make a quick escape, he'd simply run out, hop on and bugger off.

On foot now, Hari negotiated the disorderly traffic, dodging a decorated elephant headed to a temple festival nearby – it was that time of the year. Thanks to his alert senses and decent karma he had, so far, always survived the Bengaluru streets.

On the first floor of the building there was a chit fund company optimistically named Interesting Pyramidal Investment Scheme Pvt Ltd. He headed up the stairs to the next floor, where he noted a firm that went by the somewhat cryptic name of Telegraphic Intimations. Hari had read about telegraphs on Wikipedia but had no clue they still existed in the IT capital of India. Up a final flight of stairs, he spotted an unglamorous glass door with a low-key sign for Total Safety Security Agents & Services stencilled across it. There he stopped and hesitated for the second time.

Considering that the Bengaluru police force only had 16,109 men and women in its service, private security was big business, employing hundreds of thousands of people if you counted every guard at every ATM, jewellery shop and posh residence. So if almost everybody else worked in the security industry, then why shouldn't he get his share? Besides, it'd be a safe employment as the demand was only going up with the population. Just in Hari's lifetime, Bengaluru had grown from a million or two to over ten, rowdy-sheeters of no fixed address and other floating population counted.

He stopped to contemplate a notification painted on the wall, stating that applicants were expected to be well-groomed, clean-shaven with sober haircuts, dressed tidily in ironed shirts and formal pants in a colour no brighter than brown.

Rolling his head sideways to loosen up the neck, he pepped himself, checked his looks in the door glass: no matter how much coconut oil he used, an uncontrollable protuberance stood up from his forehead as if he were born on a bad hair day. He was wearing his showy nylon shirt and frayed stonewashed jeans. Plus, he had grown a trendy moustache. One of his friends had one, so he'd followed suit. Perfect disguise, nobody would think of him as a potential detective. Would-be movie star, yes. Detective, no.

Trouble was, Hari had never applied for a job before because he'd been too busy staying alive. However, at the age of twenty-eight, it seemed to him that only salaried people mattered in the matrimonial ads. In fact, most people of his generation, born in the 1980s, were married and had kids, mortgaged homes in apartment buildings with 24-hour security and decent jobs with the possibility of receiving a pension before God took them off to their next reincarnations.

Somehow Hari had found himself left behind on life's backburner, as if he were starring in a movie that nobody wanted to produce.

He dug in his jeans' pocket for the printout of his bio data. The CV was almost truthful. In Math and English, two subjects he had a bizarre aptitude for, he really hadn't been at the bottom of the bin in elementary school, though he had got expelled at the age of thirteen. As an adult, he'd spent very short stints in jail so there wasn't much of a rap sheet to speak of. In the CV he listed it as 'judicial training' and, indeed, he had aided the police as a snitch.

At the end of the list of professional experiences, after 'tourist guide' (euphemism for tout) and 'investment adviser' (ditto for two-bit conman), it read 'hero'. That was where he saw himself heading. However, hero jobs didn't come knocking on a daily basis.

No point worrying too much, he told himself. Then he pushed open the door, ready to face whatever waited on the other side.

Hari took in everything in a semi-split second. A lifetime's worth of street smartness had given him a phenomenal analytical capability. It was an open-plan office and could have been, say, a cheap travel agency for indentured labourers to go to the Persian Gulf or a low-end call centre, if it wasn't for the fact that so many of the staff looked like ex-army men – very orderly, no anarchy, matching haircuts.

The receptionist was the token woman and she added a touch of colour to the scene: curly hair with henna and dolled up in a blue sari, green eyeshadow and golden eyeliner.

'*Oota aayita*?' he greeted her cheerfully, enquiring whether she'd enjoyed her lunch already, and handed over his CV.

She glanced at Hari, the way you did at an insect in somebody else's tiffin box, before she grabbed the paper, put it in the in-tray on her desk and went back to battering her keyboard.

He waited politely for half a minute.

Nothing happened. He knew, judging from her position as the needle's eye that every camel had to pass through, that she was likely to keep him waiting until the end of the world or perhaps even longer if she could have her way. When Hari leaned forward, he saw that she was browsing a matrimonial website and spamming its members with special offers for Prenuptial Domestic Espionage: ₹17,999 for a basic check-up – economy, latest pilgrimage, left wing affiliations, life expectancy – and ₹27,999 for an executive package deal – CV, BP, TDS, STD, HIV, H-1B, 2BHK, etc.

'So can I go for the interview?' he said.

'We'll call you, don't call us,' she said.

They didn't care much for PR, he found, when he asked for a brochure detailing services and rates. She said, 'Not available.'

'But that email you're sending out, how about you BCC it to me?'

'Confidential.'

She was born to be a secret agent, he thought, a little impressed, but didn't give up, 'Well then, *please*, can I meet somebody who will explain the *job requirements*?' He made it a point to speak in English, to impress her.

'No.'

Limited and basic vocabulary, Hari noted and shot back some polysyllabic words using a form of highly specialized roundabout grammar typical of bureaucrats who wanted to stretch or obscure a statement – a linguistic proficiency learnt from his uncle, who, before he was arrested, had been an expert at writing unfeasible legal contracts and getting people to sign them against their better judgment. 'Under the circumstances, I request you to kindly do the needful and revert my application, because, for your information, yours is not the only agency in need of competent staff.'

She took a bored look at his CV. She frowned at something. 'Hero, is it?'

It worked. Hari learnt a first lesson about how to become a private eye: just like fire must be fought with fire, only a bureaucratic mindset can beat a bureaucratic mindset.

The second lesson followed shortly. Powerfully built, but balding, reading glasses, very clean white shirt, stainless pants, ironed tie with the 'Total Safety' monogram, the Detective in Charge of Operations (DCO) had his desk in the centre of the office surrounded by about a dozen identical men crouched behind stacks of flimsy printouts and brown files.

This detective's desk was clean: no magnifying glass, gun or anything remotely scary. A no-smoking sign and a desktop computer with smouldering incense sticks jutting out of the ventilation slots at the back of the bulky screen. An empty steel tumbler of either chai or coffee.

'Had your coffee?' Hari said, politely assuming that the detective was a fellow south Indian filter coffee aficionado, and chattered away. He introduced himself as Mr 'Harry' Majestic, a hero in the making, 200 per cent of the right stuff.

The DCO interrupted him, 'So what exactly do you want?'

Hari felt that he had been quite clear about it. But one ought not to challenge people who were ostensibly superior and senior, because the DCO might get angry if Hari pointed out a flaw in his detection skills.

Instead Hari took charge. In most organizations, whether private or public sector, the buck never stopped halfway across the office floor. He implanted a thought in the detective's head, 'Maybe it's better you take me to your leader?'

While the DCO thought this over, to test his power of observation, Hari filched a pencil from the stand on his desk. No problem.

The DCO drew his hand across his baldness as if he still had hair. However lush his bush had been once upon a time, its barren remains were reduced to two crew cut carpets of stubble that wormed their way around the high-shine pate. He cast suspicious eyes at the things on his own desk, as if they were there to spy on him, and then, finally, stood up with a nod.

'I think you should talk to the boss,' he said, picked up some papers from his desk drawer and escorted Hari to the next level of the game.

The lesson from this round was that a successful private eye was never a beggar, but a chooser, and that nobody had a chance when it came to somebody like Mr Majestic. Triumphantly, Hari felt that this was one game that he was bound to win.

Time for a third lesson: the Master Class. The managing director was dressed in a uniform-style khaki sari and enthroned in a private glass cubicle where the air-conditioner rumbled, and when she saw Hari at the door she stared hard, trying to place his face. A *woman*: Hari hadn't expected that. In his experience, women were always far more complex than men. He'd have to tread carefully. No more pencil-filching.

The DCO handed over a bundle of reports, perhaps clues to murders or bank robberies, and the responsibility of speaking to Hari. She dismissed the DCO and, glancing through the reports, went on to sign her initials in the bottom right-hand corner of each sheet.

Hari greeted her in a friendly manner with liberal displays of an ear-to-ear smile – only one tooth missing, the side effect of previous heroics – and said, 'Madam, had your food?'

She didn't reply. The Total Safety Company maintained the maximum level of secrecy. But there was a dismantled tiffin carrier, its lids and bowls littering the desk, the compartments for various food items empty. Dots of non-vegetarian gravy stained the keyboard of a sleek laptop. Being a private investigator appeared to be a job that earned you not only bread and butter, but full meals too.

Hari instantly knew that he had a lot to learn from this lady. Because it was never what you saw, but what you were meant to think you saw, that mattered. And here, that picture was almost perfect. A purring miniature waterfall added an idyllic quality to the cubicle, a soothing calmness, except when the motorized pump spluttered and hiccupped with the power fluctuations.

A shelf held awards and trophies. The Madam must have been quite the heroine in her heyday. One engraved metal sheet mounted on polished wood commemorated her captainship of a field hockey team at the Asian Games and a diploma issued by a religious organization acknowledged her eminent service to humanity.

Hari decided to break the ice with polite small talk in chaste English. 'Seeing that you're a busy lady, Madam, I don't want to disturb, but I require some clarifications. I've read about detectives in magazines and seen you people in movies, where you always are the heroes, but what does the job actually consist of?'

Her fountain pen stopped moving, it hovered above a file, the springs creaked in her office chair and the Madam turned to the window next to her desk. Those all-detecting eyes lost themselves in the distance and then she said, 'That I can't tell you.'

'Why?'

'Our profession is such that we can't discuss our work with non-clients.' Behind her back hung a poster with 'dos and don'ts' for the security-minded, but Hari had long suspected that if one were too tight-lipped for one's own good, one lost out on a lot. 'May I know why you're asking?'

'Madam, I wanted to find out if the job suits me,' he said enthusiastically.

'That I doubt.'

'How so?'

'People with criminal records are not suitable detectives and judging from your appearance you'd be on the police's rowdy-sheets. No parental guidance, juvenile delinquency and then remand home; correct me only if I'm wrong.'

She was way smarter than Hari had anticipated. He rolled his head sideways, neither quite admitting nor denying anything.

'Besides, you're scrawny,' she added.

Not ready to accept the truth about his limited muscle mass and other handicaps, Hari decided to go for another approach. If he had been pulling off a scam, it'd have been a bad idea to change tactics midstream, but this was about displaying one's versatility in order to get a job, so he ignored the warning bells. 'Madam, I appreciate your high level of discretion. I can't tell you how many detectives I have gone to, but they all fail the test. They start bragging about cases they've solved, uploading the data on every crime and victim.'

She rocked in her chair. 'So what are you saying?'

'What do you think I'm saying?'

'You want to engage our services?'

'You have the mindset of a genuine detective,' he complimented her. 'My own boss, on behalf of whom I myself have come, expects 800 per cent discretion and nothing less flies.'

'You mean that you're a middleman between us and the client?'

The way she pronounced 'middleman' sounded not much different from 'poop stuck under my boot' but Hari was used to being looked down upon so he nodded merrily. 'Correct. So how much do you charge?'

She shook her head. 'First things first. Who is the actual client?'

Hari drew a deep breath and made the logical next move. 'It is classified information and shared on a need to know basis only. If I were to recommend you to my boss, I must first know what you can do for her. She pays premium rates for premium services.'

'I see.' Cash was the key, as always. She laboured with her answer almost as if it was a trick question. Finally, she said, 'Supposing your client wanted to buy that house over there but didn't know who owns it, we'd find that out.'

Hari turned to gawk at the building across the street, outside which he'd parked. *Strange.*

'That house?' he echoed.

'Yes, that one.'

'The one right there?' He thought: *if a normal human wanted a house he or she would go to a real estate agent rather than a secret agent.*

'Or the Enfield Bullet parked in front of it,' she said.

But Hari already knew who owned his motorcycle. He couldn't help but blurt out, 'So that is what detectives do for a living?'

It may have sounded disrespectful. By then he'd been at the agency for quite a while and so far nobody had told him anything of interest and he had still not been offered coffee or tea. It was unheard of.

The Madam shook her head. 'Not at all, I said that supposing somebody wanted to know, we could find out.'

'How do you find that out, then?'

'That is a secret,' she said. 'Now what is this affair regarding?'

Hari spotted a hint of irritation in her voice and decided to stop pushing and begin pulling. But before he had time to spin a story, she continued, 'And you're involved in it somehow?'

Hari suspected that she was viewing him with increasing distrust.

'Only as an intermediary,' he said, perhaps a tad quickly. Even to his ears it sounded as if he were bluffing.

'And why exactly were *you* chosen?' she asked and suddenly the tables turned. Perhaps it had been a mistake to try and browbeat a veteran like the boss of Total Safety Security Agents & Services. The moment she caught the whiff of something suspicious, she turned into a deadly sleuth.

Before he came up with an answer, she attacked with semi-lethal force. 'For what purpose are you asking these questions about our secret work? Who are you?' Since there were no other suspects to narrow in on, Hari was put through the third degree, shouted at, and he imbibed the important lessons that a detective must:

A. Never take things at face value;

B. Never be too sure of oneself;

C. Preferably not lie too much.

The undeniable truth is, of course, that we cannot usually foresee the negative fallouts of our best deeds. The Madam's questions focused largely on his shady past and soon Hari was worrying that he had broken some invisible law by trying to apply for a job, and that his next reality check might involve basket-weaving in Parappana Agrahara Central Jail. Before he could come up with satisfactory answers to any of her questions, she demanded, 'Do you have any identity proof with you?'

Rather traumatized, he decided that this was the right point of time to take his leave. He said, 'Bye-bye Madam, and have a safe day.'

It was better to wish people well and remain friends.

2

How to Handle a Win-Win Situation

Hari thought that it was a place he could consider moving to. Known, due to its location, as the Main Drain Semi-Slum, it was a warren of narrow residential roads that were neither a complete slum, nor quite part of the city plan. There was no water supply. Women and girls carried drinking water in colourful plastic pots from the hand pumps near the railway station and the sewage drained out of the alleys into a canal, the eponymous Main Drain that mercifully – during this time at the end of the monsoon – had been properly flushed by the rains, so didn't smell as bad as one would have expected.

On closer inspection, the area was quite pleasant. About quarter of a furlong from the bazaar, the lane widened into a community chowk with a tailor's workshop, a shop called Hot Chips with its oil on full boil, a liquor shop and a banyan tree girded by a low platform on which were bidi smokers, coffee drinkers and an outdoor barber. A wholesome scene, save for a lending library renting out tattered pulp at a nominal cost.

Hari's associate detective, Mr AC Gaadi, had parked his autorickshaw in the middle of the square as if to take a nap. His acting was too realistic, thought Hari, who spied on him through a pair of binoculars that his technical expert Doc had found in an army surplus shop.

Hari and Triplex had set up the Position Alpha surveillance station on the shell of a partly collapsed brick shed at the corner of the square. They chose it because it was one of the few taller buildings, a forgotten Bengaluru Electric Supply Co property. It housed a large transformer on its flat roof. Downstairs they'd hung a handwritten sign saying: *Repair Work in Progress. No Admission without Permission. Trespassers Prosecuted. Bye-bye and all the very best.*

They pretended to fix broken power lines, though of course, all the electrical installations were illegal, a lethal mess of cables strung from house to house, a multitude of highly personalized connections to the grid where it passed through the transformer.

In the afternoon, they saw the woman come out again to bring home water from the hand pumps. She walked with the delicate gait of a lady elephant, the water pot resting against her gently swaying hip. Triplex almost electrocuted himself on a loose wire.

Any man would believe in the power of love upon the sight of her. Except, perhaps, her husband, who'd naturally do his best to suppress any powers that love might aspire to … considering that here she was, alone at home, and there might be potential fun on offer for a lovely, lonely woman.

A week earlier, fleeing from the Total Safety Company office, Hari had been blasting himself for the colossal failure he had made of the job application. It should have been a simple thing. Crossing the road again, he had glanced over his shoulder. *Was he being watched, were they perhaps going to frame him as a scapegoat in some investigation?*

Then he told himself to be sensible, he had merely asked for information and one can't be put in jail for that. The Madam's attitude may have been a brusque way of telling him to find work elsewhere, but the paranoid fool within Hari wasn't listening to reason. Paranoia being one of the most contagious diseases known to man, Hari surmised that a detective's actual job might be to instil it in people, so that they behave.

Only when he got on his bike and strapped his second-hand military helmet on, did he feel in control again. He gunned the engine and to be on the safe side he returned to Uncle Mamool's office via a roundabout route. He drove up and down streets, past the futuristic ISKCON temple twice, crossing and re-crossing the railway tracks, to make sure that nobody was following.

In his absence, Hari treated Mamool's office like home – the location was ideal, in a somewhat rundown commercial complex in CD Road, one of the busiest streets in the town's scruffier parts, not far from the railway station. Mamool wasn't Hari's biological uncle, but the lover of the woman who had adopted him. After she died, Mamool had let him sleep by the door in a cardboard box stuffed with old newspapers and sawdust, and taught him many legal and illegal things.

He felt a bit bad about not having visited Uncle Mamool for weeks. But with Mamool festering in rehab, the bills were piling up: office rent and medical fees. Hari's liquidity was low and it wasn't as if the coffee-wallah was going to give unlimited credit.

In moments of distress, his closest friend Triplex – who was intellectually incapable of worrying about anything – was the only one who could offer solace.

'How is that possible? The secret spies didn't want to hire you?' asked Triplex, who had goaded Hari to go and apply in the first place.

It was later that same day and Hari was still stressed out after the encounter.

'To begin with,' he said, 'there's a *difference* between spies and detectives.'

'Same difference,' said Triplex.

They had met up as usual at Deluxe Bar. It was a cut above the other shady bars on CD Road and the perfect place to take stock of the failures of one's life. One sat in a creaky cane chair and nursed one's beverage instead of tanking up quickly at a counter before some other drunk rammed an elbow into one's gut, causing the rocket fuel to ignite and projectile. Triplex guzzled super-strong beer, while Hari ordered a fresh lime soda with gin. Sweet and salt.

He tried to learn life skills from Triplex who was a true artist when it came to surviving the odds. His childhood friend was much like the brother Hari might have had if he'd belonged to a proper family. In earlier days, they used to peddle VCDs on the streets, sourced from Triplex's father's shop, and later in life, while Hari did his best to move up the food chain, so far unsuccessfully, Triplex stayed faithful to his video piracy. He was nowadays so deft that he could film in the dark of a cinema hall even if the attendant was standing right next to him. His real name was Neel Yeenappa, but in film circles everybody knew him as Triplex because of his fondness for triple-X movies. His shop had been seriously raided by cops sometime back, the stock confiscated. Yet he remained remarkably optimistic.

Triplex was out on bail, but you wouldn't have known it if you saw him – flamboyant as ever in stretchy white and red nylon garments and white cowboy boots that squeaked with every step. He wanted even blind women to know when he stepped into a room. He talked about the possibility of taking over another shop in the Bilateral Market Shopping Complex and risk going back into business. However, as long as he was still waiting for his court hearing, reopening the shop was a strict no-no. He'd go to jail.

He also often said he'd take a bullet for Hari. So far, he just hadn't had an occasion to do so. Actually, one of the few things Hari could be happy about was that very few people planned to murder him.

'Then what?' said Triplex.

'And then: not hired but nevertheless fired,' said Hari and filled him in on the spooky experience.

'But you still want to become a full-time hero, right? Why not open your own detective agency and pocket the profit?' Then Triplex added, as an afterthought, 'I take that back. Bad idea. It means that you'll have to follow lots of, what's it called, laws and regulations.'

It was a fantastic plan. In a flash, Hari saw the neon sign: *Mr Majestic, OK & Co, Heroes for Hire*. 'OK' were his uncle Ontappa Kallappa Mensinkai, alias Mamool's initials and as the detective bureau would have to be headquartered in his uncle's office it would be a good idea to include him on the signboard.

'You're a genius,' he said.

'I always was.' Triplex grinned and ordered more beer.

'You see, when people refuse to explain what they do and how it is done, it means that there's nothing to it. Because if the customer knew how simple it was, they couldn't charge money for it, could they?' He excused himself.

At the cybercafe across the street from the bar, Cyberspaced-out Internet Paradise run by Hari's old friend, the hi-tech whiz, Doc, he rented a booth. The computers were slow because the users downloaded too many viruses, but on the other hand, Doc gave Hari unlimited credit. Hari did a quick search and found hundreds of websites belonging to a huge number of detective agencies and private security bureaus, and going through the FAQs and promotional hyperbole that marketed their services, he found out exactly why companies such as the Total Safety Security Agents & Services prospered these days. He made mental notes and prepared a sketchy plan.

A few minutes later, he stepped back into the bar with a smile wider than his face. In the meantime, Triplex, always supportive of Hari's schemes, had saturated his beer glands and was extremely open-minded when Hari told him about his findings.

Detectives were in high demand now that the massive middle class had got into the habit of spying on spouses, servants and employees. Any class-conscious family worrying about its social status was a perennial source of revenue. Therefore, an estimated 60 per cent of investigations were related to grooms and brides. Was the bank balance, as stated in the marriage proposal, actual or fictional? Did they drink, smoke, eat non-veg or have other immoral habits? Had there been prenuptial romantic liaisons with the maid or driver? Postnuptial infidelities in turn led to divorce-related muckraking and bonus work for the detectives.

The remaining 40 per cent consisted of corporate chores such as verifying the CVs of candidates applying for jobs, but didn't end with that. Once they hired, companies took out contracts for employee surveillance to prevent godown pilferage and industrial espionage. On top of this, agencies supplied watchmen, bouncers and bodyguards at daily, weekly or annual rates.

There were thousands of detective bureaus – nobody knew exactly how many since there was no licensing authority. Hari, therefore, concluded that being a detective wasn't much different from going on being oneself, it wasn't even necessary to be adept at martial arts – actual detectives rarely jerked somebody's eyeballs out of their sockets while taking down confessions in shorthand. He'd only have to make some changes to his lifestyle, but then again Hari didn't see much of a future in scams and touting anyway.

Regarding other highly specialized skills, like fingerprinting techniques, they'd simply consult with Aunty Pushpa, the Sub-Inspector at the local police station. Hari could ask her for free advice the next time he went there to snitch on somebody. There were ways, if one knew the ropes.

'We're going to do all the stuff that the cops don't, can't or won't. We'll be just like James Bond and Agent Vinod.' Since Hari had to employ a DCO to act as his deputy director, he naturally thought of the resourceful video pirate as the best candidate.

'Oh yeah?'

'Sure,' said Hari. 'Don't you also want to become a hero?'

'Right, so let's simply do what makes sense to us,' said the newly appointed DCO as he burped alcohol fumes into the air.

'That's what I'm talking about,' said Hari.

'We can do everything we want to do,' said Triplex.

'Yeah man,' added Hari to encourage him – after all, the pay packet and perks might not be so competitive.

'Anything at all,' said Triplex, 'and nobody can arrest us because we are detectives.'

'Eh, but within limits,' said Hari.

'But almost anything?'

'Kind of almost,' Hari clarified and felt his gloomy mood vanish.

That was how they'd play it then: unlike the Total Safety Security Agents & Services, there was going to be nothing furtive about their detective business. They'd go high profile and be real life CD Road heroes. He was going to save the world, or, at least, suitably small bits of it, and get well paid for it too – for according to the law of karma, the best long-term profits were for the good guys.

In the dimness of Deluxe Bar, they went through the plan in detail, with Triplex, the visionary, faffing, and Hari making calculations on a paper napkin. The main initial investments were glossy visiting cards and a stylish signboard, in flashing neon, to hang outside the office from the veranda railing. Hari had a small cash buffer kept aside for his uncle's medical bills, but he would stake it all on the new detective agency.

It was a clever move on the part of the receptionist at the Total Safety agency to send out spam to users of online matrimonial bazaars. Websites for finding prospective spouses, such as ProperDesiNuptials.org and BluruTechieSeeksTechieToWed.co.in, had upwards of forty million registered customers resulting in an estimated million weddings per year. As both parties needed to hire detectives, it meant there were millions of job opportunities. According to Hari's findings, some clients bought prenuptial check-ups in bulk, testing a dozen suitors in one go before deciding on the best buy. Getting such clients meant striking gold.

Supposing they undercut Total Safety, whose cheapest prenuptial package came at ₹17,999, and sold budget check-ups at ₹15,000, they should find plenty of takers. It was a small sum considering that the average middle class family borrowed hundreds of thousands of rupees towards wedding costs. Dowries included cars, or at least a Japanese scooter, and washing machines, if not an imported German bathroom. There were trousseaus consisting of silk and gold-embroidered saris and jewellery, and wedding guests expected to be treated to five-star multi-cuisine banquets at the cost of ₹999 plus taxes per plate – or ₹4,999 if the groom or bride was from Delhi or Mumbai – so what was an additional ₹15,000? Even if they priced their services at rock-bottom, they'd still be looking at a decent annual turnover provided they found one new client every day of the week – except Sundays when Hari himself planned to trawl online for a suitable bride.

With only a limited number of auspicious wedding dates during any given year, people couldn't afford to dilly-dally either. If Hari partnered with his own astrologer, Sri Pandit Pundit could pass on clients against a commission.

It was a win-win business. They came up with the dirt, they got paid and the customer told other potential clients the juicy gossip that turned up on so-and-so, averting a potentially scandalous marriage. If they didn't find anything, they'd still get paid but the customer would be so much happier ever after.

Triplex, of course, saw great prospects too. Here was the profession that allowed him to act as a decoy and seduce any number of brides to check for loose morals and film it all to supply the waiting client with video proof. Plus there was the chance of getting famous. He was a true tapori: a santoor played in the hot tandoor of his head; tablas hammered out an arrhythmic beat in his heart; and like everyone else in CD Road, he dreamed that one day his life would be turned into a blockbuster talkie with song-and-dance numbers. He quickly counted on his fingers and whooped.

'Bombaat! If I find one hot chick that can't be schedusched, I'll make her my dove! *Defectives*,' Triplex wisely pointed out with a hiccup, 'are born, not made. Schorry, detectives.'

The same week marked the onset of the October puja period – one celebration followed by another, auspicious days for slaying mental demons or starting a new project – so Hari worked fast on the design for his posh signboard.

He headhunted all his friends to work with him. Their get-ups and perks forced him to blow what financial buffer he had. Expenditure didn't end with that, anybody who was anyone hit him up for cash. He had to book advertisements to get press coverage and was advised to staple ₹100 notes to the hand-delivered press notices. Otherwise the journalists didn't read them. Then there was catering for the inauguration, it cost a bomb.

Hari revised his budget and found that he couldn't afford the classy signboard he'd spent days designing. Instead he used the inkjet in Doc's cybercafe to print an A4-sized nameplate that read *Mr Majestic, OK & Co Proper Investigations by Heroes for Hire (Confidential) WE HAVE NO BRANCH* and borrowed a roll of tape. Things can only get better he kept telling himself while trying to position the makeshift sign outside the office in a manner that wasn't seedy.

Then he went down to the street and looked up at the railing where he had dreamt his neon sign would be. The A4 didn't look too bad; after all it was a start-up. Seeing his own name in print, in bold type, was the first step on the career ladder and hopefully there'd be cash inflow soon or Hari was going to have to move out of the Puncherwallah Complex.

This was his personal to-be-or-not-to-be moment.

3

How to Throw a Deadly Party

Hari studied the pink concrete hut which had such a beautiful name: Prem Vilas or 'the abode of love'.

Huts in the Main Drain Semi-Slum generally had one or two rooms, but were homes to joint families of up to five generations. Housing in central Bengaluru was dear and even a businessman, the owner of a coffee mill, say, had to make do with a minuscule plot in an area like this.

The couple they were spying upon, a coffee miller and his wife, were privileged as only the three of them – they had a small daughter – shared the dwelling. It may have been named Prem Vilas in bygone days when the inhabitants believed in love, speculated Hari. It was fortunate from the detectives' point of view that there were no windows to the hut and just one door: it would have been tricky to keep a larger residence under round-the-clock surveillance. And luckily, the puja period coincided with the bright half of the lunar cycle, when the October moon was at its fullest, which compensated for the absent municipal streetlights.

The miller had told Hari that his own parents stayed with his older brother, who managed a coffee plantation in the hills, while his wife had a few sisters and a mother who all refused to move away from her native place, a small town where the pace was slower than in Bengaluru. It struck Hari that one problem was the complexity of modernity: they were a nuclear family, which was a very un-Indian thing from the point of view of social stability. If there had been in-laws in the picture, she wouldn't have been able to have fun – or be suspected of having fun – of her own.

If the wife left the house while her husband was at his mill, then AC Gaadi, with his rickshaw conveniently parked right outside, would offer her a discounted ride. If she went to a cybercafe, Doc would sit in the next booth and spy on her online activities using special software. He'd pretend to be a computer engineer proposing to scan her computer for viruses, for her own protection, while he'd do the very opposite – install the correct viruses. If that didn't work, he'd get into her booth after her. Most people never erased the cache memory and cookies, so the browser gave a detailed account of everything they had viewed online.

That was the basic plan. If she did anything a decent wife wasn't supposed to, they'd find out. If she was cheating on her husband, Hari would buy a box of disposable napkins and deliver the bad news to the client.

On some level it was quite wonderful how far he had advanced, having just opened his detective bureau the day before.

The inauguration stirred up interest on CD Road – a crowded street of cinemas, small shops that sold everything under the sun, shady drinking dens, manic-depressive traffic and hordes of floating populace. The office lay in an old building called Puncherwallah Complex, on the first floor, which Hari shared with Cyberspaced-out Internet Paradise, the astrologer Pandit Pundit and Suleiman's canteen which was also known as Veg Non-Veg Friendly Mess. On the ground floor was a garage. In the alley behind, bumpers and wheel rims, carburettors and mufflers, rusty crankshafts, dented bonnets and worn tires were stacked along the walls.

At the bottom of the alley, Hari put up a party tent with a snacks table and two outsized stainless steel thermos vats of coffee and tea, breathing steam like improvised explosive devices. Freeloaders milled about, munching from trays of Bombay sandwich, cocktail samosa, mutton puff and sweets such as cashew barfi and Mysore pak procured from a sweetmeat vendor in Mysore, where Triplex had relatives.

This was all part of a strategy. It was rare to get a free lunch on CD Road, but any well-wisher who dropped in at the Mr Majestic, OK & Co premises that day returned home with a full tummy. To them, the launch of a detective agency was like the opening of a grocery store, except that it had nothing to sell. But people would adjust their mindsets – as soon as they faced a problem, they'd come to him. Word of mouth was, as everyone knew, the most powerful marketing tool. And a burp was just another way to say it.

He scanned the crowd for local VIPs. They were all here for his sake. Whenever he spotted a prospective client, he picked up a platter with mixed snacks and set off to network. A minor hazard, Hari acknowledged to himself, since the snacks were either deep-fried or made from pure ghee, was that the clients were more likely to need a cardiologist than a detective.

On this big day, Hari had dressed up in his most formal outfit: a pair of silvery, shiny pants and a golden shirt that made him look like he had come from outer space or a 1970s movie. He was pulling at his moustache to make it grow another inch. It was still downy. He had just wrapped garlands of marigold around the handlebars of his motorcycle. It had been scrubbed and polished – the toughest bike in the universe, a gleaming black Enfield Bullet 65 bought third-hand. Its 499cc single-cylinder cast-iron engine gave off a loud thump – unlike the later models that had aluminium engines – and it could hit 100 mph when used by Special Forces to patrol the Thar Desert or the Nagaland Hills' wilderness. Though in Bengaluru, of course, the streets were so constipated that you'd be glad to move along at 5.7 mph which was the average traffic speed within city limits. Nevertheless, it was a hero's bike, and now, on this day, it had become a blessed bike.

According to the venerable telepathic soothsayer of CD Road, Pandit Pundit, picking the right inauguration day and hour would guarantee Hari many clients and massive cash inflow. Thus, the chosen day was the Ayudha Puja, or Worship of Implements, when every vehicle, whether motorbike or bus, was given a thorough wash and transformed into palm groves on wheels, festooned with banana leaves and flower garlands. Fat pumpkins were smashed before them like crushed traffic victims, the juice splattering all over.

After throwing the pumpkin, Pundit turned to Hari and made a mystical statement, 'Welcome to the life of a grown-up. Please don't waste more time on pointlessness.' He was right as always. It was high time to grow up and Hari had been postponing it for too long.

Hochiminh Meshtru had come. Hari touched his old schoolteacher's feet and received a gift in return, a poster to put up in his office. This was a surprise because till the point of time when Hari was expelled, Meshtru used to call him an 'illiterate ignoramus' and predict that he'd end up in jail.

Then Hari noticed that the poster was one of those graphically illustrated ones issued by the Bengaluru Police and written in poetic rhyme to make it easy to memorize:

ALERT! ALERT!! ALERT!!! He is a Cheat. Don't get Beat.

A Rupee in your Hand, is Worth Two in his Hand.

If you care for this caution, you become Hero.

If you ignore this caution, you become Zero.

'Thank you Meshtru ji, you're far too generous,' said Hari, hoping that the poster wasn't meant as a rebuke for his past sins.

Meshtru lectured him, 'You're still full of that restless energy that always made you such a rascal, boy. But I have a case for you to work on. Have you been to a hospital lately?'

'No, but eat some fresh snacks and you too will stay hale and healthy,' said Hari cheerfully.

The old teacher couldn't resist having a few of the cholesterol torpedoes – fat green chillies coated in golden deep-fried gram-flour batter.

'Ah! Think you'll live forever? You're so lucky to be young and ignorant,' Meshtru said as he studied Hari's new business card. His eyes were tiny, yellowish and far apart, reminiscent of germs trapped in test tubes, searching for human tissue to infect with something incurable – like lack of self-confidence. His Adam's apple was huge and it bounced up and down when he harangued Hari, who got a sinking feeling that his achievements amounted to nothing.

Meshtru gave him an endless, convoluted account of how he had been experiencing throat pain and the hospital that treated him wanted to sell him an overpriced plastic surgery to reduce the visual impact of his Adam's apple. Hari heard him out, he didn't want to appear impolite, not on a day like this and not to somebody who exerted a certain influence in the local politics.

'Meshtru ji, if there is a requirement to investigate maltreatment of your esteemed character, we will need sufficient data on the crime and crime scene,' said Hari.

'Sickly Hospital,' Meshtru said in a conspiratorial voice. 'It's been our neighbourhood clinic forever. Can you believe it's been sold off to some foreign venture capitalists and renamed Globalized Style Super Speciality Hospital? But what good is that supposed to do us common people? I'm telling you something fishy is going on, boy.'

'Is that so?' said Hari. So the slummy backstreet clinic was being upgraded. Cool, he thought, the city was developing.

While Meshtru rambled on about the commercialization of hospitals – which made him see the red flag of Maoism on the horizon – Hari wondered what was wrong with Hochiminh Meshtru. Ex-firebrand and Apparatchik, in the 1970s Meshtru had walked optimistically from village to village like so many urban idealists, including, briefly, Hari's uncle, OK Mamool. They had taught the rural folks to read and write their way out of oppression. Then, after the collapse of communism, he became religious and had taught slum kids like Hari. And now here he was today, raving, 'Isn't it your *duty* as a detective to ensure that the working classes also get their healthcare provisions? In this world of increasing privatization, don't you think it is a matter of *solidarity*?'

Hari suppressed a sigh. He didn't want to admit it, because it wasn't good PR to be bored with the public already, but he regretted the choice of motto for the agency, 'Don't Worry, Everything Can Be Fixed by Mr Majestic's Heroes'. Not every damsel in distress was going to be in a push-up bra like in the movies. If sundry people began to regard him as some altruistic psychotherapist who'd listen to their woes free of charge it all might backfire.

'Solidarity is top class, have some coffee, Meshtru ji,' said Hari and handed him a tall glass of filter coffee from the wire basket that a child labourer was carrying around. He added, 'I've never been sick anyway.'

Of course, he was underplaying it – he'd had his fair share of fine-calibre bullet holes, cracked ribs, blunt-instrument brainings, animal and human bites, general evil … but the only telltale sign of a rough life was a broken tooth in his ear-to-ear smile. Then Hari took off with a hearty, 'We'd be happy to take on any assignment Meshtru ji may have for us and our fee structure is a very modest fifteen grand per week.'

That silenced Meshtru.

In another corner of the back alley, AC Gaadi's autorickshaw was being decorated with jasmine garlands tied to the roll bars. It was a beautiful and agile vehicle quite famous around CD Road for its high-decibel in-flight karaoke entertainment system that always blasted the timeless tunes of Michael Jackson. Its three wheels had been shoeshined. It had got a fresh coat of paint, bright yellow on top and black on the bottom half, symbolizing its nature as the king of the day and the lord of the night.

Although Hari had his Enfield Bullet, a detective agency needed more than two wheels – in short, it required a company vehicle, so when Hari started recruiting, he first spoke to the deadliest driver he knew to increase their total number of wheels from two to five. Fearless but not godless, Gaadi was tough as an old ball of chapatti dough, but within his rough-and-ready exterior lurked a gentle heart of fourteen carat gold. Today, he had dressed for the occasion in a starched white dhoti, bare chest. He'd even taken a vow to remain vegetarian for the duration of this current auspicious lunar cycle.

Hari observed how lovingly Gaadi unscrewed the retractable machete blades attached to the vehicle's nose wheel and washed them to remove traces of cartilage belonging to the occasional rash driver who'd had the audacity to overtake him. There were new stickers on the vehicle. Gaadi had renamed it 'Volvo' and an advertisement covered the rear window: *Mr Majestic OK & Co: Proper Investigations (Confidential), the Only Fully Computerized Detective Agency – CHEAPEST Hourly Rate, Weekly Assignment Minimum 101% Discount, Everything Can Be Fixed, WE HAVE NO BRANCH.*

Gaadi had demanded a SATNAV device upfront, in case the job took him and his rickshaw into uncharted territory. Hari pointed out that in Bengaluru a SATNAV was of no use because roads were constantly dug up at random by various inscrutable authorities and declared one-way or were rebuilt into underpasses or flyovers. So no electronic map, however hi-fi, remained up-to-date. People were used to this and navigated by enquiring, which is why directions between any two points in town, no matter how complex the route, involved no more than two words: 'Ask anybody'.

But rickshaw drivers were non-negotiable by birth. Therefore Gaadi became the first rickshaw-wallah to have a SATNAV and Hari had made it a point to mention this in his press release.

He helped Gaadi tie some palm fronds to it so that the rickshaw looked like it had sprouted out of a coconut.

The 'Fully Computerized' claim was something the agency's cyber expert, Doc, had suggested they must advertise – as proof of being with the times. As far as Hari knew, Doc was born as KF Pinto, a Catholic of Goan ancestry, but he preferred to be called Doc, or, in his online avatar, as '.doc', which sounded technically advanced. His Internet-chat-download parlour in the Puncherwallah Complex was full of somewhat antiquated computers that often hung. But Doc insisted that these comps be included in the venture and so Pandit Pundit was sent upstairs to bless them, smear their screens with kumkum powder and sacred ash, so that they'd surf on for another year.

This auspicious October day was not only for the worship of detective equipment. Tools of all trades were given their dues: shopkeepers humoured their swipe card machines with an extra swipe, doctors prayed that their scanning machines and defibrillators would meet many new patients, and in the underworld rowdy-sheeters sharpened their machetes and tested them on rival history-sheeters. All the little things that modern man relied upon, for survival and death, took centrestage.

Of course, Doc too wanted special electronic gadgets in order to sign up as a detective. Although his requirements were too complex for mortals to understand, he assured Hari that they'd make a difference. For $29.99 only, from web shops abroad, one could get surveillance kits containing the latest top secret equipment developed for the CIA and MI6: surplus equipment was sold online for half the price of the government-issue version. When they arrived, Doc's bugs looked cheap and plastic, and were made in China, but they nevertheless cost a load of money.

Since their use was strictly prohibited in India, everything had to be smuggled through Nepal.

Triplex very reasonably asked for nothing but aphrodisiacs from the famous wedding bazaar in the old town of Delhi, where all manner of gilded condoms and gorilla costumes were peddled to lovers who wished to have more romance in their day-to-day life. To prepare for his new heroic career, Triplex had waxed his chest and pierced his nipples with brass miniature beer cans.

It started to get crowded in the alley by the time the Sub-Inspector from the neighbourhood police station, Mrs Pushpa, arrived with her entourage of banana leaf decorated Hoysala jeeps and garlanded Cheetah motorcycles. She was no more than half an hour late, which proved that she respected Hari more than if she had been many hours late.

Some shady acquaintances of Hari's ran off at the sight of the uniforms, but other passers-by got curious and thronged the alley to see if something terrible had happened.

A hush fell. The dais had a background of purple velvet with the tinselled Mr Majestic logotype on it. Howling with distorted feedback, AC Gaadi's karaoke microphone was hooked up for the speeches – later there'd be a Michael Jackson singalike contest.

'*Yellarigu vandanegalu mattu Hari-ge hrudayapurvaka abhinandanegalu*!' said Pushpa by way of greeting. She wore her parade uniform. This was her first time as a chief guest on a dais. She was after all only a Sub-Inspector at one of the town's approximately 150 police stations. Then she added, 'Ready for the bad news?'

People squirmed nervously, fearing a scolding. Hari beamed at them.

'The crime statistics are going haywire. From having been a backwater town inhabited by pensioners and gardeners, Bengaluru is booming when the rest of the world is crashing. But as you are well aware, money will attract unlawful elements: thieves, burglars, scammers come by train and bus and plane from distant places for looting purpose.' In her view, the city, and the rudeness of urban life, had eroded the trust that survived in the villages of India. In the lengthy speech that followed, she emphasized the importance of every citizen taking responsibility for creating a society free of law and order problems.

It was hard-hitting. Within a few minutes most of the audience, an assortment of CD Road lowlifes, drifted off to the snack table again or were talking loudly on their phones.

Hari kept the Sub-Inspector company on the dais, it never harmed to be a sycophant. She usually watched out for him and he tipped her off when he heard anything of interest. And although she, as a police officer, couldn't formally support Hari's project by passing on jobs to him, she had mentioned, in confidence, that she viewed it as excellent rehabilitation for the boys, because they'd almost certainly lower the crime rate simply by going straight. So it was good to be friends with the law, definitely better than going to jail. She held the same view, which was why she had agreed to be the chief guest.

She continued, 'We pride ourselves on being modern, but then you only want this, then only that and you don't want to earn it by honest labour. When you finally get it, you merely want the next thing on your list, okay?'

The audience rolled their heads sideways, they didn't simply want things, they craved them – and that was why they had moved to the city.

'What happened to honesty and diligence? I can't see it anymore here on CD Road!'

There was a murmur but she ignored it. Hari smiled at various hostile faces, to defuse the insult. He prayed that nobody would throw a sandal. Finally, she addressed Hari and his colleagues:

'Whatever you do, you must do it without breaking the law … or you will be put away alongside any criminals you catch, okay? Follow my advice and become the solution, instead of being the problem.' The last words were spoken with a significant glance at Hari. After what seemed like another two hours she finished her list of complaints against the male half of the population with the words, 'Remember, you may be reborn as women in your next lives and then we'll see – drunkards and hooligans will molest you all. Then we'll see, okay.'

Hari nodded solemnly. It was a well-known fact that the Sub-Inspector's own husband had deserted her, hopped onto his brand-new scooter one evening shortly after their honeymoon to go buy betel nuts and vamoosed. Therefore, Pushpa Aunty loved to give every man a good dressing down and on a day like this she savoured the opportunity. After her speech, Hari almost thought he knew why he'd done it. People who travelled northwards returned to CD Road with stories about him living like a fakir in a cave in the Himalayas.

After the booing and hooting stopped, Hari stepped across the dais to declare a vote of thanks and present the Sub-Inspector with a bunch of freshly stolen flowers. He cleared his throat and spoke as pompously as he could, this being the highpoint of his life, 'When we connect the dots here, we have drunk in so much wisdom about the malefactors who hide amongst us, and their malafide racketeering, but we assure you that crime in this town will soon be a thing of the past.' He went on to give a brief introduction to the core operative team, who got their fifteen seconds of fame when Hari invited them to the dais: Video Surveillance Specialist Mr Triplex who was wearing his white cowboy boots; CCC-S, or the Cyber Crime Cell Supervisor, Mr Doc and Mr AC Gaadi, head of HR, the Hit & Run division.

The last crew member was a minor embarrassment on a day like this. Hari announced that the Legal Senior Director, or LSD, was on temporary loan to another institution – in fact OK Mamool was becoming a long-term research project at the detox facility where he was incarcerated. The scientists were amazed at his seemingly indestructible liver and several institutes wanted to buy it for medical research. There was some applause at this wonderful thought that somebody from CD Road could be so important.

Once the police left without arresting any of the guests or detectives, Gaadi brought out two plastic barrels of spurious bootleg from under the passenger seat of his rickshaw.

He demanded that Hari drink with him. Hari was hesitant; he knew who his friends were and alcohol wasn't one of them. It was fun at first but always got him into trouble later. However, Gaadi didn't take kindly to those who refused a toast. 'You got to be a little humane,' he said.

So Hari gulped it down. He immediately felt that familiar lurch: a rapid sinking through rubbery softness and then being catapulted upwards in a bungee-jumpy motion. Soon he was very upbeat, his tensions gone; the unruly lock of hair on top of his head stood remarkably erect and his moustache slithered like a furry worm on his upper lip.

What a day! Again there was a surge in guests as word spread through the bars that somebody was plying people with free drink. Hari staggered about dancing and singing 'doesn't matter if you're black or white or brown' on Gaadi's karaoke system. It was a night to remember, but by the time Hari woke up his memories had disappeared down one big black hole.

Happiness ended the moment he opened his eyes and two fluorescent scalpels of icy strip light sliced into them while the spittle-stained concrete floor of his office pressed hard against his face. Home sweet home, he thought because the dark cloud had a silver lining: at least he didn't wake up in jail.

4

How to Avoid Taking Tension

'There, I see them,' said Triplex. 'Will I get a Diwali bonus?'

'Who are you looking at?' asked Hari, still struggling to overcome the titanic hangover.

'Lover boys at three o'clock. I solved the case on the first day, Majestic. I'm a natural.'

It was getting hot on the brick shed's roof. The afternoon air felt like the detectives were imprisoned inside an idli steamer. Smoke from innumerable households wafted up. The odour of kerosene and cow dung blended with the tasty fumes of cooking masalas.

Hari shifted his binoculars to check out the two young men in tight jeans walking towards Prem Vilas.

Triplex was zooming in with the camera, but Hari – always aware of the big picture – noticed that they stopped at every door.

'Triplex, lesson one in detective work is to pay attention in order to interpret what you see correctly.'

'I just did.'

'And what do you see?'

'They're collecting funds for a community puja.'

'Which means?'

'That they're probably under cover,' said Triplex. 'Like we are. Aren't they?'

'You simply watch too many movies. The lover, if he exists, won't be under cover – he'll simply be a normal guy, a postman or a milkman with his cow, making a house delivery.'

'Or a woman,' said Triplex and licked drool from his chin. He had spotted a female neighbour who interested him.

'The wrong kind of movies too,' said Hari and noticed smoke coming out of a hole in the front wall of Prem Vilas. Either she too had started cooking or she was heating water for a bath. *Did she expect a visitor?*

'Shall we throw some crackers then?'

'Why?'

'To see what happens. Maybe she'll get scared, come out and do romantic stuff with those two.'

'In your dreams.'

Thus the afternoon played itself out, school kids walked past, barefoot, many of them lugging schoolbags almost double their size, squealing with delight at the thought of tiffin at home.

It was getting late in the day and the light turned golden and mellow. Darkness fell with its smells of frying onion, flickering cold light of televisions, FM music from radios and the cows coming home. Model slum, thought Hari. Finally the coffee miller too returned after shutting shop and nothing of interest had happened in his absence.

'When do we eat?' asked Triplex with a wistful rumble from his tummy. He never ate anything that didn't swim in animal fat and he, of course, expected to be treated to non-veg at company expense. The perks had been one of the important negotiation points when Hari hired his employees, since he couldn't guarantee salaries. They all worked on a commission basis.

'Dinner break is at midnight.'

'Come on, Majestic. The bars will be shut. That's unfair.'

'That's reality. It'll be good for your liver and other organs. Do you have any idea what a liver transplant would cost you? You should take good care of the one you have,' preached Hari.

'You're so mean,' said Triplex.

Sullen silence on the roof for three seconds, until Triplex forgot he was supposed to sulk. He dug out a pack of Gold Flake and lit a cigarette, smoking it in his cupped hand, the way it was done in gangster movies. He was flamboyant, bought cigarettes with filters, while the normal thing to smoke would be bidis.

'Isn't it awesome,' said Triplex.

'What?' asked Hari.

'We're detectives now, Majestic. And to think how the other day we were total losers.'

'Yes, hard to believe,' said Hari to his second-in-command. But he knew that the visible world contained within it a deeper truth – veiled and arcane, glimpsed now and then, usually offline, if one was perceptive. This hidden truth shaped one's destiny and through it the cosmic chaos was processed into order.

The whole surveillance operation had been initiated that same morning. Unbolting the office door, he found that the day outside was unfolding at full blast, as it usually did – but today was one of those days when life was no joke. His tongue appeared to be unshaved, his skull was a mass of writhing angry wasps stinging from within. There were no customers at his doorstep: CD Road was full of people but nobody was headed for the stairs up to Hari's detective bureau.

That was a bit lucky, because his flashy new clothes were covered in gore, shirtsleeves torn off and buttons missing. Walking down the stairs was an uphill task. Even a simple thought was excruciatingly painful; the wasps inside his head constantly upped their ante and attacked every lobe of his brain, molesting it ferociously with their stings.

Hari went to the alley behind the office and saw that the boys must have had a lot of fun. The area bore the typical signs of a theatre of war, a direct bomb hit, say, in downtown Kabul. The legs had been ripped out from the snack table, the richly decorated rented shamiana was partially burned and the beautiful flowers had been stomped into the ground. Among all the broken glass, he noticed shards of Peter Scot bottles. He remembered that cases of the not-so-cheap whisky had arrived from somewhere.

He was having flashbacks. *Had the night ended in a series of explosions? Oh no … but … yes*, thought Hari as he did his forensic analysis, recalling through the mental haze how Gaadi and Triplex had fired rockets, forgetting that the shamiana formed a ceiling over the alley. The missiles had put the cloth on fire. The thermos vats had come to use as protective headgear.

AC Gaadi slept wrapped in banana leaves in his autorickshaw, on his cheeks were knife cuts smudged with dried blood, but he was alive enough to speak up when Hari prodded him. Luckily, no hearses were required.

'That was the best party. Let's have another one soon. What's the time?'

'October,' said Hari, who was still suffering from the semi-black out and his voice made a hollow echo inside his head, the wasps getting restless again.

'Too early, swami, don't wake me up yet,' said Gaadi and turned his back to Hari who felt the burden of directorship acutely.

His second-in-command might help them see things through.

'Where's Triplex?'

Gaadi shrugged. Where indeed was Triplex when he was needed? Hari checked his two mobile phones, office and residential numbers, but there were no new messages. In his pockets, he found a notebook and a Reynolds pen with red ink, red for highest priority. He had bought sets for his staff, different colours for each so that they needn't sign their names: blue for Triplex for obvious reasons, green for Doc and invisible ink for Gaadi who anyway didn't know how to write. He noticed that pages were torn from his notebook and recalled vaguely that there was something he mustn't forget, but he fed the ominous thoughts to the mad wasps in his head and went across the road to Deluxe Bar to breakfast on a pint of Thums-Up cola, which contained no fruit and had no nutritional value, but was sugary enough to set his head straight.

The soupy dusk of evening lived on forever inside the bar, dim and merciful to the hangovers of men, protecting their puffy faces from carcinogenic sunburn. The bartender was at the counter, eating an omelette with lots of green chillies straight from the frying pan, the spoon scraping off the non-stick coating. There was nobody else there, except for a sweeper sweeping up the cigarette butts of yesterday – smoking in public was prohibited, so it was always a good idea to sweep the evidence under the carpet.

'Guru...' But Hari was interrupted by the much too talkative bartender who informed him that somebody had busted the backdoor the night before, after closing time, woken him up – he slept in the bar for security reasons – and bought, on credit, two cartons of fine whisky. Now he wanted the money. Although the info-dump made Hari suspect the worst, he said, 'Since I am a professional detective, I can help you track the defaulter down.'

But the case had already been solved. The bartender produced an IOU that Hari apparently had authored. It was in his own handwriting, with red ink no less, and when he compared the chit with the tear marks in his notebook, he knew that things were going to get worse and worse. Whisky worth ₹15,000 or what was earned on a week's investigations blown on one party.

Shortly afterwards Anand, the coffee-wallah, burst into the bar.

'AC Gaadi told me you'd be hiding here,' he shouted.

He was only about thirteen and too young to set foot in an establishment like this, but his face was able to convey such mature suffering that Hari did his best to be nice. The conversation was stiff at first.

'Had your breakfast?' said Hari.

'Had it, and you?' said Anand and handed him a scribbled bill. The sum was surprisingly huge – another week's worth of investigations would go into paying it off.

'Having,' said Hari and rubbed his sweaty forehead. 'You're trying to cheat your most loyal customer?'

In his characteristically caffeinated rapid-fire way of speaking, Anand itemized the amount, every single broken glass and the two badly dented stainless steel thermos vats that were practically scrap metal.

'Boss, that's horrible,' said Hari and groaned. 'I simply can *not* believe it.'

The coffee-wallah stood arms akimbo, eyes accusing Hari.

'Sorry, Anand,' said Hari and dug after his wallet, a very nice one that he had bought to keep his new business cards in. It was empty save for the cards.

Broke as usual, Hari promised to pay for the damages with a free consultation, if Anand ever needed a detective's services, and wrote another IOU at the back of a business card.

'Is the consultation transferable?' For such a small kid Anand was very sharp, he was going to have his own coffee estate one day.

'Does it say non-transferable anywhere?' said Hari to humour the boy and wished him bye-bye and all the very best.

Hari breakfasted on credit and in the company of self-pity.

He was nursing a final tumbler of fizzy beverage, when Anand turned up again. He hadn't come alone. A big monster of a man was with him.

Previous incarnation? Hari had this habit of cataloguing people by determining – intuitively – what they had been in earlier lives: it helped him figure out whether they were a threat or not. If, for example, somebody had been a reptile previously, Hari knew that the person would be slippery. A poisonous snake was dangerous. A frog, on the other hand, suggested a Francophone colonial connection; many Frenchmen had settled in the south Indian town of Pondicherry and practised their exotic culinary culture, including frog-hogging, and some of them therefore obviously took rebirth as frogs before they got a chance to become humans again. It was a well-established theory and almost certainly correct, too.

This gent made Hari think of a bull, the Spanish kind that wrapped bullfighters around its horns. Hari's initial impulse was to run, but his legs were too weak and he merely resigned unto his poor karma.

There was the heavy rosewood table between them, a solid bullet-proof obstacle, and in the worst case he could slide under it and play dead. The one thing that reassured him, however, and made him stay put, was the plump little girl that held on to the hem of the bull-sized man's tent-like shirt. She wore her hair in plaits, with bright ribbons, and in her other hand she had a two-rupee plastic bag of colourful bonbons.

'He needs your help,' said Anand.

'Oho. Can I offer refreshments?' said Hari, relieved. Frankly, he didn't think it was appropriate to consult with customers in a bar. But he adjusted; there wasn't much else to do.

The prospective client asked for a Limca for the girl, rum for himself. Hari convinced the bartender to extend his credit to also include a peg for Anand. Had a concerned citizen set foot in the bar right then he'd have been perfectly justified in filing a case – for serving alcoholic beverage to minors – but when the peg was set down before him, coffee-wallah Anand's eyes forgave Hari some of the morning's shocking stuff. So perhaps one could say that it was a good thing that concerned citizens were rare in the vicinity of CD Road.

Anand introduced them. The free detective consultation was going to be traded off to the proprietor of the Supernice Sugarcandy & Coffeeworks. That way Anand was going to clear his debts with the coffee mill and so the IOU business card Hari had given him was now placed on the table between them.

'Bhaskar, how can I be of help?' asked Hari.

'That's Bhascar with a C, my numerologist suggested the change.'

How he knew that Hari hadn't pronounced his name with a C was a mystery, but Hari didn't fuss about it.

'So tell me, Bhascar…' said Hari.

'That's *Mister* Bhascar to you. And if you wonder, the C is a Roman numeral. So that I will earn in hundreds of rupees, as if the cow of plenty herself moved into my house.'

'Oho, you must have a big house then,' said Hari.

'I hear that you own a detective agency,' said Mr Bhascar who sipped the Old Monk with a grim expression. 'What exactly can you do for me?'

Hari rattled off some spiel as if he was an old hand in the business. Life was about acting; performing the part allotted to one as best as one could, in the hope that the theatre management extended the run of one's show. Hari had always held this to be true and studied and rehearsed his role, though unfortunately his show didn't have a coherent script. While speaking, he discreetly pressed a speed dial button on one of his phones; the other, on the table, rang. He picked it up, adapting a businesslike tone:

'Majestic and Company, how may I help you? … Good Lord! There's strong reason to suspect that you are bugged if there are breathing noises on the phone line. I'm in a top-secret meeting right now, but this is a clear-cut case and I'll dispatch our team to dismantle the concealed surveillance equipment within seven minutes.' Hari had read somewhere that it was a statistically proven fact that people who believed in numerology felt the mention of seven was preferable to any other number. So he used it liberally and he could see that the auspiciousness of the number made Bhascar warm up. 'We wouldn't want those lovely seven daughters of yours to be all over the Internet in their birthday best. Your Holiness, it is always a pleasure to be of help to you and give my regards to the queen when you cut chai with her in London next.' While he pretended that he was listening to the static noise, he formulated a plan, and then he clicked off the phone. 'Sorry, it was a world leader whose identity I cannot divulge. Where were we?'

Bhascar turned to the coffee-wallah. 'Anand, will you take Galata out to play.'

'But…' said Anand and reached for the rum, then let his hand fall and stood up – trying to pass on a bad debt, his leverage was low. 'Galata, come, we'll buy candy.'

'I already have bonbons,' said the little girl, determined to stay on and hear the grown-ups talk. She had been twisting her head this way and that, thrilled by it all. 'And I want to finish my cool drink.'

As Hari compared daughter to father, he found that apart from certain features – big eyes and a tendency for corpulence – their personalities differed. He presumed that the girl had inherited her chirpy nature from the mother's side.

'Be a good girl, Anand needs somebody to play with. You're both too young to be in here anyway,' said Hari in an attempt to help out.

Grudgingly, she went with Anand.

'So you're having a problem with your missus?' said Hari, turning to Bhascar.

Bhascar's eyes grew wide and Hari noticed how red they were. 'You don't know how right you are!'

'I know exactly how right I am,' said Hari.

'But how can you tell?'

'That's a detective's job.' It was a gamble, but he knew that in a majority of the situations when men came to talk to detectives it had something to do with women, and vice versa. Besides, he had spotted a few telltale signs, 'That you love your daughter is obvious from the way you prevent her from hearing the wrong things. If your dilemma concerned business you wouldn't have sent her out. Also, if you didn't have a family problem, your missus would have been minding your daughter right now.'

Bhascar rolled his head sideways in appreciation, his bull's neck impressively flexible.

Hari did likewise, but a shorter, more professional head-waggle. It hurt when he rocked his head abruptly, but thankfully the wasps were gradually going back to their hellhole and ideas were on the move again.

The client's face crumpled up. 'Uh … but I can't tell you about it, you'll think me crazy.'

'No, I won't, I'll simply solve your problems,' said Hari. 'You have to trust me enough to provide me with a complete upload of what troubles you, crazy or not.'

Bhascar gazed down into his empty tumbler, then he grabbed the absent coffee-wallah's drink and downed it in one go. He studied Hari's visiting card. 'This consultation is free of charge?'

'Ninety-nine point nine per cent.'

'And how much will I have to pay then?' asked Bhascar, his eyes narrowing. The man was a businessman up to the nails of his pinkies.

'Don't worry, when your problem is fixed to your fullest satisfaction, we may consider a mutually acceptable bonus, but we never overcharge – you pay as you like. Nothing if we cannot solve your problem,' said Hari magnanimously.

'Is there any chance that my wife will find out that I've hired you?'

This man had many doubts – about his missus, about Hari Majestic as a detective. But at the same time, Hari realized that even a cheap client was a client. Although he was technically offering to handle the case for free, to pay back damages to the coffee catering equipment, he'd have to sell himself hard. To prove that he was a private eye it wasn't enough to create the impression that he knew what he was talking about. He also needed to implement the hypothetical knowledge in such a way that it proved useful to the client.

Hari lifted two fingers and the bartender repeated the drinks plus gave them a complimentary steel plate of sliced onions.

'No chance whatsoever,' said Hari. 'With us you are in safe hands and I will be the only one who knows, not even the field agents will be aware of your good name.'

Bhascar started munching on the onions. 'So what you're saying is that…'

'Let me share some basic facts. Statistically, one third of all humans are habitually and morally corrupt. There was a time when people trusted each other. Not so today, distrust is all we can take for granted. All the same there's less need to worry in Bengaluru than if you lived, suppose, in Los Angeles, since a population increase by a 100 per cent here only results in a 15 per cent increase in crime, while it's the other way around in America where criminals are much more efficient. How can you be sure who this person you call your missus is, who you share your home with, unless you engage us to scrutinize her activities? Only fools are trusting.'

'I'm not a fool,' Bhascar said.

'Not to worry, boss. There's no stigma attached to hiring a detective to check on a spouse's fidelity; on the contrary, it's completely normal and we recommend every happy family to go through it now and then to ensure that the happiness is everlasting. Our IT department will hack her email account without leaving a trace, ferret out data to prove it, if it is so, that she engages in lewd cyber romance. Our surveillance staff will use their telescopic camera to document her movements from a distance and special microphones to tap her conversations. We will put a practically invisible man on her tail, maybe, for example, dressed up as a rickshaw driver. If it comes to divorce proceedings our senior legal director – he's currently on a secondment but will be back in service by the time we need him – will oversee the preparation of the documents so that your case will hold up in court, the settlement shall be in your favour and you will win custody of the child.'

That last statement stirred up mixed emotions and Bhascar quickly downed his new drink, 'I'd rather die than find out that my wife loves somebody else.'

Hari saw that the deal was practically settled, 'It needn't come to that. It is our policy to hope for the best, but be prepared for the worst. It's called situation one-oh-one.'

'Situation one-oh-one?'

'Yes, somebody may have inserted himself like a zero between the happily married ones, but we just can't know – that is why there is a zero there, signifying the unknown factor. I'm a bachelor myself, but that doesn't mean I don't care for marital obligations. In the best case, we shall find that there is nothing to find, and that you have been worrying unduly, as the solid evidence may show that your missus is not guilty of any wrongdoings.'

'Uh,' said Bhascar, 'if you don't find anything, how will it prove that there isn't something going on?'

'I think you answered your own question.'

'How?'

'Boss, you see, for something to be going on, it has to be an ongoing activity. It is in human nature that a habit, whether good or bad, manifests with certain regularity. If you are a saint, you will do one good deed every week. If you are prone to vice, say if you have the drinking habit,' said Hari and made a gesture to the booze tumbler, 'you will take the drink minimum once a week, more likely more often, yes?'

Bhascar moved his hands away from the tumbler. 'Yes?'

'The same goes for any habit. People who monger mischief by nature partake in the mongering once in seven days – whether it is love affairs, drug habits or robbing banks. Anything that is not happening on a weekly basis, does not qualify as a habit; for example, you see that I am drinking a soft drink, hence we deduce that I am not an alcoholic. So if we keep your missus under round-the-clock surveillance for a week and nothing suspicious surfaces, no email or call or meeting of illicit nature, then it is safe to assume that she is not what we in the trade call "BC".'

'*Busy?*'

'No.'

'Uh, Before … Christ?'

'Bad character.'

Bhascar pushed the tumbler away from his side of the table. 'Looking at you one wouldn't think it, but your understanding of human nature is truly profound. I'm so grateful to have met you.'

Hari rolled his head sideways. His headache was gone and the adventure was about to begin. He whipped out his notebook and the red Reynolds pen.

'No mention, boss. So, her name is…'

So her name was Apsara. As Mr Bhascar spoke, Hari felt an unaccountable sense of honour – this stranger trusted him for no reason at all.

It appeared that Apsara spent her days at home happily and didn't mind being alone while her husband was busy roasting and grinding at the small coffee mill that he owned on the main bazaar corner. Their only child, Galata, went to a preschool across the road from the coffeeworks and, in the afternoons, she sat in the shop with her father, eating bonbons and helping him pack the coffee powder until it was time to go home for supper.

The food was always ready on the table, sometimes chicken, always ghee rice, at least two vegetables and homemade mixed pickle – and never any leftovers from the day before, always freshly cooked food. The wife sang to herself as she rolled out hot chapattis.

Bhascar revealed that earlier, when they were newlyweds and before Galata was born, they used to go to Lal Bagh Botanical Gardens on the weekends or sometimes to Nandi Hills by bus, but that had ceased.

'How did that happen?' Hari asked.

Once their daughter was born, Bhascar told Apsara that they couldn't afford outings, what with the dowry they must save up, if they wanted to buy the child a decent groom by the time she came of age. Apsara accepted his decision. After that they hadn't had any more fun together.

As the next step to curb his wife's unreasonable happiness, he stopped giving her spending cash and took care of the grocery shopping himself when the tarkari-wallah pushed his vegetable cart past the coffee mill. If she ever asked for money to go to the tailor to mend a salwar, he handed over the cash in carefully counted ten-rupee notes on the condition that she produced a bill. Even then she never threw a tantrum.

'Is the house clean?'

'She does the laundry every morning. Then she sweeps the house before she has her bath in the afternoon.'

'Oho. Does she care for her hair, take headbath and put coconut oil?'

'Yes, why?'

'Of late, does she do it more often or increasingly rarely?'

'Twice a week without fail since we got married.'

'Boss, you don't suppose that she has simply adjusted only too well to married life?'

'What do you mean, Majestic?' asked Bhascar. His face drained of all blood until his skin turned grey, his eyes were round and red as tomatoes, his hands grabbed at the rum tumblers, but both were empty.

'I'm asking for your opinion.'

'How am I supposed to know?'

'So what's wrong then?'

'That is what is wrong, she's making me suspicious. She never asks me to take her to the Botanical Garden anymore. Why is she so happy all the time?'

Hari thought about this. Lal Bagh was a place where people in love went. He nodded. 'I see your point. Boss, tell me more.'

'I must be in the shop from morning to evening, but sometimes I go home early to surprise her, and she is always doing something like stuffing masala into chillies, or darning and mending, and lately she started knitting woollens to sell in the neighbourhood this coming winter in order to help save money for Galata's dowry. My digestion has gone totally haywire. Do you think I'm able to sleep? Frankly, what would you do if your wife was happy with so little?'

Life was perfect, so something had to be wrong. Hari instinctively knew what. Bhascar sat all day at his mill, busy with product adulteration, mind idle. Obviously, a man like him was going to get paranoid about what went on behind his back.

'It is admittedly suspicious,' said Hari and rolled his head sideways. 'Most women expect to get some adventure out of life. Let my agency undertake an investigation to find waterproof evidence of whether madam is or isn't enacting infidelity schemes.'

Hari was fairly sure that an investigation wasn't going to turn up anything, but the husband's jealousy might nevertheless escalate and take a dangerous turn. It was important to save the marriage if for no other reason than to ensure that little Galata didn't grow up an orphan due to some horrible tragedy. Perhaps, if he proved that the missus wasn't cheating, the coffee trader would give Hari free coffee for a month. He said, 'Meanwhile, you'd want to tell her that there is a sudden rush at the shop due to the festival season, you will work extra long hours and Galata must also be there to help.'

'Why?'

'It will give a window of opportunity. If your missus is having an affair, we will know like that only. I sincerely hope that nothing untoward will come up, but in case something is there, we will show photographic, videographic, audiographic and computergraphic evidence of her with suspicious gents.'

'I'm not sure I want that.'

'Brace yourself. Or how will you be able to ever eat your tiffin if you go on worrying? We will help settle your divorce out of court,' said Hari, thinking that perhaps divorce was the best solution – at least for the missus.

'I've already said I don't want a divorce. I want her lover eliminated. You catch him and then…' said Bhascar, breathing heavily.

He did the clichéd finger across the throat that he must have picked up from B-films. Real gangsters did it with two fingers.

Hari completed the sentence rationally, '…*then* we'll see to it that everybody gets what they deserve.' Although Hari should have rejoiced about getting a case already on the first day, the situation made him feel a bit low – it was dawning on him that this kind of sad infidelity and distrust investigations was what he was going to spend his working life dealing with.

When he got back to the office, he found that Triplex had resurfaced like a stubborn Trojan virus and was bragging to Gaadi about some chick he had eve-teased the night before. His face was variously distorted by green, blue, black and red welts, and only a few spots here and there retained their original skin colour.

'Love came and went?' said Hari.

It transpired that rich boys had objected to his presence outside a posh college and hostel for modern girls, and physically prohibited him from setting foot on their hunting ground. But Triplex was a man who lived for his dreams and he planned to have a tailor stitch him a college jacket and climb up those hi-fi rungs of society as soon as his face healed.

He had stolen a bunch of bananas on the way back, now they ate a couple each. It was the best hangover food. Hari congratulated Triplex on his resourcefulness and reported to his crew that they had a case to crack.

'But what … swami, are you saying we're not getting paid?' interrupted Gaadi.

'Please work with me on this one. This is what our job is about, what we're meant to do. It may appear as if we're unpaid, in terms of cash, but think of the opportunity to make a name for ourselves. And maybe we'll get free coffee.'

Gaadi wasn't convinced. He tore a slip of paper from his notebook, rolled it up tight and started cleaning wax from his ears, as if he couldn't believe what he was hearing.

'Majestic,' said Doc. 'I have a plan.'

'What?'

'Give me her phone number and I'll hack into her mobile, install this spyware I've got and it'll enable the camera to stream video to us. We'll get images of everything she does and where she goes. Cheapest and best solution.'

'Boss, trouble is that hubby is so suspicious that he doesn't let her keep a mobile. This demands legwork.'

Doc chewed his lip. He lived in a tech-savvy future and found it hard to believe that there were medieval people around who didn't.

Triplex got fired up. 'But I can use my camera to film her! It'll be great to put a hot promo on YouTube, we'll go viral.'

'*Chup*!' said Hari. Although he didn't want to appear a prude, he was sceptical about his associate's moral fibre. 'When we investigate, we are going to do it the proper way.'

'Come on, Majestic. I've always wanted to take snaps of somebody called Apsara.'

Because Apsara wasn't just an ordinary name, but it also meant 'heavenly damsel' or 'celestial nymph'.

'I am telling you we are not YouTubing anything,' said Hari, 'we're simply going to save this lady from a tragic destiny.'

'Let's do it then, swami,' said Gaadi and wiped off the earwax from the piece of paper, daubing it on the wall, where it left an orange stain, and then he carefully fitted the slip back into his notebook.

5

How to Find the Clue That Matters

They heard Bhascar rant loudly for some time, then the lights disappeared in the cracks of the door and finally it was quiet.

The plan was that Hari and Triplex would take turns to stay awake on the rooftop through the night, but Hari suspected that none of them would end up sleeping. Triplex was a chatty fellow, liked to discuss which hair gel had the most macho scent. And if Hari didn't listen, Triplex would snooze too.

Hari did his best to keep Triplex awake by sharing nuggets of forensic wisdom gathered over the years as an ardent student of criminological literature such as the *Crime & Detective Magazine*. Triplex, of course, didn't see any point in reading when there were movies and YouTube; it wasn't dyslexia or illiteracy, no, it went deeper than that.

Later, Triplex took off to get dodgy over-spiced tamasic non-veg fare to ruin his karma, and Hari leaned on the parapet, watching the house.

After midnight, he heard voices and observed three men walk towards Prem Vilas. They stopped at the burnt-out power shed, right below Hari's position. For a moment he worried that they were going to come up. But they were just taking a break and Hari smelt hashish mingled with rancid body odours. They talked loudly, the way addicts do, planning a theft at the railway station where the ceilings were dotted with 32-inch digital display monitors. Hari recalled having read that in just the last couple of months some half a dozen such monitors had been looted from the high security terminus despite the closed-circuit surveillance. As a matter of fact, just the other day the security cameras had been stolen by some audacious burglar, which was why the thieves he was overhearing felt that the railway platforms were becoming a free for all.

Hari took down the details with his red Reynolds pen in the notebook. He'd throw the information in Sub-Inspector Pushpa's direction. This was completely safe – he didn't know the perps, they didn't know him, and would never guess how the police found out, and all the while he tried his best not to suspect his electronics expert Doc's involvement in it. As soon as they took off he text messaged Pushpa. It might turn out to be worth a couple of rupees in tip-off money.

Nothing happened for the longest time after that. Triplex was gone and Hari had to stay up, hungry and sleepy. Alone in the dark, he wondered again if this was how he was going to spend the rest of his days. Spying on married people? Selling petty criminals to the cops? That didn't seem so heroic. But he told himself that every hero had to start at the bottom.

In a way he envied Bhascar, who had a gorgeous wife, a home, his own business and everything else that a man could wish for, except perhaps male offspring. What sort of girl would pledge her heart to somebody like Hari, where to find that girl willing to love a person whose life was like a prank the gods had played on mankind…?

His gloomy musings were interrupted by scraping noises from the corner where the ladder led down.

'Who's there?'

'Triplex,' said a hoarse voice.

'Password?'

'I don't remember.'

'Say the secret password or I'll shoot.' Hari didn't have a gun, but he wasn't planning to break protocol. He made a mental note to speak to Doc at the tech department and perhaps get a taser or some other kind of stun guns issued for select personnel. Or pepper spray. It could be used to spice up food too, in boring restaurants.

'Something or whatever.' The DCO came crawling, drunk as a deep-fried skunk. He must have visited some bootlegger's den.

'Did you parcel for me?' asked Hari, who had given Triplex ₹100 as a joint food allowance for the two of them.

'I forgot that too.'

'And what am I supposed to eat?'

Triplex dug a boiled egg out of his pocket. It was chopped in two and seasoned with chilli powder and chaat masala.

'I've had enough of these,' he said, farted egg-smelly and started snoring.

'Lame,' said Hari.

But letting him sleep it off was preferable to having to listen to drunken remembrances of erotic YouTube clips.

•

Triplex didn't wake up even when the cock crowed and the birds in a nearby palm tree babbled in a burst of sunrise agitation. Some coolies walked to their work at the railway station, while rickshaw drivers returned to their homes. They were the only ones who were up so early. *They and detectives*, Hari thought as he scrutinized every man who passed outside Prem Vilas.

Soon the flower-garland man came on the mud track that snaked between the huts, carrying a basket of flowers on his head. Apsara stepped out to buy three feet of flowers. Later the milkman pushed a bicycle, a plastic crate strapped to its carrier, with sachets of milk and curd, shouting, '*Haalu! Mosaru!*'

Apsara drew the rangoli in front of the door, she made the pattern of rice flour more intricate than necessary, including tiny hearts filled in with vermilion powder, and Hari snapped a few pictures for reference, in case the rangoli held a secret message.

Zooming in he saw deep into her cleavage when she bent forward, and noticed that Triplex had been correct in his assessment, but he refrained from clicking right then. Though she wore a paisley-patterned baggy nightgown and hadn't yet brushed her hair, Bhascar's wife was adorable, an exquisite creation liberally endowed by Lord Kama.

She gossiped with her neighbour, a lady who apparently saw herself as Apsara's guru and thus had a lot to say. She counted out points on her fingers and did elaborate gestures that Hari interpreted as cooking instructions. After a while Apsara glanced towards her own door. Bhascar was shouting for breakfast. Apsara excused herself and went in.

The morning sun baked the roof.

Some kids got the day's first cricket championship started in the lane. At their shouts, Triplex woke up complaining that he was thirsty. Hari let him go off duty under the condition that he went straight home and slept, so that he'd stay awake on the next shift. The coming evening they'd bring tiffin carriers and a flask of coffee Hari decided, wiser after the first night's mistakes.

The female neighbour was a potential source of information. An undercover operative from Mr Majestic, OK & Co must visit her. Hari wished that he had female staff on the payroll, for in a situation like this a woman could make a more direct contact.

He called Doc.

'Tell me, Majestic?' said Doc.

'Use codenames, idiot. This is Royal Flush speaking.'

'Okay, don't take tension. Speaking of which, had your bowel movements, Flush?'

Doc was living up to his nickname. Skipping the preliminaries, Hari explained the deal, using the codename given to Doc, 'Get over here, Dotcom. There's a neighbour who needs to be investigated.'

'How am I supposed to do that?' Some felt that Doc was pessimistic, because he had a clinical way of thinking about problems and didn't believe in easy answers; everything had to be solved through the most complex means and technologies possible. Everyone else prayed to suitable gods, sacrificed coconuts, trusted the stars, used black magic and hoped against hope, but Doc was born to be a scientist. Hari liked to think that there were uses for such ungodly types too.

'Bring your toolbox with all that junk we bought on the grey market and tell them you're from a TV servicing company.'

'These are precision instruments,' Doc protested.

'So tell them that you can upgrade their black and white TV and make it show high-definition pictures in colour.'

'What if they already have a colour TV?'

'Then tell them you'll turn their mixer-grinder into a DVD-player, boss. Lie if you must, but the mission is to get inside and dig out everything.'

'Everything?' He'd take time to get used to having Hari as his superior. Doc always thought of himself as special because he owned several computers – just like in the old days when the owner of many camels and elephants was the biggest shot.

'Hurry up, do you have a pen so you can note down the address?'

'Don't bother. I know exactly where you are.'

'How?'

'What you call junk has already triangulated you to the rooftop of a slum shed.'

He disconnected the call.

Half an hour later, Doc arrived carrying a black doctor's bag. He took his nickname seriously enough. Hari saw him faff his way into the chatty neighbour's house and disappear for quite some time. On the plus side, he was a convincing expert, that Doc. It wasn't unthinkable that the family had invited him to have breakfast with them in return for changing the gender of their TV or whatever it was that Doc had promised to do.

Meanwhile, Bhascar emerged from his home in crisp, clean kurta and loincloth, holding Galata by the hand, and they walked across the hearty rangoli outside their door and off in the direction of the coffee mill. Right then Doc left the neighbour's house and Bhascar glared at him. Doc asked him if he too needed a TV tune-up.

Bhascar barked, 'No.'

He refused to be a happy man.

Minutes later, his wife was out of Prem Vilas again and Hari perked up. She started doing laundry on the flagstones near a gutter. Nothing more suspicious than that. It really was odd how she seemed not to detest her humdrum life.

For Hari it was time to go back to office – to sleep. He called Gaadi to tell him to get into position and Gaadi did a fine act of arriving and stopping his rickshaw with a roar at the same spot where he'd been posted the day before, and acted as if he couldn't get a signal on his phone, shouting, 'Hello? Hello?'

People hereabouts generally didn't look twice if they saw somebody do something strange, as long as one didn't give the appearance of having a purpose with it.

He'd barely had time to spend an hour in his dream movie and it had just reached the first song-and-dance number featuring him and the dream girl. A trifle groggy, it took him a while to understand when, where and what he was.

The caller-ID showed it was Gaadi. Hari picked up. 'Royal Flush. Tell me.'

'Target moving, target moving.'

'Roger that, boss.'

'No stupid, this is AC here.'

'Codenames, use the secret codenames in case enemy agents are tapping our phones. Yours is Rick.'

'But you called me Roger.'

'Don't waste time on things you will never understand,' said Hari and wondered briefly what he'd achieve surrounded by a flock of morons who didn't follow basic protocol or remember their designated codenames. 'What's going on?'

'Target is moving.'

'You were supposed to offer her a ride if she was going someplace,' Hari said.

'I did. But target told me to stop following her, threatened to call the cops, then turned a few corners to lose me. Very suspicious, must be up to something. Should I grab her and take her to Command Centre for third degree?' Command Centre was the codename for the office in Puncherwallah Complex.

'You're forgetting that this is not a Sandalwood movie,' Hari said. 'Which way is she heading?'

'Your way, swami. I'm at the urinals on Tank Bund Road and can see her walk in the CD Road direction. You can intercept her at KG Circle.' Like all auto-drivers, Gaadi was an expert at giving directions.

'Roger that. What is she wearing?'

'Clothes,' said Gaadi but sounded puzzled. 'Who is that Roger-da you're talking to, swami?'

'Roger means "okay, I hear you" in code language. Colour of clothes?'

'Oh like that.' Hari heard Gaadi speak to somebody who was urinating next to him. 'Bloody colour,' he reported back.

'Red, you mean? Boss, are you colour blind?' Hari had always wondered why Gaadi never stopped at red lights but sometimes blocked the traffic unnecessarily when it was green to take a power nap.

'No, no *Roger*, I wanted to double check. I don't know all the names of different colours.'

Hari headed out of the office and ran, no, practically stampeded down the crowded street to KG Circle, through the area known as Majestic because of one popular cinema. Of course, that cinema was gone now, having had to give way to video piracy and shopping malls. But that was where Hari had been found by his adoptive mother, abandoned, under a second row seat in the cheapest ticket class, and so he had got his surname, Majestic, from Majestic Talkies.

The only clue to Hari's identity had been a used ticket from Khatpadi Junction, a small town in Tamil Nadu, to Bengaluru. It was strange, and unlikely, that parents travelled so far to dump a boy child in a cinema. It was unheard of. Had they tried to find him later? Or had they gone back to Khatpadi Junction after misplacing their offspring? There was no way of knowing.

KG Road, that crossed CD Road at the KG Circle, was the main drag where buses passed in an endless stream on their way to the central bus station.

The footbridge that straddled it, near the roundabout, was occupied by peddlers who sold cheap phone accessories: one of the more infamous products here was batteries that exploded, often mutilating the person carrying the phone in his trouser pocket. Many of CD Road's most notorious perverts had been cured that way.

He climbed up on the footbridge and kept watch until he spotted Apsara, walking with a dignified gait. She was easy to track since her sari was freshly laundered, maybe silk, definitely polyester at least, shiny red and she stood out like a beacon in the pollution.

She stopped briefly at a pavement vendor's tarpaulin sheet that had various travel items on offer – chains to secure suitcases and comb and mirror sets. She didn't browse or bargain, no … She bought a small padlock worth fifteen rupees.

Mysterious, was she planning to lock her husband out of their home? Hari was surer and surer of one thing: her pre-lunch stroll wasn't for building up an appetite, it had a definite purpose. He climbed down from the footbridge and followed.

He moved fast, but with caution, keeping all options open. If Apsara happened to turn around, she might see him come towards her on the pavement and then, in the blink of an eye and without breaking his stride, Hari could vanish down an alley. *Now you see me, now you don't.* He knew these mean streets – their sounds, vapours and flavours – having spent all his life roaming them.

He'd hate to bust such a clean wife with a secret lover in one of the area's many semi-budget lodging houses, but it would mean that her husband had been right. One could hope that she planned to catch a matinee show at a KG Road cinema and just dream of love, like Hari himself often did. It'd also give him an excuse to watch a movie. But she didn't so much as glance at the poster-plastered Sangam Talkies, festooned with huge cut-out stars, showing a new hit film with superhero Upendra.

She weaved her way past the ubiquitous pavement vendors and through jungles of merchandise that spilled out of the shopping complexes, pirated DVDs cluttering folding tables, vegetables on pieces of cardboard, makeshift kiosks displaying shirts and pants, a vendor of broken wall clocks sitting in a corner, one bearded trader had hundreds of pairs of sunglasses tucked into his beard, Chinese electric shavers were piled up on the roadside, competing for space with three-legged stands laden with snacks ranging from spicy churmuri mixtures to sweet fly-encrusted jalebis, but she walked on without stopping.

The Majestic area wasn't salubrious and women were in fact warned against being here alone. It was a mathematically interesting fact that out of all the bars and booze shops in the state of Karnataka, some 38 per cent were located in Bengaluru, and the majority of them concentrated here, near the bus and railway stations. Therefore, many of the city's rowdies, goons, thugs and con artists frequented the neighbourhood, on top of the thousands who came hoping for a break in the city, dream realization-cum-implementation or cheap action in any of the downmarket joints.

It was a place where small sins were no sins at all, a place for business and pleasure, the embodiment of the wonderful and the weird, and turning a corner there could change one's life forever. What might Apsara be in search of?

She walked down one of the quieter back lanes until she came to a street corner Sufi tomb, where she spent a few moments in contemplation and then locked the padlock to the metal grille whispering a wish. Apsara didn't make contact with anyone; she was simply devoting herself to devotion.

And then she walked home again right past Hari, who busied himself inspecting the chewing gum selection at a cigarette stall. On the way back, she lingered at a tree where several snake sculptures stood guard.

From there he followed her back to her house, where AC Gaadi was lolling on the passenger seat of his autorickshaw.

6

How to Deal with Accidents That Don't Come Alone

A week later, Hari woke up at his desk.

He saw his uncle's old alarm clock on the floor, smashed to bits, the result of some nightmare. So he had started having nightmares? The time, the time ... It must be half past hell o'clock or something. He checked his phone and saw that he had missed breakfast but it was too early for lunch.

He thought of his next move. A full seven days and nights, and the routine investigation had only served to invade a poor woman's privacy for no good reason at all.

All right, so he had in principle solved his first case, by virtue of which he was – what his lawyer uncle would call – a bona fide detective. Today was their last day on 'Operation Way-Too-Happy-Wife (Op. WTHW)' and he was to meet Mr Bhascar and deliver the final report.

Hari picked up the broken alarm clock and flipped its fingers forward by some hours. 'Lunchtime,' he said and headed out to grab a bite and energize himself – because in the absence of any damning evidence he must compile a report that was empty of substance yet solid enough to convince Mr Bhascar of his wife's purity. Despite the husband's suspicions and Triplex's conviction that a 'bomb' like Apsara had to have a secret lover, it was Hari's hunch that she was completely innocent. But Triplex wanted to go on with the investigation until his camera caught Apsara in a compromising position together with one or more moustachioed strangers.

He padlocked the office and went next door to the Veg Non-Veg Friendly Mess, where he had a running bill. Suleiman was busy cleaning out and chopping up yards of bloody intestine. It was the main ingredient in his famous spare part masala, one of the best in town.

Of all his neighbours in the Puncherwallah Complex, Hari especially liked Suleiman, whose food was as uncomplicated as the man himself. Suleiman's ambitions were limited to buying, some day in the future, a chapatti maker of the same model that the Indian army used, that turned out 8,000 chapattis per hour. Not that he ever served so many even in a month, but Suleiman always hoped that the next month would see a higher turnover.

While Hari gobbled up his brunch of dal fry with chapatti, he reviewed the reports by Triplex – SMS printouts, Gaadi – audio tracks recorded with his phone with snippets of karaoke thrown in and Doc – who had a preference for writing everything in Java Script, plus himself – inspired poetry.

Hari pushed Triplex's theories out of his mind as unproven and focused on the facts. They knew exactly what she ate and approximately how many calories she burnt on her daily routine of kitchen work, laundry and house cleaning, and that she preferred to listen to suitably conservative radio stations that played light Carnatic music, rather than filmy beats. They had rifled through the garbage every night and there was no evidence of illicit psychotropic substance abuse or West-inspired junk food, only wholesome home-cooked leftovers and the occasional empty box of pure ghee sweets from Blissful House.

One day she had gone to use a public phone at a Xerox shop to make a call. Hari bribed the PCO attendant to get the billing slip.

Then he had dialled the same number on the pretext of offering zero interest loans due to the coming Diwali season, when household items were on massive discount sale, and found that the number belonged to Apsara's widowed mother in a nice nearby town without an underworld and where the old lady lived with Apsara's sisters. Pretending to help her to make up a shopping list, he got to know more or less the entire family saga including what their Diwali priorities were. Apsara's father had been a construction worker in Dubai. The Gulf money had bought Apsara a coffee miller husband and upward mobility to fast-paced Bengaluru, but recently her father had had an unfortunate accident, falling off a 200-storey skyscraper. Due to the Arab Spring recession, the building contractor in Dubai had used substandard scaffoldings and neglected to insure his staff ... and besides there was no male heir in the family tree, the mother complained. Hari wished her happy puja and hung up.

As expected, Apsara's neighbour whose curiosity encompassed everything within sight turned out to be an excellent source. According to the interview by Doc, she was thrilled at the idea that her TV might soon be hooked up to the gossipy Internet. So, while Doc was tinkering, she uploaded everything about everybody she knew, data ranging from the make of their TVs, how many channels each household received, what soap operas they preferred, plus food habits to marital status and so on. It amounted to a fairly detailed census.

In the name of honesty, she had to admit that her dear friend Apsara was stuck up and far too saintly. She had no business relations with bookmakers or bad characters – there were many of those in the neighbourhood according to Mrs Luxmy, who had of late noticed two corrupt degenerates lurking on the roof of the old power shed, knowing that they weren't up to anything good. To be fair, Hari would have wanted to let her know that only one of them was a corrupt degenerate.

But nobody except Apsara's own husband and the envious Mrs Luxmy cast evil eyes on her. The character verification was beginning to suggest that Apsara was far superior to anybody on the payroll of Mr Majestic, OK & Co – indeed, she was a saint.

Hari himself had witnessed Apsara spending time at the shrine once more during the week. She was checking that her padlock was still in place. It being a Sufi shrine, it didn't matter if the devotee was Hindu, Christian or Muslim, for according to local tradition anyone could be blessed with a healthy fat boy child by praying there.

He discussed her visits to the shrine with Pandit Pundit, the honorary spiritual advisor of Mr Majestic, OK & Co. Although the guru didn't endorse any cults but his own, he admitted that Hari had a point: since the lady already had a daughter, she obviously needed a son next.

Inputs from the gossipy neighbour confirmed Pundit's theory. The dowry for the son would suffice to buy Galata, the daughter, a decent non-alcoholic non-beef-eating husband with a safe government employment.

Once Apsara's wish was fulfilled, she'd remove the padlock and sacrifice it to the Naga snake stones. Meanwhile she ate calorie-rich sweetmeats made out of pure ghee to improve the odds. Hence, she did what was the duty of any wife, but the yearning for marital happiness and sheer homemaker enthusiasm had been misinterpreted as nymphomania.

All was fine with Mr and Mrs Bhascar, and yet nothing was. Sometimes mere distrust was enough to ruin a perfect marriage, observed Hari. He wanted the end to be happy: 'the investigation didn't unearth anything untoward' were the words he planned to conclude his report with, determined to pull the plug … well, unless Mr Bhascar insisted on paying them to continue.

Because, there was always a but – and Hari foresaw one major problem: objectively speaking the outcome was the best possible, and he was convinced that no matter how much they dug in the mud there'd be no traces of love, illicit or otherwise, but he still doubted that a man like Bhascar was going to feel that such a happy end was satisfactory. Why pay for nothing? Hari had to admit to himself that any normal person around CD Road would ask the same question, including Hari himself. And even if it was the truth and nothing but the truth, a jealous husband was probably going to remain jealous.

And although he wasn't keen on carrying on, he conceded that Triplex may have had a valid point when he said that they must put doubts in Bhascar's head and offer to go on for as long as it took – it made business sense because such an operation could in theory last for years. The first week had been free-of-charge according to the IOU undertaking, but if the investigation dragged on they'd get paid.

It was a serious headache. He found that he detested himself more and more. But if he were to close the case and drop Bhascar as a client, he needed to find a paying customer right away. He was beginning to realize that he must go like a door-to-door salesman to sell his services to prospective clients. He picked up the phone and started making appointments, while he nursed three or four coffees and digested the food. Suleiman put too much chilli and oil in everything so as to give his customers value for money.

That's the way great businessmen worked. They gave their customers an illusory sense of value for money.

After a number of calls, he had a meeting set up with a prospective client in the afternoon. He had an hour to kill and he knew that there was one task he had postponed for too long. But in this moment of existential crisis, when he began to view the detective agency as a potential failure, Hari needed to visit his true guru. So he asked Suleiman to fry up a stack of oily keema parathas.

In the alley behind the office, he handed out a few parathas to the pack of dogs that guarded his Enfield Bullet 65. Their leader was a hairless mutant mongrel that Hari had adopted when he was a deviant puppy; judging from his apparent DNA profile his father had been a pit bull terrier that went about romancing bandicoots. His name was Underdog and he pretended to be Hari's best friend. In fact, for some reason all stray dogs were fond of Hari. Perhaps they thought of him as a fellow loser. In which case they were mistaken.

Nevertheless he fed the dogs every day, because he believed that what went around came around. If he, for example, took rebirth as a dog in his next life, he would want fresh food now and then.

Hari took off on his motorcycle, brooding over the imminent bankruptcy of his detective agency, and zigzagged dejectedly past the modern Mantri Mall – where he'd never afford to shop – and the old Malleshwaram Market, separate worlds located in the same street, and he was almost crushed by a bus. Reflexes saved him.

He drove up the road to the De-Addiction Medicine & Neuropsychiatry Department, which had a very inauspicious acronym. So unlike practically everything else in town, its name was never abbreviated. The institutional campus was big, built as it was to care for all of Bengaluru's mental problems. A pathway led to a melancholic concrete block, where he nodded to the guard, who didn't bother to look too closely at the bulge in Hari's shirt made by the contraband non-veg greasy food, that according to certain well-known psychiatric and spiritual theories perverted the mind – you just had to look at Triplex to see the truth of that.

On the second floor of the inpatient ward, OK Mamool had a private room. 'How is Uncle feeling today?' said Hari cheerfully.

Uncle Mamool used to complain, rant and rave, and get worked up, blasting the whole world and everything in it, especially Hari, calling his nephew a 'vegetarian' and 'teetotaller' and 'carpet salesman' and 'son of a bald mother'. Today: nothing.

Not too good, then. Uncle sat on a grey plastic chair, staring at the bare wall with one of his sandals in his hand as if he had forgotten whether he was about to take it off or put it on.

'Did Uncle step out for a walk?' asked Hari and took the sandal away from him, and put a soft rubber ball with a painted smile in his hand instead. It had been Hari's get-well gift to him.

'Bah.'

'Uncle is looking good today, a man about town,' Hari lied. 'Can Uncle guess what we're celebrating?'

He couldn't and wouldn't. In the ensuing silence, Hari wondered if a similar fate awaited him too. Although it was an inauspicious thought, he'd rather die than be hospitalized. He just couldn't see himself handling such a non-happening life.

'Got a job now. So don't worry about me, Uncle. Lie down and chill,' said Hari. He told him about the agency, and that Uncle too was going to be employed by it. 'Does Uncle think it a good idea?'

'Bah-bah.'

Hari listened closely to determine if this was a more encouraging 'bah-bah' than Uncle's usual laconic 'bah'. Today's wasn't the angriest he had heard. OK Mamool was a fount of incredibly flexible advice handy for whenever a rule had to be bent to fit realities. Unfortunately, he had been disgraced and debarred from practising law by the State Bar Council after a failed attempt to start a riot in order to stall court proceedings that weren't going the way he wanted. At Halasur Gate Police Station, they had registered cases under the Prevention of Damage to Public Property Act 1984, Indian Penal Code sections 147 – rioting, 148 – rioting armed with a machete, 307 – attempted murder, 353 – assault or criminal force to deter public servant from discharge of his duty, 435 – mischief by fire or explosive substance with intent to cause damage, 437 – mischief with intent to destroy or make unsafe a decked vessel of twenty tons burden or more and 506B – criminal intimidation. They also charged him with dacoity, but later withdrew that charge, since the minimum requirement was to be part of a gang of no less than five miscreants. Uncle was a lonely wolf.

'I brought some goodies,' Hari chirped and for a moment there was a dim light in the old man's rheumy eyes. It extinguished as soon as Hari unwrapped the plantain leaves around Suleiman's coconut-oily keema parathas, and Uncle saw the goodies weren't bottle shaped. 'Now we'll taste some yummy non-veg.'

Uncle's lower lip quivered as Hari stuffed a soggy paratha into the toothless mouth. For dessert, he gave him a strip of big pink antacid tablets – he wouldn't be able to digest the food otherwise.

Hari felt sorry. In theory, spicy meat-stuffed parathas were a strict no-no because of the depraving effects, but stopping drinking, smoking and non-vegetarian habits at the same time might put Uncle's body in detox shock. More drink and Uncle died little by little, but without bad habits he had nothing to live for. His brainwaves had apparently ceased to be visible on scans.

Hari didn't want to lose him, his only almost real family member. Although he felt that some of the things Uncle did were wrong, he still admired Uncle for having such simple and clear male ideals: his only ambitions were to eat chicken every day, get drunk every night at 6 p.m. and shout at his wife. Uncle's wife had, of course, left him long ago, so he was unable to fulfil all three ambitions, but the remaining two he did, or had done, until Hari put him into detox. That's why Hari felt sorry, as if he had betrayed him, but he tried to convince himself that it was for Uncle's own good.

The first week of the rehabilitation had been all right. Uncle had been full of anger and begged Hari to bring him a quart of Old Monk, which Hari refused on account of the random breath and urine tests that patients had to go through. Being caught would result in immediate discharge, putting Uncle back in square one.

Hari had suggested, 'Pretend that it's a holiday away from the bottle. The booze will be so much tastier when Uncle comes out again.'

Uncle hadn't been convinced. *So this is what the end looks like*, Hari thought. He heaved a deep sigh when he was back on his bike. Visiting Uncle had made him really depressed. *Uncle is Uncle and tomorrow is another day*, thought Hari to himself and forced a smile to his lips.

'If you're serious about being a spy…'

'Hero,' Hari corrected him.

'Well, hero, you should investigate why, instead of going to the bonesetter who charges twenty-five rupees, we end up paying lakhs of rupees at the hospital. Vested interests are there to lure people away from natural cures, like Homoeopathy.'

Talk of the Town was around the corner from CD Road. It had upholstered sofas rather than wooden benches and tablecloths that were only a little unwashed, so it was suitable for a business meeting. The appointment had been made for two o'clock, so Hari made sure to reach before three. It turned out that Hochiminh Meshtru was already there enjoying tiffin at Hari's cost.

Hari apologized, 'Sorry, I didn't realize that Meshtru ji would be on time.' His plan was to get contracts from the local municipal ward and Meshtru, who had taught many of those who ran it nowadays, could recommend Hari's agency to supply security and bodyguards, or probe malpractices like the water mafia that thrived off the perennial water shortage – even during the monsoon when dogs drowned in the bazaars, the taps had a tendency to run dry.

But for a full hour Meshtru ranted against modern medicine. It was the familiar tirade that Hari had heard before and Meshtru argued for a 'return-to-the-herbs' policy that had worked well for thousands of years to treat anything and everything. His Adam's apple jumped in excitement.

Perhaps it had been a mistake to offer Meshtru a glass of caffeinated beverage. Now and then, his Adam's apple turned into a hysterical ping-pong ball. Although Hari was dead tired from a week of all-night vigils, he did his best to avoid getting hypnotized by the pinging and ponging, and stop himself from yawning in deference to the man's age and social standing.

Instead, Hari waited out the rant the way one waits out a cloudburst during the monsoon, unable to see how the fact that he was a detective had anything to do with healthcare. 'Can Meshtru ji be a little more specific?'

Meshtru's Adam's apple went ballistic. 'Pretend to be sick, snoop around the hospital and if you come up with anything scandalous, there's a finder's fee – I wouldn't dream of asking you to do anything for free. You also have a living to make, boy.'

Hari smiled. This was too good to be true.

Meshtru put ₹200 on the table.

'I'm taking it from my own pension.' Meshtru leaned back, very satisfied with himself over the munificent offer.

'Per hour?'

'No-no-no.'

'Oho. Per day, I see.'

'Of course not.'

'Per week, Meshtru ji?'

'For the assignment, rascal.'

Hari didn't quite like it when people called him things like rascal. But he smiled.

'That is mighty generous of you.' His fee structure wasn't going to cut it with a person who thought in terms of 1970s monetary values, when paisa coins actually bought you something. 'But our base cost per week is fifteen … eh, thousand.'

'I know that, of course. The remaining funding you may raise with my blessing through an awareness campaign within the community, because you're doing this for a public cause,' said Meshtru. 'That is what we used to do in the good old days.'

It sounded very easy when the words came from the mouth of an antiquated idealist.

'Correct, Meshtru ji, absolutely. So if all this malpractice is well-known, then what exactly do you need our services for?'

'There's no evidence.'

'Then how do you know it is true?'

'Because everybody knows.'

'I see. Somebody must have poured buffalo milk in my coffee this morning, because I'm a bit slow. Give me some hints.'

'Have you, for example, noticed how Sickly Hospital,' said Meshtru, 'has re-branded itself? The other day I went there to get a prescription for my throat and they had put up a new board with the name Globalized Style Super Speciality Hospital … *Globalized?* It smells of black money in Swiss bank accounts but they do no restoration work on that decrepit building, they just inflate the fees according to the euro exchange rate.'

'That's probably a scandal,' said Hari. But to him it sounded natural that a hospital made money out of its services, especially a no-questions-asked local clinic like the one in question which mainly catered to gangsters and rowdies after they were bashed up in street fights. The problem was that Hari didn't quite see how his agency could gain from that. The old teacher's pledged remuneration wasn't worth spending a day in hospital for and risking antibiotic-resistant super bugs. But … he'd have to adjust. He could trawl Wikileaks for related stories, cut and paste together a report worth ₹200. He sighed and said, 'We shall do the needful.'

In the end, when he footed the tiffin bill, he observed that the more one paid, the less one got, which was perhaps the main reason why free lunches were out of fashion. The snacks cost ₹198 or almost as much as he'd make from this case, leaving him with a profit of two rupees.

'Bye-bye and all the very best,' he said and made a mental note to take out health insurances for himself and his operatives as soon as he had enough cash. In case something untoward happened, it'd rattle the agency's balance sheets if even the cheapest hospital charged euro rates.

Stepping out of the restaurant, he told himself to stop procrastinating. He had to go deliver his report to Bhascar and close the case. And if this meant that his first paying case wasn't going to net more than two rupees, then so be it, he decided.

Looking at things from a more optimistic perspective, there were plenty of would-be clients around. He'd never thought of it that way, but it now occurred to him that if one were to count them, the CD Road area hosted more than a dozen pharmacies, a handful of piles and fistula clinics, and at least a pair of competing minor hospitals. The unhealthy CD Road lifestyle made for good medical business. Maybe he should offer to protect the clinics against litigious dogmatists like Meshtru?

He took out his phone to call Triplex and discuss the matter, but then he saw his second-in-command – the typical trademark swagger, colourful clothes, the white cowboy boots – on the opposite pavement of HM Road, a parallel street to CD Road that was lined with lodges, bars, several tandoori eateries, a few film distribution companies and one big green-painted cinema hall, and three air-conditioned indoor bazaars for grey market goods. He was about to call out, 'Had your lunch, Triplex?'

But his smile froze when he spotted, a few steps *behind* Triplex, none other than Apsara walking with a determined expression on her face. *What was going on?* For a quarter of a second, Hari blanked out. Then he set off after them to try and figure it out.

7

How to Get or Not to Get Love

This was a catastrophic worst case scenario. Apsara may have suspected that she was under surveillance and started watching the detectives: maybe the gossipy Mrs Luxmy had tipped her off.

If Apsara found out that her husband had put detectives on her trail, they'd be royally toasted and jammed. Failing a simple routine investigation would destroy their reputation among CD Road's business people – and no reputation meant no clients.

Triplex passed 3rd Cross Road, where there was a sandwich griller on the corner, a waste paper recycling shop, yet another piles clinic, an agro seeds and a cashew nut trader – shops typical for the area – while Apsara followed. No doubt about it, she was going after him. *But where was he headed?*

He seemed to be on his way towards the race course. Then he made a quick deviation into the entrance of a nondescript lodging house in the block between 3rd and 6th Cross Roads. Trying to shake off the shadow, Hari presumed.

A man was lying on the pavement outside a crowded booze shop, one door down from the lodging house, babbling to the smog above. Apsara skirted the drunkard and passed the Kama

Boardless Lodging Hotel. Maybe she wasn't following Triplex and Hari had overreacted? He relaxed.

But she only took a few more steps and then stopped … She started to turn. They'd be face to face right then, so in half the time that it took her to turn around, Hari fluidly made a beeline for the street side boozer. Drunks who had downed their liquid lunches were squeezing out from behind the counter, gingerly stepping over the man on the pavement, while other thirsty gentlemen were pressing to get inside and the ensuing pavement traffic snarl gave Hari cover.

'Here or parcel?' asked the shopkeeper.

'Parcel.' If she saw him, Apsara had no reason to believe that he was anything but another alcoholic. The shopkeeper wrapped up a grenade-shaped 375 ml bottle of cheap rum in a sheet of newspaper and Hari glanced sideways to see what Apsara was up to.

She was nowhere, not up the street, not down the street. The hallucinating drunk was rolling off the pavement onto the road, and cars had to brake, drivers honking angrily.

On his phone, he hit the speed dial button for 'Operative Codename Blue'. The phone rang, but Triplex didn't pick up.

Drastic measures were needed. Hari followed into the Kama's lobby, empty save for a man watching a loud song and dance program on a small black and white television. A corridor led deep into the building, dark and empty, and a staircase climbed to the floor above which had an upper veranda facing the street. He thought he heard somebody walking up there.

'All full,' said the man and glanced at the telltale shape of the liquor bottle in Hari's hand.

'But I just saw new customers walk in,' said Hari. Unfortunately this wasn't one of the hotels he used to bring tourists to in the days when he was touting around the bus and railway stations. Otherwise he could have cashed in a favour. This was way too downmarket for commissions; according to the rates posted on the grooved felt signboard, a single/double was no more than ₹149/₹169.

'Maybe you're drunk and seeing things.' The man was as unhelpful as hotel staff around CD Road could be.

'Come on, he's my friend, Triplex … ah, proper name is Neel Yeenappa, tell me the room number and I'll reimburse you for the trouble…' He dug into his pocket, empty. Like an idiot he'd spent his last rupees on booze. 'Business is dull, but how about a sip of fresh rum?'

When Hari spoke the words, he saw the futility in even trying: this sort of place didn't maintain a register, it was practically a brothel.

'If he's your friend,' said the man, 'why don't you call him on the phone, find out his room number?'

Game over. Not so long ago, nobody would have been hostile towards Hari, but now that he was acting like a nosy detective, he was an outsider on his own turf. He stepped out onto the street and crossed to the other side.

He reached in time to spot Triplex and Apsara on the upstairs veranda. Triplex was unlocking the padlock on one of the doors. He then motioned her inside and she didn't mind the fact that he touched … no massaged … her elbow. *He had crossed the line and made direct contact!*

Hari pressed the redial button. He saw Triplex glance at his pocket. Apsara stopped in the doorway.

The call made her nervous. Triplex smiled his lopsided movie star smile and shook his head, killed the call and adjusted his testicles in one swift move. Then he ushered her inside and shut the door.

Hari had the sinking feeling one might get if one's heart was surgically removed and chucked into a sewer. He called 'Operative Codename Dotcom', who was next on the speed dial, and Doc picked up.

'Tell me, Royal Flush.'

'Do you know what Codename Blue is up to?'

'He's solving the case.'

'What case?' echoed Hari and clutched his rum bottle so as not to hit himself over the head in pure frustration.

'The case we haven't solved yet.'

'Oho! How is he doing that?'

'He's infiltrating the enemy side with the help of a bottle of Goana wine.'

'What nonsense, has Triplex lost his mind?'

'He's working undercover. Don't compromise him; use the codename, Royal Flush.'

'Since when did *Codename Blue* start drinking red wine?'

'He doesn't,' said Doc who was an expert on everybody's dietary habits. 'It's part of plan B and he's implementing it.'

'Abort mission, abort,' Hari shouted. The wavy curl on his coconut-oily head turned into a mini tsunami. People outside the booze shop stared. Even the miserable drunk stopped crawling around in the street.

'Too late, Flush,' said Doc, 'the snake has entered the pit. We'll get the evidence we need to nail her.'

'What evidence? Don't tell me. At a lodge on HM Road?'

'So he told you the plan? It was meant to be a surprise, Majestic, sorry, Flush. He's too much, yah! First he got me to wire a room with closed-circuit cameras he stole from the railway station. Then he convinced the suspect that he's a Tantric and can provide her with a fertilizing therapy of alcohol that guarantees male offspring. Poor thing fell for it.'

Hari felt the brain getting sucked out of his head, as if somebody had stuffed the hose of a vacuum cleaner up his nose.

'I have to say I'm impressed at what I'm seeing on my screen. She's already rolled off three yards of her sari. He's a fast one.'

Hari scanned the surrounding buildings until he spotted Doc on the roof facing the hotel. Camera in hand, an antenna beside him on the parapet.

He knew then that Bhascar was going to roast all of them, including his missus, and grind them down and blend them with his coffee powder.

Triplex was remorseful when they held a staff meeting back at the office. At least for two seconds, then he started arguing that the missus wanted to get pregnant and he only carried out his male duty.

For the first time in history, Hari lost his temper with Triplex and called his best friend bad names, 'carpet salesman' – Triplex protested, 'vegetarian' – Triplex was traumatized at the thought, 'teetotaller' – Triplex was almost in tears, and 'politically incorrect' – Triplex had no idea what it meant, and 'son of a bald mother' … until Triplex looked fully devastated.

'I bet you don't even know what a *misogynist* does for a living?'

'Don't take tension, Majestic,' said Triplex, shocked at being yelled at. 'She was in on it.'

'As if,' said Hari who shook with rage.

'I did this for your sake, so that you'll get a fee from the customer, you can't say I'm not a loyal employee. Those pics are worth money!'

When Triplex saw that Hari was unable to speak because he was hyperventilating, he continued:

'Starting an agency, acting big hero, big inauguration, then failure. No way, Majestic, you know it as well as I that this was the only possibility.'

As always he was like the total Immaculate Conception. Hari felt like smashing one of the office chairs over his head. But he knew he couldn't afford to buy a new one and Triplex did his shamed dog act, and Hari had a weak spot for brainless creatures.

Besides, the surveillance images from the hotel room proved that she had imbibed wine and taken off her sari in the company of a seedy man. None of which becomes an honourable housewife.

He sighed.

Triplex went on, 'Majestic, you've got to be realistic. Now we have proof. Exactly what her husband wanted.'

'So what do you suggest?'

'Majestic, he's right,' Doc said. 'Now the husband will find that his suspicions weren't unfounded, so he can digest in peace.'

Hari had to admit that his colleagues, logically speaking, were correct. He dismissed them and sat alone at his desk thinking whether to write the report or not. Morally, every answer to the question was equally wrong, but at the same time equally right. He turned his eyes to the pictures on the office walls, of saints and gods, movie stars and mahatmas, and asked himself what they would have done.

He leafed through the printouts from the spycams in the hotel room. He toyed with the cigarette lighter, but no. Can't do. He had a code of professional ethics to follow as a detective – to act in the client's best interest and hence not falsify the result of the investigation.

He took out his red ballpoint pen and wrote across a sheet of foolscap: 'Top Secret Highly Classified Report of Operation Codenamed WTHW'. What he felt privately had nothing to do with the matter. He decided to name Triplex as 'Mr XXX' in the report, and keep his identity a secret.

'Boss, the investigation unearthed something untoward,' said Hari, after he finally mustered up his inner bullfighter and rode over to the Supernice Sugarcandy & Coffeeworks to take the client by its horns with a preamble long enough to soften up the horns in question.

Out of decency, he made it a point to turn away after handing over the select photo printouts, the bottle of rum he'd bought and a pack of extra-soft paper tissues.

'Have a little beverage,' he said indicating the Old Monk, smiling half-heartedly. 'Drown your sorrows.'

He anticipated some harsh language and was glad that the daughter wasn't there, listening. Galata had been sent off to the juicer-mixer stall with ten rupees to drink some pulped papaya and then play with the other slum kids.

Hari watched them kick around a ball among the rusted car wrecks on a garbage strewn, abandoned construction site. He sat on the narrow ledge outside the sales counter, on a stool kept there for the convenience of the coffee mill's customers. Apart from coffee, Bhascar sold condiments and boiled sweets, and there were gunny sacks with chicory on the floor, next to the grinding machine.

Strangely enough Bhascar hadn't started crying or screaming. After a long silence, a few ice-cold words popped out, 'This evidence hasn't been tampered with?'

'Photos never lie. People only do,' said Hari matter-of-factly. Of course, he could have asked Doc to doctor them if he had wished to do so, but there was no need. He added, 'If you don't mind me giving you a piece of unsolicited advice, boss, don't do anything drastic.'

'What are you talking about, Majestic? Like divorce her?'

Like kill her, Hari thought but didn't want to plant stupid ideas in Bhascar's head. He smiled sweetly. 'With all due respect, if you examine the forensic report closely, you'll find that our expert panel has scrutinized the materials in detail and concluded that she's suffering from a temporary mental imbalance resulting from a strong urge to conceive a male progeny, so however bizarre this must seem, what was done was done purely out of love for you, boss.'

Bhascar didn't reach out for the tissues Hari had put on the counter. Or the rum. 'For love's sake? Your expert thinks I can't satisfy my own wife?'

'No such allegations have been written in the Top Secret Highly Classified Report of Operation Codenamed WTHW,' Hari solemnly declared. He cleared his throat and reeled off more: 'What has happened is that sometimes ladies have a strong craving for babies; they get it about once a month according to the Wikipedia, at a critical stage of the ovulation cycle. This unknown individual took advantage.' Hari blurred the bad aspects by ladling it on. 'Shall I pour you a peg? No? You see, boss, if she'd had means of her own, she'd surely have gone to a clinic, but test tube babies have a costly price tag. So she must have thought, foolishly, that she can solve this cheaply on her own by using traditional, time-tested methods.'

Bhascar didn't look too happy about the explanation, but it was important that he understood that according to the findings, Apsara was blameless in principle, even if she wasn't entirely innocent of the incriminating act of having stepped into a hotel room with a man of bad character. For a long time Bhascar sat in silence on his side of the counter. Hari itched to quickly hand over an invoice to cover unexpected expenditure – hotel room, booze, paper napkins and so on. *Or maybe he shouldn't have come at all?* Instinctively, he knew that he wasn't going to get any bonus in the form of cash or coffee for solving this case. He was about to bid farewell and wish the coffee miller all the very best, but Bhascar gave him one of his evil eyes and Hari stayed put.

Bhascar slapped a hand on the counter.

'Look, Majestic, how often has she been meeting this bastard?'

'Only once in a lifetime, as far as we have been able to ascertain.'

'How do you know for sure?'

'We had our musclemen put him through the fourth degree,' said Hari, improvising. 'He confessed to everything between the fifth and the sixth degree. Due to the mutilation he suffered, you'll never need to worry again.'

'Mutilation?'

'Castration. It hurt.'

'Is it in the report?' asked Bhascar, browsing through the pages.

'No, if I had written about that in the report, boss, and it subsequently fell into the hands of the police, we'd run the risk of having legal action taken against us.'

Bhascar mulled this over. 'So you have musclemen in your service?'

Hari nodded gravely. 'Of course, just like the CIA and MI6, we too have special agents who perform operations for which we need deniability and discretion. But these are dangerous people so a good man like you, boss, wouldn't want to encounter them even in your worst nightmares. But I'd like you to understand that we've used all our resources regardless of expense to solve the case and if you so wish you could contribute with a suitable amount. It might be appropriate, considering that we did prove that your suspicions weren't entirely unjustified.'

'So they torture and kill people for money?' Bhascar went on.

'It is a question that is best left unanswered unless I feel sure you're not wearing a concealed mike.'

'Come on, Majestic. You want money?'

'Yes.'

'I'll give you money. But then you've got to give me something in return.' Bhascar went on, 'Off the record, who is this fellow?'

Hari shook his head. From among the surveillance images, he had deliberately selected those where it was impossible to identify Triplex: in the first one he was turning into the dingy lodge and all that was visible was the back of his purple nylon shirt with Occult embroidery and stonewashed jeans with fake diamond studs and the white cowboy boots. Behind him one made out Apsara heading in the same direction and Hari a few steps after her.

In the second photograph, Triplex was on the upstairs veranda fiddling with the lock, his head bent, while next to him Apsara was casting a nervous eye down the street – her body covering most of his.

The photographs from within the room were poor in quality: the lights had been off, the resolution of the closed-circuit cameras was low, but one could make out Apsara on the cot and

Triplex doing some hocus-pocus with her. The time code printed in the corner placed them in sequence with the telephoto images and taken together their evidence value was difficult to ignore.

'He needn't ever know who told me.' Bhascar put a muscular finger on the topmost photograph, 'How much for his name and whereabouts?'

'Sorry, boss.'

'You're not covering up for him, are you?'

Hari felt trapped. He reminded himself that there was no such thing as objectivity. Whatever you wanted people to believe, was what you put into their heads – whether you were a detective, psychiatrist or a scammer, it was the same thing. Truth was a matter of persuasion, not of fact. Persuasion, in turn, was all about talking faster than people could think. 'Why would I do that? We have ensured that he never approaches your missus again … when he gets out of hospital.'

'Which hospital?'

'That's between him and his insurance company.'

'But you see my problem, don't you, Majestic? I only have your word for it. I want to be sure that that man is gone for good, even if it means I will have to hunt him down myself and chop him into kebab pieces and feed him on a platter to his mother and his father and his sisters and brothers.'

'Due to our stringent code of ethics, I must counsel you against any such course of action as it may land us all in jail.' The entire thing was about to backfire.

'Look, we're both businessmen. Name your price.'

'That is unfortunately not a good idea.'

'You understand, Majestic, that I can go to another detective agency with these photos. They too will have musclemen. And they will force you to talk. So why not make it easy for yourself? *Where* is he?'

'He is in Mysore to do penance and eat vegetarian kebabs. Vegetarianism is the best.' He hadn't had the time to prepare proper lies so he was thinking on his feet, and as Mysore was where Triplex had most of his relatives, in theory, he could therefore have gone there. While speaking, Hari locked eyes with Bhascar for an endless twenty-second period, signalling honesty, hoping that he, like all normal people, was given to wishful thinking.

Bhascar finally said, 'Now we're getting somewhere. Mysore, you said?'

'Yes. May I, by the way, have those snaps back?' Perhaps it would be the best for all concerned parties to destroy them.

'I need to think this over.' Bhascar made no attempt to return the camera printouts. Instead he handed over a ₹500 note. 'That should be enough and I get to keep the evidence.'

'So how about one kg of free coffee as a bonus? No? I thought so,' said Hari who then shot off a big smile, wished Bhascar all the very best, bye-bye, and hoped that it was the last they'd see of each other. While mounting his bike he couldn't help blasting himself.

He ought to have put in a better performance back there.

'So I can't upload the clips?' asked Triplex when they met later in the evening.

It looked like it might rain any minute so Hari shovelled in the watery pani puri. He loved the complexity of the flavours: hot, sour, murky, marshy, sickly-sweet, everything at the same time. He swallowed and said, 'No, you are not putting anything on YouTube.'

Hari had used some of the money Bhascar gave him for the printouts to buy his friend a plate of samosa chaat, the rich, oily snack that Triplex relished and, in his own crazy way, had deserved.

'You're so mean,' said Triplex, unhappily. 'It's such lovely romantic footage and I worked to get it. It's my debut as a movie star.'

'Thanks but I prefer not to hear anything more on this subject.'

'Just think about it, Majestic. A video that goes viral is a great way to promote our services. Can I have one of your puris?'

'Have. But it would also mean a speedy death for both of us.' And they'd be lucky to be reincarnated as tapeworms in their next lives.

The skies were full of dark clouds. It would rain. Triplex looked pitifully sorry.

'Hey,' said Hari, 'let's do something fun. How about if it starts to rain we catch the late show of Upendra's flick *Topiwallah*?'

'Majestic, you have no sense of business, you're unable to pay salaries to your staff and you want to go watch some movie?'

Hari chewed and thought it over. Blissful House remained one of the most well-liked eateries near KG Circle, where the rush hour traffic honked its way into and out of CD Road. It was popular with local families who came there to demolish plate after plate of sweets and savouries.

The chaat counter was adorned by a metallic baboon. As children, Hari and Triplex loved to watch the pulpy mango juice flow from the monkey's mouth and fluffy popcorn pop out of its ears even if they could afford to buy neither. Currently, Hari missed those innocent days. But they were grown-ups now and the good news was that they could eat as much unhealthy junk as they liked.

Trying to mend the growing rift between them, Hari decided to treat Triplex to something special. As he went towards the cool counter to see if they had ice golis, he found himself face to face with Mr Bhascar who was, at that very moment, coming out of the family dining hall. His breath reeked of cheap rum and his eyes were redder than usual.

The temperature fell. Hari's blood curdled into frozen yoghurt. No need for ice golis. After the initial near-heart attack, Hari saw that Bhascar had his missus and daughter in tow.

This night had turned out even worse than bad.

8

How to Live and Let Die at a Chaat Counter

Apsara was wiping ice-cream from Galata's frock and brushing away puffed rice that had somehow nestled all over her hair. She hadn't spotted Triplex yet. Hari felt rather than saw Triplex stiffen behind him: the sound of munching was replaced by a perceptible vacuum.

Dying wasn't necessarily a bad thing as long as you were reborn as something better, he reminded himself. But the problem was that you could never be sure. Suppose one ran the risk of taking rebirth as a tapeworm, to use a not entirely unlikely example, one had good reason to cling to one's present incarnation, so he greeted Bhascar in a most friendly manner:

'Good evening, Mister Bhascar, good to see you're out gallivanting with … eh, the family tree.'

'Majestic…' Bhascar was mining his cavities with a second-hand matchstick. Even that makeshift toothpick looked potentially lethal in his hands. 'Fancy crossing paths with you again.'

Apsara glanced up, saw Hari and frowned – was there a hint of recognition? – and then her eyes darted past him and she quickly pulled the sari pallu over her forehead, low enough to hide her face.

'My good self I am simply taking in the healthy evening air,' said Hari somewhat awkwardly. 'Had your tasty tiffin?'

'Yes.'

'And had your coffee too?

'I only drink my own coffee.'

'Oho, why drink adulterated coffee here when you can blend your own?'

Bhascar took the matchstick out of his mouth and snapped it in half. 'Introduce me to your friend, will you, Majestic?'

Hari was about to claim that he had no friends, detectives were loners, but he knew that the only way out of this mess was to play the bluff game – audaciously – so aloud he said, 'Yes, this is Sri Neel Yeenappa. Associate, freelance, not fulltime. You might recall…'

'Yes?'

'…what I told you about torpedoes and musclemen? It is advisable that you immediately forget ever setting eyes on that man. For your own safety.'

Hari glanced over his shoulder. Triplex had turned his back to them and put on sunglasses. He was less brave in reality than in his fantasies.

'Those white leather boots must be very fashionable since I seem to have seen something similar recently,' said Bhascar. 'What is that goat head design on his nylon shirt?'

It was unfortunate that Triplex wore exactly the same outfit as in the surveillance pictures.

'Please come.' Hari lowered his voice and dragged Bhascar with him, a few steps away. 'The earlier owner of the clothes actually … doesn't need them anymore. And you know why, don't you? He's a *eunuch* now. Let's keep the subject confidential.'

Bhascar bent down to face Hari and he too whispered. 'Say, Majestic, there was one thing that I was wondering about.'

The man's self-restraint was scary. Also, judging from his breath, he had polished off the entire bottle of rum. Hari's only hope was that Bhascar would refrain from killing collateral victims in front of his daughter. He was a doting dad after all.

'Yes?'

'You say the bastard had been turned into a eunuch?'

'Yes, that's exactly what happened. Very sad case.' Hari put on his gravest face.

'I see. How do you explain that, when according to the time data printed on the surveillance photos they had been snapped earlier today? You mean to say that in the span of one afternoon he did that business, got beaten up by your men, was castrated, put in hospital and … didn't you say he's gone to Mysore? Do you want to know what I'm thinking right now?'

'Not necessarily.'

'I think you think I'm stupid.'

'Absolutely not. Must be a technical goof up at the lab where we got the printouts done. These things can be fixed. I'll get you a fresh, correct set of prints free-of-charge.' *Don't panic, not good.* Hari mustered up all his ex-conman talent to play this right. Apart from changing the dates and times, he'd get Doc to photoshop a random head onto one of the surveillance images of Triplex in the hotel room.

'Explain it one more time. Is he in hospital or is he in Mysore?'

'Bit of both, perhaps.'

'Or perhaps neither? I think you're a pathetic liar, Majestic.' Bhascar turned to his wife and raised his voice, 'My dear, would you trust this man?'

She was evasive. 'He seems like a fine young man. Are you planning to hire him as a delivery boy? Looks a bit old for that job … and weak.'

'What about the trustworthiness of his…,' said Bhascar and turned back to Hari, but in the meanwhile Triplex had slunk off into the crowds, '…bastard friend?'

Hari nodded his head sideways in concern. 'Oho? That bastard, not worth trusting.'

Bhascar was about to say something but Apsara interrupted him:

'I think Galata must go home to sleep.'

'No, I don't,' said Galata who sensed that some adult drama was being played out before her. But their daughter's voice deflated Bhascar's attitude.

Apsara dragged her away and started walking ahead. Bhascar had to follow. As a parting shot he said to Hari, 'I have no reason to trust you anymore. You'll soon find out what I'm capable of.'

Hari smiled and said, 'Bye-bye and wish you all the very best.'

'Majestic, I swear I didn't touch her.'

'But I saw you. There's photo proof,' said Hari with pity and sorrow to his best friend.

He had found Triplex cowering behind the next corner, his macho bravura wiped out.

'I didn't touch her like that. I just got her to drink wine to make her uninhibited and get the sari off. For the sake of the cameras.'

'What nonsense are you talking?'

'It didn't work the way it was planned. Photos lie, you know it as well as I.'

Hari checked behind his back. Bhascar and his family were gone. This was mad. He and Triplex went in the opposite direction, to where Hari had parked his Enfield Bullet.

'What do you mean?' said Hari as he strapped on his military style helmet.

'It was obvious that she didn't want to go to bed, so I did some pretend Tantric stuff for the camera. But nothing happened.'

'Now you're telling me!'

'I was doing my best to help. I gave you something to show the husband, didn't I?'

'False evidence! And you lied to me,' said Hari and gunned the engine.

'What to do?' said Triplex as he jumped on behind Hari.

Of course, it had never occurred to Triplex that somebody might take out a contract on a man who just did what a man had to do.

'The best would be if you went on leave for some time,' said Hari as he drove towards the KSRTC bus station. 'Go and stay with your relatives until Diwali. That's the only place where he won't go hunting for you now that he knows I lied about you being in Mysore. The rest of the world is going to be turned upside down.'

'Paid or unpaid leave?' said Triplex.

'What do you think you deserve?'

Hari felt sorry for him. Sometimes he found it hard to understand how Triplex had been reborn at all. When they got to the KSRTC terminus, Hari used up the last of the money Bhascar had given to buy a one-way ticket and explained to Triplex that he must count himself lucky that Apsara and Galata had been present. Without them there was no telling what Bhascar might have done – a good guess was that he'd have nailed the makeshift toothpick into Triplex's roving eyeball.

'And you better get rid of the shirt and boots,' Hari continued. 'They're all over those snaps. If that guy hires thugs, you're going to be cremated in your fancy garments.'

'This is a brand new shirt!'

'You went and bought it for that purpose!' exclaimed Hari who found it hard to believe how meticulously Triplex had planned the seduction. That was the problem with him. In the wrong circumstances, Triplex could be very crafty.

'Just because you never get any girls you shouldn't be so envious. Can I at least keep the boots? Please.'

'The boots will have to go too.'

'You're so mean.'

When it came to facing consequences, it was as if he had the mind of a child. On the other hand, Triplex never hesitated to help Hari with his schemes no matter how dubious they were…

'And don't come back until I say so,' Hari sighed.

Finally, after Hari had pushed Triplex onto the shuttle bus for Mysore Road Satellite Bus Stand, he wiped sweat off his face, the perspiration mixing with rain drops. It wasn't as if he'd lost a friend permanently. Triplex always turned up again, the way a spam email for cheap Viagra popped up in one's inbox no matter how many times it was deleted. But it had indeed been a rough day and he ought to get back to office before there was a complete cloudburst. He kicked life into the Bullet's engine.

•

The motorbike rumbled up CD Road through one of those sudden and intense post-monsoon showers when it not only rained cats and dogs, but bandicoots, cheetahs, Bengali swamp adders, inflatable crocodiles and baby elephants too.

Even if he was wet and miserable, Hari Majestic thought of himself as the king of these parts, a troubled king, but nevertheless the king.

His phone buzzed in his pants. He checked the screen and saw 'Codename Rick' … that would be AC Gaadi. He decided not to take the call. One day he'd teach Gaadi how to write by using predictive text and then he could SMS instead of eating into Hari's mental bandwidth.

He felt sick and tired of detective work. A big mess, that's what he had made of his first case. The downpour grew heavier and heavier. CD Road was getting flooded. It looked like it had rained ten inches already. The streetlights flickered and there'd be a blackout any minute.

He parked his Enfield Bullet in the alley at the back of Puncherwallah Complex and handed out the half a dozen samosas he had parcelled for his trusty stray dogs. On his way to the office, he glanced across the street at Deluxe Bar where a big bunch of huge thugs stood in the doorway … And one of them was Mr Bhascar.

Running was the wrong thing to do if he wanted to prove his innocence, so Hari took a brave step into the street to resume their earlier conversation.

He stopped when he heard somebody shout 'Majestic!' from above. He turned his head up. It was Doc on the first floor veranda of Puncherwallah Complex, outside his cybercafe which was adjacent to Hari's office, waving. It looked as if his nose was wrapped in tissue paper. Maybe it had been mistaken for a ball and struck with a bat?

At the same time the drunken thugs spotted him, so Hari didn't have the time to make sense of what Doc was up to, playing cricket with his own nose.

He assessed the scene and noticed that Bhascar held a cricket bat. Hari connected the dots. Something seriously bad was going on. And Hari had a sudden feeling that he knew what, as the gang of heavy-built thugs started moving like fuelled-up tanks towards the battlefield, in Hari's direction. The skies cried as if the gods were already mourning him. If life was a movie, this kind of heavy rain would have been an ominous sign. Luckily, he was still wearing his helmet.

When Bhascar came close enough for them to have a civilized conversation, his first words were, 'Bastard, I'll kill you.'

It wasn't as if it came as a surprise to Hari, because ever since the day they first met, he had known that Bhascar wanted to kill whoever was trying to make his missus happy.

Hari attempted his broadest smile, the one that stretched from ear to ear, until his lips hurt. 'I'm actually not a bastard. I'm an orphan.'

Smiling didn't help much, because Bhascar continued along the same track, 'It doesn't matter what you were before, but now you're dead.'

'What have I done?' asked Hari and took a step back, always the sensible negotiator.

'You set my wife up in order to take compromising photos of her.'

'With all due respect, it was that other bastard,' said Hari.

But the situation was not in his favour. The thugs fanned out in the street, stopping the sparse traffic. Some of them were giants. Tattooed. Their moustaches were a hundred times bigger than Hari's downy upper lip fluff. He had to retreat, like an abdicating emperor, back into the alley.

Bhascar came after him, 'And where is *that other* bastard?'

'Out of station. Why don't you save yourself trouble and simply believe me when I'm telling the truth?'

'Where?'

'Mysore, of course,' said Hari retreating another step, but they all moved a choreographed step towards him.

He knew that these thugs were not going to be happy unless somebody suffered a great deal, it was unmistakable from the way they unsheathed their long swords sharpened out of strips from a car chassis, known in street slang simply as 'longs', and how their bicep muscles were tensing inside their soaked half-sleeved safari shirts. Until they laid hands on Triplex, he'd have to substitute for his friend.

'Don't lie to me, Majestic! I just saw him with you.'

Hari heard somebody scream 'Help!' but it turned out to be just himself. Some loiterers on CD Road stopped to peek into the alley, but when they figured that it wasn't a film shoot, they hurried on in the relentless rain. This wasn't their riot.

The thugs blocked the entrance to the dead-end alley. There was only one way he could run. He did a turn and rushed behind Puncherwallah Complex. The thugs followed, mud splattering as they ran.

Hari ran towards his motorcycle.

The pursuers were a few steps behind him, when the stray dogs started barking. The thugs stopped, hesitant to enter further into the noisy darkness. But Bhascar, face red with rage, attacked Hari, smashing his cricket bat against the motorcycle helmet. It sent Hari staggering.

Suddenly there was an eerie howl and an organism hurled through space and landed spread-eagled across Bhascar's face, its claws sinking deep into the fleshy head meat, as its razor teeth cut into the coffee miller's throat.

Underdog! The fearless mutant mongrel proved that he was the best friend of some men and the enemy of their enemies, and did his usual antisocial thing by urinating into Bhascar's sinuses.

He then snarled at the other thugs, bared his bloody incisors and gave them the I'm-rabid-and-you're-dead glare. The thugs debated among themselves whether the risk of getting chewed up by disease-ridden dogs was worth the free booze they'd been treated to.

Feeding snacks to the dogs had proved to be a better investment than any health insurance policy, thought Hari.

In that moment of chaos, Hari jumped on his bike. He kick-started the engine that was still hot and the Bullet shot through the lines of men. Then he did a googly around the corner and was cruising down CD Road.

Death had been postponed. He glanced back and saw Bhascar and his men with their swords and bats. They were running to a row of two-wheelers outside Deluxe Bar.

He took a sharp turn at the next corner into SC Road and toppled over the bhajji-wallah's boiling oil vat and stacks of batter-coated eggs. The hard-working man had found a dry nook from where to peddle cheap junk food to the few hobos that risked the pouring rain.

'Sorry,' Hari shouted. 'I'll come and pay later.'

Somebody always had to pay … Scary thoughts filled Hari's head. *Had Bhascar beaten up Apsara to get the truth out of her? Maybe she lay hurt in their hut?* He went through his options. Her safety was his responsibility now. He could only think of one honourable thing: he must rescue Apsara and take her to a hospital. Then he'd be ready to die a hero's death.

Plans were forming in his mind. In case he found her unharmed, he must warn her that if the gang couldn't lay their hands on his own good self or Triplex, they might target her next. He'd drive Apsara to the police station and get Sub-Inspector Pushpa to help her. She could be locked up in protective custody, Hari thought as he swerved into Tank Bund Road. He speeded so fast in the rain that he almost skidded and fell off the bike.

The engine stalled. Everything was going wrong. He looked back to check how far they were. Half a block. They were riding slow scooters. That was a clear indication that they weren't professionals, just a bunch of bad buddies Bhascar had rounded up and plied with booze to jack up their machismo.

'You'll too be reborn as a scooter if you don't cooperate,' he told his bike as he tried to wake it up.

It worked, it started. He drove out of the way of a lorry that came blasting down the road in the wrong lane the way they do at night, when the drivers are half asleep.

He recalled that during their surveillance work he'd noticed a fenced in compound that had been marked for the construction of Garden-city Residence apartments, but that was being used as a garbage dump and children's playground. There'd be plenty of hiding places. He could lose them there.

It'd buy him time to fix this mess. Hari took a side lane into the semi-slum, cruised between rickshaw wrecks and then switched off the engine and rolled the bike through a gap in the fence at the end, across chemical puddles, and did his best to look like he and his bike were part of the trash. He pushed the two-wheeler into a dark corner and squatted behind a rusted car carcass.

He waited.

The rain poured. After a few minutes, he peeked through the holes in the Hindustan Contessa, a vintage model.

The thugs had stopped outside the fence. They were spreading out to surround the compound. Smart thugs, smarter than he'd thought. They'd cut off the escape routes and wait him out.

'I know you're there, Majestic!' Bhascar called out.

No, you don't, thought Hari but managed to keep his mouth shut.

'We'll catch you and you'll regret.'

Perhaps Bhascar was right. No point waiting for all that to happen and then regret it, so without starting the engine, Hari got up and pushed his motorbike along the dirt track, deeper into the darkness, behind stacks of steel beams and other construction material. By the time they figured out that he'd moved on, he'd be long gone.

For some distance the abandoned construction site remained a rubbish dump. Then it merged, seamlessly, with the semi-slum. Where the garbage mounds ended he found himself in a narrow lane by the main drain. The rain stopped, he wiped his face. Things were looking brighter.

When he thought he was out of earshot, Hari jumped onto his bike and kicked life into it. He rode on, hoping to lose them by taking random turns to the left and right. Slums were always a bit of a maze with very few straight roads. Soon he barely knew where he was.

He zigzagged madly along the slippery paths, way too fast considering there were no municipal streetlights. Sometimes he crossed through tiny backyards with collections of empty coconut shells and soggy washing that had been rinsed by the rain.

Finding himself in an alley that didn't lead anywhere, except in circles, he opened the nearest door without knocking – the lower-end housing was made of tarpaulin and palm leaves and so there was no point putting padlocks on the doors. That would only lead to the locks getting stolen by scrap metal dealers. Hari pushed his motorcycle through a home, apologizing to the women for disturbing while they were busy cooking dinner. Luckily, their menfolk were out working in the rain – perhaps hunting him – or he'd have got himself into more trouble there and then.

All around the slum dwellers went about their evening activities. Because the huts were so tiny, much of people's lives took place outdoors – retired uncles sat under palm trees smoking, chai in flimsy plastic cups was bought from pushcarts, children gathered round the sellers of hot boiled peanuts. Life, pure and simple.

Hari saw all this in amazing detail, the way one tends to do when one regrets the many wrong choices in one's life, and he wished then that he had followed a 101 per cent righteous path – then he'd have been one of these normal folks. Instead of always finding himself in trouble, he'd be sipping tea, watching some stupid stressed out loser trying to run from a gang of thugs.

He suddenly recognized a building, a burnt-out shed in the front of which he had himself hung a sign prohibiting trespassing, and he knew he was back at the pink concrete hut that used to be the abode of love, or Prem Vilas.

He stopped in the tiny square. His pursuers were nowhere to be seen. He took a deep breath and then slowly drove his bike through the sticky mud into Bhascar's lane. The moment he reached Prem Vilas, he pulled up close to the door and banged his fist on it, calling to Apsara to step out.

'Don't be afraid, missus. We met before. I need to talk to you.'

Nothing happened. He hoped that he wasn't too late.

'I have an important message,' he shouted. He kept banging on the door. He had some Diwali crackers left in his pocket, in a plastic wrapping, and lit the fuses, throwing them on the threshold of the house. When they went off, she'd hear the explosions, if she was alive.

But the fuses must've been wet. There were no blasts. Instead he blasted himself for having bought such shoestring budget crackers.

He decided to go get the police to break down the door.

He got on his bike.

Meanwhile, the door opened and it turned out that Bhascar was home, towelling rainwater off his face. His cheeks bore the bloody scratch marks of Hari's stray dogs. Or were those the marks of Apsara defending herself against a beating to death? It was a thought that Hari didn't want to think, but couldn't put out of his head. Bhascar greeted him coldly, 'There you are, bastard. I was getting worried that you may have lost the way.'

'Not to worry, I used to be a tourist guide, boss.' But Hari rolled his bike back from the door, things weren't going right.

Bhascar came nearer. 'Think I'm stupid? Did you think I wasn't going to suspect that you too were wooing my wife?'

'Oho. Let's not mistake,' said Hari and smiled – to keep smiling even when you were facing death was a survival tactic he had already learnt as a child. But when he looked around, he saw that his escape route was being cut off.

Bhascar's thugs came from the slum square, armed with long swords. They weren't as many now. The rest must have stayed back at the construction site, but even the three that he could count outnumbered him – and Hari was very good at math.

It was a trap. He should have anticipated it.

'You're a clever man, boss,' said Hari. 'I think we can discuss this issue between mature gentlemen.'

Bhascar finished wiping his face with the towel, then he wiped his hands. But said nothing.

'With all due respect,' Hari went on, 'killing one's missus or other civilians is not advisable. Let me point out one thing to you, honestly, everything you saw was an illusion. Your missus was faithful and if you hadn't doubted her devotion and hired detectives, there would have been no problems.'

'Don't lay any blame on me.' Bhascar threw the towel on the ground between them.

Hari worked harder. 'Try to see the moral of the story: never distrust your loved ones … Where is she, by the way – madam Apsara?'

'Don't drag my wife's name into the mud with you, bastard.'

'I already told you I'm an orphan…' he started but then he was bereft of speech.

Because she came up behind her husband and Hari was pleased to see that she was alive and well, until he noticed that she was holding a cricket bat. The odds in favour of his survival had been under 5 per cent until this point, or the same as the percentage of alcohol in a mild UB Export beer, but he feared he might have reason to lower those odds very soon.

I'm dead, he thought.

No, worse, he rethought.

Taking a good look at his ex-client's scratched and bruised face, Hari instinctively knew that Bhascar wasn't going to forgive and forget. When he gave it some further thought, he couldn't fault his client, not after what he and Triplex had done to destroy the family. But it was good that Apsara wasn't dead. A child shouldn't have to grow up without a mother.

As Bhascar took it from her, she resisted for a short while but then she let go of the cricket bat. She wasn't as merry as she used to be, but more like resigned to fate. It appeared that her husband was now going to use Hari's head as a cricket ball. It was the sad end to a bad game.

9

How to Impersonate a Dead Hero

'Tell us where your bastard friend is hiding and we'll let you go, Majestic.' Bhascar slapped the bat against the palm of his other hand. A perfectly reasonable deal under the circumstances, but it was getting repetitive. 'And if you say Mysore, it'll be your last words.'

One's last words were only spoken once in a lifetime, so Hari cleared his throat and chose them with care, 'Can't we reach some form of gentlemen's agreement? Out of kangaroo court justice, boss.'

Surreptitiously, he felt around with his foot for the kick-starter. But one of Bhascar's thugs reached out a meaty hand and when Hari evaded it, another massive thug caught him in a firm grip from behind. Hari turned his head only to, literally, face death.

Behind him stood the biggest of the gang's men, a giant who sported the grandest moustache that Hari had ever seen – outside the silver screen where moustaches always were larger than life – and his bulging forearms were decorated with impressive skull and crossbones tattoos. As he pulled Hari up close to his reeking mouth, the fumes made Hari a bit tipsy, 'We like to keep the area clean. That means if dirty boys like you, who dare try molesting our wives, come here, we clean you up by dipping you in acid.' He laughed at his own joke and Hari noticed that he had gold teeth. Some kind of slumlord, he probably hoarded his criminal earnings in his mouth.

'That's quite hilarious,' said Hari and tried to laugh with them, while looking around to see if any of them actually carried a canister with acid.

'Don't kill him yet, Deadlyappa, let him speak,' said Bhascar.

Deadlyappa was a suitable alias for a person like that, thought Hari who knew the kind of guy fairly well, the kind who shaved his balls with one hand while dipping losers in barrels of acid with the other, but aloud he said, 'Seeing that you're anyway going to rip me apart, I'd rather not betray my colleague due to the karmic repercussions and my future rebirth options, if you get my point.'

'No problem. So say goodbye then,' said the giant with the gold teeth.

Hari regretted his words almost immediately, but couldn't take them back. So here it was, the end, he thought and felt sorry that he'd never had time to travel around the world and all the other things he hadn't done. How sad.

Suddenly, there were loud blasts like gunshots and the thugs threw themselves to the ground. Mud splashed. Hari too was mildly shocked, but in less than a second he realized that it was the Diwali crackers that had been smouldering and now had finally gone off.

He saw his chance.

Leaning down low on his bike, he gunned the powerful engine and the Enfield shot off like a bullet. Its back wheel bounced on something. A foot must have gotten under it. He heard Deadlyappa cry out loud. The thug in front of the bike rolled out of the way and Hari yelled, 'Bye-bye and all the very best!'

He did his trademark zigzag in case the pursuers were good at throwing swords. He planned to return with the police in tow. He dug for his phone to give Pushpa a call; he had the Sub-Inspector on his speed dial under the codename 'Wrong Number'. He noticed there were lots of missed calls. Right then the mobile started buzzing.

He glanced at the screen and saw 'Codename Rick'.

AC Gaadi again.

He was about to divert it to a psychiatrist who could write out a prescription for some pills to calm the rickshaw driver down, but then he thought better of it and took the call. Hari squeezed the phone between his cheek and shoulder as he cruised down the alley, his bike skidding on the muddy lane. At the same time, there was a thunderclap and then rain began pouring down.

'Swami, it's me.'

'Yes, I can read,' Hari said grimly. 'Had your dinner?'

'Listen, swami. They want to take care of you. They beat up Doc at the office.'

'I know … with a cricket bat.'

'I've been looking all over for you. You okay?' asked Gaadi.

'Not to worry. Just got a little bit ambushed.'

'Where are you, swami?'

'Driving away from Stakeout Position Alpha. The thugs were going to dissolve me in acid, turn me into tooth paste or something.'

For once he hadn't exaggerated much. There was a brief silence.

'Okay, swami, sounds bad, even if it may be good for your teeth. According to my SATNAV, there's a narrow lane to the right after you pass the tall toddy palm. Drive down there. Park your bike in front of the Hardly Country Liquor Shop. I'm just a few blocks away and I'll pick you up around the corner in a minute. They'll think you're hiding inside the bar and by the time they've asked all the drunks they won't know what happened to you.'

'Great plan,' said Hari and swerved into the lane after the toddy palm.

The road ran between ramshackle huts. He clicked off the phone when he smelt putrid arrack and then he spotted the liquor shop and that was about as much as he managed to do before the ground gave way under his motorcycle. Its wheels were spinning in thin air.

Oho, thought Hari as he saw the earth rise to kiss the moon.

It was a kaleidoscopic experience. The headlight of his Enfield Bullet played on the sheets of rain that fell over the slum. For a split-second his brain tried to process what was going on. Then everything flew up fast, or rather, he fell down.

With a screech of metal, the bike bounced on the paving bordering the edge of the uncovered main drainage channel. He smashed into the ground, hitting his side, his teeth rattled as he banged his head on a concrete slab. His helmet was ripped off. Luckily, his head stayed on.

Twinkling lights. *Stars or raindrops?* For a moment he didn't know what was up or down, and he held on to his bike for dear life as it skidded down the muddy embankment.

As the motorcycle tumbled into the main drain from which the semi-slum derived its name, he fell along with the heavy machine into murky storm water. The engine hissed when it died.

As he sank, Hari reminded himself that in his next reincarnation he'd fix everything better if he only came back as a human, and not repeat the same mistakes, and then he thought: *Here we go, bye-bye and all the very best.*

The motorcycle's wheels hit the bottom that was covered in debris and so it toppled over against the drain's sidewall, but he was still in the saddle, and unable to move because the weight of the bike squeezed his leg against the slimy concrete. He was stuck.

He heard voices.

'Is he dead?' asked Bhascar and somebody shone a torch into Hari's eyes.

But he wasn't dead, not quite; he was still breathing. Waves of sewage lapped his face. His head was above the surface. Somehow he felt very lucky to be stuck, for the current might otherwise have swept him away. As long as the water level didn't rise, he'd stay alive. But he couldn't move. Through half-shut eyes he saw the beam of light hit the raindrops that appeared almost suspended in the air. The thugs walked around on the embankment. Bhascar looked down at him.

'Hey, bastard! Are you dead?'

Hari reminded himself to stay optimistic, say nothing, do nothing and they might go away.

'Bastard looks dead.'

'You sure? He's one devious bastard.'

'I'm not going to climb down and find out, if that's what you're asking.'

'How about we throw something at him?' another man said.

'Why?'

'Timepass.' Laughter.

'Let's not waste more time. If we leave him like that, it'll look like a traffic accident.'

'Okay, come on before anybody sees us.'

One by one, the gang members took off. The last one to go spat at Hari, satisfied with a good night's work.

However, thought Hari to himself, they obviously weren't used to killing people. Most people weren't. Hari knew from experience that it could actually make one feel quite sorry afterwards, especially the first time. That was the main difference between professionals and amateurs when it came to these things. Professional killers would make sure that the target was properly dead.

There was silence again. The bad part was that he didn't know how to swim. He tried to pull his leg loose, but it was stuck. With his heart thumping hard and his blood rushing, Hari felt himself drown slowly as the muddy water rose around him.

Somewhat later, he heard AC Gaadi's autorickshaw come thundering down the alley, a sonic boom blasting the hubbub of hell on top volume, which was really a distorted karaoke version of Michael Jackson's 'Bad'.

The rickshaw was near. Hari tried to shout, but the music was too loud. He heard the sound of the engine grow softer as Gaadi drove on. He accepted his karma and saw death ahead of him, a bull's-eye that he was flying towards like a dart and he tried to focus on hitting a higher score for a better rebirth. Maybe he should have chosen a different set of last words – something more heroic? Anyway, now it was too late.

Then the rickshaw returned.

Was he hallucinating? *No* … It stopped, the engine switched off, and Hari heard Gaadi talk to somebody. Punters from Hardly Country Liquor Shop, perhaps, but the voices were distant, blurry. Soon Gaadi had gathered a group of people to help him search, there were shouts, they shouted his name. *They were looking for him!* Gaadi was a well-known character hereabouts, his reputation as a man of action had spread across the slums. Nobody dared to contradict someone like him.

The voices came closer. 'You saw them chase the kid in this direction?'

Indistinct reply.

'Help me!' Hari called out, trying to avoid swallowing too much water.

But when Hari looked up it was to see Gaadi's happy face. He was having a laugh at Hari's expense. 'Taking a bath, swami?'

'Extra witty. Pull me up.'

With two other men holding on to him so he wouldn't fall, Gaadi reached down into the drain. But Hari's leg was stuck. It felt elastic. Almost as if it was stretched out and about to be torn off.

'Hang on a sec,' said Hari.

He fumbled around under the surface, got a grip and pushed the motorcycle away from the side of the drain. Finally his leg came loose. It wasn't excruciatingly painful, thank god. He held up his hands again, Gaadi caught them and fished Hari up and out of the mucky yuck in one swift move. The leg that had been stuck was numb.

'My bike is down there,' said Hari. It was the most expensive thing he owned.

'Don't blame me. The SATNAV wasn't up to date with that open drain, any chance we can upgrade our systems?'

'The day I make money I'll definitely consider it. Right now rescuing my motorcycle is a more pressing concern.'

He felt dizzy. Gaadi helped him stand up. 'Don't worry, swami. We'll fix your bike, catch those thugs and disembowel them organ by organ, and have too much fun doing it. Revenge is always the best cure.'

But unlike Gaadi, he didn't believe in scorched earth policy, so rather than pulping misguided gentlemen he felt like going home, rinsing off, having some piping hot coffee, seeing if his mobile phones could be dried and putting on clean clothes.

In a perfect world, that would have been the next move. But it wasn't. When Gaadi let go of him, Hari's leg unexpectedly folded under him and he collapsed.

To his astonishment, the earth came flying up again in a rerun of the previous accident. He could only watch the calamity stupidly, unable to make sense of it. Gaadi caught him before he smashed his face into the paving slabs a second time.

Sitting down, Hari was initially a bit puzzled, but then he made the observation that his right leg was missing – or rather it wasn't where it should have been but was bent at an unnatural angle as if there was an extra joint between the knee and the ankle.

Although still attached to his leg, his foot was lying sideways next to him. Without being a medical expert, Hari guessed this meant that he had broken some bones.

'I'll take a rain check on the pulping expedition,' he said.

'Ayooh, swami,' Gaadi tried to cheer him up, slapping him playfully.

'No-no, I think my leg's actually broken.' Hari pushed him off.

'Looks to me you have two feet, two hands, but perhaps too much imagination.' Gaadi found it hard to believe that recreational violence could be that harmful.

'I don't want to die.'

'Of course not,' said Gaadi and grabbed Hari's arms. 'Come on, cheer up.'

Hari head-butted him on the jaw. Instead of hitting back, Gaadi analysed the sight of Hari's strangely and inappropriately bent leg. He said, 'Shit happens.'

Hari tried to feel consoled. Weird – the leg was broken, and yet he wasn't screaming his head off. Maybe because he was born to be a hero? Or was it that he was in too much pain for his body to feel it? Intellectually, he was completely there. He knew, for example, that life was never going to be the same. His next assignment was going to be as a maimed beggar, pushing himself up and down Brigade Road into the paths of tourists, tripping them as they came out of shops in the city centre. No woman would want to marry him. Maybe Gaadi should throw him back into the drain, wish him all the best and then ... then Gaadi asked,

'So what do we do now?'

Hari had a sudden idea. He should have listened more carefully to his old teacher Hochiminh Meshtru when he had gone on about hospitals. Now the finger of destiny was pointing him in the right direction. On his quest to do good for mankind, this was going to be his last and most important case – before he joined the ranks of the beggars.

Yes, this was how it must be.

'Let's go to Sickly Hospital,' he said.

This was the perfect cover for the job: a broken leg. The best plan under the circumstances. Besides, he figured that he would be safe in the hospital and Bhascar's thugs wouldn't find him there.

Gaadi bundled Hari into the back of his autorickshaw. The passenger seat was wide enough for him to sit sideways with the leg stretched out.

Thus it was proved once again that rickshaws, like the one Gaadi owned, were what kept this city and its inhabitants alive. The three-wheeler roared out of the shantytown and up to KG Circle where it cut through the traffic like the last of the man-eating tigers of the erstwhile princely state of Mysore. The rest of the traffic treated it accordingly.

Gaadi drove around the temple in the square the wrong way and, turning and shouting to Hari, explained that some holy man had told him to always go against oncoming traffic in order to reverse any bad karma.

If karma was involved then surely this was it, thought Hari, as the centrifugal force threw him into the guard rail, leg first. Now finally the pain hit him. He screamed, every bump in the road making him feel like he was a masala ingredient in a mixer-grinder.

Gaadi screamed back, 'Yes! Just shout, let it all out. It'll make you feel good, swami.'

Hari went on screaming but it didn't help much.

Minutes later they negotiated some roadwork – the old bazaar areas were being upgraded to the new millennium with underground broadband cables – and screeched to a halt in Balepete's narrowest bazaar where the Sickly Hospital lay wedged between single-storey neighbours.

Karma, it has to be karma. Hari felt the new case being placed before him like a challenge from the gods, making his senses acutely alert to everything.

The former Sickly Hospital looked the same as it had always done. The iron railings were rusty, giving it that Bollywood B-grade horror movie look that certain lower-class lunatic asylums took pride in maintaining. Only the signboard was freshly repainted and now this was GSSS Hospital – Globalized Style Super Speciality Hospital. It was flanked on one side by a pharmacy, Sickly Medicals, to which patients were sent to buy their own medicines, and a booze shop on the other, MRP Drinks, handy for bedridden rowdy-sheeters and goons like Hari's uncle who simply threw down a rope with money tied to it from their ward window and hoisted up beverage and mixture to supplement the hospital fare.

A few steps away from the entrance, a man lay face down on the pavement. Perhaps he'd had a peg too many and done something stupid, and then hadn't made it to the hospital in time. For it was a fact that Sickly Hospital used to be the traditional healthcare centre for crooks, thugs and rowdies: no questions were asked as the staff was accustomed to the chop-chop injuries of the CD Road lifestyle.

It wasn't that the area lacked better places to go to. Right opposite a fancy new establishment was under construction.

Mediclinix Resorz™ seemed incongruous in a bazaar like this with its glass facade. A luxurious franchise catering to the local sick rich. But nobody that Hari or Gaadi knew ever went to such places where they probably asked for an ID before you were admitted.

Hari turned his attention back to GSSS Hospital and saw an orderly come out carrying an ominously red bucket and for a moment he wished he could afford something classier, something like the medical resort across the street, and get taken care of by a luxury doctor. He should have bought a medical insurance when there was time, now he was paying the price of procrastination. Well, too late for regrets.

Then he noticed there were cute nurses by the entrance to GSSS Hospital. In their uniforms they looked too good for health and quite attractive as well. He'd at least die surrounded by beauty, if he did. Meanwhile AC Gaadi barked orders in a manner that made it clear that 'No' was the worst possible answer. After some negotiations and a growl from him, two orderlies in lab coats – hopefully they weren't on the morgue staff – were bullied into submission. Initially, they refused to touch Hari, pointing out that he was covered in slime and didn't smell nice. But Gaadi just growled once more and Hari was quickly prised out of the back of the rickshaw.

They reluctantly held on to his arms and told him to climb up the steps.

No way. He refused. So the orderlies carried him indoors. The sewage made his body slippery. Every time they lost their grip and his foot hit the ground, he cried. It wasn't exactly a hero's entry but it drew the attention of a pretty nurse and a gurney was found for him.

The waiting area was swarming with wailing patients and one man was panicking, 'I'm not screaming. I'm talking normally. Why do you accuse me of screaming?' Hari agreed. People shouldn't be wrongly accused of screaming when they were only shouting.

Then Gaadi issued loud threats left and right until Hari was rolled into the emergency room. A middle-aged nurse arrived on the scene, stern, matronly, bespectacled, her grey hair cut short, with a Florence Nightingale cap firmly in place. Her nametag identified her as 'Head Nurse Kolaveri' and she told Gaadi to shut up or leave the premises.

That silenced him. Perhaps she reminded him of his mother and it was a universally accepted truth that a man always had to obey a mother's voice. 'Give this one an injection so he stops crying,' said the nightingale to one of her nurses.

Hari was given one huge injection, so powerful and quick-acting that it was like having a coconut smashed over one's brain. Due to the resulting grogginess, the nightingale gave Gaadi an admission form to fill out on Hari's behalf. He sat down on a plastic chair by Hari's gurney, daunted by the sudden paperwork he was saddled with. It was a known fact that he disliked bureaucratic order.

However, it turned out that Hari had underestimated him. He took out a pair of reading glasses from the breast pocket of his uniform shirt, then he squinted at the papers.

'I didn't know you were literate,' said Hari, stoned from the massive injection.

'Don't tell anybody or I'll have to kill you. People will start thinking I'm a soft guy and take advantage,' said Gaadi. 'Anyway, what's your name, swami?'

'You know my name, boss.'

'Ah yes, in all this excitement I forgot: M-E-Z-E-S-T-I-C, right?'

'Quite right,' said Hari. Checking in under a slightly false name was always the safest.

Stealthily, he infiltrated the globalized hospital system, watching everything and everybody. Of course, his body was genuinely messed up, which made the undercover act more convincing.

The gurney smelt of disinfectant and dead bacteria. The walls were plastered with posters – 'the Wonder of Herbal Medicine for Childless Infertility Sexual Disorder' … 'Yogic Therapies for Alcohol Addiction Hairloss Weight Gainloss' … 'Conducting of sex determination test of the sex of the foetus is officially prohibited and therefore it is not officially done here.' Everything seemed normal and overboard, so Hari's first impression was that his teacher Meshtru may have worked himself up unduly.

Then he caught sight of a familiar moustache. *Oho!* One of the other patients who had come in was a friend of Bhascar's, Mr Deadlyappa who had been hostile a little while ago. He was more humble now. Listening to his conversation with the nurse, Hari understood that the back wheel of the Enfield Bullet had apparently crushed Deadlyappa's foot. According to Wikipedia, a foot contains 26 bones and many ligaments that can get damaged.

That's the thing with these classic motorcycles. They were heavy. Especially when they roll over feet. To be on the safe side, Hari snatched a roll of bandage from the instrument trolley next to his gurney and wrapped it around his head so as to stay incognito. The battle wasn't over until it was over.

Then he made an inventory of the staff. His eyes were twice their normal size as he studied these cute nurses who were so unperturbed by the body's frailties. They went on piecing together broken skulls like 3D puzzles, stapling cut up faces, band-aiding the ailments that were typical of CD Road people.

The pretty one, who had found him the gurney and kept glancing curiously in his direction, was almost certainly from Kerala. The other one with long wavy hair was so obviously from Kerala. The voluptuous goddess … ah, got to be south Kerala. Then there was the head nurse, the nightingale with forbidding, conservative eyes, looking like she was … *Tamilian?* Better be careful. One should always make friends with the bosses, thought Hari and started planning some witticisms to entertain her with.

One of the nurses, the pretty one with the toothy smile, came to him and removed the bandage from his head. Hari breathed in her delicately complex scents of talcum powder, coconut oil and something else, something spicy. With a wad of cotton wool, she daubed disinfectant on the bruise he'd got when he smashed into the slab by the main drain. Or maybe it was from when Bhascar tried to knock him out with that cricket bat. Luckily, he had worn his helmet at all times.

'Don't worry, sir; the doctor will soon be here.'

He did a 360 degree head turn. There were no other patients within hearing range. She called him 'sir' for some unaccountable reason. Did he look that old?

'Are you talking to me?'

'You're that detective Majestic who was in the newspaper last week, aren't you, regarding some inauguration of a new secret agency?'

Blasted, his cover had been blasted.

10

How to Be Patient

He analysed the situation. The nurse evidently read the local papers about neighbourhood heroes and she also had an extremely beautiful big smile with a chipped front tooth. He felt as if she saw right through him … the dirt, the sewage and saw the real him.

'Is this accident the result of some hero stunt?' she went on, casually.

He meditated for a fraction of a second. *What would Triplex have done in the same situation?* The truth was that women scared him. He had so little experience of them. His own Mum had deserted him. His adoptive mother had died prematurely. All potential girlfriends had said no when he asked them to say yes. Cautiously, he rolled his head sideways.

'I thought so.' Her voice was a bit like what you'd expect to hear if a girl added sugar, honey *and* jaggery to her coffee: energetic, melodious, deliciously sweet. She held up five fingers and asked, 'Sir, can you count my fingers?'

He did his best to interpret the situation correctly. *Was she flirting with him?* 'Yes…' he confirmed. He read the nametag on her chest, discreetly. By mistake he spoke her name out loud – '...Diamond.' He went on, lowering his voice, 'As a matter of fact, I would appreciate it if you didn't mention to anybody that I'm here. Can't start writing autographs. It would draw unnecessary attention.'

What a name! She even wore a tiny diamond stud in her nose, set in a gold flower.

'Kindly focus on my fingers.' She was obviously used to being ogled at by boys. 'Count them.'

Hari thought furiously and asked himself: *What would Triplex have done?* Counting to five was hardly going to impress anybody. He wished he could call his deputy director and take his advice. *Call?* Maybe that was the answer. So he blurted, 'Nurse, why don't you ask me to memorize your phone number instead?'

'How many fingers do you see now then?' she spoke with that delectable Malayalam lilt. She held up one finger, the middle one.

Everything was great about her! She was not only incredibly stunning, but thoroughly hardboiled.

When Hari continued his surreptitious survey of the emergency ward he noticed that Bhascar's injured friend was scowling. His big moustache was drooping. Uh. Hari smiled back, did an innocent shrug. It was a game of survival and everybody had lost a little.

Mr Deadlyappa then leered so that all the golden teeth showed and he shaped his hand into a gun, and with the forefinger and middle finger erect he drew a line across his throat, and then he pointed at Hari. He was definitely more than a semi-professional rowdy-sheeter, possibly a history-sheeter.

There was a sudden clatter as AC Gaadi jumped up from his chair, knocking it over in the process. Happy to have something better to do than fill forms, he walked across the emergency ward like a thunderstorm, rolling up the sleeves of his uniform shirt. He growled a few quiet words to Deadlyappa with a fist in the air. All patients turned to look the other way. That was how you stayed alive hereabouts.

Right then the bossy head nurse with the Florence Nightingale cap walked in. She had fetched a big pair of scissors.

Gaadi quickly shaped his fist into an extended paw and shook hands with Deadlyappa. It was the forceful, menacing type of handshake of a temporary, fragile truce. Then Gaadi returned to the chair in the corner and twiddled his thumbs with an angelic expression on his face. At least somebody was having fun tonight.

Head Nurse Kolaveri busied herself with cutting off the leg of Hari's jeans with the scissors. Down below his knee there was a dark red mark. Up on his thigh there was a purple bump the size of a coconut on the spot where he had hit the side of the drain. Things were not looking good at all. His two mobile phones, coated in brown slime so they looked like chocolate bars, fell out of the pockets.

'You're smelly,' she said, quite unimpressed by him.

Hari didn't dare to contradict. She had a strong personality. He asked, 'Is it serious?'

'Save your questions for the doctor.'

'But will I die?'

'In the long run, most likely from lack of hygiene.'

'Will I walk again before I die?' Hari hoped he wouldn't have to hobble out of the hospital with a strap-on Jaipur foot.

She looked at him, matter-of-factly, 'I'm afraid you'll be back on the streets sooner or later, none the wiser.' She had, in no time, formed herself an exceedingly unfavourable opinion of Hari, and to her his present condition was the natural result of antisocial activities.

On the positive side, she clearly didn't suspect at all that he was there to spy on her workplace. So far only Nurse Diamond and Mr Deadlyappa knew his real identity. Deadlyappa wouldn't go high-profile and kill him in the emergency ward but bide his time until he got an opportunity to quietly stab Hari in the back. Regarding Nurse Diamond he'd have to wait and see.

Sometime later, a doctor came to examine Deadlyappa's foot and Hari's leg, and to check out all the other human wrecks that had drifted into the emergency ward on a stormy night like this.

About Hari's own age but well fed, indeed fat, like educated people with good pay packets usually were. The doctor's body was full of curving S-like patterns – his nose was like the lower half of the S, the brow the upper half; his moustache was two tilted Ss head to head; his double chin a series of intermingled Ss. Past life: perhaps a boa constrictor that had died from indigestion after swallowing a hippopotamus. He even had a tattoo on his lower arm of two intertwined snakes. The thing that worried Hari wasn't so much the doctor's young age – or whether he was fresh out of medical school – but his nametag that gave his name as 'Viral'. It was a common enough name and in any other line of work it'd have been perfectly ordinary.

But Dr Viral acted competently; he looked at Deadlyappa's foot first and sent him off for treatment – one worry less for Hari – and then he came over, pressed around Hari's ankle with both thumbs, performing a thorough leg examination. 'Move your foot sideways.'

Hari doubted it was possible but fixed his eyes on his foot. And he made it a point not to crack a joke about the doctor's name.

He willed the foot to move. And it did. It moved left, then right.

'Very good. You haven't damaged the muscles or the nerves,' Dr Viral stated. 'But it is nevertheless a serious bone fracture.'

The doctor declared that this required super-specialist surgery and that the operation must be done immediately. Hari agreed. Head Nurse Kolaveri came back with more papers on a clipboard. 'We need to confirm your Medi Assist card particulars.'

'Simply haven't had time to fix one, but printing out the insurance letter is the first thing on my agenda.' He'd get his uncle to forge some semi-authentic insurance papers.

But it wasn't good enough for her. She explained the deal. For an expensive surgery they required an advance cash security deposit from patients who didn't have insurance, because a rowdy-sheeter treated on credit wasn't likely to come back and pay later – he might well be dead by that time. The estimated cost for the procedure was ₹60,000, out of which a third had to be paid in cash upfront; the rest to be settled before he was discharged.

'Without a leg, how will I run without paying?' he argued. 'The only way I can skip the bill is by dying on the operating table.'

'Be that as it may, the question remains: how will you pay?'

It was easy. There was no way he'd hand over 20,000 to them. He decided to call their bluff and turned to Gaadi, 'Let's go, boss. I think the leg is fine now.'

Miracles did occasionally happen, especially in India. The pain was gone. He swung his good leg down from the gurney, a bit light-headed from the injection with the strong painkiller and reached out for Gaadi's shoulder.

Gaadi steadied him. 'Sure you're okay, swami?'

'About half-half, give or take. The quack misdiagnosed me.'

He took one step and the broken leg folded like a three-way jack, first at the knee, then again between the knee and the ankle, and Hari started sinking towards the floor. The doctor hadn't tried to cheat him. They had to lift him back up on the gurney.

Gaadi took off to get cash. Not from an ATM, because none of Hari's friends had a credit or debit card, but from loan sharks who advertised 'no security required at weekly interest' with stickers on lamp posts, urinals and bus seats.

Gaadi came back a little later, not so upbeat.

'What happened?' asked Hari.

'Swami, they're willing to lend towards buying a vehicle or a house or something that can be used as collateral. But no moneylender would risk a rupee on your life.' Gaadi shuffled his feet. 'I collected as much as I could from Doc and the others, but it doesn't come to more than a grand.'

Hari tried to smile. 'Thanks.'

'What to do, want me to sell my auto?'

'No, not that, absolutely not,' said Hari – he was touched by the gesture but knew that Gaadi's identity and his autorickshaw were one and the same, without his three-wheeler he'd be a lost soul.

The head nurse returned again, assistant nurses in tow, to find out if Hari was planning to vacate the gurney. She informed him, 'There is a traditional bonesetter down the road. He'll "fix you" for fifty rupees.' It was brutal but at least she was honest – people had survived in the many millennia before Western medicine came along, and by cheaper methods.

'But please, Kolaveri Didi,' gasped Nurse Diamond.

Hari considered the time-honoured budget option, but the way Diamond covered her worried gasp by pressing a hand to her lips made him think twice: did she visualize him as a cripple? For it was a well-known fact that people who went for traditional remedies, where the broken leg was put into bamboo splints, often limped for the rest of their lives.

'Aunty, *swalpa* adjust-*madi*. Is there no other option?' Hari finally said, the tension returning bit by bit, pain stinging his leg again.

Head Nurse Kolaveri gave it some thought. Then, for some strange reason, she started shooting off questions at him at a speed that Hari had difficulty keeping up with.

'How's your health other than the leg?'

'I follow my astrologer's advice and he says health is wealth, so by that token I'm rich.'

'Do you smoke?'

'What's that got to do with my leg?'

'The doctor will need to know everything, so, for your own safety, answer the question honestly.'

'I've no unhealthy habits,' lied Hari.

'Drink?'

'Never anything but fresh lime soda sweet and salt,' he lied again. Small lies: the occasional bidi or drop of gin surely couldn't matter? Hari chewed his lip, hoping that the random meaningless questions might lead to a reward of some sort.

She snapped, 'Any existing medical conditions: infections, hepatitis, HIV, cancer?'

'No, Aunty.'

'And your family?'

'Not that I know of.' Absolutely true, since as an orphan he'd never met his biological parents. 'Aren't you going to ask if I have allergies?'

'Do you?'

'None whatsoever.'

'Then why should I ask?'

'For fun?'

She turned to the nurse, 'Diamond, run urine, serology and blood tests. We also need chest and kidney X-rays, and abdominal ultrasound.'

'Why?' asked Hari. This didn't sound like it was going to come cheap. They were planning to rip him off big time.

'We want to eliminate any possible risks.'

'What risks?' It was indeed beginning to sound risky.

'None as long as we do the necessary tests to eliminate them. So how old are you?'

'How does it matter?'

'You want the surgery or not? Age?'

'Sorry, won't interrupt again. But you see I don't have a birth certificate, though I have reason to believe that I'm twenty-eight.'

'What do you mean – "reason to believe"?' The nurse stared at Hari for a beat, 'You think this is a joke, huh?'

'That's the truth. I was adopted.' He gave her his best smile, the one where every tooth showed.

'Let me see what I can do,' she said.

She walked out of earshot and made a call, standing under a sign that proclaimed mobiles must be switched off. After a few minutes she was back.

'It's your lucky day,' she said. 'There's a foreign surgeon in residence at our sister clinic across the street. We pool our resources. He's willing to perform the operation together with our own Doctor Viral.'

Hari remembered having noticed the posh Mediclinix Resorz under construction bang opposite. Jackpot indeed, sometimes the worst day of one's life could turn out to be the luckiest one. He noticed that Diamond smiled too.

'Okay, what's the catch?' asked Gaadi.

His sober growl reminded Hari that strings were attached to every special offer. 'Yes, why would he do it?'

'Goodwill work under our charitable slum-dweller scheme. Since you obviously don't have a medical insurance or cash, it won't cost you a thing. Doctor *Glas Philipovich*,' she pronounced his fancy foreign name with care, 'will do this for a bit of exercise.'

'Is he going to experiment on me like some kind of guinea pig?'

'Don't talk nonsense. Doctor Philipovich comes from an old aristocratic family and happens to be one of the world's topmost surgeons, trained at UCLA…'

'Doctor of liposuction or what?' said Hari to add a light remark, so as to mollify the grumpy head nurse.

'Behave yourself. You can take it or leave it. But if you have the surgery, you're going to be walking again in about three months.'

'Three months!' To somebody with his restless temperament that was equal to serving a life sentence in Parappana Agrahara Central Jail. But then again … *international expert?* When the choice was between a foreign style luxury surgery for free and a bonesetter who'd tie a bamboo stick to his leg and give him an eternal limp, the choice was easy. This also meant he'd get to investigate two hospitals at a go, a great gig – like killing minimum three birds with one stone.

'So what do we do next, madam Head Nurse ji?'

Head Nurse Kolaveri fetched a document consisting of two stapled pages. 'Put your thumbprint on the form. Our nurses will run tests while the operation theatre is made ready.' She seemed to take it for granted that someone like Hari didn't know how to read legal documents.

But she was wrong. Hari glanced at the 'Charitable Slum-dweller Scheme' application form. It contained a lot of gobbledygook that he was supposed to accept, but thanks to his advocate uncle he understood that it absolved the hospital of any responsibility if something bad happened during surgery. 'What if I don't accept?'

'Then nothing happens.'

So the irony was that after all he had no choice in the matter. Might as well auction off one's soul on eBay, he thought as he pressed his thumb on the dotted line.

He was swiftly admitted, his body was washed and disinfected by the orderlies, the tests were run and he was given a private room on the ground floor, rather than a bed in the common ward. Nice, he thought: it also meant he wouldn't have to sleep in a cot next to Deadlyappa. He observed that the door couldn't be bolted or locked from the inside, but then again as long as Gaadi was there they'd outnumber Deadlyappa.

Another doctor came with Viral to look at him. An older man, thin and tall, greying at the temples, with the indeterminate face of a multinational corporation, and the only disturbing characteristics were the Band-Aids that covered much of his hands and even neck.

'Why has he cut himself so badly?' whispered Hari to Viral in the local language, Kannada, getting apprehensive about the surgeon's scalpel skills.

Viral replied in a mixture of Hindi and other languages, like the cosmopolitans did, 'Voh nicotine patches hain. My colleague is trying to give up smoking. Just don't do anything that might irritate him and you'll be fine.'

'Oho. Will the surgery be painful?' Hari asked.

'You'll be sedated while your bones are realigned and a rod is inserted to keep them from moving out of position during the period it takes to heal,' Viral said.

'And you're sure I won't die?'

'Doctor Philipovich never makes any errors.'

The eminent Philipovich listened to Hari's heart and gazed into his pupils while humming to himself. Thorough. Philipovich mumbled in some singsong lingo and Viral appeared to understand what he was saying. Hari's own European vocabulary included words like 'spaghetti western', 'pizza delivery' and 'mafia', none of it useful there and then.

But he presumed he could not be in safer hands.

When he was wheeled into the operation theatre, the sedative was administered by Head Nurse Kolaveri and he drifted out of consciousness, as spaced out as a cartoon character.

There was no turning back, he thought in one of his last lucid moments before his eyes glazed over with the transparent screensaver that most people are equipped with by nature.

Maybe better that way. He heard the drilling and hammering, drowning out the beeps of the ECG. Whenever the doctors spoke to each other, they did so in their secret foreign language.

Later he woke up for a fraction of a second to see the doctors wash their hands. The surgery was over. The last he noticed was two red plastic buckets filled with ice in the corner of the operation theatre, by the washbasin. Then he fell asleep.

Being under sedation was like visiting an alternative reality. Everything merged, his imagination, the Wikipedia, all the googling he'd ever done. A human is nothing but a virtual extension of the Internet. *One is nothing but an extension of the Net?* He must have read this somewhere or was it the dream talking?

His eyes popped open and he saw his body crucified on the hospital cot. His torso was feverish as if filled with stir-fried adrenaline. He tried to change his position. *What was this?* He couldn't feel a thing in the lower body! He forced his head up from the pillow, about to cry. He envisioned himself in a wheelchair, everything amputated from the nipples down, a vegetable with USB dongles plugged into his ears.

Looking around, he found that he was back in his private room. He made out his body, it was hooked up to two needles sunk into his hands, transparent rubber tubes ran to a stand and hanging plastic bags with liquids in them, plus two more hoses draining fluids from lower down. One of them was scary, filled with a gore-coloured fluid. *Had he been contaminated by something when he fell into the drain?*

He tried to shut his eyelids but he was still in post-traumatic shock, his eyeballs pushing out of their sockets and making it hard to avoid the horrific sight. He counted and re-counted the limbs.

There were four of them – two arms, two legs – yes, way to go! No need to overreact. The broken leg was bandaged and propped up on pillows, but otherwise very solidly where it belonged. He was in hospital, safe and being nursed back to health.

Then he took in the private semi-deluxe room. The walls were bare, whitish with darkish palm prints here and there. No attached bathroom, but a washbasin and a trash bin by the door. A limp wall bracket indicated where a TV set had once been. Now the only entertainment was a window with a vertical pattern of iron bars on it, through which faint streetlight seeped in. It was quiet outside, early morning as far as he could tell.

Gaadi sat in the corner next to the door, on a plastic chair, snoring in a low key. He'd hopefully wake up and protect Hari in case Deadlyappa came knocking.

Royally loyal, thought Hari, *should sleep, me too*. But all the drugs in his system made his thoughts spin in a most surreal manner.

He simply couldn't get the cute nurse out of his mind. He remembered that one of her front teeth was chipped, the only flaw in her beauty. He let his tongue play along his own teeth until it wriggled its way into the gap where a tooth had been knocked out during a street fight – a strange coincidence, but their mouths were indeed compatible, made for each other like filters and cigarettes.

What to do? Trying to figure out what Triplex would have done in his situation, he tried out some tentative pickup lines. 'Your smile is the world's second biggest.'

'What's that?' said Gaadi, sounding suspicious, suddenly wide awake. No smile. He clenched his fists. He was grumpy too.

'Sorry, talking in my sleep,' said Hari, on the defensive.

'You woke me up.'

'So sorry about that too. Just a nightmare, boss. But I'm all right now.' However, when he tried to sit up, his head began to spin. The pain was returning, not just to the leg but the sides of his stomach too. 'How many days have I been out?'

'Your surgery lasted until three in the morning, swami. So go back to sleep.'

'I can't.' Too weak to be up, but too worked up to sleep.

Gaadi started to push Hari down on the cot. 'It's 6 a.m. and if you don't stop talking nonsense, I'll ask them to put a stitch across your mouth.'

But Hari was genetically unable to shut up. The eagerness to talk nonsense was boosted by all the drugs that had been pumped into him.

Gaadi went to the door and shouted into the corridor for a nurse to come fast. He must have woken the entire hospital. Hari noticed then that there was no buzzer at his bedside. But he started smiling in anticipation of Diamond entering his room, even though he wasn't quite done rehearsing yet. He said to Gaadi, 'Get me a glass of water, will you, boss.'

'What … water?'

'What if they give me sleeping pills to swallow ... you want me to shut up, right?'

Gaadi went to the washbasin in the corner.

'Not regular tap water,' said Hari. He wanted Gaadi out of the room. 'Filtered water.'

'What nonsense!' said Gaadi, as if Hari had asked for perfumed sherbet.

'I'm fragile, I've had surgery and I'm afraid the smallest bacteria might kill me.' It was a small lie, he actually felt quite heroic.

Gaadi thought it was thoroughly uncool to display emotions – like fear, worry, love, whatever. But he took off to go find the nearest water dispenser. Hari straightened his hospital gown and licked his teeth clean of night fluff. Then he remembered his hair and ran his fingers through it to put all the curls in place. He heard girlish footsteps.

11

How to Know the Difference between Real Love and Stockholm Syndrome

When Diamond crossed the threshold, his smile stretched until the corners of his mouth got hooked around his ear lobes. His mental cameras zoomed in on her face from multiple directions, in the blockbuster version of existence that constantly played in the sold-out theatre of his mind.

'How are we feeling, sir?'

'I can't sleep.'

'Not to worry, we'll give an injection.'

'It is as if the ache is spreading.' *To my soul.*

His grin froze when Head Nurse Kolaveri followed Diamond into the room. She positioned herself at the doorway. Of course, any nurse would take care to never be alone with a male patient hereabouts. So he didn't dare to flirt as much as he had planned. It was too risky.

'It's your nerves replaying the accident,' said Diamond.

'But it's hurting all the way to my chest,' he improvised. He spoke in code: a nurse would know that the heart is situated in the chest. There was some truth to the claim, too, as his body felt like one big bruise up to the neck. Especially, it seemed that the lower part of his ribcage had been pummelled badly. Hari fingered the rubber hoses that pumped stuff into and out of him, 'And what are all these doing in my body?'

'Fluids to hydrate you and antibiotics go in through the two intravenous lines, the catheters drain out urine and bile.'

'I see,' said Hari although he didn't quite get it. But he guessed everything served some purpose – removing bile sounded top class, even though he wasn't the bitter type. One shouldn't be too suspicious, not when one got cut and pasted for free by foreign diploma-holding medical experts. 'But why am I so sore all over?'

'Probably just some *allergic* reaction,' said Head Nurse Kolaveri snidely. Hari hadn't thought of her as the type who'd cut jokes, but she was hopefully just trying to tickle his funny bone with her remark.

'In my stomach?'

'We'll increase the dosage of the painkiller.'

'But won't that make it an overdose?'

'Be strong, sir,' said Nurse Diamond, preparing a syringe. 'This might hurt a little.'

This was not at all romantic, Hari thought to himself as she wiped a portion of exposed skin with disinfectant and then jabbed the hypodermic needle in. While she went to dispose of the syringe, he got woozy. He dreamt that she removed his hospital gown. Or was it Head Nurse Kolaveri doing it?

They uncoiled a length of bandage from his abdomen – bandage? *Abdomen?* They spread greasy ointments on him. It was a vivid dream. He may have tried to speak. Uninhibited by drugs, he thought he said, slightly embarrassingly considering that they weren't alone, 'You have the second biggest smile in the world so … uh, so being a professional nurse do you want to practise the mouth-to-mouth method with the one with the biggest smile?'

Hopefully it was just a dream.

He smelt something burning, smoke in the air and opened his eyes. Gaadi had lit a breakfast bidi by the window.

On the bedside table there was a steel plate with an idli on it, plus, according to a swift forensic examination that Hari made, rice crumb traces of two more idlis and driblets of coconut chutney. Gaadi had been considerate enough to leave one for Hari.

Daytime traffic outside: scooters sputtering and whining as people drove to work and clinking of bottles being transported in tempo trucks. Not the night time racket of drunk driving and rowdy thugs. There was construction work going on nearby, the persistent shriek of a cutting machine mixed with the loud grating of a borewell drill. All the noise made the windows rattle and his bed shudder. Strange place to build a hospital, this unquiet bazaar, but it wasn't any concern of his.

Time for work. To be on the safe side he counted his legs and his arms again. All fine, all still there. He pulled up his gown to have a look at the spot where Nurse Diamond had touched him – whether in a dream or reality.

Strange … There was a bandage wrapped around his abdomen just like in the dream. Why had the doctors performed surgery so far up from the leg? Had he cracked a few ribs too? He made a mental note to ask somebody.

Hold on, he thought, *this made no sense*. His uncle had damaged his ribs in drink-related accidents and had never been given anything but painkillers, and told to rest and stop drinking. He knew it was a genuinely bad idea, but curiosity got the better of him and he unwrapped the bandage from his torso. Then he studied his abdomen. There were two sterile cotton pads on his stomach, one to each side. The compresses, held in place by adhesive strips, were situated too low to be broken ribs.

When he pried off the compresses it didn't hurt, the painkillers took care of that, but he saw dark bruises extending down from below the lowest rib and across the midriff. At the centre of each bruise was a big scar. The larger one was almost a foot long from end to end, wrapping around his body towards the back. Many stitches and some dried blood. No sign of inflammation, but then on the other hand he was on an antibiotic drip. What were these scars? *Allergy?* Hardly. What then? *Stigmata?* Had he become a Western saint all of a sudden?

This was absurd.

'Slept well, swami?' asked Gaadi, interrupting Hari's stream of consciousness.

'Yup. I thought I was dreaming but … do you see what I see?'

'Depends entirely on what you see.'

'Look. My tummy has been stitched up.'

'What's the problem? You're in a hospital and for your information they stitch people in hospitals.'

'It's a problem since it was my leg that broke.'

Gaadi barely glanced at Hari's scars and proclaimed, 'You think too much, swami, that's your only problem.'

Hari had heard that one before. Almost everyone, including his astrologer and spiritual adviser Pandit Pundit, kept telling him to stop thinking unnecessarily. 'But…'

'Surgery is surgery and if you don't come out of it with scars then it is no surgery. Got your money's worth, haven't you, swami?' said Gaadi and lit another bidi.

The sun was shining on half of his face and Hari could tell from the dark bags under his eyes how extremely worn out he was. He decided not to argue any further.

Later Dr Viral came on his rounds together with Head Nurse Kolaveri. Viral looked as if he hadn't slept much that night. He'll go far, thought Hari, be the owner of his own hospital one day.

'So how does the leg feel?' asked Viral, while strapping a cuff onto Hari's arm to check his blood pressure.

'Absolutely fine but I think I may have developed an *allergic* reaction.' Since he was there undercover working on a case, he had to play his cards with care.

'What's that?' Viral removed the stethoscope from his ears for a second.

Hari pointed to the bandaged mess on his tummy. 'There was some discomfort here this morning.'

'What kind of discomfort?'

'The head nurse thought it might be allergy.'

Nurse Kolaveri gave him a toxic glance.

'Right, nothing to worry about. I'll prescribe something,' he said and plugged the stethoscope into his ears again.

'But what's wrong with me?'

'Nothing. No bleeding – that's a good sign. The operation was successful and you may experience nausea currently, but everything will be perfectly fine, don't worry.'

How bizarre! Emphatic insistences of nothing to worry about always made him suspect that the matter involved some ultra fine print that was invisible to the naked eye. But he was too stoned from the medication to put his finger on the problem.

Viral washed his hands at the basin in the corner of the room, squeezing liquid soap out of the dispenser, rubbing his palms together. He was either very clean or liked to pretend so. Hari saw his snake tattoo and was reminded of his initial impression – the doctor was a snaky type, hard to get a grip on, shedding his skin every now and then according to Hari's analysis.

He remembered how the doctors washed their hands … vigorously in the operation theatre, at a washbasin in a corner … It seemed to him that he had observed something significant there and then. But his mind was covered by a thick drug haze.

Viral finished his meticulous handwashing. 'Nurse, make a note. In addition to the steroids and broad-spectrum antibiotics, the patient is to get medication for epidural pain, morning and evening, heparin injections, Punarnava tablets and Liv-52, the strongest capsule to be taken thrice daily for four weeks.'

'So I'll be here for another four weeks?' said Hari.

He seemed to recall having been told something different the night before.

'No-no, you can say goodbye to Nurse Kolaveri after a few days.'

'Now you're telling me! I was informed earlier that it'll take months to heal.' Blasted, he had expected to spend ages flirting with Diamond and investigating the hospital.

'The entire healing process will take that long, that is so,' said the doctor, his earlier reticence replaced with a medical advisory tone – possibly to avert later patient complaints. 'But you don't have to stay here for that to happen. What you must decide soon is whether you want to use a walker or crutches, and as soon as your stitches heal you must practice a few physiotherapy exercises, and then you'll be fit for fight in about twelve to sixteen weeks, I'd say. Until then, it's advisable that you don't take coffee, don't put too much strain on your body – no rough sports like boxing or wrestling.'

'No coffee?'

'Absolutely not. What work do you do, by the way?'

Hari was about to say hero, but made a tactical diversion, 'I'm a consultant.'

'Very good. Carry on then,' said Dr Viral and left.

Meanwhile, Gaadi had been loitering by the door, but now he came in again. It was time for another bidi and since smoking was prohibited in the hospital he could only light up in Hari's room. He looked bored.

'There is one doubt,' said Hari.

'Tell me, swami.'

'You'd never lie to me?'

'Why would I?' said Gaadi.

Yes, maybe he wouldn't, but who knew? 'For no purpose,' said Hari. 'But you'd tell me if I was…' he hesitated, 'was having a nightmare?'

'You had one in the morning.'

'Correct, boss. But am I having one right now?'

'What do you mean?'

'The doctor and that nurse were here, weren't they?'

Gaadi nodded but looked oddly at Hari, who decided that it was time to be proactive.

'So I am awake then. Okay, boss. Priority number one: take my mobile phones and get them repaired. The Enfield Bullet must immediately be pulled out of the drain and given to Puncherwallah's workshop for a bit of tuning up. Have him disinfect it – especially the handlebars. Drive by Bhascar's place and check on his missus, speak to the neighbours and ask them to keep an eye on the family. Urgently. After that, have a nap so that you can be back on duty in the evening again.'

Gaadi looked like he was about to say something, but kept quiet.

'Was there something I forgot?' said Hari.

'Your enemy is in the common ward with a broken foot, same corridor but two doors down. Right now he's not walking. Sure you will be fine alone?'

'Excellent human intelligence gathering. Now get me a dozen glasses of coffee and I won't be alone.'

'No coffee for you said the doctor, but you can binge on filtered water.'

Was Gaadi being sarcastic? Before he could figure that one out, Gaadi was gone. Minutes later he heard the familiar rumble of the autorickshaw through the window and a blast of Michael Jackson on the karaoke, Gaadi roaring along to the music, and then the comforting noise vanished in the distance.

Hari was alone. The medication kept his mind fuzzy, it was difficult to focus. Without coffee, it was hard to do anything at all.

Now and then he heard steps. But they passed his door. Once in a while he worried that Deadlyappa might get stupid ideas and try to take revenge. But he wouldn't be foolish enough to do anything in broad daylight, not if his foot was injured and he couldn't run away from the scene of the crime, and soon Gaadi would be back for the nightshift.

Unlike his uncle, who was frequently hospitalized, Hari wasn't used to being sick. Peculiar thoughts were clicking in his head as if a rusty crankshaft had been inserted through one of his ears to turn the brain upside down. Maybe it was the shortage of visitors and the lack of coffee and no Internet – but as there was nothing else to do, he went on obsessing, calculating and crunching the numbers. He was staring at a sum where the factors didn't add up.

It was generous of the hospital to bill his surgery to a charitable scheme. The leg was going to be fine, the doctor had said. And he hoped that the doctor was trustworthy. But he had doubts … The medical advice didn't seem consistent with a broken limb. It was more like the doctor had been talking about hernia, an illness that Hari's mildly decrepit uncle suffered from. If he wasn't so stoned … He battled with his mind, told it to focus.

He wriggled the toes at the end of his bandaged leg. The abdominal scars were a fact and there was nothing he could do to wish them away. *What had really happened?* Sometime during the hours when he was under sedation somebody had done some extra cutting on his body. It was another fact that couldn't be ignored, however weird it seemed.

'Wake up, sir!' To see Nurse Diamond in the doorway was like watching a beam of sunshine come dancing into the room. 'Time for lunch.'

Of course Hari hadn't been asleep, just pretending. He yawned, acted the part of a tired weakling, while he scrutinized her, read her body language, looked for signs. In her starched uniform, Diamond was lovely, like one of those celestial beings in Christian paintings that missionaries sometimes brought to CD Road in order to save a handful of sinners. But he simply couldn't get used to being called 'sir'. Before he met Nurse Diamond, nobody had ever addressed him that way.

Since Head Nurse Kolaveri was nowhere to be seen – she must have gone to her quarters to sleep after a long shift – he flirted. No harm in trying, as Triplex always said.

'You can call me Harry, the hero from the newspaper, remember?' he said.

Diamond's backup consisted of a skinny ward boy who emptied the garbage and pretended to do some room-cleaning. He didn't seem particularly concerned about Hari. Nurse Diamond brought the lunch tray to him – palak paneer, rice, curd and two mandatory chapattis.

'How's the "hero" doing then?' She had attitude, she didn't go first-name basis just like that only. No, she was proper.

'*Enikku sukhamaanu*,' he said, using one of the phrases he'd picked up from Kerala people.

'Oh, you speak my native tongue,' said Diamond, delighted, clapping her hands together.

Of course he did, he was an ex-tout, wasn't he? 'To tell you the truth I've felt better. But it's all part of the job. Trouble during a case. It was a high-speed motorcycle chase.'

'A "case-chase", it must have been exciting,' she said, playing along. 'But why take a job where you break your bones?'

He had no good answer for that. But the sun shone through the broken pane of glass, making the whole room shimmer with an amber hue that enveloped Diamond in a halo. Her voice was like a sweet song from a nice movie. She hummed the theme from

Uppidada MBBS – she also appeared to like the same gangster comedies he enjoyed watching. He said, 'The *bad guys* thought I was dead and chucked me into a sewer.'

'Sounds very dangerous.' He felt a sting of jealousy at the thought that she might be equally cheerful when talking to other patients – many of whom, like Deadlyappa, were bad characters from CD Road.

'I do what I must do in the line of duty.'

'Eat your food then, that's your duty for today.'

'By the way, thanks for saving my leg,' he said, while scooping up some of the curried spinach with a chapatti even if he had no appetite. 'We heroes do much legwork, you know, so we need to mind our legs.'

'It's okay. We get many similar cases. Routine matters, Bengaluru traffic mostly, rarely as exciting as yours.' She checked the numerous rubber tubes attached to him and changed the infusion bags dangling from the drip stand. Then, measuring out pills into a small plastic cup, she said, 'Once you've eaten, it'll be time for medicines.'

Voltage and wattage was in the air, low perhaps as of now but it was there. He felt torn between his logical and emotional sides. *Was she as innocent as she appeared? Could it be love at first sight or was it Stockholm syndrome? Trust nobody*, he reminded himself. Perhaps it was time to use his deductive skills, because the only way to find out, as Uncle Mamool usually said, was to find out. So he tried another approach. 'So at ₹60,000 for routine leg surgery, the hospital must be raking in the profit then?'

'What's that supposed to mean?' She set the last of the pill bottles down and handed him the cup with medicines. There were many pills in funny shapes and colours. 'Take these if you're not planning to eat more.'

'Your salary must be quite decent and you probably get provident fund and a pension too?' he asked.

'Much of the work here is charitable.' She took the hospital's side.

'Tell me, what are these medications good for?'

'So that sir will be out of here faster,' she said politely. Among the pill bottles he recognized one – the herbal wonder drug Liv-52, typically administered to alcoholics with liver diseases and of course, Hari's uncle Mamool had one at breakfast, lunch and dinner.

'I thought I was getting all the antibiotics and painkillers I needed through these tubes.'

'Don't worry, herbal tonics are never harmful.'

'And what does this one do?' he asked pointing at the Punarnava bottle.

'Hogweed,' she said, 'has diuretic properties and is good for maintaining kidney function. Besides it is anti-inflammatory and will protect you against urinary tract infections.' She knew her stuff.

For some mysterious reason, her home state Kerala supplied a large number of nurses, doctors and pharmacists to the healthcare sector, and it was also the source of the many millennia-old Ayurvedic tradition of natural medicine. Hari was ready to bet his money, had he had any, that an understanding of herbs and their medical usage had been passed on in her family for hundreds of generations.

But considering that he had never suffered from kidney ailments or liver disease, it was strange that the doctor had prescribed these two tonics ... unless there was a direct connection to the two suspicious surgical holes in his abdomen.

'What's your last name, Diamond?' he asked. He needed it for his report. 'Mine's Majestic.'

She hesitated. Then she said, 'Mol.'

'Diamond Mol,' he echoed.

'Swallow the pills,' she said as if talking to a patient awaiting a brain transplant.

He said, 'Is that Aunty-nurse your Mum or something?'

'You mean Kolaveri Didi?'

'Yeah.'

'No, sir, why do you ask?'

'There's something odd about her but I can't put my finger on it,' he said. 'She is a bit … bossy.' He had meant to say 'scary' but changed his mind.

'I get your meaning, sir. She's a real mother hen, takes care of us nurses like an older sister. That's why we call her Didi.' Diamond flashed him a toothy smile. 'She's been working here longer than anybody and you couldn't be in safer hands. Sir, now if I may be excused, some of us have work to do.'

So did Hari, so did he.

A faithful old retainer, but he couldn't shake off the feeling that there was something creepy about 'Didi' as the nurses had nicknamed her: Big Sister.

He wondered if 'Big Sister' held the key to understanding how his bonus scars had come about.

12

How to Lose Friends and Make Enemies Fast and Easy

After she left he was alone again and worrying about what Deadlyappa might be up to. Probably making plans for how to take care of Hari. He'd be defenceless if the thug decided to call in his gang. If they were really professional about their rowdy-sheeting, they could storm the hospital, chop him up with machetes and escape before the cops reached. Such things happened hereabouts.

Sometime later, the painkillers kicked in again and hallucinatory images of Diamond, feeding him pills to strengthen his kidneys and liver, were screened in his internal cinema hall. What was the worst case scenario?

Like any twenty-eight-year-old, Hari had seen it all. It was just that it typically happened elsewhere – not in Bengaluru proper, which was an enlightened metropolis. But he'd read about the illegal organ trade in the local newspaper and learnt that, like hamburgers and hotdogs, it was global business. A single human body such as his own, the body of somebody who wasn't a CEO, a film star or champion cricketer, even if it looked useless to the layman's eye, was a rich natural resource waiting to be plundered – it contained many yards of intestine, a lung or two, a heart, pancreas, arms and legs, a variety of glands and eyes including two corneas, also nerves and bone marrow, tissue and about a dozen pints of blood. There was a fortune inside him waiting to be harvested.

Had he spotted Head Nurse Kolaveri on a wanted poster in the police station, for having peddled stolen kidneys on the black market? Maybe that's why there was something so familiar about her? After all, she had been present during his surgery; in charge of anaesthesia, she would have had reason to be both the first and the last at the crime scene.

Yes, of course he could scribble something negative about her in the hospital's Complaints & Suggestions Book. But no, it'd be prudent to maintain a low profile: undercover detective work was required here. One thing was clear. For once in his life, Hari Majestic was the right man in the right place.

It started out like a really nice evening. Around dinnertime, the natural born subversive Gaadi smuggled in Hyderabadi mutton biriyani, Andhra-style lemon chicken and several bottles of super-strong Knockout. Hari was happy to see Gaadi's jolly face and for a moment everything felt normal and the hospital wasn't scary at all.

'Party time,' said Gaadi and opened a bottle with his teeth. 'To your health.'

'So how are Bhascar and missus doing? You went and came?'

'All right, playing happy family.' Gaadi reported how he'd got the slum dwellers to go get ropes and lift the motorcycle out of the drain. 'You will have to invest in a new phone, but your two-wheeler is at Puncherwallah's garage and by the time you're out of here it'll be waiting for you like a long lost lover.' In his bachelor world, vehicles were like spouses, but better.

With his stomach filleted, Hari didn't have much of an appetite. Considering that he probably didn't have a liver either, he thought it unwise to drink beer.

'Sure you don't want, swami?' asked Gaadi.

'I'll pass,' said Hari.

'Okay, more for me, then. What a day!' Gaadi guzzled it down. About one minute later, eyeing the mutton biriyani, he asked, 'And you're not eating?'

'I'm good,' said Hari.

'I'll taste then.'

'I thought you had taken a vow to only eat vegetarian during the pujas.'

'Relax swami, a chicken is a vegetarian and so is the goat, hence I'll help you finish your meal. It's no big sacrifice.'

Time to change the topic, for now the foreplay of light banter was over, with the question he really wanted to discuss, 'What would you say if I told you that I suspect my liver and kidney may have been stolen and that I'm pretty sure the Head Nurse has made non-veg curry out of my body?'

Gaadi chewed his food a little slower, 'If I were you then I'd avoid the grub here.'

'Point taken,' said Hari and waggled his head. Not that he had expected pity. And Gaadi was so right. 'Is that all you have to say?'

'Shit happens.' Gaadi shrugged and gestured with a chicken wing at Hari's leg, 'Take this as a lesson, swami. If you had done what that nurse suggested and gone to the bonesetter, you'd have had none of these problems, both kidney and liver would have been there. But now that you are where you are, you must view this as an opportunity. You'll get stronger by small setbacks. The bone will grow back and be harder to break next time.'

'Please, work with me here.'

'Are you planning an insurance scam?' Gaadi seemed to think he knew Hari well enough to spot a number of opportunities in the situation.

'Me? I'll tell you what I'll do – I'm going to solve this mystery,' Hari declared. 'The question is what you're going to do about it.'

'I'll drink to that,' said Gaadi.

There was an awkward silence when only Gaadi's burps could be heard. Hari felt a little sorry for himself. Deep inside, he was dismayed at the notion that a colleague of his could think him the one pulling a con job here, when he was so obviously the hero *as well as* the victim. And, being without his two trusted phones might, in a worst case scenario, turn him from a manic into a depressive. Gaadi thought aloud. 'So now let me … *belch* … if I've got this right. Somebody removed parts of your body without taking your permission? And you suspect the nurse? But why would she do such a thing?'

'That's what I'm going to find out.'

'And it was done with no written approval from you?' said Gaadi who was eternally sceptical about bureaucracy.

'My mistake. I may have given it.'

Hari recalled in a flash that prior to the surgery he had put his thumbprint on a 'charitable slum-dweller scheme' application which doubled as a consent form that absolved the hospital of more or less everything that might go wrong, and that it had included a clause according to which tissue removed during surgery became the hospital's property to dispose of or use for medical research, and so on.

'What's the problem then?' said Gaadi. 'I thought you got the surgery for free and it was a square deal? And now you're regretting. Is that it?'

And that was, in a sense, true. The problem was that Hari had been preoccupied with getting his leg back at the time. Now he wished that he had paid closer attention. After all, his Uncle Mamool was an expert on impossible paperwork and kept telling Hari that if he ever had to choose between signing a contract and getting shot in the head, the latter was the less bothersome option. At least you had a chance of surviving the bullet.

The situation was both good and bad. More bad than good, perhaps, because suddenly the nurses, Diamond and Kolaveri, were scowling by the door. Diamond carried in a tray with more of the regulation palak paneer.

'Visiting hour is over,' the head nurse announced as she took in the mess of beer empties, food wrappings and mutton bones, and signalled to Gaadi to get lost.

'He's my bodyguard,' said Hari.

Right on cue, Gaadi flashed his Bengaluru Autorickshaw Drivers' (BAD) union membership card which looked like it had been through at least three world wars.

Head Nurse Kolaveri frowned.

'Bodyguard?' She turned to Nurse Diamond. 'Who *is* this patient?'

'Sir seems to be a local VIP … of sorts, Didi,' said Diamond.

'He may be the peg pasha of Patiala, but now he's under my watch,' said Kolaveri. 'Who gave permission to bring drinks here?'

'No problem. We were just about done anyway,' said Hari cheerfully.

'Be that as it may, the drunkard must leave the room, and … from now on he's strictly *banned* from entering this hospital.' She glared at Gaadi who quickly put out his bidi in an empty bottle and was trying to look innocent … but with an incriminating piece of chicken neck sticking out of his mouth.

'But why?' asked Hari. 'Am I not entitled to have a personal attendant with me?' He didn't want to be left alone at the mercy of Head Nurse Kolaveri.

'You should have thought about that before breaking hospital rules.' She picked up a beer bottle. 'Now please tell your … bodyguard to get out before I call security.'

'What if I refuse?'

'You're free to leave this hospital with him.'

Hari would have wanted to have a quick powwow with his number one trouble-shooter. But the ban took immediate effect. No point creating a scene. Gaadi downed his last beer in a rush, sending the bottle clinking under Hari's cot, asking, 'You'll be all right, swami?'

'Not to worry,' said Hari and waggled his head.

Despite having an uneasy feeling, Hari decided that this was the time to get down to business rather than chicken out and decamp with Gaadi. Of course, it may be a bad decision to stay put, he thought but then again, he had often done the wrong thing before and survived.

Right then the situation was further complicated. Dr Viral walked in.

'Doctor ji, what an honour.' Whenever Hari felt the urge to speak, his mouth took on a life of its own. His wit was unstoppable.

It decided to probe as deep as possible. 'How come a talented gentleman like you works in a slum clinic like this?'

'I don't work here,' said Viral. 'I own the hospital.'

Hari was surprised for barely a second, then he exclaimed, 'Oho, how is that?'

'I bought it.'

'But why this slum … why not a proper institute where you can pursue Nobel Prize winning medical research, Doctor ji?' Being a veteran scammer Hari knew how to embed any perceivable cynicism among innocuous words such as 'Nobel Prize'.

The head nurse's blood pressure seemed to shoot through the ceiling while listening to the conversation.

'What's your name … *Mezestic*?' Viral said and busied himself with studying the chart at the foot of Hari's cot, and then finally turned to face his patient, 'What kind of cartoon character name is that?'

'My own good name,' said Hari – and he was proud of it, too.

Behind the doctor's back Gaadi was making gestures. Hari broadcast warning signals to get him to shut up and go, but he probably thought he'd help by acting as an agent provocateur.

Viral said to Hari, 'You live nearby, is it, Mezestic? Then you should be happy and understand that I want to do something for the people in the area. That's what my supervisor at the university hospital always taught me. He said that one must place the greater common good before one's own interests and that if everybody did so we'd soon live in Utopia instead of India.'

Hari was impressed. Some people did work on improving their karmas.

'I don't think your guru meant it literally,' Gaadi butted in.

'What's that?'

'What I'm saying is: how can you study to become a doctor and then throw it all away treating these bad characters whose names are on the police department's rowdy sheets and who never pay?' Here Gaadi made a completely unwarranted gesture at Hari as if they were doing the good cop–bad cop routine – with Hari as the baddie.

'Who are you?' said Viral and stared at Gaadi, then at Hari. Then at Gaadi again.

'He's leaving,' said Kolaveri and started pushing Gaadi out of the room and called in two ward boys to tidy up the beer empties and oily plantain leaves that were spread all over.

'You didn't answer his question,' said Hari who had decided that he might as well play with the highest stakes.

Viral got agitated, his spare tires wobbled and some spittle flew in Hari's face. 'Listen, I too grew up in these parts. My little sister died exactly because she wasn't given proper treatment when she was admitted to this clinic. Dysentery, a simple case of dysentery, and it shouldn't have had to happen. I don't want any more sisters to die ever again; so you see I'm improving conditions here by providing cheap but good healthcare. Ask yourself this – have we demanded one single paisa from you? No, I have operated a broken leg and put a stainless steel rod with state-of-the-art titanium locking screws, waiving all charges.'

Hari heard him out and in the doctor he recognized another self-made man, somebody who had emerged out of the slums, overcoming every obstacle. The situation was developing in an interesting direction. He winked, 'Doctor ji, I have something of great importance to say. Can we have a word in private?'

'Why?'

'I'm one of the good guys, like your good self,' Hari assured him, lowering his voice to a whisper, 'Doctor ji, we're in the same boat, fighting a mutual enemy.'

The doctor looked confused. 'Nurse Kolaveri, will you all please step outside?'

'But we have to tidy this mess,' she said. 'I'm telling you, Doctor, these goons and louts make too much trouble.'

'Nurse, please. This is a patient-doctor consultation that demands privacy.'

That's the way, thought Hari. He knew that, statistically, at least one of the hospital personnel might be involved in the theft of his body parts. Without hard evidence, he couldn't know for sure which of them had taken which organ, and if more than one was guilty.

He hoped that Diamond was innocent or there'd be problems in their future marriage – if it ever came to that. In the best of worlds, Bengaluru arguably being close enough, they'd fall in love. But problems such as distrust, as he had learnt from the recently concluded Operation Way-Too-Happy-Wife, could lead to many sad things.

Just now Dr Viral had delivered a great speech full of altruism and dedication. The question was if Hari's gut feeling – emanating from roughly somewhere between the two big surgical scars – was right and Viral was innocent. Viral appeared to be a good doctor, if a bit daft. His ambition to provide the slum dwellers with proper healthcare was laudable – but investing in a bad clinic like this was the wrong way to go about it.

That left one obvious culprit who had the possibility to commit the crime: Head Nurse Kolaveri. If Hari was right about the situation, Viral would soon see that he owned a hospital full of not only crooked patients but equally nasty nurses. As if she knew of Hari's suspicion, Kolaveri took off in a huff, motioning to the ward boys to follow her. Diamond glanced back at Hari before shutting the door. Hari was ready to pull his ace out of the sleeve. But of course, his hospital gown was sleeveless.

'Okay, now,' he said, 'listen Doctor ji, you can't trust anybody but me. There are criminal crimes going on in your hospital, right under your nose and I can prove it.'

Viral wasn't amused.

'No, you listen to me,' he said angrily. 'I don't know what scam you're trying to pull, but I've met people of your ilk before, Mezestic. I've heard enough of your perverse lies and warped ideas. Let me give you one piece of advice.'

'But Doctor ji, you've got to...' Hari started but then he hesitated and the doctor interrupted him again.

'I mean it when I say it. Don't try to threaten me. Whether you're a mythomaniac lying to yourself and need psychiatric care for your mental problems or you're dishonest because you think that you can extort money from me is beside the point. You're a bad character, you've most definitely got criminal genes.'

'How can you say such a terrible thing?'

'Because I can tell it from your dishonest eyes, your broken teeth and the unintelligent shape of your skull.'

'I don't believe you.' He had, of course, been confronted with similar claims before and sometimes wondered if there could be any truth to these.

'I'm a doctor and I know what I talk about.' Probably, and not without justification, the doctor was concerned that his hospital's bad reputation might take a turn for the worse – a hospital that he had sunk his life's savings into. For a moment, Hari actually felt sorry for him when he saw Viral's face. Viral was learning the hard way that altruism and humanism were still in the pipeline.

'But you don't see…' Hari was himself now beginning to catch glimpses of what was hidden behind the veils of illusion.

It was him who had been blind for too long and presently Dr Viral confirmed as much as he went on, 'You're the one who doesn't see. Now get this – you need to ask yourself if you want to keep that leg, which I've saved free of charge because I am a good man, or if you want to pay the price for trying to ruin my reputation. If need be, I can reverse the operation and remove the titanium screws. Am I making myself clear?'

'Yes, eminent elocution.'

'So behave yourself.'

The backstreet diplomat within Hari told him to behave sensibly: grin, bear it and maybe this was one occasion when he should follow a doctor's advice.

'Yes, Doctor ji.'

'Carry on then.' Viral left.

In fact, he should have listened much more carefully to his old school teacher Meshtru who had warned him of this particular hospital, of things being not quite right. The city had some 2,447 registered super speciality hospitals, and out of those, he had to book himself into the one that was a front for a criminal operation. What were the chances – less than 0.04 per cent? He'd played for the highest stakes and lost it all.

13

How to Learn from Self-help Books

Darkness had already slithered down from the tropical sky. All over town nightlife went on except in Hari's room, a sad, lonely place where he lay awake staring at the limp TV bracket protruding from the wall. Even with the TV long gone, the force of habit was strong. An antenna cable dangled out of a hole next to it. The detective in him concluded that some unhappy patient must have stolen the television from the room, or smashed it in retaliation for getting his organs stolen, after which the room was downgraded to its semi-deluxe status.

The racket from the construction work had died down to a single drilling sound, that too faltering as the sole worker took more and longer smoke breaks.

A radio jockey played Sandalwood cinema songs on somebody's transistor.

Rickshaw horns honked.

A vegetable vendor pushed his cart, shouting to find buyers for what was left over from the day. Voices floated up from the nearby stores, laughter from the booze shop next-door, loud haggling, somebody getting socked on the nose, then the sound of pumping blood.

An ambulance arriving, somebody wailing.

The smell of frying garlic, MSG, food colouring – somebody was cooking gobi manchurian. But he wasn't hungry, barely remembered what having an appetite felt like.

Even later, the last shops were downing their shutters with loud rattles.

A lone man raved in the street. 'Why this misery?' he shouted in Tamil, a refrain sometimes heard in these parts to where migrant labourers travelled from far and wide. The poor man must have realized a fraction of a second too late that the last drink for the road had cost him the bus fare back to Vellore or Villupuram or whatever the name of his native place was.

The blurry voice was like an echo of Hari's own desperate thoughts. The difference was that he was sober. A man without a liver had no choice. Right then, alone in the middle of the night, he'd have given anything, but another organ, to be sitting on a semi-Volvo to Vellore.

He kept awake, listening for steps outside. Would Deadlyappa have found out by now that Hari was without a bodyguard? Hari didn't dare close his eyes.

Hours later he heard the call to morning prayers and knew that it was around five in the morning. Shortly after that somebody blew on a conch and there was temple chanting, distant but soothing. Some people had friends in gods.

The blackness outside the window turned grey and he smelt mustard seeds being popped in sizzling oil and curry leaves frying, the pungency of red chillies and then the hissing of a pressure cooker as people prepared their breakfasts.

He asked himself what the movie stars would do if they were in his situation. He had seen thousands of Sandalwood, Bollywood and Hollywood action movies where heroes were almost killed, repeatedly, and yet they got back up and fought. But he was beginning to comprehend that the actual human body was breakable – and how brittle it was.

Was it possible to have post-donation blues?

The following days were among the most depressing in Hari's life and little by little his resolve started to give away. It was just the thought of saving his leg and tracing his organs that kept him going. Nobody visited because anybody who claimed to be his friend was immediately blacklisted by Head Nurse Kolaveri. Nothing else happened. Dr Viral had stopped coming.

But the wounds healed, he got better. He was served idli or bisi bele baath or upma for breakfast, and palak paneer twice a day, tea at fixed hours, but no coffee. Whenever Diamond and Kolaveri came, Hari pretended to be fine and collaborated nicely. They had told him that he'd be out in a few days, but now a few days had passed and he was still here. At night, weird thoughts crawled around in his head like crabs in a bucket, none making any further headway than another because the others would pull down every escapee. What was going on?

Did they keep him back to stop him from reporting the theft to the police? In a hospital like this, where second-rate killers occupied many a bed, a contract on Hari's life would have been cheap. They'd only have to cut a deal with Mr Deadlyappa in the common ward, who'd probably do it for free … or at a hefty discount. But taking out contracts on patients' lives were against the regulations at most hospitals and Hari counted himself lucky that the Globalized Style Super Speciality Hospital played by that rule. At least so far.

As the hours crept by, he reminded himself who the biggest enemy was: it wasn't necessarily Mr Deadlyappa with the crushed foot, or the snaky Dr Viral, or the sneaky Head Nurse Kolaveri, but his own brain. According to the self-help books he loved to read, the brain conspired against itself, clung on to bad thoughts and tried to lead its possessor into defeat. If there was a dark spot ahead, a negative option, you could be sure that your brain was going to seek it out.

Think positive, he told his brain, which seemed to have a life of its own. Another night, when he found it hard to sleep, he started plotting. Lying passively on a cot, wishing to get well – Hari hated it, it was so not him. It was perhaps a sign that he was getting used to the drugs they stuffed into him, because suddenly his thinking was almost coherent and lucid. Or perhaps they had stopped putting buffalo milk in his tea?

While others might go on cribbing and complaining, hoping that *somebody* would do *something* about it, he knew that it was *he*, himself only, who had to do something about it. Nobody else was going to come and help. Soon that was the only thought left in his mind. In short, idleness didn't become him. He slapped himself, like his uncle used to slap him and told himself to do *something*.

So he started filing an imaginary case report. Visualizing a computer before his eyes, he opened a blank document, naming it 'OperationOperation.doc', and as he went through events in his mind he saw the text appear in the air before him. He had suffered an accident and was brought to the hospital for treatment. No, that wasn't how it happened – for it had begun even earlier … when headmaster Meshtru asked him to investigate the hospital.

Starting from that fateful meeting in Talk of the Town restaurant, he reconstructed the series of unfortunate events that made him act like an idiot and put himself in this position. When his accident happened, Hari had persuaded Gaadi to drive him here as a result of the conversation with Meshtru. He was made to put his thumbprint on forms that he didn't read carefully, but whereby he lost ownership of his own body. The morning after, everything was different. Either he was a certified idiot or ... He preferred *or*.

He filled in the crimes in the report that was growing in his mind, described the appearance of the crime scene, his body, and added specific details about injuries sustained as result of the offence. Two holes. A list of missing items.

Certain things were making a lot of sense now. As far as he could tell they were all profiting from this. The nurses, like everybody at the hospital, received their salary from Dr Viral so it was fairly obvious on whose side they'd be when it came to the crunch. *Would anybody but an idiot trust Diamond?*

Well, Hari still wanted to. The major question remained: *what had happened to his organs?* If he could prove that they had been sold on the black market, then it wouldn't matter that he had signed a consent form, because commercial trading in human organs was a crime.

To make the case solid, he needed to collect more evidence before he talked to the cops, ascertain the exact extent of interior damage, perhaps by obtaining a copy of the surgery report or, even better, by finding the missing body parts.

•

Don't wait to get it, just take it. And do it fastly. That's what his uncle used to say. Rather than willing any inheritance to Hari, he said he would hand down the truth, and nothing but it.

The hospital had promised him physiotherapy but he hadn't been offered a single Kerala style oil massage or anything nice so far. He simply had to cure himself. He removed the bandage and plucked at the scars; the scabs came off. The wounds were dry to the touch. Very good, whoever stitched him up had done an expert job.

Cautiously, he moved around on the cot. It hurt but not too much. He wriggled his toes and lifted the injured leg up in the air, gently. *Top class*, he thought, as he watched the leg tremble in midair, holding it there until it shook uncontrollably. He lowered it then and rested it until the pain drained off.

He was a man with one leg of steel. Half a superman. Or quarter at least. He lifted the foot again, then a third time, and so on until he had done ten. He was exhausted, panting.

Then, after a bit of rest, he struggled to test his limits again. Very soon it really hurt, but he did twenty more leg lifts. It felt good to have a stainless steel rod inside. Super good. Steel was great, it made him tough – like heavy metal.

He felt every bit the hero again.

A hospital was a big place. How to even start digging for its secrets? While doing his leg exercise, he focused on the useless TV bracket on the wall. His sight wasn't blurry anymore.

An eye there. A good position for a surveillance camera.

The room could become a perfect trap if it was wired.

In fact, Doc might be able to bug the whole room, just like he had bugged the Kama Boardless Lodging Hotel. Record everything that happened next time Viral came to threaten

Hari. Doc was talented when it came to electronics. People said he had been born with a microchip on his shoulder. He could pretend to be a computer engineer, ostensibly servicing the hospital's system, but instead installing spy cameras in the operation theatre, spyware on every terminal, cloning hard disks, or if there was a central server then infecting that with a Trojan and accessing security camera files from the night of the surgery.

There were obstacles. First of all, Hari needed to get a message through to Doc. How to do it? Gaadi wasn't allowed into the hospital premises and Hari's two mobile phones had died a sad death in the drain.

Odds simply weren't in his favour.

He decided to do some more leg exercises. He sat up on the side of the cot facing the window. It was going to be a sunny day. The window had a view of the alley at the side of the hospital, but he could also glimpse the bazaar street and the facade of the Mediclinix Resorz on the opposite side. Like many buildings around here, the hospital appeared to be around 70 per cent built up, at which point somebody seemed to have lost interest in completing it.

A cow stood in the middle of the street, waiting for housewives living around the bazaar to put out yesterday's rice and banana leaves.

He lifted his leg. Then he knew what he had not been able to see clearly. A ward boy came out from the still-under-construction Mediclinix Resorz, its gleaming glass wall suddenly looking very open-for-business, and furthermore the boy had an empty red plastic bucket in his hand. Hari had seen those buckets before … in the operation theatre.

Follow the red bucket trail he told himself. So obvious everything was the moment you figured it out: it had been right there under his very own nose all along.

At seven o'clock, the rest of the hospital woke up. The noises from the construction work also grew louder which started to give him a mild headache. Although he had barely slept, he was wide awake and saw everything plainly now. As he sat and stared out through the window with his new-found clarity, he clocked a familiar character walking down the bazaar. Looked a lot like his old teacher, Hochiminh Meshtru. Massive Adam's apple and all. As he came closer, Hari was sure that it was him. Without doubt. Meshtru stopped outside, looked around before he headed for the Globalized Style Super Speciality Hospital.

Something was going on.

The morning routine was the usual one. Nothing out of the ordinary. Diamond and Kolaveri came on their rounds with a tray of spicy bisi bele baath, but at the door, Kolaveri got a call on her mobile.

'It's the doctor, I've got to take it,' she said. She stood outside in the corridor.

Diamond entered the room alone. Under ordinary circumstances, he'd have used the opportunity to declare his undying love and done many beautiful things within the shortest possible time, but now he merely curled his toes in anguish and studied her, hawk-eyed.

'Good morning, did we sleep well?' She behaved too normally. She tilted her head. 'How are we today?'

She pretended to be friendly, as she measured out his medication, the variety of jolly pills, and said, 'Doctor Viral has been irritated for days.'

He didn't touch the food, but popped the pills. He rolled over on the cot, pretending to be the strong, silent type of hero.

'What happened? Did we get out of bed on the wrong side this morning? Please, to get well you have to eat. If you want something else I'll go to the canteen and fetch. Would you like some juice?'

'I'd rather … *ennha oru kaapi aayikote*,' said Hari, who'd have given his left foot for a cup of coffee, but his saying it in Malayalam didn't create any deep feeling of bonding between them that day. Then he added, 'My dreams are all right, it's being awake that is proving to be something of a nightmare.'

'No coffee, definitely not until recovery is over. It can lead to undue excitement and disturbed sleep.'

'I know what's going on here,' he said. 'And I trusted you like a fool.'

She said, 'But what did I do?'

The head nurse was still talking loudly in the corridor. He smelt Diamond's closeness, her intimate scents of sandalwood soap and coconut oil, and tried his best to stay ice cold.

'Nothing.'

'What are you saying?'

'That's the problem,' he said.

She sat down on the far end of his cot. 'You'd let me know if I could do anything to make you feel better? Anything at all.'

'Why would you?' He wasn't a fool. Diamond was a minor cog in the sinister machinery, doing what she was told in order to get her pay cheque. He found it hard to forgive her for looking the other way or whatever it was that she did to endure.

'I don't like it when patients are sad.' She put her hand on his arm, lightly, like a butterfly.

Then their eyes met, properly. Not merely a glance, but a soul fondle. Every moment in life was a choice. And one needed to choose well.

The head nurse was still in the corridor, busy with her call, so Hari decided to risk it. He didn't know whether to trust Nurse Diamond even 50 per cent. Then again, 49.9 per cent should be good enough to gamble on.

He hoped that she would choose to be good to him. And that again was something insufferable. *Hoping* struck him as a mindless activity. Knowledge was the true way, mathematical calculation of karmic fallouts, based on a combination of data from the Internet and the movements of stars, but he didn't even know her zodiac sign.

He took the plunge. 'Diamond, there's one thing you can help me with.'

'Yes?'

'Something about this hospital where you work is … how to put it? Not quite right.'

'No?'

'Sort of wrong, and I think you know it.'

'I do?'

'Possibly illegal, let's say.' He pulled up his hospital gown to confront her with the evidence.

'*Chee*, dirty boy!' she said. She stopped doing 'sir' this and 'sir' that and he was, to tell the truth, more used to being called 'dirty boy', which was fine.

He put his forefinger to his lips. Kolaveri was still having an intense conversation out there. The doctor must indeed be extremely upset. Hari pointed to his abdomen. He drew lines with his fingers along the two scars.

'See these. You yourself said those herbal pills you're giving me in addition to the antibiotics are tonics for the liver and kidneys.'

'And you're saying?' Her eyes grew bigger.

'Yes, exactly what you're thinking. I was admitted for a broken leg. These scars constitute evidence of punishable offences.'

He could have told her the relevant section numbers, too: Sections 319 and 338 relating to causing grievous bodily hurt, Section 336 for endangering the life or safety of others, and Sections 378 to 381 regarding theft, robbery et cetera, in addition to which the law also has provisions applicable against perpetrators of criminal conspiracy, criminal intimidation and commercial dealings in organs according to the Transplantation of Human Organs Act of 1994. Somebody would have to go to jail for about seven years.

Hari had his Uncle Mamool to thank for a lot of useful data. They had often played a game, when Hari was a kid: one said the number and the other had to remember the law. Hari generally won, because he had something of a calculator mindset so he knew all laws by number and their maximum penalties, and only broke them when the situation demanded. It never ceased to amaze him that behind an innocuous number like 420, for example, was a law that could put an ex-tout like him in jail for having cheated far too many tourists and other gullible people.

She connected the dots. Not that difficult considering that she had a medical education. 'And do you want to lodge a complaint?'

'Not my number one priority.'

'Then what?'

'Deliver a message to a friend of mine: Doc.'

'Another doctor?'

'Ah yes, my regular GP, Doctor Doc Dotcom. I want a second opinion. Can I borrow a red pen from you?'

'Red pen, what for?'

'A lipstick will do.' But she wasn't the type of girl to share her lipstick with boys though she did actually have a red pencil which she was happy to hand over. Hari wrote a quick note on a slip of paper, using a code that Doc would understand, 'Bring medical kit'.

She watched him fold the chit. 'So where is his clinic?'

'You know Puncherwallah Complex, near Movieland Talkies and opposite Deluxe Bar?'

'Yes, but that's a terrible area. I had no idea there was a hospital there.'

'It's not exactly a hospital, it's called Cyberspaced-out Internet Paradise.'

Diamond bit her lip. 'I guess I shouldn't ask what kind of doctor he is.'

'That is a very good idea.'

'So what do I tell this doctor?'

'Give him this slip. Ask him to come ASAP. Your Kolaveri Didi and Doctor Viral will not like what I'm proposing, so I beg you to keep this a secret.' If she delivered the message to Doc rather than Viral, he'd be able to trust her. If not, then he'd soon be reduced to a non-veg gravy item.

'I'll go as soon as I can, but that'll have to be after work, I'm afraid,' she said.

'Be careful. Maybe you should avoid going at night. You know how the men on CD Road have a reputation of misbehaving after dark. Best you go first thing in the morning when the crooks are napping. I'll compensate you once this case is solved.' He planned to take her out for lunch, dinner and maybe even breakfast, every single day of her life.

She smiled.

Hari was stressed. Although he still heard Kolaveri speaking on the phone and pleading with the doctor, the conversation might not last that much longer. 'Do you happen to know what the head nurse is talking with the doctor about?'

'I think it's regarding some old schoolmaster who has been complaining repeatedly about the hospital.'

'Oho, is it so? Is it something serious?' said Hari.

'I'm not sure. I saw him come in this morning and he was claiming that he'll hire detectives, have the hospital investigated and expose malpractices. The doctor is terribly upset and we've been ordered not to talk to strangers,' she said and then she stared at Hari, a little bit amazed at the thought, 'Are you the detective he's talking about?'

She was sharp. Meshtru was a moron. Hari waggled his head sideways.

14

How to Handle the Third Degree

He hoped that the old teacher hadn't totally blown his cover. Maybe he should have informed Meshtru about his progress and instructed him not to poke his nose into things. Too late now.

He strained his ears – and heard the head nurse go on with her phone conversation. Trust ladies to make the telecom industry the most profitable in the world. But her agitated tone did sound worrisome. In which case, Hari's time was running out. Diamond was his only hope and as she had already agreed to carry his message to Doc, maybe she could be talked into doing more than that. 'You really want to help me?'

'You're offering me a detective job?'

'We're currently not hiring staff. Besides, I'm not sure if women in Bengaluru should be detectives. It's a very risky job, we deal with criminals, break legs and stuff. Detectives need to be scary, like men.'

'But you need my help. And there seems to be a puzzle here that you'd find hard to solve without me.' She flashed that 10,000 volt smile of hers and he caught a dazzling glimpse of her chipped front tooth. 'My Mum constantly tells me that I'm far too curious for my own good but I've always preferred detective stories to that romantic mush they peddle in women's magazines. Keeps me awake on the late shifts.'

Puzzle was the accurate word for his cut up belly. He calculated. She could be a valuable asset. In thrillers, the secret agents had a word for enlisting an agent from the enemy side. They called it to 'turn' the agent. And in the process, if they happened to get married, she wouldn't even have to change the monograms on her hankies – Diamond Mol or Diamond Majestic, the initials were the same. 'Yeah, so there may be temporary vacancies at the agency. My deputy director is on an assignment in Mysore so I might have use for a secretary. So while I give the matter due consideration, will you help me with one more thing?'

'What?'

'Yes, what is that?' came Head Nurse Kolaveri's stern voice from the doorway. 'What are you two whispering about?'

'Nothing, Didi.'

'Don't trust these filthy people,' said Kolaveri. 'Is he trying to befriend you?'

'No, Didi, he's nobody to me.'

There and then Hari experienced sudden cardiac arrhythmia and for a minute he thought himself in need of a triple bypass operation, until he noticed that Diamond had crossed her fingers behind her back. Head Nurse Kolaveri glared at him with the most evil of evil eyes.

'May I add something?' said Hari, thinking on his feet.

'What now?' said Kolaveri.

'Perhaps I might need physiotherapy. How will I get well otherwise?'

He was looking forward to therapy sessions with Diamond who might rub him with scented oils and medicated ghee, a Kerala style Ayurvedic massage which in turn would be a great start of their epic love affair.

Kolaveri crossed her arms over her chest. 'You don't say?'

'I expected that to be a part of the treatment.'

'You seem to be much less stupid than you seem,' Kolaveri said and Hari cringed a bit. She continued, 'So you're ready to begin with physiotherapy?'

Yahoo.com! thought Hari optimistically. But he exercised self-control and aloud he just said, 'That sounds fine.'

'Good. Doctor Viral is planning to come see you later today, so I will suggest to him that it will be a good time to start working on you,' Kolaveri said. 'He may as well oversee your physiotherapy in person. Nurse Diamond, come along then. Don't waste time on this good for nothing type.'

Things finally started moving. Whether it was in the right or wrong direction mattered less to him. But she was on his side, Diamond, and it was wonderful. He took a nap, after all he'd been awake all night, and he slept peacefully after a long time. He dreamt of Diamond. She was going to help him. She'd massage his leg until it healed. Sometime in the late afternoon, judging by the light from the window, he woke again.

He noticed there was a vase of flowers. The card was from Diamond and she hoped he'd enjoy the gift – a walking aid: an ugly contraption with four legs attached to two handlebars. What kind of gift was that?

He pushed himself up from the bed and sat on its edge, staring at the walker. It was the kind he had seen elderly people use. He reached for it. It had a light metal frame, but felt sturdy. What would his neighbours on CD Road think if they saw him totter about with that thing? For months to come, the jokes would be on him.

He held on to the handlebars and balanced on his good foot, the toes on his broken leg dangling an inch above the floor. He moved the frame one step. Then he straightened his arms, lifting his own weight and swung his body forward and set his good foot down. He reached back for the drip stand. It had wheels. He pulled it closer. So far so good, there was no pain. Just a buzz. Probably his nerves telling him that it'd hurt if he weren't on painkillers.

He repeated the action until he had crossed to the door, several steps from the bed. It took him no more than a minute and wasn't painful, only a little tiring.

There was a slip of paper on the floor by the door. Hari bent down and picked it up. Another love letter from Diamond? He unfolded it and found that it was a kind of hate letter. It said: *'Bustard, U will B killed B4 U live.'* Live? Oh, leave.

He got the feeling that Mr Deadlyappa was up on his feet again and had somehow found out which room he was in. Hari had to make escape plans.

On the door was a sketch map showing the emergency exit routes. His room was in one long ground floor corridor with two larger wards and a few private rooms, and there was a fire escape at the far end – as seen from the main entrance – leading to a stairwell. One should be able to get out of the hospital that way if the need arose.

He felt the door handle. It turned, but the door was bolted from the outside: it had sturdy hinges and no glass pane, and couldn't be locked or opened from the inside. He was virtually a prisoner, then.

He turned around to survey the claustrophobic room. Nothing usable as a weapon: only the cot, a bedside table, washbasin, the window with its sturdy iron bars. Frustrated, he banged the walker into the door. It bounced back and the recoil took him with it, he lost his balance, powerless to break his fall. The drip stand toppled and knocked him over the head.

He lay on his back, helpless like an upturned cockroach, the walker next to him. Stupid, ugly, useless thing. He tried to climb up without letting the damaged leg touch the floor, but it was impossible.

He dragged himself across the floor towards the bed, when … he heard … somebody … draw back the door bolt. *Oh no, not Deadlyappa, not now*, he thought.

Seen from his cockroach's-eye view, Head Nurse Kolaveri filled the doorway. Hari felt relieved.

'What's this hullabaloo? You're disturbing the other patients.'

'I fell out of bed.' Hari decided to downplay his activities.

'And what were you doing trying to get out of bed? In your condition, you should be careful or you may meet with a serious accident.'

Was that a veiled threat? Aloud he said, 'I couldn't find the buzzer.'

'It was removed because we are too understaffed to answer random calls. Imagine if every patient rang at all odd times.'

She was fast, but he was faster, 'But what if nature calls?'

'I'll show you what if…' She made a gesture which he misinterpreted as an attempt to slap him.

He did what he could to resist but was too weak, and managed only to tear off the Florence Nightingale cap she was wearing.

'Stop acting like a fool,' she said, lifting him up with her surprisingly powerful arms, as if she was a mother and he was a baby, and dropping him on the bed.

He gave her the cap back meekly. She flattened a wave of hair that stood up over her head, and although Hari had a similar wave in his hair, he doubted that it was enough to awaken any feelings in her towards him.

Head Nurse Kolaveri righted the drip stand and checked that the needles hadn't come loose. 'You better behave as long as you're in my hospital, young man.'

'Yes,' he said and tried to defuse the situation. 'I'll be a model patient from now on.'

But it was too late. The door was thrown open again and more trouble walked in: Dr Viral and his colleague Dr Philipovich. Viral looked grim, as if he had been brooding a lot about Hari's insinuations and connected them to Meshtru's visit in the morning. Whatever went on in his head, it certainly gave Hari an uneasy sense of foreboding.

'Good evening, Nurse Kolaveri,' said Viral.

'Doctors…' Kolaveri was a completely different person in their presence. Soft-spoken, god-fearing.

Hari did his best to sound cheerful. 'Hello, Doctors! Thanks for the surgery. I feel fine and maybe I could go home soon. Had your coffees?'

The tall, elderly Dr Philipovich didn't seem to notice him; he did his best to look anonymous, hiding behind the nicotine patches that covered his skin. Perhaps the situation embarrassed him. He was, after all, a foreigner with a fancy degree and probably not used to slum hospitals and rowdy patients. But if that was so, then what was he doing there at all? Good question, thought Hari and jotted down a quick mental note.

'How do you enjoy your stay in our incredible country?' Hari went on, doing his best to bond with the foreigner, the way he used to in the good old days when he worked as a tout.

Dr Philipovich still didn't look him in the eye, but seemed instead very much in need of a cigarette.

'He doesn't speak English,' said Viral, quashing Hari's hopes of building up a rapport. 'Nurse Kolaveri told me you insisted on getting physiotherapy. Now remember, while your body requires a lot of rest, it is important that you exercise your leg or it will become stiff and you'll walk like a duck. And you wouldn't want that to happen, would you?'

'No, Doctor ji,' said Hari and wondered if he should be afraid.

Viral instructed Kolaveri to help the patient sit at the edge of his cot. Hari decided that for the time being it was best to follow hospital protocol and do what they told him, so he dangled his legs and relaxed the muscles.

'This may get painful, but I'm sure you're used to that,' Viral said. 'Straighten the leg, slowly.'

Hari decided to show them what tough stuff he was made of. He flashed a smile at Head Nurse Kolaveri. He put the foot up, piece of cake. It was a lucky thing that he'd had the foresight to exercise on his own. When he was about to lower it, Viral interrupted:

'Keep it there.'

Not so difficult. Dr Philipovich mumbled something as he busied himself pulling out another nicotine patch from a box and searching for free space on his skin to put it.

'Does the leg hurt?' Viral translated while he felt Hari's pulse and listened briefly to his heart through a stethoscope.

'It's top class,' said Hari through clenched teeth. It was actually painful. But he was determined to survive.

The doctors conferred in their mystery language.

'Professor Glas Philipovich says that you may lift it higher. Don't bend the knee. Keep your leg straight. That's the way to do it. And then … higher again,' said Viral.

Hari couldn't – the leg trembled violently, the pain was way above his threshold level. 'Doctor ji, I think it is impossible.'

'As long as there's a will, there's a way. Or don't you want to walk again?'

Hari nodded vigorously. He felt flames shoot out around his face and the deep-fried eyeballs popping out of his head as he lifted the leg another few inches.

'The more you exercise the leg, the faster you'll be on your feet.'

'That is a wonderful thought,' said Hari, but his leg refused to follow orders.

'Lift it,' said the doctor, and added, in a by-the-way kind of way, 'I thought our confidential conversation the other night had clarified our respective positions.'

'Oh, yes,' said Hari.

'But what is this I hear about you being really famous here in the neighbourhood? Or infamous, some kind of loose cannon for hire – and the cheapest one around, according to somebody who came to speak to me.'

'Me? Yes, I'm quite well known. If Doctor ji ever needs to find a cheap hotel room or the best souvenir deal, I'm the one to speak to.'

'Should I trust you?'

'Most certainly,' said Hari as the bells of a fire engine were clanging not so far away, his body was burning up from the inside as if he had swallowed a crematorium by mistake.

'I don't think so. By the way, this old headmaster of yours made allegations. He even threatened that an investigation would be launched. He *threatened* me! Can you believe it?'

Hari had had a bad feeling about Meshtru ever since he was a schoolboy, but now it turned infinitely worse. He tried to ignore the matter and pushed himself harder, despite the throbbing pain in the tightly bandaged leg, to show how earnestly he obeyed the doctor.

'Oho, I'm fully shocked, Doctor ji. Don't take him seriously, that senile fart reads too many pirated Dan Brown novels,' said Hari, wishing he knew what Meshtru was planning next, but then again it was quite possible that he wasn't planning at all. Some people simply knee-jerked their way through life. 'Gets ideas from bad books, sees conspiracies everywhere, talks too much rubbish. I surely disown him.'

'Be that as it may, there's some confusion around here. As a man of science, I don't like confusion,' said Viral. 'You must keep the leg up much higher or you might never walk again. What do you prefer?'

That sounded like a threat. Though he wondered if perhaps his perception of the situation had been warped by all the drugs they had stuffed him with. However, watching his foot quiver halfway up in the air everything felt very real, and he expected the stitches in his tummy to open up in an involuntary disembowelment. 'I'm as confused as you are and I simply … have … no idea.'

'If you say so. How does your leg feel?'

'I think it is cured. Halleluiah, I can walk.'

Viral exchanged a few words with Dr Philipovich, who looked Hari up and down, his eyes rested briefly somewhere around the middle of him, the gaze of an organ kleptomaniac. Then Viral turned to Hari, 'You're not putting your heart into this. My colleague says he's afraid that we'll have to take you into the operation theatre again.'

'What for?'

'Amputate your leg. How will you pay for that surgery?'

'Slum charitable scheme?' suggested Hari and struggled with the leg exercise, until saltwater squished out of his tear ducts, dousing some of that burning feeling. He was used to taking a macro-perspective on things and knew enough about the problematic human nature to suspect that an unfortunate chain reaction had been started.

'Up.'

Down, it wanted to rest.

'Up, I said.'

The air was humming with bad vibes, like an out of tune orchestra that improvised the soundtrack to the film about his life. He wished superhero Upendra would come and save him. Viral conferred with Dr Glas Philipovich and then turned to Hari.

'You can relax.'

'Thanks, Doctor ji.' Another second and he'd have had a full body haemorrhage. Hari lowered the foot until it hung limply over the edge of the cot. What relief, what instant relief. He smiled through his tears.

'That wasn't so painful, was it?' said Viral. 'How do you feel now?'

'Very much alive,' he said. He was pretty hardboiled after all. He forced the corners of his mouth upwards, but silently he cursed Meshtru. He said, 'May I go home now?'

'You will give up your amateur investigation first, yes? I hope you understand that there is nothing to find here.'

Not at this hospital, thought Hari, *but what about the other clinic across the bazaar?* But aloud he just said, 'How can I find anything if there is no investigation in the first place?

'Should I believe you then?'

Hari upped the stakes – the rule of any game was that when you knew you were going to lose anyway you might as well bluff harder, 'If you don't believe me then kill me. But don't forget the karmic repercussions.'

Viral scratched his head and added, 'While I give it some thought, we should finish your physiotherapy so that you get well.'

'No wait!' Hari wanted to erase what he had just said.

'Yes,' said Viral, 'and lift it a little higher this time.'

'You can't be serious.'

'You prefer amputation?'

Hari kept his mouth shut. He stretched the leg so that it felt like a pillar of undiluted pain. The room started spinning as if he'd mistakenly been prescribed an airplane propeller instead of a suppository.

He stared at his toes. They were at eye level. Practically inside his eyelids. His heart had apparently burst because its shreds were seeping out through his mouth, along with a scary metallic taste of frothy blood.

'That shouldn't be necessary,' wheezed Hari, sweat pouring down his face.

He kept the leg up for what felt like forty-five hours but was more like forty-five seconds. Both doctors took it leisurely. Viral stooped to feel Hari's pulse and listen to his heart again. Hari was shaking violently. Dr Philipovich mumbled something.

Viral nodded. 'The operation was highly successful, if I may say so myself. And you seem to be recovering fine, any *complaints?*'

'No,' said Hari between clenched teeth. 'No … complaints, Doctor ji.'

'Is that so?'

'Uh-uh,' Hari sobbed.

Head Nurse Kolaveri looked uncomfortable. To the doctor, she said, 'Should it really hurt so much?'

'This patient …. is the worst type of slum-dwelling rowdy-sheeter according to my diagnosis. No manners, unable to feel pain, so trust me, nurse, this is only good for him. But you wouldn't know nothing about it so don't interrupt me again if you want to keep your job.' Viral turned to face Hari again. 'This is what I'm talking about. Lift your foot higher.'

Hari lifted it another few inches.

'See what I mean?' said Viral.

If only he could use his toe as an earplug and cut off the sound of his own sobbing. He had seen yogis hook their legs behind their necks, but never thought that one day he'd do it himself.

'Stop it, Doctor!' Kolaveri insisted.

Hari agreed.

15

How to Fully Comprehend the Meaning of Horror

'Nurse, are you implying that you don't trust my judgement? You know how hard I work to save this hospital and I'd advise our patient here to do likewise – to work that leg, to save it,' said Viral, matter-of-factly.

She stood her ground, 'Please, Doctor, let the boy rest. Not everybody can handle your vigorous therapy.'

'How many times do I have to tell you, Doctor ji, it's all a big misunderstanding,' added Hari. He felt like a cactus that was missing its desert. But he finally realized that what Viral was waiting for was a sign of unconditional surrender. He tried one last bluff, '*There is no investigation.* My firsthand experience is that your hospital is very charitable to have given me a free leg surgery and I am so happy and grateful to you.'

Viral smiled then, pleasantly. 'That's what I like to hear. We'll prepare a special notarized discharge document on which you will sign that you have no complaints whatsoever about the treatment you've received, no?'

'Oh yes,' said Hari, palpitating, but managing to speak in snatches. By then he was quite ready to be referred to the morgue anyway. 'I'll do whatever … you tell me … sign anything. I'm a very … cooperative person. Fully 1,000 per cent.'

'Very well. I'm so glad we all agree.' Viral spoke in his formal, normal tone, as if nothing untoward had taken place. 'Continue with the exercises, morning and evening, do as many leg lifts as you can. Otherwise, there's the risk of atrophy and you wouldn't want that. Nurse, please give him something for the pain. I think he has learnt the importance of physiotherapy. Carry on, everybody.'

'Yes, Doctor,' Kolaveri said. To Hari, she added, 'You'll feel better soon. The doctor knows what he's doing.'

Hari felt, or he felt he ought to have felt, happy to be alive. If only there had been a spycam in the room he would have had all the evidence he needed. Now it would be his word against theirs, he needed hard evidence and would have to provoke the doctor to go through this routine once more, to get it on tape. He'd wait until they brought the affidavit, then he'd make them bully him again in front of cameras before he signed it, and thus he'd outsmart them. But aloud he breathed softly, 'All the very best, boss, goodbye.'

Morning again, D-day. Hari felt a strange mixture of relief and dread when he saw Diamond in the doorway and everything was normal again – she was carrying a tray of upma with spicy mixed pickle and piping hot chai. He glanced behind her, half expecting the head nurse to follow and bust his plans. Diamond offered him a broad, disarming, multi-toothed smile. She said, 'I was worried about you.'

Was that love in her voice? He adored that chipped front tooth of hers. He mustered up something resembling a grin, and lied as usual, 'I've been through worse. So tell me.'

'Mission accomplished,' she chirped. 'Your Doc is here for a second opinion.'

'And what did Kolaveri Didi say to that?'

'She's home, she had a bad migraine attack,' Diamond said.

Hari rolled his head sideways.

Doc walked in. His nose was still bluish and greenish, and somewhat flatter than usual, from the night when Bhascar tried to take revenge.

'Tell me, Majestic?' He was carrying his black medical bag, looking professional, and he immediately observed the vase of flowers on Hari's bedside table. 'Nice flowers. Oh, and before I forget, the other day our old schoolteacher came to look for you. Remember that lunatic? I hope it's okay that I told him you were here. I thought you might enjoy a visit. Did he bring you the flowers?'

'No, and, speaking of which, he's the last person I'd like to share a desert island with. Remember how he used to cane us in school? One thing I learnt then is that he's bad for my health. This time he almost got me killed,' said Hari and pulled his hospital gown up, displaying his abdomen, the gauze and cotton pads. The cuts.

Doc waggled his head. 'I knew he was a crazy man, but this...'

'Doc, the door,' said Hari.

He moved back to the doorway and glanced into the corridor. 'Clear.' It was that time when everybody was taking tiffin. They could expect to remain undisturbed. Doc sent Hari a quizzical glance, Hari nodded quietly and Doc stayed at his post by the door, but pulled out an MP3 recorder which he switched on. Hari turned to Diamond.

'Listen, Diamond. The truth is sometimes uncomfortable, but the problem is that it remains the truth, whether you want it or not. Yesterday you wished to be a detective. So what do you say today, time to stop sitting on the fence, eh?'

She shrugged almost imperceptibly, but Hari saw that she was ready for serious talk.

'I'll lose my job, I guess…' She looked him in the eye.

'Good point.' Was she stupid or conscientious enough to throw away the entire lower middle class dream of a career, credit card, et cetera?

In that case, they were really made for each other. She sighed and sat on the corner of his hospital bed.

'Just trust us and tell all,' said Hari.

'Yes, you can trust us,' said Doc.

'You'll find that it improves your karma,' added Hari.

She wiped a tear from the corner of her eye.

'I joined this hospital because I believed it was a noble thing.' She put her thumb to her lips and chewed on its nail. 'But now I almost feel like going back to Kerala and becoming a nun.'

'That may not be necessary,' said Hari because he suspected that a nun might not be permitted to fall in love with a common man. He grabbed her hands to prevent her from chewing up all her nails. He said, 'Listen, is there a water shortage at the hospital?'

'No, why?'

'I keep seeing these boys running across between here and that building on the other side of the road with plastic buckets.'

'Buckets?'

'Yes, red buckets.'

'Oh, it's not for water.'

'Then what?'

'It's something to do with the charitable surgical work.'

'That's what I thought. Do you want to tell us what you know?'

She bit her lip. He too wanted to nibble on that luscious lip. Then she spilled the beans. 'Hari, you must think me naïve but … I kind of didn't know exactly or I think I knew partly, but ever since you started asking these questions I've been thinking a lot. Yesterday, when I accessed your file in the computer at the nurse's station, I found that the surgeries that are done for free involve a voluntary donation, and in your case they took one kidney and 70 per cent of your liver to cover the cost of your leg surgery. Titanium screws are very expensive per piece, you see.'

'Voluntary donation, huh?' Somehow he wasn't totally surprised.

After having spilled the beans, she next spilled the chicken gravy and curd rice too. When he asked her about the organs he had lost, what exactly they were useful for, if at all – because most people he knew had nothing but problems with their livers – he received a full-fledged medical tutorial.

Diamond explained that the liver is a spongy multifunction organ that recycles the blood. Blood collects dirt and gets infected with poisonous impurities when it passes through the intestines, and must be purified before it goes back to the heart. Hence, the liver is a laundry service for the inside of the body, cleaning out all that toxic waste, debris and foreign particles from the bloodstream. If the liver stops working, it essentially equals what'd happen to a city without adequate garbage and sewage disposal.

The kidneys work in tandem with the liver, Hari learnt: the body contains 6 litres of water that must be re-filtered every hour, amounting to almost 150 litres per day. Kidneys thus separate about 1.5 litres of waste daily – which is also known as 'committing nuisance' if the cops catch you expelling that waste liquid against a public wall and then you'd be liable to pay a fine under the Karnataka Municipal Corporations (Amendment) Bill. Healthy kidneys have a capacity of filtering up to 200 litres per day. Even if one of them fails it doesn't mean that a person dies, although the filtering process of course takes twice as long, so a person with one kidney does well in eating only very healthy food and drinking fresh fruit juices.

He absorbed the data. This girl was better than the Wikipedia, the previous love of his life.

She pointed out, 'I guess with only 30 per cent of your liver left, you must cut down on alcohol consumption by approximately 70 per cent.'

'Okay, I hear you,' he said, frowning a little, 'and so then what – they sent my body parts to some international organ supermarket on the Internet, or?' Though he could make a guess, he wanted her to confirm it.

'The harvested parts were put in sterile containers in buckets with ice. I've never been inside the new Mediclinix Resorz, but according to your surgery summary they were taken there,' she confirmed. 'I think they want to keep donors and recipients away from each other, it is probably better for business.'

'Oho. So I've been harvested in a businesslike manner.' He didn't mean to sound cynical. It certainly was preferable to being cut up in some Russel Market butcher's shop and left to die among the other useless animal spare parts. The red buckets constituted a strangely primitive way of transporting stolen body parts, but sometimes the simplest solution worked best – especially if you wanted to hide something of this magnitude: an illegal trade in human organs. Nobody would question a red plastic bucket.

'To satisfy my curiosity: if one gets, for example, a new kidney, how many days will one stay in that clinic?'

'The recuperation takes a few days. If the person has to travel far, it is recommended that one allows about a week for the healing so that there's no complications.'

'They travel … *far*?'

'Yes.'

'You mean the recipients are not local people?'

'They're medical tourists,' she said. 'That's apparently the way we raise funds to subsidize this hospital.'

He had read about medical tourism and how it brought in hard currency. If he hadn't stopped working as a tout, he might have benefited from it too – in those days when his conscience was more flexible.

'I'd like to have a look around that Mediclinix Resorz to find out exactly what happened to me after the surgery. Maybe find my lost kidney. What do you say?'

'However, I was wondering,' she said, 'maybe there shouldn't be such a ruckus made about it.'

'Why not?'

She struggled with the words. 'You can't just walk in and take your kidney back because it'll already belong to somebody else.'

'Why, it's originally mine, isn't it?'

'First of all, you'd need surgical skills to retrieve it.'

'Don't worry, I'll think of something,' said Hari. 'If kidneys can be replaced, it should work both ways, shouldn't it?'

Diamond cast a look at Doc in the doorway who pretended to be busy listening to MP3s of Sandalwood film hit songs on his headset while he was actually recording her statement. Doc removed one of the earphones, 'What?'

'*Are* you a real doctor?'

Doc waggled his head. As if in a chain reaction, Hari waggled his head too and continued, 'This is something more than a routine investigation, it's personal. I want my body back intact.'

Hari figured that he could google for instructions on how to perform a reverse transplant. Usually essential information – how to make bombs with chapatti flour and Knockout cans, how to protect your computer from the evil eye, how to print yourself a BCom diploma – was freely available on the Net.

Diamond said, 'Can I help you then?' She hadn't smiled for a while but now she tried a consoling little cheerful face.

'Perhaps. When did you say your Kolaveri Didi is expected back on duty?'

'After lunch.'

'Perfect. The trick with working undercover is to create an identity as close to your own as possible so that nobody will see through it. So I want you to come with me to that luxury clinic, act your part as a nurse while I'll pretend to be a medical tourist. And as a token of gratitude, I'll treat you to Sunday brunch at a gourmet restaurant. Are you veg or non-veg?'

'You're supposed to be a detective so I leave that to you to figure out. But you need something to wear.' She indicated his lower body that was unclad.

'Great thinking. You'd make an excellent detective too.'

'You would be unemployed if I was. Just teasing,' she added when she saw his face.

'That's hilarious,' said Hari. 'Let's get to work. I want eyes all over this place, covering every inch of it. Whatever espionage equipment we own must be deployed. Anything the hospital staff does or says, I want to be the first to know.'

'He's not a medical doctor, is he?' Diamond crinkled her pretty forehead.

Hari and Doc exchanged glances and then turned in unison to waggle their heads at Diamond. She was a very clever girl.

'I thought as much.'

'Listen, I must access the computers,' said Doc and took out a USB pen drive from his black bag. 'Any bright ideas?'

'Let me do that,' Diamond volunteered.

'Don't take unnecessary risks,' said Hari. Having found potential love, he didn't want to lose the potential even if the love wasn't forthcoming.

'There's a computer at the nurse's station and after my rounds I'm supposed to key in the medicines I've given to patients into the billing software. I'll do it then.'

'Great, so connect this, run the software on the flash, it won't take any time to install itself and then give it back to me.'

'What software is it?'

'It's called "jab.exe" and it's the opposite of an inoculation, it opens up the computer so that I can remote-access it and infect it with whatever I please.'

'Are you sure that it won't be dangerous to our patients?'

'It's not that kind of infection,' said Doc, though he didn't sound so sure.

'And see if you can find out the name of my organ recipient while you're at it,' suggested Hari.

After she left, Doc opened his black bag and took out an electronic kit which included what essentially were tweaked regular cheap Chinese semi-smart phones turned into espionage machines. They had wireless Internet and grainy cameras and reasonable sound. Plugging in a mike and a button-sized video lens on a cable improved the quality of the footage according to Doc, who explained that the instruments recorded the surveillance files to 4 GB memory cards, which held upwards sixty to seventy hours of video and sound each. Simultaneously, they buffered the recordings, compressed them and uploaded them to a cloudserver – so even if the devices were discovered, nobody could destroy the evidence.

He beamed at Hari, assuring him that it was so idiot proof that Hari needn't worry at all. Just charge the battery pack when the juice ran out, there'd be a discreet soundless vibration against his spine – because that's where the instrument was to be located.

Doc used double-sided tape to fix one instrument to the small of Hari's back and then covered it with bandage so that it blended in with the surgical ones. Only a person who knew what to search for would find it.

To connect the miniature lens and mike to the handset was trickier. It involved running thin black wires up along Hari's spine, under the hospital gown, and masking them with skin-coloured Band-Aid strips, all the way up to Hari's head – luckily his hair was thick and lush thanks to all the coconut oil he put in it, underneath which the cables were routed to his ears. The lens was clipped to the right earlobe. Doc had covered it with silver thread in a pattern making it look like a ladies' clip-on earring. He'd fashioned an almost identical pair out of the microphone and it was clipped to the left ear. Slightly outlandish gear, but if one was born to be a detective one simply pulled it off.

They did a sound and image test – 'we're online, check, check' – and using Doc's phone they logged on to the cloudserver and Hari saw that the test clip had already been transmitted to the backup account.

'Impressive. Remind me to mark you out for an increment when we do our next appraisal. Now I need a camera there on the wall.'

'We never do appraisals,' Doc complained, the eternal pessimist, but followed Hari's instructions and put up one of the closed-circuit cameras in his arsenal, and a microphone, feeding the signal to a second handset taped underneath the washbasin. He covered the camera in black tape until it looked like it was a part of the broken TV bracket and used white masking tape to hide the cables on the wall. It all appeared like a slightly shoddy repair job; nobody would look twice at the installation. 'Or when were you planning the next appraisal?'

'In this lifetime, don't worry.' A stretchable but precise timeframe.

'By the way,' said Doc, 'if you recall, you've borrowed money from me. But since you ended up here I haven't bugged you about it. Just so that you know.'

'I'm paying you back ASAP. And boss, didn't I buy you all these bugging things?'

'Some, but Triplex had to steal the CCTV system for me. Okay, now we have one camera that travels with you wherever you go and this one here covers the room. If anything at all happens, I'll see it, okay?'

'Point taken.' Hari had been thinking of borrowing money from Doc but scrapped that plan.

16

How to Find Good Food in a Bazaar

After the morning rounds, Diamond returned with a pink sari covered in purple flower patterns. She hadn't had the time to go to a garment shop so she popped around the corner to her paying guest accommodation and selected it from her own wardrobe. This sari was one that she kept for special occasions.

And she lent him a single girlish slipper.

Although Hari was moved by the gesture – that they'd gotten so intimate they shared garments and footwear – he knew, as he wrapped the sari to wear it like a lungi, that his reputation was going to suffer irreparable damage. On the other hand, he couldn't go out in just the hospital gown. It barely covered his groin.

'Coincidentally, it does match those funny things you're wearing on your ears,' she said, amused.

The pieces of homemade jewellery weren't that bad, but combined with a purple-pink flowery loincloth: what would people think? That he was a foreign tourist who'd mistaken

Bengaluru for Goa? Actually, a perfect disguise if he wanted to pass himself off as yet another medical tourist.

'They're part of my disguise as an alien,' he said and took the top secret executive decision that there was no point in telling her that he was recording everything she said. Like all professional agents, he operated on a need to know basis and Diamond hadn't yet been formally employed, so she didn't have the necessary double-0 security clearance. 'So do you have any fresh data to upload?'

'According to the report, your organs were healthy. If not, the patients would have died,' she said and explained that in the consent form Hari had been given when he was admitted, there was a box for the name of his next of kin. Two fictitious foreign relatives of his had been named as recipients.

Technically it was only legal to donate to close relatives, while commercial sale was strictly prohibited under the Transplantation of Human Organs Act. But according to the file, A Frankenheimer, fifty-nine years, Hari's third cousin once removed, had got the kidney and Baiju Ganbei, forty-four, his co-brother on the maternal side, had got his liver, or strictly speaking, 70 per cent of it. Everything she said went into the recording device. Besides, the relevant files would be copied by Doc's malware. Once Hari was discharged from the hospital, he'd walk out with rock solid evidence.

The first name sounded vaguely European or American and the other had a Chinese ring to it, which meant that parts of him were poised to travel far and wide. Hari said, 'So if DNA tests prove that they're no relatives of mine … and they are attempting to take my body parts out of the country, then we have a watertight case. Well done, Diamond, top class investigative work.'

Diamond electrocuted him with one of her powerful smiles. She had got her happiness back.

She helped him get up and handed him the walker. Once one got the hang of it, it was possible to move at a good pace with the contraption. She pushed the drip stand.

When they passed the common ward the door was open, so out of curiosity he glanced inside. And locked eyes with Mr Deadlyappa who was sitting up in bed, drooping moustache, deadly tattoos. At first Deadlyappa's eyes were clouded by some confusion, as if he couldn't believe what he was seeing – and Hari did feel terribly self-conscious in his garish get-up – then Deadlyappa smiled that nasty I'm-gonna-share-your-snap-on-Facebook smile.

However, Hari thought that they shouldn't have to be Facebook enemies just because of a broken leg and a crushed foot, so he stepped into the ward, where the presence of so many other patients would guarantee his survival, to announce that their little war was over because he was leaving to fight a bigger battle. Deadlyappa would then wish him all the best. In the movie version of his adventures, which constantly played in his mind, it would be the perfect beginning to a grand happy ending. He greeted the rowdy-sheeter, 'Came to take your leave. Had your breakfast, Deadlyappa ji?'

Deadlyappa's foot was in a lump of plaster. *Ouch*, that must have been painful thought Hari and shot off an affable smile. Deadlyappa's moustaches twitched.

'I'm going to have *you* for breakfast one of these days,' said Deadlyappa and flashed his gold teeth in a bloodthirsty grin.

'With pickled toes as a side dish or what?' joked Hari in a most friendly spirit.

'I'll pulp your brain into chutney,' said Deadlyappa and started to look for something – he definitely wanted to throw an intercontinental ballistic missile at Hari. But weapons of mass destruction were not allowed in the hospital. 'I'll take care of you…'

'Boss, no time for that, got important stuff to do.'

However, Deadlyappa wasn't willing to forgive and forget. 'You think you're going to be safe out there, but I'll come after you wherever you go. And I'll kill you, and when you're reborn I'll kill you again and then again until you stop coming back.'

'Oho, is that so?' said Hari and wondered whether he should point out to Deadlyappa that they had an audience who witnessed their altercation and his threat of committing a triple murder on Hari. But looking around he noticed that the dozen or so amputees and other traffic victims in the ward did their best to pretend they hadn't heard a thing. Of course, if you had just lost an arm, you'd want to keep the other. So instead he said, 'Thanks, that'll give me some excitement in life after life.'

He saw Deadlyappa lose his temper and reach for his mobile. Unfortunately, all the people in the world couldn't be best buddies. Some conflict was inevitable; it was part of the cosmic order. News of Hari's escape from the hospital would reach Bhascar in another second and then they'd be after him again, and things would be back to normal. This was clearly one of those juggling days when all the balls were going to be in the air at the same time. So he said the only thing that made sense:

'Bye-bye and all the very best.'

Outside, in the bazaar, the construction materials that cluttered up public space and caused rickshaw and bullock cart jams, forced Hari to walk slowly. But at least he was out, away from the claustrophobic hospital, a free man. He could do anything he wanted. Go anywhere in the world. It was an amazing feeling … to see people shop at the bazaar stalls, labourers pour sand into a concrete mixer, a postman riding his bicycle down the narrow lane, the sun shining.

'What's the plan, hero?' asked Diamond.

Hari liked it when she called him that. To live up to it, he gave the state of affairs mature deliberation.

'We'll wing it,' he said.

'You can do better than that,' she said.

He gave the state of affairs even more deliberation, and said, 'Since I'm a man of my word, I shall take you for that meal I promised.' Perhaps it was the non-veg food discussion with Deadlyappa that had given him an appetite, but he was all of a sudden salivating at the thought of eating something other than hospital palak paneer. 'Does that sound like a plan to you?'

'I thought we were going to do detective work?'

'The A and O of detective work is to sit down first over a good curry and plan the operation in detail.'

'I had no idea.'

'Lots of people haven't got the slightest clue but luckily I know everything. And didn't you just say that the head nurse isn't expected back until after lunch? She won't notice a thing.'

'I don't know if restaurant food is advisable. A patient's diet during recovery...'

'You must be missing your native food, no? There's an alley where you get the best fish thalis with lots of coconut oil.'

To somebody from Kerala the flavours thus conjured up were irresistible. Hari guided her a few blocks down the bazaar and into a narrow and winding backstreet, the 6th Main, which was lined with Malabar-style canteens.

'How wonderful!' she exclaimed. 'I had no idea you could get proper food in Bengaluru.'

Hari smiled to himself. 'If you need to know anything, ask me before you google.'

He directed her to one particular mess which was a little clean with bathroom tile walls around the entrance and three tables in a windowless backroom. Its grand name was Nandana Biriyani Palace. There was a tray of deep-fried masala-covered mackerels on the counter. A poster of a mosque on the wall.

She said, 'You can't imagine how much I miss Kerala,' as they each got a plantain leaf and a waiter ladled on reddish, plump grained rice, steel bowls of fish curry, beef fry and velvety appams.

The proprietor came and greeted Hari warmly, tactfully ignoring his burlesque costume which Hari didn't bother to explain either. They were offered free dessert, paper cups with payasam. Then, after a few hearty morsels, Diamond observed casually, 'Say, you seem like a reasonably popular guy around these streets, yet I haven't noticed any family members coming to see you at the hospital.'

'I'm actually an orphan.' While Diamond ate, Hari entertained her with the incredible but true account of how he had been found as a baby under seat number B-16 in Majestic Talkies by the cleaning lady on the same day that the Internet was invented, AIDS was discovered and *Jaane Bhi Do Yaaro* was released, fastforwarding through the making of a hero while glossing over the darker points, until this very day. All people had a native place to be nostalgic about, except Hari Majestic. Nobody had come looking for him in all these years, not as far as he knew. Was he perhaps a Tamilian? The evidence was insubstantial and circumstantial: a train ticket had been tucked into his diapers when he was found in the cinema. A used ticket for a journey from Khatpadi Junction, a small railway station in Tamil Nadu. At times Hari fantasized that he had a more spectacular pedigree – that his mother was a real Mummy, an Egyptian, in which case his father may have been a Pharaoh? But it was just a fantasy.

Diamond stopped eating. 'That's a strange coincidence because Khatpadi Junction is near where Nurse Kolaveri hails from. Perhaps you could enquire if she ever met your parents.' When she started asking follow-up questions that might shed too much light on the myth he'd built up around his past, he tactfully changed the subject. Certain aspects of his doings shouldn't go on record, especially if there was a chance that any such recordings could be played back in a courtroom.

'What's your zodiac sign?' he asked instead.

'I don't believe in all that superstition.'

'But you were born?' He ought to have the data handy so that Pandit Pundit could draw up a matrimonial horoscope and match her with him.

'Of course.' She gave him her date of birth.

He calculated fast. She was a kanya, which was good: analytical, practical, diplomatic, meticulous, and dreamy – the perfect partner … for Hari. 'And where?'

The homely grub made her recall Tellicherry, her small hometown in Kerala. People from there became either acrobats or nurses. She chose the latter, because the circuses were being shut down. She went on talking, sharing the smallest details of her life – typical kanya behaviour. A kanya could, in a worst case scenario, actually bore people to death. But one did well in never complaining: the kanyas were also known to be vindictive, impulsive and tense.

She didn't mind that she hadn't seen so much of her motherland, she substituted it with detective novels from which she learnt the ways of the world – like all Malayalees she was a voracious reader – and she had been *so* thrilled when she read in the local newspaper about Mr Majestic, that there was a detective to protect her neighbourhood, and to think that she now had an opportunity to work with him on an investigation!

She was her parents' only child because people in Kerala were enlightened and didn't produce dozens of kids. Hers couldn't afford to feed more than one anyway. Her father was originally from the state of Nagaland, a travelling salesman of the world's hottest chillies who married a local girl and settled in Tellicherry. So they were quite cosmopolitan, too. But once, on a visit to Bengaluru, her parents were caught in a stampede at the railway station. Some commuters trampled them by mistake.

Whenever she crinkled her nose at some tedious or particularly sad memory, the diamond stud in her nose flashed with a glimmer of light. They broke a few bones and were taken to the hospital which at that time was still known as Sickly Hospital. She had just joined the hospital and so her parents were treated well. Hari was gladdened to hear that their organs were still intact. But ever since then they refused to set foot in Bengaluru again. Her Mom was troubled by her hipbone after the sad incident. Her Dad kept writing to newspapers trying to get stampedes and riots prohibited. He'd gone a bit crazy after Bengaluru; it could be a deceptive city that sometimes afflicted people deeply.

Diamond supported them by sending her salary home or what was left after she paid her living costs. She stayed in an ₹800 per month paying guest accommodation around the corner from the hospital, on the floor above a noisy weaving mill. 'I miss the sea and the fresh air. I wish there was an easy way to make a load of cash and go back home. One employment agent I spoke to suggested I rent out my womb for surrogate pregnancy. If the customer is a foreigner, they give you two thousand US dollars plus free boarding and lodging for nine months.'

Luckily, she had no idea that he was wired with a recording device. Hari gulped. 'What do you have to *do* to earn that much?'

'It's not what you think,' she reiterated. 'It's a clinical procedure where they mix the ovule and sperm in a lab, and only then is it inserted. But I don't see myself working at that kind of clinic even if the pay is high, so I turned the offer down.'

His heart had almost stopped there for a bar of beats. He kept watching her as she spoke and he felt certain she must have been a peacock in her previous life, she was so full of grace and she held her head high. She'd never contemplate trading her soul for a few thousand dollars … unlike him. He liked the fact that she didn't affect modesty, but said whatever she thought.

'Boyfriend, you have had?' he blurted out, his pulse galloping.

She eyed the fried mackerel on his banana leaf. He wondered if he should offer it to her.

Eventually she said, 'There have been temptations, but I've … I guess I ought to get married soon. But the way things are with my parents, there's no money for dowry.'

'Why don't you pick a good man who doesn't demand dowry?' He gently put the mackerel on her banana leaf.

'Where to find that man?' she said to the dead fish.

'Want to have babies?' he said, in an attempt to implant ideas in her mind, to which she said nothing. But sometimes people spoke without words. Hari knew that every normal mind came preloaded with data that determined its functioning, reaction patterns and so on, and usually the human configuration was opportunistic. A glib talker turned this to his advantage, inserted certain codes into the data stream and thereby changed the functioning of the mind. He added, 'Me too.'

'How many?' she said.

'One ladies, one gents. Plus minus one.' He waggled his head sideways. 'As long as the mother is all right with it.'

'That's very enlightened of you,' she said, fishtail sticking out of her mouth, 'So what do we do next?'

She was a practiced fish-eater and used her tongue to dislodge bones that got caught between her teeth, purging them through the left corner of her mouth. There was something very sensuous about it. He knew what he wanted to do. While listening to her, he'd had time to think. There was one sure way to get to spend more time together. 'Now shall I teach you the basics of detective work?'

She nodded enthusiastically. He had to wrestle his eyes away from her lips.

'Detective work is rarely action-packed like in the books you read but more a matter of methodical analysis. We must collect evidence about the transplant racket, Xerox handwritten surgical memos from both hospitals, or whatever it is you call those papers … We'll copy those and the related account book entries to get a complete picture of their illegal operations. You see, I need hard evidence to bring to my police contact. Then we'll put it onto DVDs that'll be delivered anonymously to TV channels and everything will be okay.'

He noticed her frowning.

'You were about to say?' he encouraged her.

'But it isn't important.'

'Even the smallest lead can be of vital significance.'

'You might not want to hear it.'

'Tell me, nevertheless.'

'I don't understand how your detective agency makes any money from its work. How do you pay your own salary for example?'

Good question. She was too clever.

He rolled his head sideways. 'By not taking undue tension over it. We can auction the DVDs to the media.' But when the bill arrived, a slip with the figure 256 scribbled on it, he groped for his wallet. Then he remembered. 'Eh, can I borrow from you?'

Summing up the day so far, and if one were optimistic about the way things were going, he'd got a free meal and a first date with his wife-to-be.

Next it was time to solve the crime. When they were walking back through the bazaar, Hari asked, 'Diamond, to clarify any doubts, you're sure you want to go through with this? This is the last chance to turn back.'

'Don't you want me to be there with you when you catch the crooks?' she said.

'Of course, but it can get rough.' In fact, his gut told him that since he had got out of the hospital alive, and if he were an intelligent being, he had better leave and stay away. But it wasn't always possible to make intelligent choices.

'You just said that detective work rarely gets as dramatic as in the books, and besides, you're here to protect me, hero, aren't you?' she challenged him as she helped him steer his walker and drip stand past two healthy cows that snacked from a garbage heap.

'That is also there,' he conceded. He ignored the loud warning bells; they were anyway only inside his head.

The glassy facade of Mediclinix Resorz soared before them. It was a veritable tower compared to the cramped bazaar houses surrounding it. According to the municipal bylaws, buildings higher than two storeys were not allowed to be built on thirty by forty feet plots, so house-owners hereabouts usually built three storeys, the third one being a semi-basement that housed shops. That way they almost kept within the limits. Any structure taller than fifty feet was deemed a high-rise. The medical resort, at six floors, was a bazaar skyscraper. But Hari was going to bring it down.

The neon-sign was turned off in the daytime but the flashy design – green coconut palm, blue lapping waves against a smiling sun – grabbed Hari's attention. Bamboo scaffolding climbed up walls, reinforcing iron rods jutted out, women labourers in shiny saris carried wok-shaped troughs with mortar on their heads.

'Strange to build an international luxury clinic in the middle of a noisy bazaar,' he spoke for the sake of the recording. 'I'd have assumed they'd pick a quieter street for their upper-class customers.'

'It's not strange at all if you think about it,' said Diamond and went on to explain how one of the difficulties with transplantations was the time factor. The longer the organ was out of the body, the greater the risk that it rotted. Storing it in a sealed, sterile container inside an ice bucket was one way of keeping it fresh. 'But in our climate it's tricky even then. So the best solution is to create a close connection between supply and demand – as in having the recipient staying next door to where the harvesting is happening.'

She told him that for the past year, or about as long as she had been employed here, this upcoming luxury wing had been Dr Viral's pet project. Not only were the rooms air-conditioned, those who worked there got better pay, she explained, including tips in hard currencies from the patients who were called 'guests'. 'But Kolaveri Didi, because she's old-fashioned, feels that things were better before they started curing the rich, the way she sees it is that it's at the expense of the poor.'

'How do you know how she feels?'

'We all know. She's that kind of person.'

Hari said, 'You'd make a fantastic detective if you worked on it, Diamond.'

At the entrance they negotiated heaps of sand that was used to dilute the concrete. As soon as they entered through the glass doors, they were inside an already fully operational zero-bacteria hospital. Nobody paid much attention to Hari and Diamond. She seemed like the nurse she was, attending to a weirdly dressed and therefore foreign-looking patient.

The lobby was white-panelled with black sofas and a small souvenir counter with Channapatna wooden toys and sandalwood incense packets. It looked all the more like a hotel because of the tastelessly dressed foreigners in flowery hippie pyjama pants and spaghetti strap tops who kept the lady at the reception desk busy.

A tourist in a motorized wheelchair was complaining. 'So can we do the beach resort, then a jungle with wild elephants but not the bird sanctuary, then *one* historical monument to understand your culture? My grandkids prefer to start with the beach, kids are kids.'

'Yes, but there'll be an extra charge,' said the receptionist.

'If the package is all-inclusive then how does it matter in which order we do it?'

The receptionist tolerantly explained, 'The Meditourism ambulance bus departs weekly and will be going to five heritage sites and two wildlife sanctuaries on the way to the beach, which for natural reasons comes last since it's furthest away from Bengaluru. The packages have been designed to make it more economical for you.'

'We don't want cheap stuff. Why are you so bureaucratic about every bloody thing?'

Diamond led the way through the cluster of foreigners, pushing the stand with the drip bags. Because of her uniform, she wasn't stopped by the guard at the doors separating the lobby from the clinic's innards.

Through the first door down the corridor, they caught a glimpse of a closet with mops and brooms, dirty bed sheets piled on the floor, and Hari spotted an orderly scrubbing one of the red buckets with a disinfectant soap bar. Evidence to add to the collection. Hoping that the camera captured it, he told Diamond to ask the orderly to hand over the bucket.

Watching her, Hari was impressed again. She was a natural, simply pretending to be far higher up in the food chain than the lowly nurse she actually was, and the orderly didn't dare to dispute her. She gave Hari the red bucket.

'What will you use it for?' she said.

'Who knows, I might need something in which to carry my kidney back?' Hari said, hooking the bucket to the walker's handle.

17

How to Stage a Showdown at a Medical Clinic

Starting at the top seemed the best strategy to Hari. The lift took them to the Penthouz Wardz where the best paying customers were likely to stay. It was also where the chief surgeon, Dr Glas Philipovich, had his private office according to the floor indicator – perhaps to keep an eye on his investments.

When the doors opened with a merry chime, they got out in a corridor with only five doors. Hari looked around. No sign of the doctor or any guards. The far end housed the office and along the sides were four Executive Deluxe Special Business Class Patient Suites. The nearest suite, EDSBCPS-4, was empty, its door open, perhaps it had belonged to the patient downstairs who was in the process of checking out.

The next room, EDSBCPS-3, was occupied. They knocked and entered, and Hari took it all in. It was an old habit of his, taking him no more than 0.6 seconds to ascertain whether a situation was good or bad including determining the previous incarnation of every human in sight.

Flat-screen TV by the bed, desk with a power saving lamp, rumbling air-conditioner by the window, fridge, but no jacuzzi or anything over the top fancy – not exactly five-star but standards comparable to hotel rooms in the ₹3,999 to ₹5,999 range, which in Bengaluru terms was either higher low budget or lower high budget.

On the walls were gilt-framed advertisements for Economical Bone Marrow Transplantation, International Standard MRI Scans, Cardiopulmonary Bypass Family Package Deal and Medically Supervised Recuperation in a vegetarian resort starting from €99 per day.

The occupant was a man, aged around fifty, in a light blue tracksuit that was too tight. His long blond hair was brushed back from his deeply tanned face and held in place by a sweatband. He wore sunglasses even indoors and reeked of a perfumed suntan lotion. He may have been a tandoori chicken in his previous lifetime and for all that mattered he looked like his name could be Frankenwhatever.

'Who's there?' Had the patient had a cornea transplant? Then Hari should count himself lucky that they hadn't removed his eyes on top of everything else. 'And what's that squeaky sound?'

Diamond stopped pushing the drip stand and the sound died.

'That's the tea trolley coming down the corridor with tiffin you're hearing,' said Hari. 'Meanwhile, before you gobble down your snacks, I'm here from the Hospital Quality Control Board with a few routine questions.'

'Why?'

'Why not? Doesn't matter if you've just had a brain transplant, answer the questions and you will win a guaranteed holiday…'

Hari deliberated for a fraction of a second: the customer didn't look the ashram type, nor the Taj Mahal type, '…to Goa.'

If his analysis was correct, the patient was the type of tourist who'd enjoy grilling himself in the Indian sun, with or without tandoori marinade.

'Goa?'

'Don't like Goa?'

'Yeah, Goa, man … I love free holidays.

'Your name, please?' Hari made it a point to sound through-and-through bureaucratic.

'Why?'

'Standard procedure. For the air ticket to Goa.'

'First what's yours?'

'My good self is Doctor Harry.'

The patient leaned forward, lifted his sunglasses and strained his bloodshot eyes. After blinking a few times when he seemed to take in Hari's garish sari, not particularly well concealed by the hospital gown, the single girlish slipper and jewellery clipped to his ears, he said, 'Cool man, I didn't know there were gays in India.'

Hari was about to say something but thought better of it. Guy had some problem with his eyes.

'And the hot chick is?' So he hadn't had a cornea transplant then if he saw that Diamond was a stunner.

'Nurse *Sugar*, as in sweet.' She was a clever girl, she used an alias.

'You can call me Armcandy. So when do I get the ticket? You guys wanna come along? I'm a swinger.'

Hari did a double take. *Foreigners!* If one were to trust the file and the names recorded in it, no person named Armcandy had received any part of him. But he had lived long enough to always assume that any name might be faked. 'Tomorrow morning, first thing, a team of flower girls will garland you. Mister Armpitcandy, is that what it says in your passport?'

'It's kind of an artist name. You need my actual name for the raffle? Okay, I'm Edipo Papas.'

'And what kind of artist are you?'

'I'm a connoisseur of the art of loving.'

'We have that art in India too. So you're from where, Greek?'

'Yes, lots of women say I look like a god. Don't I? But nowadays I'm based in Pattaya, Thailand, where I work as a personal trainer in a gym. The European economy went down the drain so I outsourced myself. But you didn't come to find out about that, did you?'

Hari nodded. 'No, the question you must answer to win your free holiday is have you had a transplant and were you satisfied with the result?'

'No.'

'No, what?'

'If you work here, man, I'd have expected you to know I came for body rejuvenation.'

'It wouldn't look good if a hospital assessed its own quality, would it? So for obvious reasons, the work is done by independent investigators like my good self. That explains my undercover outfit. What's rejuvenation about anyway?'

'My man, I availed of a speciality-of-the-house Tummy Tuck offer which included toughening of the removed fat with an extract from Malaysian organic rubber trees and re-injecting it into the upper arms, a technique pioneered here at the clinic or so I've been told.' Mr Armcandy showed off his disproportionately thick upper arms.

'What was the special offer?' asked Hari, still suspicious.

'The deal included a free eyebrow tweak.' His fluffy eyebrows fluttered.

'No new organs? You're sure?' said Hari. Wrong room, then. Just to get some extra sound bytes for his report he said, 'No complaints you wish to lodge?'

'If you're a quality control man, can you do something about that constant construction noise? That drilling drives me up the wall.'

'No problem,' said Hari, 'I'll ask them to switch India to silent mode for the duration of your stay.'

The doctor's office was locked.

'Pity I forgot my crowbar,' said Hari.

'No problems,' said Diamond and kneeled before the door. She used a hairpin to open it. Took her no more than half a minute.

'I'm impressed. Where'd you learn that?'

'I was a mischievous child. So my parents often had to lock me up in the pantry. But the door never held me too long.'

He peered inside. The office was empty. Airy, with a leathery examination couch, a huge desk with cash lying about in the drawers – it took all of Hari's self-restraint to leave the evidence where he found it – an old KGB identity badge with the doctor's name on it, a Sony laptop covered in nicotine patches and sacred ash from the pujas a few days back, and a panoramic window overlooking the decaying rooftop of the GSSS Hospital across the bazaar.

'It's an absolute madhouse, this place,' said Diamond as she studied the wall decorations. Strange old pictures. 'I had no idea.'

He took a closer look, too. Possibly in an attempt to cheer himself up on days when he got tired of the rundown vistas, the doctor had covered his walls with framed sets of black-and-white images of patients. There was a sketch of a man who had four arms and four legs within a circle. Another picture was of a cut open skull with what looked like brain curry in it – but it was labelled 'The Circle of Reason'. It was the office of a man who loved his patients the way Taison, the chicken butcher of CD Road, posted colourful blowups of mutant broilers with two heads, the ideal fatty lollypop or the perfect wing outside his shop.

It all struck Hari as somewhat spooky.

EDSBCPS-2 was next. A very rich-looking Chinese or Japanese gentleman was half-sitting in bed, dressed in a silk kimono with cartoon characters printed on it, rocking slowly back and forth – sumo-wrestling with himself or doing physiotherapy? So this would have to be Baiju Ganbei, forty-four years old, who had bought 70 per cent of his liver.

'Bee you-mister.' Hari tried to pronounce the name but couldn't get it right.

'Baiju Ganbei,' the man confirmed.

'That sounds very much like a foreign language. Myself I'm from the Quality Control Board.'

Mr Ganbei pointed at the sari that draped Hari's lower body and said something more in his own tongue, 'Geisha?'

'I'm fine, but how do you do?' Hari replied.

'I don't think he understands English,' said Diamond.

'*Liver*,' said Hari and pointed to his own abdomen. 'Do you have a word for it in your language? It is a non-vegetarian body part.' He tried to think of words from that part of the world, but apart from *hara-kiri* he couldn't come up with anything really suitable.

Then he made a charade of taking a pair of scissors, cutting up the skin, gingerly prying the sides of the cut apart, lifting out something about as big as a portion of keema kaleji – a spicy, minced mutton liver snack – serving it on an invisible platter and pushing it across an imaginary dining table towards the Oriental man, who was befuddled, the way tourists often were in India.

Hari held up two fingers and scissored in the air, then he pointed at Mr Ganbei.

Mr Ganbei imitated the gesture. 'Chopsticks?'

Hari shrugged. No need to disturb Indo-Chinese diplomatic relations. The two countries already shared a highly sensitive border.

He'd just have to sober up by 70 per cent from now on.

The last room was EDSBCPS-1, with a window facing the flat low roofs where laundry was drying and children flew kites.

The woman by the window looked like … *a woman?* This was a bit of a problem. The file had said nothing about a woman, but then again some foreign names sounded very unisex to Hari's ears. Women were complex beings. Well, at least more complex than men.

'Madam Frankenstein…'

'It is *Frankenheimer*, but you can call me Alice.'

She had large spectacles and was arranging photographs into a scrapbook or a diary that lay on a desk, other photos were blu-tacked to the wall next to the window – mainly Indian street scenes.

'Alice, is it?'

'And who might you be?' she said.

'The name's Harry.'

'Really … as in that Potter?'

'But better, welcome to Bengaluru, the city at the centre of the flat world,' said Hari, it was one of his riffs and it usually worked on foreign tourists.

'Thanks. So, Harry, what's that red bucket for?'

Hari waved a hand at Diamond. 'Don't you recognize legitimate medical staff on duty when you see them?'

'Well, I haven't seen you here before, have I? You look a bit sick.'

For a moment, Hari was taken aback by her standoffish tone. Then he improvised, trying his best to come up with suitable things to say, 'Don't mind the clothes. My job has to be done undercover.'

'No, I meant sick in the hospital way. Or why else would you be on drip?'

'Don't worry, madam,' Diamond said, softly. 'He's got an allergy.'

Hari thought fast and clarified, 'It is all part of the disguise – the bandaged leg, this walker. I'm a very professional medical investigator. So like the nurse said, not to worry.'

There was an awkward moment after that. Hari hadn't planned this operation properly. He looked around the room that Alice had tried to make homely by putting up stuff on the shelves, mostly souvenir things, the kind of cheap keepsakes sold in the nearby Avenue Road bazaar. Save for the thick glasses, she herself looked younger than her fifty-nine years, peering at them with curiosity. Finally, Alice broke the silence.

'I'm so sorry for you. Must be terrible to be allergic in a dirty country like this. Hey, if you are an investigator, can you come here and help me investigate something?'

Although he would have wanted to protest against her sweeping statement that India was 'a dirty country', he took the cue from Diamond to proceed with caution. After all, it was his kidney talking. Since they had been more or less invited into the room, Diamond and Hari walked closer to the table where several photos were laid out.

'Do you know this place?' She tapped a finger onto one. It appeared very much to have been downloaded from the Internet. A vegetable market – carrots fashioned into picturesque cones on the stone slab counter, next to a square-sided pyramid of tomatoes and a bunch of bananas dangling from the bamboo pole that held up the awning. The vegetable seller smiled invitingly into the camera. It was a generic postcard picture, could be anywhere.

'It's some old market,' said Diamond without hesitation.

Hari studied it for another two seconds and pronounced, 'Maharajah era.' After all he was an expert on tourist attractions.

'Which Maharajah?'

'Why do you want to know?'

'I keep seeing it in my dreams.' She peered at him, nearsighted.

'Maybe because you looked too many times at the photo?' said Hari.

'No, I used to see it in my dreams *before* I found this picture online. That's what's puzzling me. Anyhow, I recognized it instantly. I just can't figure out where it is. Know what I'm saying?'

'So why not email the photographer and ask?'

'He's dead, isn't he?'

Her enthusiasm about the photograph was infectious, especially since Hari had a strong belief in karmic repercussions and had this theory that tourists often came to India to pay for misdeeds from previous births. He felt the adrenaline pump through his bloodstream. He was thinking on his feet now. Or foot.

'Oho, that's too bad karma. But what if you were the photographer in your past life and that's why you recognize the snap?'

'Amazing! I think you're reading my mind!'

'Great minds think alike,' said Hari and rolled his head sideways.

She went on, encouraged, 'I've been collecting photos of India ever since I knew I was coming here for the surgery, and more and more I'm feeling some mysterious connection to this country and its people … know what I'm saying?'

'Better than you think,' said Hari. The main problem was that he instinctively liked most women; this one reminded him of many of the motherly tourist ladies he had found wandering in the streets in those days when he was touting, and if the circumstances had been different he would have happily guided her to the best Kashmiri souvenir shops in town. Barely missing a beat, he went on, 'Never doubt mysterious connections. This is the land of karma.'

'Really,' said the woman. 'You people are so full of wisdom.'

He had a plan shaping in his mind. 'Thanks to the great merits of our previous lives, so many of us lucky ones live here, one and a half billion they say.'

'I never knew.'

'Actually nobody knows the exact number. It may be that some of us were foreigners in our past births, but now we're not, not anymore, now we're ourselves.'

'That's so interesting. Harry, tell me if I'm crazy but I'm a vegan and I don't quite feel at home in the materialistic West.

Anyhow, what if I was an Indian photo artist in my past life, specializing in vegetable photography?'

Interestingly, she accepted him as a medico-psychological expert although he wore funny things clipped to his ears and was wrapped in a flowery sari. No Bengaluruan would have done it.

'Doesn't sound crazy at all,' said Hari. 'The only doubt is why anybody would take rebirth in the West in the first place.'

'You think it's possible that I did something bad? Maybe while taking photographs the camera sucked the souls out of the vegetables…?' When she saw the nonplussed expression on Hari's face, she took it as an opportunity to deliver a soliloquy which basically comprised her complete autobiography as she imagined it and it ended with, 'And then due to that bad karma I was reborn in Minneapolis?'

'Almost certainly that is the case,' Hari countered in his most professorial tone. He had met people from those parts before and knew they faced cold, harsh winters, and that life there wasn't cheap like in India. 'Most bad people are reborn in places like that where they contribute to the godlessness. And they are forced to do other unnatural things that lead to stress and get kidney diseases due to unhealthy lifestyles, toxic food and drinking alcohol, and need transplant surgery.'

'Oh my god, that is so absolutely true. You won't believe it but I've just had a *kidney* transplant.'

'When did that happen, if I may ask?' said Hari, to confirm that it indeed was the right kidney they were talking about.

'Just this week. Earlier I was sick and tired, in constant pain, doing dialysis for three hours every second day, and now it's … I'm so full of energy I can't sit still. I love it here in India.'

His stomach gave a sudden brutal lurch. He started to feel bad about taking back his kidney. But one had to strive on with a pure mind.

'Glad you enjoy visiting our country. But here comes the crunch: have you thought a few steps ahead?'

'About what?'

'What this may do to your future rebirth options?'

'What do you mean?' She picked up some of the photo printouts from the table, moved them about as if they were pieces in a jigsaw puzzle.

'Good question,' said Diamond.

'Standard procedure,' he said. It was time to strike the hot iron. 'Did madam ascertain that the kidney came from a willing donor who was correctly reimbursed for his suffering?'

'Now I don't get you,' she said.

'No joke to get, madam. There are some doubts, whether it is bona fide or not, and the maximum penalty you're facing is seven years in Parappana Agrahara Central Jail.'

18

How to Multitask in a Broom Closet

Alice closed her eyes as if she had just had a terrifying vision. Then she shook her head. She faced Nurse Diamond and her cold tone was borderline rational.

'Nurse, this person frightens me, I demand that you remove him from my room or I shall have to summon the police. I don't want to get involved in your internal affairs and how you run this business, but I was shown papers that certified the kidney to be organically harvested from a vegetarian teetotaller. There was a lot of paperwork.'

'Summon as many police as you like, madam Frankenstein or whatever it is that you wish to call yourself,' said Hari who wasn't sure whether to feel flattered or offended at being called a 'vegetarian teetotaller'. There were two sides to each coin. 'You see, it has happened in the past that documents have been forged by racketeers.'

'I'm not listening to this anymore. I can't hear you.'

Hari added, 'Better pay attention, because the thing is that you seem to have no idea where that kidney came from, or who, or for that matter *what species* the donor is.'

Alice studied her hands. They looked healthy, like she used expensive skin creams. She tried to stay quiet but couldn't do it for long. She exhaled. 'I heard you do things differently over here, but … I googled on my iPad and came across weird stories … Do you think I was cheated and the kidney came from a chimpanzee? If that's the case, I'll sue. I love animals. I wouldn't want to hurt one. Anyhow, I'd die rather than have a chimp inside me, I'm a vegan.'

'Do you feel a strong craving for bananas?'

'No.' She cast an odd look in his direction. 'Can't say I do. May I ask: are you stoned?'

'No, I'm a "vegetarian teetotaller", so don't worry about that,' lied Hari in a quick diversion of attention before he attacked with renewed force. Despite the hints he had dropped, she hadn't yet connected the dots, but soon she would have to face facts. 'There are worse scenarios I can think of.'

'Such as?'

'What if the kidney was stolen from a sedated slum dweller?'

'Anyhow I didn't do it,' she said. 'It was paid for.'

'Madam Alice, then let me ask you: did you hand over the cash personally to the slum dweller?'

'I don't understand a word of what you're saying.'

'Hari, please,' said Diamond.

'Hold on a minute, Nurse. Can you, madam Alice, swear that you took the trouble to meet the donor and establish a just fair trade relationship? I don't think so. They have hoodwinked you with body parts bamboozled from some … some orphaned child.'

'Oh no. How can you say such a terrible thing?'

'Oh yes,' said Hari. 'And that is what will put a weight on your karma so heavy that you can never again expect to be reborn as a human, but count on being an *insect* for a *minimum* of a *hundred lifetimes.*'

Alice blinked to suppress the tears that had appeared in her eyes. 'What makes you say all these horrible things? You don't understand, back home this surgery would have cost a quarter million dollars not counting pre- and post-operative care and medicines. Coming here sounded like a great solution to the insurance company, they were happy to pay when I told them that it's easy to find donors abroad…'

'What sounds too good to be true usually is.'

Alice went on without bothering unduly about the minor immoral aspects, '…and I get a holiday thrown in at a vegetarian beach resort. Anyhow, wouldn't you have done the same in my place?'

He probably would, but aloud he said, 'You still haven't justified why you think you have a right to do what you did.'

'Why would I justify anything to you?'

He put a hand over his heart and fiddled with his nipple like a kamikaze pilot clutching the control stick of his airplane, time to drop the bombs. 'Because I'm the one whose kidney you stole.'

She paled. 'I thought you worked at the hospital.'

'Yes, it is what you may call a temporary gig as an involuntary organ donor. But she works here fulltime and she'll confirm that everything I'm telling you is true.' He pointed at Diamond.

'Who is he?' said Alice to Diamond.

'He's a hero,' said Diamond.

'Victim,' added Hari and pulled up his gown to show the scars.

Alice paled even more, almost as if she had dipped her face in rapid action fairness cream. 'I'm so sorry to hear that. You're missing a kidney?' she said. 'Is that what this is about? You think I took it.'

'Correct. Now, ideally I'd like you to give it back. Please.' He indicated the red bucket.

'But it was *paid* for, so don't you think I am entitled to a kidney?'

'You may well be, madam, but not necessarily *my* personal kidney. Couldn't your insurance company have paid for a proper non-stolen kidney?'

'One can't buy it over the counter, one has to wait in a transplant queue for years, because there's a limited supply of brain-dead donors...'

'Hari is not brain-dead!' Diamond blurted out, crossly.

'*That* organ is still with me,' affirmed Hari.

Alice responded emotionally, '...but I may have had to wait for decades hooked onto that horrible dialysis machine, and may not have survived. Harry, to be honest with you, I did it mostly because of one reason.' She was going into confessional mode. 'I don't have children. If I had, my life would continue in another form in them, and I'd have died knowing I'm leaving an inheritance to them. Anyhow, so then I thought I'd better hang on for as long as I can. Keep doing good, know what I'm saying? I wish I could give the kidney back, seeing that you're unhappy about it.' She thought for a minute. 'But I suppose wishing isn't good enough for you, so how about I give it to you right here and now, and I die?'

Hari felt a massive lurch in his stomach again. It was as if the cavity that had held the kidney was telling him something, maybe saying goodbye and wishing him all the very best.

'No, keep it,' he said addressing the empty red bucket.

'Say what?' asked Diamond and Alice in unison.

Hari shook his head; this wasn't working out the way he had hoped. However much they argued about it, there was no sign of an appropriate solution. He wouldn't want anybody to die because of him, for that made him as nasty as the organ racketeers.

'Diamond, we're wasting our time. Alice madam, kindly take good care of my kidney. I shall miss it. Bye-bye then, all the very best and see you again in about a hundred lifetimes. If it is of any consolation, an insect's lifespan is short, so it'll go faster than you think.'

Alice sat with her mouth open, but no sound came out.

'Hari, we should carry on,' Diamond interrupted, sensing that he was drifting from the subject.

She grabbed his drip stand and when he felt the pull of the hypodermic needles he followed sheepishly with the walker. Giving up was so not like him, but this time he had lost the game.

Diamond escorted Hari down the corridor. They stopped before the lift. According to the indicator panel, it was coming up.

'Damn it.'

'Why do you use such dirty language?' asked Diamond. 'And what was all that about, harassing the poor woman, in the end for no purpose?'

'It couldn't be helped.'

'But can't you see you made her very sad?' Diamond sounded irritated for some strange reason, as if all this was Hari's fault. 'Operation: Operation' had run into a dead end and turned into a farce of an investigation. A tactical diversion was required.

'I hope that's not the good doctor on his way up here,' said Hari and nodded at the large red digits changing.

There was no time to run. There was only one lift and the fire escape wasn't an option for a legless man. Being a super quick thinker, Hari suggested a detour into the empty EDSBCPS-4. Diamond dragged the drip stand with her.

'Do you even believe in that reincarnation stuff you go on talking about?' Diamond blasted him as she shut the door. 'Isn't all that made up by superstitious gurus and astrologers to control the gullible, like opium for the masses?'

She was from Kerala, the land of communism, rationalism, feminism and guru-busters, so he felt he must point out, 'Just because you work in a scientific job doesn't mean that unknowable mysteries don't exist in our world.'

'I thought you detectives were committed to solving mysteries, not messing around with poor women's minds.'

'Please be quiet,' he said, 'I'm working.'

There was an ominous chime from the lift doors. They heard steps outside. Heavy footfalls, had to be at least one of the doctors, Hari guessed. They waited another few heartbeats, until it was silent, and then Hari mouthed the words, 'Let's go,' and she proceeded to roll the drip stand towards the lift.

There was nobody in sight.

The lift doors were closing. Hari pushed on faster.

He wasn't planning on waiting for the lift to return so he used his good leg to kick the red bucket between the doors in time to prevent them from shutting. The bucket made too much noise. But the sliding doors stopped when they touched the bucket and reversed. Diamond picked up the bucket, then Hari walked inside and hit the ground floor button.

The doors stayed open long enough for it to feel uncomfortable. In hospitals, the lift doors were set to be slower, to give patients time to exit and enter. Hari counted the seconds. Finally they started closing again.

Right then, Dr Glas Philipovich came out of Alice's suite and caught sight of the bizarrely clad Hari, all dolled up like a drag star, and Diamond. He looked angry, as if he'd misplaced his box of nicotine patches and suspected that Hari had stolen it. Dr Viral was with him and acted as a translator. Coming towards them, Viral shouted, 'Stop! What's in that bucket?'

But then the doors finally shut and the lift shuddered downwards. Diamond fell back against the metal wall. 'That was close.'

'You got scared?' said Hari.

'No, but what an adventure this turned into.'

Hari watched the numbers count down the floors, but wasn't sure that this was the end of the story.

They got out on the ground floor and she led him towards the exit. The security man was slumbering, a ring of empty paper cups around the legs of his chair. Hari handed over the red bucket to him.

'Boss, will you take care of this?' he said. He didn't want to give the doctors a reason to accuse him of bucket theft. Not after yesterday's physiotherapy, when they showed him that they meant business.

'What do I do with it?' asked the puzzled guard.

'Mark it as evidence, specimen number two,' Diamond ordered him. She was almost as quick a thinker as Hari. 'Keep it safely.'

'Okay, madam.' The guard got up and lumbered off to the office.

Hari scanned the lobby: it was deserted. Luck was on their side. The tourist group was gone and the receptionist must be somewhere powdering her nose. Behind them in the corridor, the lift doors were closing. No doubt to return to the top floor. But they had a short respite.

Hari said to Diamond, 'We better move out of here faster than the Mysore Shatabdi Express when it passes through Cantonment Station. What's the evidence number one, then?'

'You,' Diamond said as she assisted him across the lobby.

Hari pushed open the glass doors to the street and looked around in the noisy bazaar which, after the air-conditioned hospital interiors, slapped him in the face with its usual happy chaos of wheeling and dealing. He was accustomed to making quick threat assessments. That was the approximate nanosecond when he saw Mr Bhascar, the coffee miller, come out of the GSSS Hospital bang opposite.

Luckily, Bhascar had his back to them as he was helping his friend, the rowdy-sheeter Mr Deadlyappa, negotiate the steps one at a time. Deadlyappa was walking with a cane, his foot in its bulky plaster cast. It took Hari no more than a quarter of a second to figure that Deadlyappa must have decided to get out of the hospital to pursue him and settle scores.

Any second now, one of them might look up at the luxury clinic and spot Hari. Which would be a bad, bad thing. Judging from Deadlyappa's gestures – two fingers cutting across throats and a hand shaped into a pistol – he hadn't yet decided on what murder method to use: whether to chop off Hari's head or shoot him in the brains, or perhaps a bit of both. In fact, Deadlyappa looked so mad that Bhascar had to restrain him physically from running amok there and then and killing innocent bystanders.

Hari ducked and backed in through the glass doors into the air-conditioned lobby. Unprepared for the sudden retreat, Diamond pushed the drip stand into him and they collided.

'What's the matter?' she said.

'I'll explain later.'

He headed back to the corridor from where they had escaped. The guard hadn't yet returned to his place. The lift doors chimed, they would open any second.

Diamond grabbed Hari's elbow, 'We have to get out of here. It's foolish to stay.'

'Don't worry, heroes do foolish things all the time,' he whispered.

'Why?'

'We do what we have to do. That's rule number one in our job.'

Hari heard the voices from the lift. The doors had started opening, slowly. Diamond froze as she too caught the doctors yelling at each other. She was of a very practical turn, because in less than a second she pushed Hari through the first door in the corridor, into the broom closet.

The orderly who had been washing buckets had left. It was a tiny space that contained shelves, a sink, detergent bottles and a pile of unwashed sheets on the floor.

She helped him sit down on the sheets. Then she quickly folded up the walker and stuffed it in after him, keeping the drip stand upright, so that the flow of antibiotic fluids wasn't interrupted.

'If they ask you anything, pretend you have no idea,' he whispered. 'You took me for a therapeutic outing and I forced you to go up there in the lift. You won't lose your job if you've done nothing wrong.'

She checked the corridor left and right. Then she stepped into the closet after him and pulled the door almost shut, leaving a narrow chink. She sat down next to him on the dirty bed sheets, pulled a clean sheet from a shelf and draped it over the two of them. She whispered, 'Can't desert you at the point when it starts to get interesting.'

For the time being they were in near total darkness.

Distantly, they heard the doctors argue. Hari made an educated guess: they were unhappy. He stuck his head out from under the sheet, moved closer to the door trying to remember which ear the microphone was in. He listened intently and hoped everything went into the recorder too.

Viral dragged the security guard out of the lavatory, threatened to fire him and interrogated him about who had left the hospital in the last few minutes. The guard hesitated. His replies sounded evasive, the way people speak when they don't want to be made scapegoats. Then when he finally understood that he wasn't going to get court-martialled, he told them that one eunuch had been taken out by a nurse. Though he admitted he hadn't seen them leave the hospital, so it was quite possible that they were still around.

Viral made a call on his mobile. Minutes later, Kolaveri came running from the other hospital. She wasn't so bossy now. Hari hoped everything went into the microphone.

'How is it possible that a legless patient walks off with one of your nurses?' asked Dr Viral.

'Administrative mishap,' said the head nurse. 'Won't happen again. Diamond is only twenty-six and you know what these young girls are like, doctor.'

'No, I don't know what they are like. Would you care to explain *why* I should turn a blind eye to dereliction of duty?'

'She's innocent and trusting, poor thing.'

The doctor got really angry. 'Whether she is stupid or not isn't the question … with her assistance that pathological liar managed to gain access to Mediclinix Resorz up to its highest level, and he tried to swindle one of our guests. Who knows what he's up to next.'

It satisfied Hari to hear that he had infiltrated the highest level, even though he hadn't achieved anything by it. He squeezed Diamond's hand. It was the excitement. Her hand was hot, soft and somewhat moist, and she squeezed his hand back. She too was thrilled.

The doctor shouted at Kolaveri for some time. Then he stopped, caught his breath and said, 'I want that invertebrate back in his room, I want him safely locked up, strapped down in bed and use a straitjacket if you must. It is unsafe to have these rowdies running amok. Have I made myself clear?'

Clear enough thought Hari and made a mental note to google 'invertebrate' to learn more about his own specific medical condition.

The head nurse mumbled something about them not having any 'straitjackets' at the hospital. Viral issued further orders. 'That man is a danger to himself and his surroundings. I expect you to turn the whole hospital upside down if need be, question everyone and find out everything he's been up to, Nurse Kolaveri.'

Kolaveri said, 'I'll take care of that, Doctor.'

'For your own sake, I hope you will,' Viral raved on. 'We plan to give the hospital a complete makeover. We'll install modern surveillance systems and your entire nursing staff will be upgraded. We need educated people with a professional mindset. Not village girls like that one. We can't afford another security breach.'

'No, Doctor,' she said.

'Right then, carry on.'

They heard the footsteps recede, then all was quiet. Hari almost felt sorry for the head nurse and whispered to Diamond, 'We better lay low. Until we know it is cool out there.'

In here, he was feeling the heat.

'Yes,' Diamond agreed softly. Being called a 'village girl' and 'that one' couldn't be uplifting.

'Tell me more about Kolaveri Didi,' he whispered. 'Do you think she's on their or your side?'

'She has a sad past.'

'Why, something happened?'

'She never got to complete her nursing education.'

'That's why she gives off the impression of being somewhat incompetent? But it needn't be a bad thing. Look, I never finished school and I've done well.'

'Also … she doesn't trust many people.'

'What people?'

'Male people. She says that most men aren't trustworthy.'

He could have guessed. 'I'd say she's right.'

'But I want to trust *you*.'

They held hands in the dark. 'Why does she have a problem with men?'

'She's always been like that – she escaped a rural native place she doesn't want to go back to, is lonely, with no kids … For her, life's been a raw deal. But she hasn't given up, she works hard. She's a source of inspiration.'

'And because of *that* you trust her?'

Diamond answered the snide question with a profound question. 'What else can we do but trust each other? Don't you think mankind would be beyond salvation if we stopped having faith in our fellow humans?'

Hari could have enlightened her, but thought it prudent to let her keep her illusions. 'So what brought her from god-knows-where to Bengaluru? The prospect of making money?' Basic questions were the best if you wanted to get somebody talking, whereas putting problematic existential subject matters before anybody most often only served to shut that person up for good.

'They say, though I don't know the details, that she dropped out of nursing school because of some trouble. She never told us about it, but we think she had a fling with somebody who was already married. You know how conservative people were in the old days.'

'It would make a nice plot for a nostalgic movie.'

'You're so sweet,' she said, amused. She gave him a girlish peck on the cheek.

'It's because it is getting hot in here,' said Hari, 'and I feel like a boiled candy.'

'In Kerala, on the coast, we're used to much hotter,' she said.

'Yes, I can imagine that,' said Hari. He had too many unsown wild oats within to stay unaffected by her presence. Squeezed close to her under the sheet, he felt her breath like a warm breeze on the nape of his neck, and the coconut oil in their respective hairdos thawed and started to run, trickling down their ears, juicing them up and making strange thoughts flow. Intellectually, he knew it was still October but in his heart it was May, it was that hot. Hot like chillies from Nagaland.

His fingertips moved across her palm in gentle strokes.

'Don't get fresh with me, hero. Or...'

'...Kolaveri Didi might come. Oho, you got me scared.'

But she didn't do anything to push his probing fingers away, she didn't break a single one of them with a sledgehammer, didn't slap him even. Instead she giggled. So did he, and he cautioned himself that in situations like this, and no matter what, it was vital to stick to the general censorship criteria set by the Board of Film Certification. Perhaps it would be an appropriate time to disable the camera and voice recorder. But Doc had cautioned him that the system was idiot proof. He sighed; the two of them were so close, and yet so far – kept apart by an idiotic gizmo. Although he doubted that the poor light in the closet was sufficient for the video to capture anything, he couldn't bear the thought that uncensored MPEG files of their private moments might be downloaded to the computers at Doc's cybercafe.

'Are you uncomfortable?'

'This frock is strangulating me,' he said, to hide the fact that he was attempting to unplug the mike and camera wires. Another white lie followed, 'Claustrophobia, some people get that in hospitals.'

'Do you want to get out of here?' she asked.

A minute went by, two, and then he suggested, 'Perhaps we should wait just a little longer to be on the safe side.'

'Want me to help you loosen the gown?' She started untying the ribbons at the back. She did it with a nurse's clinical touch. Used to patients' bodies in all shapes and sizes, this probably wasn't what she counted as a romantic moment. But for Hari it was.

He calculated the odds for her also stripping off something. Group psychology dictated that if one person yawned, the tiredness spread through the room and everybody started yawning; or if a person talked on her mobile, her companion was likely to make a random call while waiting. On TV too they used taped laughter, so that TV addicts sitting at home wouldn't feel sad about laughing alone.

Therefore, Hari pulled the garment off and in the process tore at the cables taped to his neck, to rip out the video and audio feeds from their jacks. With some luck the device wouldn't switch over to its built-in microphone.

'Better now?' she said.

'Muchly, thank you,' he said in English. The gentle and occasional touch of skin, when hers accidentally rubbed against his, caused him to moan. 'How are you doing?'

'Don't worry about me. You're the sick one,' she said. He wondered: *was there a double meaning?* She continued, 'How's your leg? Is the pain great?'

'A little great.' He shifted uncomfortably; he didn't want her to think that he was taking liberties. 'I'm not as sick as you think.'

'Why do you men always have to be so macho? If you're in pain, admit it. Here, let me massage your leg.' She reached down to rub his thigh. The stiff cloth of her uniform, stretched across her breasts, tickled his upper arm. 'This should aid blood circulation.'

She worked on him with nimble fingers and it exhausted her so much that she was panting. Soon he too found it hard to control his breathing, feeling like a donkey that had seen a carrot for the first time in its life, 'I always used to dream that I'd meet someone like you, one day.'

'What, a nurse?'

'No, the uniform doesn't matter so much. You can take it off and I'd still feel the same.'

'So you like me…?'

'Yes.'

'…to take it off?'

'No, I didn't mean that.' If the microphone was recording, Doc and Triplex would have the laugh of a lifetime. Usually he shared everything with Triplex, even the most embarrassing experiences, but there were things that weren't meant for the ears or eyes of Triplex. Like this. He made a mental note: *Top secret.*

'Then what are you proposing?' she said.

'Why do you think I'm proposing?' he said, to prove conclusively that any dirty thoughts were in her mind, not his.

She went silent.

'If I may say so…' he started.

'Shut … up,' she said with emphasis on each word.

For perhaps the first time ever, Hari was tongue-tied. Before he was able to rework his strategy, she kissed him.

19

How to Say No to Offers That Only Idiots Would Refuse

Her lips were lusciously hot, the way he imagined the beaches of Kerala to be, and as soft, although with a surprisingly passionate strength.

His tongue probed the jagged edge of her chipped front tooth. Every moral fibre in his body went offline. *Had she planned to seduce him all along?* When he came to, about thirty seconds later, he knew that love was nothing like watching a dirty film with Triplex and Doc, but something sublime.

'Shall we kiss some more?' he said once he caught his breath.

'I surely suppose we shall,' she giggled.

They continued their experiments with mouth-to-mouth methods in the confined space of the broom closet. The only options were to swim or sink. So he unbuttoned her uniform.

'This much mischief will suffice,' she said.

'Meaning?'

'Enough is enough.'

He stopped unbuttoning her. Nothing happened for a number of heartbeats. His mind was racing. Her vital statistics were perfect. He was overpowered by her scents:

Coconut oil, *check*.

Talcum powder, *check*.

South Indian spices … he tested a line he recalled from the latest photo essay about a gangster and his moll in *Crime & Detective Magazine*, 'I've tasted your mouth and now let me taste other body parts.'

'Okay, a few buttons more,' she said.

He worried that she'd feel scandalized and scream for the censorship board to cut the scene. But she didn't. She was way too advanced for him.

'You do like me a lot,' she said, exhaling.

'Should I stop?' he whispered.

'Oh no,' she moaned.

If somebody walked by in the corridor, they'd think an epileptic vacuum cleaner had been left on in the broom closet. He continued with the task allotted to him and according to the rules of gentlemanly conduct, trying to enjoy it as long as it lasted because within another few seconds the censorship board might shut his brain down … This was the moment to pop the most important question, whether or not they were being recorded and perhaps uploaded to YouTube.

'Had your orgasm?' he blurted out. From a democratic point of view, she ought to get release from her neuromuscular tension before him, because 'ladies first' was the true gent's rule of thumb.

'Huh?' She gave an irritatingly vague response, perhaps she didn't want to be thought of as a loose woman like those depicted in *Crime & Detective Magazine*? 'I … think I'm close.'

He himself let off an unarticulated growl of hormone combustion, like an ECG-monitor flatlining. Life was too good and he wouldn't have minded it a bit if he had died in her arms right there and then.

She said, 'Hari, my hero!'

Afterwards he felt a bit smug. Feigning modesty, he said, 'Do you really think I'm a superhero?'

She wrapped her hands around his back. In all the excitement, the bandages and many of the Band-Aid strips that secured the recording equipment had come loose. Her fingers found the wires. She traced them to the telltale mike and the small spy camera lens clipped to his ears.

'What is this?' She started pulling at the wires until she had ripped the device off, tearing the strips of Band-Aid from his skin – his response: 'Ouch'; her follow-up question: 'What are you wearing?' She kicked the cupboard door wide-open to let the light in. The unromantic, harsh light from the hospital corridor shone down on their bodies, pure, white, unforgiving. She saw what she shouldn't have seen and started sobbing. Shocked, she buttoned up her uniform. 'Did you just record what we did, Hari?'

No more her hero, Hari marvelled at how twisted fate was. Here he had tried to act like the gallant type who followed the censorship rules, but people only saw what they wanted to. Had she been in the mood to listen, he'd have informed her about exactly which crimes he wasn't guilty of, paragraph number and all, including Sections 294 – filming or otherwise documenting and indecent act or song for public viewing, and 354B – act with intent to disrobe a woman. He opened his mouth to say, 'Not I, but I think my colleague did' – and was struck by how lame it sounded, so he shut up. He tried a warm and friendly smile instead.

'I don't believe it,' said Diamond. 'You dirty … boy.'

She straightened her uniform and ran out, crying.

'Is it okay if I SMS you sometimes?' he called out.

She didn't reply.

He quickly pulled on his hospital gown, putting it on back to front so as to be able to tie the ribbons more easily, which of course left a bit of a gap in the front. However, his hands were trembling too hard and all the flimsy ribbons got tangled around his fingers and the only thing he could think of was to hurry after her and calm her down. He left the ribbons untied and hobbled into the luxury clinic's lobby trying to think of a set of explanations that would work, if at all anything was possible to salvage after this. He felt his tension return with maximum force.

The female receptionist just gaped at the sight of him with his walker, dragging his drip stand by the rubber tubes like some freshly lobotomized maniac … and it struck him that he wasn't decent at all. He stopped to pull his gown together but things were rapidly getting worse; the receptionist probably put one and one together and thinking the result was three, she picked up the microphone and Hari could hear her voice on the public address system, 'May I have your attention, please? Would the security guards please come to the reception area – immediately.'

Hari wanted to yell so loudly that the whole world could hear him: *How to explain love?* But he knew none of these people would have the correct answer. Love was not a medical condition. It was a spiritual experience.

Meanwhile Diamond had stopped briefly at the doors, glanced back at him, and then making a dramatic exit she ran out, into the street, weeping. Diamond, who had been his only helper inside the hospital, believed that he had deliberately filmed her and it would be very surprising if she'd ever trust him again.

He was about to follow her. Then he saw Deadlyappa and Bhascar patrolling right outside in the bazaar, still waiting to lay hands on him. They were not as stupid as he … no. Hari knew at once that they expected the victim to return to the scene of the crime, to become the victim of yet another crime. Their minds were practically as warped as his.

What to do? As he turned to go back inside he found himself face to face with Head Nurse Kolaveri and the Mediclinix's security guards armed with bamboo lathis. He didn't know what to say.

But she did.

'What is going on here?' The question wasn't entirely unwarranted.

'I lost my sari,' said Hari who was beginning to acutely feel the inappropriateness of his lack of clothes.

'What's that supposed to mean?'

'Aunty, I'm a part-time eunuch, we all have to have a job, don't we, and I was simply looking for my misplaced work garment.'

'Where – you think it's here somewhere?' She didn't seem to believe him at all.

Diamond wasn't around to corroborate his statement which, although it wasn't strictly true, wasn't one of those lies uttered in totally bad faith either. He was simply trying to protect Diamond's reputation and he'd rather ruin his own first.

She went on to say, 'Perhaps we should go and look for your garments in your room?'

Hari thought quickly. Bhascar and Deadlyappa had noticed the commotion at the clinic entrance. They were coming in his direction. Suddenly being locked up in the hospital room seemed like the 99 per cent best option, an almost safe bet.

Besides … the head nurse's mouth was like a long straight line cutting her face in two halves. Her eyes were strangely familiar. And her hair … it was like staring into a distorting mirror, but this one also distorted age, gender…

Hari looked into Kolaveri's eyes and considered the facts for a second or two, and the strangest emotions rushed through him. His reasoning went somewhat like this: *But could it be possible? It wasn't fully impossible* … Everything he knew about her, including her hairstyle with a crazy tuft standing up from the centre of her forehead, suggested one inevitable but mind-blowing conclusion: *in her previous reincarnation Kolaveri may have been his lost mother.*

Incredible. But?

Mother of all coincidences! He'd had vague suspicions when Diamond gossiped about the head nurse's mysterious past. He and Kolaveri apparently shared a common native place somewhere near Khatpadi Junction in Tamil Nadu, they both had been born on a bad hair day, and, like him, she too had failed in her studies. *Mother of Hari!* For years he'd been wondering if he'd ever meet any of his parents again. And it had to happen like this. But then again there were no guarantees that one's mum would be one of the nice guys.

'It may be a good idea to check the room,' he agreed – since a son ought to obey his mother.

Besides, he didn't have a Plan B or C. In a best case scenario he might come up with something later. He just needed a few hours to carefully think things through. So therefore it seemed like the most excellent, if sketchiest, plan to, for the first time in his life, do as his mother told him. It might even save his life, because if he ran out of there, on one leg, he'd end up getting pulped by Deadlyappa and Bhascar.

More hospital staff gathered round and, under Kolaveri's supervision, they led Hari across the bazaar street and back to the old hospital. Then Deadlyappa hobbled up to block their way.

Kolaveri stared at him, not backing an inch.

'Weren't you just discharged from my hospital? What do you want?'

Deadlyappa nodded at Hari. 'Give him to us.'

She was quiet for a moment and Hari worried that she might agree to the proposal. Finally, she said icily, 'Why would I?'

She was used to dealing with criminal patients and most of the local crooks respected her, for her hospital was after all one of the few benign factors that kept them alive. But Deadlyappa was obstinate.

'We'll take care of him. Or…'

'Or? I think I'm going to have to have a word with your Mummy,' she said, with not the slightest hint of nervousness.

Hari was impressed. Bhascar had to use both arms to hold back Deadlyappa, who looked like he was about to jump Hari right there in front of the hospital staff. Good thing there were too many witnesses for an assassination in broad daylight.

The other good thing was that if Deadlyappa had got himself discharged, it put him firmly on the outside and Hari safely on the inside. Back in his room he should be as safe as an undertrial locked up in Parappana Agrahara Central Jail. Hari was taken to his cot, but the walker was kept out of his reach, in the corner by the door, and his hospital gown was confiscated. Instead they gave him a bed sheet to cover himself with.

'But what about my clothes?' he said.

'The doctor doesn't want to have you running around, so we have to do like this,' said Kolaveri.

'You can't leave me here naked and unprotected.'

'We'll bolt the door from the outside. This situation is *very* serious. You threatened one of our patients who is now planning to sue,' she explained to him. She sounded much like a super angry mum.

'I'm sorry if I caused trouble,' said Hari. 'It wasn't my purpose.'

'So you say.'

'No seriously, Mum.'

Her jaw dropped. 'What did you just call me?'

'I mean that I look up to you and will obey you like a mother, madam.'

She harrumphed. But she seemed to accept his answer. 'Once I've spoken to Diamond and heard her version of the story, we'll see how to proceed with matters. Dr Viral will also want to discuss what has happened. You shouldn't make a joke out of the situation, I hope you understand that. If you have anything whatsoever to say in your defence, you speak to Doctor Viral when he comes for his evening rounds.'

He nodded and thought it wise to keep his mouth shut, since anything he said might and probably would be used against him anyway. She looked a bit concerned and then she added, 'Any complaints you may have against the hospital ... you sort it out with him.'

'Yes Mum, I mean, ma'am,' he said since the complicated feeling of possibly having ceased to be an orphan, provided that some test might determine their familial relationship, had a surprisingly strong grip on him.

She gave him an odd look and then walked away in a huff. Luckily, she didn't think of searching his room and therefore didn't notice the camera mounted on the TV bracket in the corner.

There was of course no tiffin forthcoming. He heard sounds in the corridor but no steps stopped at his door. It remained bolted from the outside. He felt unappreciated. He wondered where Diamond was. Had she been fired? It was only then that it sunk in – from one moment to the next he had lost the love of his life. How would he ever find her again?

Dinnertime too came and went, and he heard the food trolley creak past without any palak paneer for him. It was worse than being in jail; prisoners at least got their tamarind rice and buttermilk on time.

Then there was the general calm that marked the end of a hard day. From the sound of it, the final rounds were over. Walls were thin enough for him to know that the other patients had been given their painkillers, sedatives, morphine and sleeping pills, because he heard echoes of their snores and farts. They thought they were safe.

And still no visits from Diamond or any of the other nursing staff, not even the doctor had come to talk to him. What were they waiting for? For him to starve to death? That'd take care of all problems.

His only hope was the camera in the corner of the room. With any luck it captured everything. Him not being given food. The thought had never crossed his mind before, but surely there was some law against neglecting patients? Being sick and scared, and alone in a hospital, it was so not him.

Later. He heard the door bolts slide. A sliver of light cut across the floor.

His first optimistic thought was that it must be Diamond sneaking in to save him. They would forgive each other. That was the best case scenario. But he couldn't smell the coconut hair oil. Instead, there was a whiff of cheap aftershave. He felt great terror.

'Napped enough?' Male voice.

Hari pretended to be practically stone dead. Preparing himself for the worst, he hoped it wouldn't have to turn out that way.

'You forget I'm a doctor and can tell the difference.'

Viral jammed two fingers up Hari's nose so fast that there was no time to react – one gloved finger up each nostril, all the way to the knuckles, poking the brain. Or so it felt during the first moment of shock.

Hari gasped. The fingers were fat and frightening, and Hari feared they might get stuck there forever.

His eyes snapped wide open. He saw a snake tattoo and a thick Rolex gold watch. The lettering on its dial spelt out Roxel. From up close, he could tell it was locally made, the kind that was sold at the Brigade Road corner, and you had the choice between fake titanium, fake platinum or fake gold. It occurred to Hari that to own a hospital Viral didn't do too well judging by his cheap accessories. He even wore imitation leather gloves.

As if he didn't want to leave his fingerprints inside Hari's nostrils.

'There, there,' said Viral. 'You should not be so obstinate. This doesn't have to get painful if we can help each other. My associate, the esteemed Professor Glas Philipovich, is unhappy with the way things are going. He is impatient. He used to be the KGB staff medical officer during the Cold War. He's going to come and settle things his own way. We have about ten minutes. So listen carefully.'

'Ah-ah.'

'Make no mistake – I'm not in the habit of issuing empty threats. How large is your team?'

'Uh ... uh,' said Hari, doing his best to deny everything.

'Two? Now we're getting somewhere. Is Nurse Diamond working for you?' said Viral and screwed his fingers deeper inside until their tips sank into the frontal lobe of Hari's brain.

Was it possible to reach the brain by digging into the nose? He had doubted it but now there were flashes of white light before his eyes, as if the optic nerves were being knotted up and he made a mental note to add this fact on Wikipedia – one learnt new things every day. 'Hooo-yoo...'

'Was that a no? Am I supposed to trust you?' Viral twisted the fingers until Hari's nostrils were crunching, and Hari nodded – with difficulty. 'You're in a cooperative mood? You have to understand that Professor Philipovich is very easily irritated – especially after he quit smoking – and the problem is that I can't afford to jeopardize the arrangement. I had to spend all afternoon dealing with a complaint from one of our paying guests, madam Alice, you happen to know her, yes?'

Hari uh-uhed. He'd be pissing adrenaline for the rest of his life, for sure.

'See, she was very grateful to receive a kidney, but she isn't so happy anymore – she believes we stole it, maybe even from a monkey, whereas the truth is, as you well know, that you signed a consent form which will hold in court. But of course, it needn't ever come to that. I have a suggestion, so I'd propose you hear me out and think about it.'

Hari had to interrupt and ask – hoping that the surveillance camera and microphone in the corner were on and recording – 'Boss, why are you doing this?' Phonetically it came out 'ohh, uh-ah uh-uing-ihi' – they'd have to subtitle that part of the video. But the doctor seemed to get his larger point.

'Unlike you, I serve society. As you know, this used to be a slum clinic that treated thugs and rowdies for gunshot wounds and machete hackings. Most of them expected to get it done without paying. But I want to help the ordinary people. However, it's not cheap to do charitable work, somebody has to pay.' He jabbed harder into Hari's nose. 'The plan is to put in place a system that makes you crooks pay what you owe to society. And in return, you people get treated for free. What poetic justice!' The doctor looked a bit like a benevolent visionary, if it hadn't been for the knuckles deep in his patient's nostrils. 'So that brings us back to the question: what do you have against it?'

Hari tried to waggle his head sideways, which was the only possible answer to something like that. He didn't mind it so much if other crooks lost their livers and kidneys, but he felt possessive about his own body parts.

'You look like you have something to say.' Viral unplugged his fingers from Hari's nostrils. The plops were enormous, like having two uncooked bitter gourds pulled out of one's head. Hari drew in a huge breath.

'Boss, that was scary.' He was making calculations; flattery was a powerful mind control tool. 'In theory, I totally agree. Your plan comes from the mind of a genius. But. .'

'Well, thank you, I'm glad you see it,' said Dr Viral and pulled out a document, what appeared to be Hari's patient journal or surgery report, from the inner pocket of his XXXXXL leather jacket, unfolded it and studied it while he went on speaking. 'Look at it this way, even if you are unlikely to ever go on a foreign holiday, your kidney will. Trust me, it is much better off abroad, getting a new life in a rich madam's body, instead of rotting away here. It'll be fed nutritious food and live longer than you, so if I were you I'd show gratitude.'

'Thank you ever so much.'

'Make no mistake, it could be worse. You could've been dead. Organs are mostly transplanted from cadavers, from whom we can harvest a lot. More than what we got out of you.'

'That's really good to know.'

'Yes, you agree? But there are too few dead around here due to the fact that most local folks are vegetarians and live to the age of ninety. Transplant organs should ideally be harvested from donors younger than sixty, for them to survive in the long run. This shortfall is a major obstacle for the development of transplant surgery.'

Viral sat down on the edge of the cot which bent under his weight but didn't break. Hari was afraid to get his nose tweaked again and crawled until he had his back against the headboard. Viral looked down at his hands, the fake leather gloves, with a tinge of regret and went quiet.

Hari knew that psychologically the most efficient battle strategy was to wait out the evil mastermind, hear him confess to his megalomania and get it all on tape. *Keep the doctor talking,* Hari reminded himself, *and figure out the financial aspects of the racket.* He'd seen it work on cinema so many times. So he pretended to be interested and nodded, 'Oho, I'm too impressed. One clarification, boss, why would a foreign doctor be interested in Indian hospitals?'

Like all megalomaniacs, Viral deemed the question worthy of a soliloquy. 'You're not getting it, Mezestic? Professor Philipovich was my supervisor at the KGB hospital. I'm indebted to him for the idea to set up my own hospital. The older and sicker those westerners grow, the greater the profits of medical tourism. It is one of the fastest growing industries in the world, clocking in 20 per cent growth. Give it another five years and the turnover will hit a thousand billion dollars. Our experimental harvesting facility is of the topmost international quality and once the construction work is over we will revolutionize the market. Our website receives hundreds of enquiries every month.'

'Oho, that's fantastic news.' It took Hari less than a second to do the numbers.

Chatting with Viral was like meeting his own evil twin. Viral didn't look Hari in the eye, instead he appeared to study the surgery report as he spoke. 'I've been rambling far too long, but I wanted to impress on you the urgency of what I am saying. You're an infamous cheat with a warped mind posing as some kind of sleazy detective, threatening to expose us even though we only do good, and what I offer you…'

'Yes, what?'

'…is a cut in return for your silence – how about a 15 per cent commission from the sale of your kidney and liver? Then if you want more money, you could work as a scout for us because we need somebody like you out there in the slums to locate more donors.'

Something within Hari, the rational side of him perhaps, told him to accept it, grab the money and walk off with a bye-bye and thank you so much. A decent profit from the market value of his own body was what he was staring at – and perhaps even a future share in that incredible thousand billion dollar business. It wasn't an easy question to reply to. In the past, he would probably not have seen any problem with it. Now he heard his own heart pounding.

The doctor tapped his wristwatch. 'Well, what do you say?'

20

How to Survive Certain Death

He drew a deep sigh. To say yes wasn't an alternative – not when the conversation was being recorded and uploaded to internet servers. He was a hero now and had to act accordingly.

'With all due respect, boss, but…'

'But what?'

'With so many laws in our country, I see great potential in the legal system, and accordingly I have doubts about your business model.'

Hari prayed that it went into the microphone loud and clear. He wanted Dr Viral to utter the clinching evidence that he needed – a deadly threat or something equally damaging. The doctor was about to explode.

'Haven't you listened to a thing of what I've been saying? You think you have the moral upper hand? *Here*, in my hospital?'

'It's been very enlightening, but there's always a but.'

'Right, have it your way. I convinced Professor Philipovich to allow me to discuss this problem that we have with you and solve it. I've offered you a fair deal. But you give me no other option, no option.' Viral pulled out his mobile – it didn't even have a touch screen – and spoke in the foreign language, Latin mixed with Russian or whatever it was. It didn't sound like a prelude to any Happy End. He snapped the phone shut and colourful disco diode lights flashed on the casing, as if to belittle Hari's tragic situation. 'Believe me that I'm sorry we couldn't find a mutually acceptable way out of this. But maybe this is for the best.'

'I'm sure it is. So what will happen now?' Hari kept praying that all of this was going into the microphone.

'I've referred your case to my esteemed colleague. The KGB has its methods.'

Hari knew how to read between the lines. He couldn't help but feel vulnerable; after all he was naked and unarmed. The foreign doctor would be with them any second. Two against one – too bad odds. He tried to will his body into producing testosterone, turn into an alpha male, but nothing happened. Somewhat anxiously he said, 'But you wouldn't kill me, would you?'

He feared the answer, though depending on what it was it'd be excellent to have it recorded.

'No. You're not going to die.'

'That's a relief.'

'I could never kill anybody. I'm a doctor.'

'I almost forgot.'

'But since you signed the consent form, we can keep you as a donor for as long as it takes to sell off every bit of you. Technically speaking, that would mean you'd be alive, even though your heart will be beating in somebody else's body.'

'Oho, I hear you loud and clear,' said Hari who was beginning to appreciate the brilliance of modern transplant surgery. In the hands of two deranged surgeons it could result in unimaginable things. Hari made a gesture to his forehead.

'For the sake of curiosity, if all of me is sold off, then what will happen to my…?'

'I'm glad you asked. Professor Philipovich has this interesting plan.'

'What's that?'

'See, he wants to be the first surgeon in the world to transplant a head.'

'What – my head?'

'Onto a dog's body.'

'Oho.'

'Great idea, yes? Surely that will get us the Nobel Prize for Medicine and wouldn't you be proud to be a part of it?'

'Lovely, I'd be so happy to share one third of a Nobel Prize. It'll buy me a nice doghouse.'

'A small sacrifice for a loser like you, but a great leap forward for science,' said Viral, straightening his tie. There was something sad about a grown man giggling to himself. 'Let's cut to the chase, as they say in cheap detective novels. Have you thought of any famous last words?'

Hari's mouth went dry. There was little he could do to stop them if they wished to hoist him off the bed, drop him headfirst onto the concrete floor as many times as it took to turn his brain into vegetable puree. Being doctors, they could then certify him legally brain-dead from haemorrhage caused by accidental fall. Looting his body while pretending to treat him was an easier crime than robbing a bank – no armed guards and lots of valuable booty.

He considered the issue at hand. Last words – this was one of those once in a lifetime things. But then again he had, of late, been forced to speak his last words all too frequently and this night didn't necessarily have to be the end if luck stood by him.

'Yes, I do have a few words that are perfect for a moment like this – I'm *so* terribly sorry.'

'You're sorry about what?' asked Viral, studying the face of a soon to be corpse. It probably held some macabre interest for the pathologist within him.

'You see, because you will not have any long-term use of me.'

'How's that now?'

'You know as well as I that there are certain mystical yogic techniques with which a person can stop his own heartbeat. And simply die. If I do that, and die here and now, you will have no use for my body because there's no time to bring in a fresh batch of organ recipients. Considering that there's no air-conditioning in this room, I'll rot in no time.'

'What nonsense are you talking? You're not a yogi.'

'Well, as they say, the proof of the pudding is in the eating.' Hari's adoptive mother had taught him meditation and he had also seen holy men enter into the deepest samadhi during sacred festivals. He'd even seen a yoga tourist try it once, rather convincingly, and if a foreigner could do it ... he'd checked online and knew the trick – at least in theory. He drew a huge breath and then said, 'Bye-bye and all the very best.'

Then he lay back on the bed, closed his eyes and willed his entire body to relax some 200–300 per cent, including the heart – which obeyed, possibly out of mortal fear.

'No,' said Viral and pinched Hari's skin hard. 'This can't be true. This is ridiculous. This is not science.'

Hari focused his mind on preserving an inner calm, where nothing that existed outside of his body could affect him.

Viral waited but Hari didn't bat an eyelid. Eventually, Hari could sense that he was moving – a sweaty body heat pattern was transmitted through the air as Viral leaned forward and pressed the chest piece of a stethoscope against the naked skin over Hari's heart. Viral was wheezing in desperation.

At that very moment, Hari grabbed his tie and yanked it. It caught Viral by surprise. Hari pulled harder, making the knot tight around the stubby neck until he started to choke.

Viral got panicky, like people often did when they lost control – and his weight didn't make him lithe and agile, but clumsy. His fat arms did a kind of ballet in the air, suddenly brandishing a scalpel he must have pulled out of his jacket pocket, trying to cut the tie off. Hari hadn't counted on him being armed.

Hari bent his good leg, pulled the knee up to his chest. He kicked as hard as he could, hitting Viral straight in the stomach. It wasn't a very powerful kick; it was more like stepping into a bucket of curd rice. Viral moved away from him, but Hari held on to the tie like it was a leash. The doctor was breathing with squeaks and a hissing sound.

He thrashed about and threw himself forward again, this time trying to slash Hari's face. But Hari was quicker and saw the scalpel come straight for his iris. He ducked, avoiding it narrowly, but it sliced off the tuft of hair that stood out like a brainwave over his forehead.

Meanwhile, Viral was regaining his balance and preparing for another attack. Hari calculated that if the doctor jumped on top of him, he'd crush him like a lizard under the butt of a rhinoceros.

Without letting go of the tie, Hari sank his good leg into Viral's solar plexus again and it disappeared knee-deep into the softness. That sent Viral reeling back, but Hari didn't let go of the tie, instead kicked him again, this time aiming at the knees, sweeping one of his legs from under him.

Viral fumbled, frothing at the mouth, grabbed the bedstead with his free hand, but he was too heavy and one hand wasn't enough to arrest his fall. He dropped the scalpel, to have both hands free to hold on with. But too late. The imitation leather glove, slathered as it was with Hari's snot and hormone secretions from his pituitary gland, slipped and Viral lost his grip. Everything was over in a fraction of a second. He went crashing and knocked his head hard on the floor and blacked out. Clutching the tie, Hari fell down with him, his drop cushioned by the folds of lard.

Hari was moaning, but being fairly used to violence he remained conscious. He spat out some nasal mucus that the doctor's fingers had dislodged. Then he tied Viral's tie to the bed's metal pipe frame. He made a series of strong knots. He pulled off the doctor's shoes (fake Adidas), undid the shoelaces and tied his hands together. It would have to do. He looked for the scalpel but couldn't see it anywhere; perhaps Viral was lying on top of it.

Hari searched the pockets of the leather jacket and found the mobile phone. He chucked it into the corner by the door, out of Viral's reach. Doing his best to keep the broken leg straight and slightly raised from the floor, he slid off the doctor's body. He pulled the intravenous drip needles out of his hands. *The pain will come later.* Now, it was just his nostrils that were raw and burning. Little bit bad.

Viral groaned. So he wasn't fully dead.

Hari crawled to his walker and, holding on to its lower sidebars with both hands, managed to raise himself up until he was balancing on his good knee. The walker wobbled precariously. His next move wasn't going to be easy.

It had to work. He thrust the walker against the door, so that the topmost aluminium pipe wedged in under the handle. It seemed to be steady enough when he put weight on it. He moved one hand up to the top handlebar, then, raising himself a bit, reached his other hand to the padded handle on the other side. He tried a few different grips until both hands got a good hold.

He fixed his eyes on the emergency exit map up on the door. No regrets. He filled his lungs and growled. And it hurt … but he had done his physiotherapy. By doing a fast push he lifted himself all the way up in one go and then he was standing on his good foot. It had worked. He turned around – with the broken leg dangling uselessly it took all of three steps to complete a half circle with the walker.

On the floor, Viral grunted. The tie kept him tied to the bed and the bound hands restricted his movements, but he was awake and looking for the scalpel to cut himself loose.

Hari needed to get out of there. But he'd get arrested or molested or both if he went out naked in the bazaars in the middle of the night. There were no clothes in the room except what Viral was dressed in. Those pants were many sizes too large, they'd just fall off a skinny guy like him.

He took a few steps with the help of the walker till he reached the cot and picked up the bed sheet that lay crumpled up at the footboard. Balancing on one leg he wrapped himself in it, pulling it between his legs like a loincloth. He could pretend to be a yogi if somebody questioned him, do the samadhi trick again if they doubted him. Near the bed he found the surgery report, which by rights belonged to him. All this while his motormouth went on talking as if by itself and he couldn't stop himself from taunting Viral a little, 'One last thing, boss, please smile at the camera there, yes … right there … over the washbasin.'

Viral stopped swearing. He saw the closed-circuit camera attached to the broken TV-bracket, and then his eyes followed the discreet cable down to the tiny recording device under the basin, in plain view for him now that he was on the floor. His face was turning dark grey, either he was angry or suffocating.

'I'll leave that one there so that my sting team colleagues can keep watch over you,' said Hari and single-footed it back to the door. He fished up Viral's mobile from the floor. He was getting better and better at manoeuvring with the walker. He tucked the phone and the report into the folds of his loincloth. He'd gathered enough evidence now.

Viral seethed, livid with rage. The idea that what had been said and done was recorded made him renew his efforts at locating the scalpel – it was a question of seconds before he'd find it and cut himself loose. Therefore, Hari decided it was time to vamoose ASAP, as it was known in detective speech, if there was to be a happy end to the movie of his life. He waved into the camera lens.

'Honourable Mister Judge ji, I hope you enjoyed the show. My name is Mister Majestic and I'm a professional hero. Bye-bye and all the very best!'

He turned the handle and stepped out into freedom. He shut the door from the outside, latching the upper and lower bolts as tightly as possible.

That had been a close call. Now he had to get out of there.

The corridor was empty save for the other patients' echoing snores. He looked up and down it, it was lit up by dim night lights, the coast was clear. *No, it wasn't.* In the waiting room, a security guard got up from his chair.

'You there, what are you doing?' He sounded annoyed at being disturbed. Bad situation.

Luckily, this guard was one that Hari hadn't seen before and so he hopefully hadn't heard of Hari's subversive activities either. He was slow, elderly, grey bearded and dressed in an ill-fitting uniform, and if Hari's leg hadn't been broken he could have outrun him without trouble. The guard carried a bamboo lathi.

While Hari worked on an answer, it dawned on him that the guard wasn't without backup either, because from out in the street, approaching fast, he heard a howl, a battle cry. Hari cleared his throat and backed off. Retreating was always safer than attacking. 'Don't mind please, I'm simply looking for the loo.'

'Call the nurse,' the guard said. 'She'll bring a bedpan.'

'I don't want to cause inconvenience and they removed the buzzer from my room … I guess they were tired of my … see I have this highly embarrassing medical problem of incontinence … and it's rather urgent.' His lips were tense but he forced them into his trademark happy smile and spoke rapidly in order to confuse the guard. 'Listen boss, I think there's something going on out in the street. Sounds like some accident or something. Maybe they need a first aid kit … or nicotine patches?'

Or perhaps the foreign doctor needed less vodka? From his days as a tout, Hari knew a thing or two about certain nationalities and had observed that some people got very noisy after a few drinks – the racket from the usually-so-quiet foreigner-going-berserk was growing louder.

The guard heard it too, but seemed somewhat reluctant about going and finding out. Disturbances in the street weren't part of his job, obviously. It could get dangerous out there at this hour. So he stalled, 'Need to do su-su or number two you said?'

'Only a quick number one,' said Hari and thought to himself that the way things were going, there would be one hell of a waterfall of adrenaline. On the positive side, he'd probably be constipated from shock, so perhaps no need for number two before November.

'Last door on the right,' the guard said.

Hari remembered studying the notice inside his room about the emergency exit being located at the far end of the corridor, near the toilets. No time to lose, he pushed on down in that direction, away from the waiting area. It was slow going. Before each step he had to use both arms to hoist himself into the air, and, dangling, swing his foot forward and only then move the walker another few inches. Then repeat the process for each new step. Avoid thinking about the consequences.

He reached the end of the corridor. On the right were two toilets and one urinal. He pondered for a moment whether to sneak in there and flush himself down the potty. Opposite these was the emergency exit, a steel door that according to the map led to a fire escape. He checked if the guard was eyeballing him, but the old gentleman had gone across to the main entrance now.

Right then Dr Glas Philipovich stormed in from the street, very mad. The guard jumped to attention. The doctor loomed threateningly, a killer whale compared to the prawn-sized guard – a hideous sight, face covered with nicotine patches, like scales, and some patches that had come loose dangled from his moustache, giving him a diseased look.

The doctor shouted at the guard, who kept saluting and talking back in a mixture of Kannada, Telugu and Tamil, trying every language known to the average Bengaluruan – so many languages in the world, but none of them universal enough. It was an impasse.

Hari tried the emergency door handle, it turned. The steel door was heavy, but he used his elbow to prop it up while he rotated the walker to back out through it.

Then there was a scream.

It came from Hari's room. It was followed by frantic banging. Viral must have found his scalpel and cut himself loose. The confused guard turned to take a look over his shoulder – straight at Hari. 'What have you done? You killed the doctor!'

His medical knowledge was surprisingly incomplete for a person who worked at a hospital, because as far as Hari was aware dead people didn't scream postmortem except in scary Bollywood movies.

Philipovich pushed the guard to the side and started coming Hari's way, howling down the corridor. To make matters worse, Hari saw a drowsy Head Nurse Kolaveri walk out of her office, adjacent to the waiting area.

'What's going on here?' She blocked the way for the raving doctor.

Meanwhile, Hari made his way out through the emergency exit and hobbled into the dark of the stairwell. He heard steps closing in. While the steel door swung shut, he fumbled around for a light switch.

Found it.

The stairwell had unpainted concrete walls. The grimy floor was covered with cigarette butts, bidi stubs and dried-up puddles of paan spittle like pooled blood.

It was half a flight of steps to the bottom landing, which was in use as a storage space for boxes with medical supplies and a narrow passage between the stacked cartons led to the street exit. He was about to head down when, craning his neck, he glimpsed a double door at the end of the passage with the words 'EMERGENCY USE ONLY' painted in red across it. But he could see that it was locked with a massive chain. They kept the thieves out and patients in. It was a death trap.

What did he expect? Hari should have known from the innumerable times his uncle had been treated here, and tested various innovative escape strategies, that patients skipping their bills were a major headache for the hospital administration.

So they had a reason to lock the emergency exit. He couldn't blame them but turned back to face the door he had just passed through. However, it couldn't be bolted from this side.

There was only one way to go, up. If he could climb to the hospital roof fast, then, maybe, he could make it across to some other rooftop and get down to the street, and … that is, if he could get up the stairs with the unwieldy walker.

The pursuers weren't far behind. He guesstimated that he had roughly seven seconds left to get the hell out of there. Seven was a neat number and a short amount of time. But impossible odds had never stopped him before so he headed across the landing towards the ascending stairs.

It took him no more than a second to cross the tiny landing.

Then he faced a major problem. The walker's four legs didn't fit on the steps. No matter how he tried it was like a puzzle where the last piece had the wrong shape. If the front legs went on the upper step, the back legs ended up on the bottom one, and the walker tilted forty-five degrees.

The fear brewing in Hari's mind multiplied by a factor of ten. Two seconds gone, five seconds left.

He balanced the walking aid at forward tilt, and jumped. During approximately one second he was suspended in the air. Then he wasn't. Before he fell flat on his face he managed to push back and put his good foot down again. The walker was useless for climbing steps. Three seconds gone, four to go.

He had to lose the walker. It slowed him down to the max. But there wasn't anything to use as a support instead of it. Four seconds gone.

Think, think: or had they mixed the buffalo milk in his tea all along to simply slow down his mind? Silence from the other side of the door. Five.

Six. The door handle started moving. Too soon. Hari reacted without thinking. He shoved the walker under the handle. Seven.

That blocked it from turning, the door stayed shut. Hari gave the walker an extra shove to jam it into place. The handle stopped moving, stuck.

That should keep them off his back. And it gave him a few seconds' breathing space. He heard their voices, muffled by the steel door. He leaned in closer to listen. Head Nurse Kolaveri demanded to know what was going on. Viral was going on about a lunatic-maniac patient who'd gone into a psychosis and had to be stopped. According to Kolaveri this had gone too far and the violent patient, if he had attacked Viral in cold blood, and unprovoked, ought to be placed in police custody.

'We must catch him first, Nurse,' said Viral.

'Why not take the lift and enter the stairwell from upstairs?' the guard suggested.

Blasted! Hari jumped on one foot across the landing again and grabbed the handrail. He aimed for the bottom step.

His foot didn't reach the top of the step but instead his toes hit the nosing which tripped him. Reacting instantly, he clutched the handrail to stop himself from plunging. He went down sideways, fast. He struck the wall. His head took the impact.

He blacked out for a second.

21

How to Fight Loneliness at the Top

Breathing heavily, he stared angrily at the wall – there was a bloody smudge on it shaped like his desperate thoughts.

Luckily, he was hard-headed. The bad leg hadn't broken again. The hospital had evidently used genuine titanium screws, not the fake ones.

He suspected that he had heard a ripping sound but didn't dare to inspect his abdominal scars. Instead, he eased himself down on the bottom step. The touchdown was hard on his skinny butt. He may have broken his tailbone.

Sitting on the step, he got an idea. He reached behind his back and, putting his hands on the step above the one he sat on, pushed himself up, and then backwards. That way he moved up one step. So far so good.

He reached behind for the next step, heaved himself up, then back and climbed another one. Once he got into the rhythm of it, of crawling backwards up the steps, it took him a few frantic seconds to reach the landing between the ground and first floors.

This was going wonderfully. He continued the same way, creeping backwards, dragging his broken leg, until his back hit the bottom riser of the next flight of stairs. He pushed himself up on it and kept going towards the first floor.

He heard the machinery of the lift rumble in the old building. It was giving off that poor maintenance rattle that indicated there'd be a 10 to 25 per cent chance they'd get stuck. Not high enough odds.

But he had got the hang of it now. He climbed another flight of stairs. He looked around for something, anything, to jam the first floor exit with and stop them from coming after him. Garbage, cardboard boxes … nothing.

After resting a quarter second, he took a deep breath and carried on up the stairs again with both arms and one leg, completely out of breath but the adrenaline was enough to keep him afloat.

Two more flights of steps … and right then he heard the steel door being thrown open onto the first floor landing below. He stopped for a second, listening.

The doctors and hospital staff were shouting randomly – the usual amateur gab: 'How did this happen?' and 'How should I know?' – and then they ran down the stairs to where he had been seconds ago. Viral panted loudly, with a kind of snoring noise, unused to stairs.

Yes! thought Hari and started climbing up again, scarcely making any noise. The only sound he produced was heavy breathing.

He passed the next landing. How many more floors were there? *Move, move and avoid thinking.* They'd soon figure out that the emergency exit was locked and that he wasn't hiding down there. And guess that he had gone in the opposite direction.

Up, up. As he climbed, he heard them push the boxes aside, making their way to the bottom of the stairwell. The medicine cartons tumbled down, crashes echoing. Then they were shouting at each other, nobody wanted to be held responsible for letting a 'mental' escape. *What a lunatic asylum this had turned out to be!*

'He's not here,' echoed Viral's disappointed voice from the depths of the stairwell.

'Shall I call the police?' asked the security guard.

That'd be perfect, thank you very much, Hari thought. The foreigner said something that nobody understood or paid attention to.

'I think that may be the only sensible thing to do,' said Head Nurse Kolaveri. 'It had crossed my mind to give the boy a chance to repent, but I'm sad to say this must become a police matter now.'

'So what will you tell them?' asked Viral.

The guard who wasn't entirely clued in said, 'Why? The truth of course … that we have a violent mental with us.'

More boxes tumbled down.

'No need for legal action,' said Viral. His panting was calmer; his was the voice of a man who was bringing things under control. 'We'll cure him if he has *mental* problems – by lobotomy.'

Hari moved up a few steps to put some distance between himself and the mad surgeons. Viral continued, 'Besides, it isn't a good idea to report this…,' he paused, for effect, '…considering that the patient is in denial about the donation being voluntary, he might accuse some of you for organ theft.'

Head Nurse Kolaveri said, 'So what am I supposed to do then?'

'You do what you always do, Nurse, keep doing your job. If everybody does their job, this will end up fine. We'll call in a psychiatrist to see him tomorrow, perform the lobotomy under our charitable slum scheme. Some people get upset after surgery, common post-traumatic reaction. Nothing strange about that.'

Hari continued climbing, taking care not to make a sound.

Viral gave orders, 'You go out and keep an eye on the main entrance in case the psychopath tries to leave the hospital.'

'And what do I do if I see him?'

'Stop him.'

'What if he demands to be let out?'

'Don't listen to him.'

'We can't force him to stay.'

'Then you'll leave with him and become unemployed. Carry on then.'

Somebody left the stairwell. At least it evened out the rotten odds.

Things were quiet for about one second.

'He's on his way to the top floor!' Viral shouted. Then, remembering himself, he repeated the same in that medieval sounding language they used between doctors.

Hari worked his muscles, mindful about his abdominal scars. He had to be close to the roof now.

The stairwell echoed with footsteps coming closer and closer – but he was on the topmost landing and his back hit a door. Attic or rooftop? He'd find out soon enough. No chain, padlock or iron slat locking it. Good sign and … also bad. It meant that this wasn't a way that thieves could enter or patients break out of the building.

He pulled the handle down, pressed his back to the door and it opened, and – there was the night sky. The air tasted like flatulence at this hour, before the freshness of the morning came, but at least he was out of the hospital, on its terrace.

He surveyed the immediate surroundings – in the faint light from the street lamps below he saw a set of three black water tanks on raised platforms and there seemed to be a two feet broad parapet running around the roof's edges.

The space was rectangular. The access door he had come out through was in the back corner. The facade facing the bazaar street was at the far end. Beyond the parapet on that side he spotted the top floors of Mediclinix Resorz, it stood about three storeys taller. But neither of the medical tourists were awake at the windows to watch over their donor.

If the doctors stopped to double-check that he hadn't gotten out into any of the corridors on the other floors it'd give him a little time to find an escape route. And if he could block this door with something … he looked around carefully. The flat roof was empty save for a pile of flexible plastic water pipes, but no planks or anything to wedge under the door handle. He had to keep running.

The parapet would be easy to climb, but from his position it was hard to tell if there was a fire ladder on any side – or anything else to climb down by – or a connecting passage to an adjacent building. He crawled to the wall at the back, grabbed the parapet and pulled himself up to have a look. Behind the hospital was an empty plot: a construction site, a mud pit full of concrete pillars, reinforcement rods jutting out in all directions. Jumping would constitute a very nasty, painful suicide – he'd be impaled or drown in mud. Some day he'd have to learn to swim.

He then crawled to the nearest sidewall and checked what was there. The seedy neighbourhood bar MRP Drinks. It was a single-storey building and thanks to the light of the street lamp he saw that its flat roof was littered with broken bottles. The narrow alley into which the fire escape exited – or didn't exit as the case was – separated it from the hospital. The dead end alley ended in a wall topped with shards of glass in the mortar. Behind that was the construction site.

If he jumped … he'd have to avoid falling straight into the alley, onto the wall topped with glass shards or on the booze bottles on the bar roof.

The only possible target area was a dumpster of hospital waste, right in front of the emergency exit. He'd have to manage the jump at an awkward angle. Practically undoable. There were easier ways to die.

He crept, in his creepy-crawly one-legged crablike style, to the opposite wall. On that side was the Sickly Medicals shop, squat and leaning against the hospital for support. It was a two-floor drop onto what looked like an asbestos roof. Soft material. He might just about survive.

He was kidding himself. Wrong, wrong, another wrong way to end one's life. He suddenly wished he hadn't climbed up to the roof. If he'd been smart, he'd have taken refuge in one of the wards downstairs and hidden among the patients. They wouldn't dare do anything among witnesses. Or maybe they would.

Too late now anyway. He had cornered himself up here. No, he wasn't going to give up. He crossed the roof back to the other side again, getting used to his insect manner of moving, and determined that the dumpster was his best bet. If he hit it, the trash should cushion his fall.

One last thing to do before he made the suicide jump. From the folds of his loincloth he took out the mobile he had borrowed from Viral. It was protected by a code, but he tested the three most common PINs, 1234, 0000, 2846, and cracked it before it locked itself.

He called Doc.

Voicemail.

Hari spoke fast, 'Royal Flush here. Download videos.'

Right then the door burst open and the old security guard stepped out, brandishing the bamboo lathi in front of him like a sword. Hari clicked off the phone and crouched in the darkest corner next to the parapet, in the shadow of the water tanks. Maybe they'd fail to spot him.

The guard looked around. The doctors must have sent him out first, scared of a crippled man.

'He's not here either,' the guard shouted.

'Are you sure?' Viral asked.

The guard returned to join the doctors. 'Nobody is there.'

Hari breathed softly. His abdomen was paining and he wouldn't be surprised if what organs were left in him started tumbling out of the holes in his body. He could all but smell his own terror: a mixture of sour sweat, unbrushed teeth and cheap nylon.

If they really thought that he wasn't up on the roof, they might return downstairs to search for him. The hospital had three floors, lots of places to hide.

'Ayooh!' The guard backed off as the foreigner pushed past him and stormed through the door.

Dr Glas Philipovich positioned himself in the centre of the roof, his silvery hair stood on end like horns jutting out of his skull. A vaporous cloud hung above his head almost as if his nicotine patches were about to catch fire. *Oho, very unhappy*, thought Hari.

'Give me your torch,' Viral demanded.

The guard shuffled his feet and said something inaudible.

'You what?' Viral shouted and took out all his frustration on the guard. 'Who told you that you could sell it?'

The guard mumbled.

'A temporary liquidity problem doesn't mean that you won't get your salary sooner or later. We've had several paying guests this week and money will come.'

Hari watched them in the light from the stairwell. Viral moved along the parapet. He was efficient, which was bad news for Hari. It'd take him a minute to search the roof. Hari made himself very small in the darkness under the water tanks.

So this was the way the biopic of the life of Hari Majestic was going to end … unless he came up with a survival strategy. He had read DIY handbooks for stunt artists and watched many films, but he was no James Bond … or maybe he was? He remembered a YouTube clip in which '007' ski-jumped off a snowy mountain. The super spy had of course been well prepared with a parachute in his backpack. But why shouldn't he try the same stunt? He untied the loincloth he had fashioned out of the bed sheet and calculated that if he held on to its four corners, it'd serve the role of a parachute. Not a parachute for high-altitude sky diving, but enough to slow down his fall and help him survive a few floors' drop. In a best case scenario, at least.

Suddenly the mobile phone he'd taken from Viral started ringing and when Hari glanced at the screen he recognized Doc's number. *Blasted twice over!* He threw the phone across the roof at Viral, yelling:

'Boss! You're getting an important call from a colleague!'

The phone flew through the air, flashing its disco diodes – yellow, green, red. Viral tried to catch it.

Hari didn't quite know what to do with his surgery report, so he rolled it into a cone and stuffed one end of it into his mouth, then hoisted himself up on the edge of the parapet, stark naked. With the paper cone sticking out his mouth like a beak, he suddenly knew what newborn birds must feel like before their virgin flight. He had learnt from Wikipedia or someplace that birds always shit before flying, to reduce their take off weight. He tried but the only thing that came out was a high-pitched fart.

Then he jumped.

As he twirled around in the air, he observed the foreign doctor closing in with lengthy strides, nicotine patches flapping crazily like hundreds of small wings all over his skin, hair on end.

Viral was busy answering his phone, 'Hello, who's calling?'

For a moment it was as if time slowed down until it wasn't moving at all. Horrors, he thought as he remained suspended inches away from the parapet in timelessness-cum-motionlessness. Some yogis knew how to levitate. But he wasn't one of them.

The last days flashed before him – the fall into the drain, the surgery, the love he'd experienced with Diamond. No regrets. Then everything started moving again, terribly fast, and he plunged downwards.

A little too late, he reflected on the fact that reality and movies were very different things, and that the classic jump scene in *The Spy Who Loved Me* wasn't performed by Roger Moore himself but was the costliest stunt of its time, according to Triplex who was an expert on cinema, and needless to say performed by professionals. It brought him back full circle to that eternal dilemma: *Reel versus Real.*

Using the bed sheet as a parachute had been a fantastic plan, except the sheet didn't unfold. It stayed bunched up between his hands. It simply wasn't made for flying with.

He lost hold of two of its corners and was tossed in any which direction, no idea whether he was flying sideways or headfirst down. Then he got caught in a giant rubbery spider's web that stopped his fall a few yards above the ground.

What in…? he asked himself in the fraction of the nanosecond it took him to grasp that it was one of those tangles of cables that hung between all buildings hereabouts.

He knew it couldn't be power cables or he'd have been grilled by now. It had to be phone lines. Thank god that everybody hadn't moved over to mobiles like he and his friends. And thanks, again, that the cables were strung up in any which way all over the place.

After that short-lived happiness, he slid through the web that kept snapping, cable by cable. That was the problem with old style phones and why so many people didn't have landlines in these modern days. The cables became brittle from tropical sunshine and monsoon rains. That's why people preferred mobiles, they didn't disconnect when somebody fell from a rooftop.

Then he was in free fall again.

Thump, he crashed right down into the dumpster that exploded under him in a brown cloud of shocked cockroaches.

He didn't die immediately.

His fall had been cushioned by trash that had, as usual, not been emptied in weeks due to the garbage strike. The city alone produced about as much rubbish as all the rural parts of the state taken together, the system always bordering on collapse, and the dumpster was full.

Hari allowed himself to sink in the softness of gauze and discarded bloodstained sheets, and a rotten cat that had used up its nine lives as a participant in medical experiments, mushy adult diapers, toxic vials and he felt something prick him. He recoiled in shock.

He saw, an inch from his face, a plastic bag with disposed syringes. The bacteria covered needles were close enough to almost hook into his eyelashes.

When he heard the doctors approach the parapet up there, he pretended to be dead. He'd played dead before; he was getting good at it.

Viral was on the phone, 'So you're a doctor? What's your name again – Doctor Doc Dotcom? Is that a Catholic name? Yes, he was a patient here, I can confirm that. Yes, *was*. No, he's not at the hospital anymore … I guess he must have borrowed this phone to call you because he wanted to be picked up. That's right – he just left the hospital … yes, one minute ago. I don't think you need to worry about him anymore. I'll let you know if I hear from him … not at all, you're welcome. Carry on then,' he said and disconnected the call.

'What do we do now?' It was the guard's worried voice.

'Nothing, there's nothing we can do,' said Viral. 'Poor bastard committed suicide. You witnessed it.'

Not bastard, Hari thought to himself, *adopted*.

'But maybe we can revive him?' The guard sounded traumatized, presumably having for the first time seen a man die a violent death before his eyes.

'Who's the doctor – you or me?'

'You.'

'So let me do my job while you do yours. We tried our best, but he jumped. He was insane and that's that. End of story. I'll see to it that you get a bonus next month.'

'Shall we go and get him then for an auto-uh...?'

'Autopsy?' said Viral. 'When did you say you got a medical degree?'

'I didn't.'

'Then will you shut up? Better let someone else find the corpse or people might ask what we were doing here letting him jump. And then you'll to go to jail.'

'Why me?'

'You're the security guard on duty, aren't you? It would seem to me that the safety of patients is your responsibility then...' Their voices trailed off.

Maybe he was dead just like the good doctor said? A medical expert usually knew best when it came to health matters.

Whatever the case, he was left to rest in peace. Rest was the best cure, he had often heard from his adoptive mother, who rarely had to go to hospitals. But then she got run over by a speeding drunk driver. Did rest cure death? Not for her, it didn't.

Lying there, wondering about his survival chances, he looked at the bright side. He could have broken his neck in the fall and become paralysed. As long as he didn't cut himself on scalpels or syringes, the dumpster was more comfortable than the cot in his stuffy office in CD Road. Here it was cool and airy, and provided that it didn't rain he'd sleep nicely. He tried to think of anything else that was good about his present situation.

For some reason, his thoughts kept returning to his dead adoptive mother. He missed her. Were they going to meet again in the next life? She had been his role model. He practised the homemade yoga she taught him when he was still a child. He breathed through one nostril at a time to soothe the vital forces, make the body immune and strong, and visualized his leg growing back.

22

How to Land on One's Feet, or Foot, at the End of the Worst Day of One's Life

Morning broke, as was its habit, and when he heard the cawing of crows he knew for sure that he had survived this too. It had been a rough couple of days. All the bones in his body felt semi-broken.

Although it was only to be expected, he was a little disappointed that not one of his colleagues at Mr Majestic OK & Co had come to his rescue. An unfortunate salary cut would have to be announced at the next staff meeting.

Scavengers came to rummage through the dumpster. Hospital waste contained left over drugs and expired medicines, second-hand syringes and other things that could be resold. This morning they found something rarer and much more valuable.

An entire organ donor. He listened to their talk and decided that he'd protest if he overheard them discuss the market value of his body parts. He'd had enough of that.

Luckily, the oldest woman saw that Hari was alive. Over her sari she was wearing a tattered T-shirt that proclaimed: *No Job, No Girlfriend, No Problem.* Hari could relate to that. She smelt his breath for liquor and when she was satisfied that although he was naked and in a dumpster behind the MRP Drinks Bar, he wasn't a drunkard, she addressed him respectfully, 'Brother, may we take you to the doctor?'

Hari considered whether it was necessary to fight back but then he figured that the question wasn't malicious – they were concerned citizens.

'Thank you, big sister, but I'm…' He paused before coming up with a suitable subterfuge, '…a yogi. Just meditating a bit. But since you disturbed me, can I borrow your mobile and make a local call?'

'Brother, we're scavengers, how do you expect us to have mobiles?'

Unthinkingly, Hari had assumed that even these poorest of the poor belonged among the 63.5 per cent of slum dwellers that had mobile phones in their pockets nowadays. But his mathematically-oriented mind had blanked out the 36.5 per cent who didn't, and who existed outside the connected world.

'Sorry, sister, no offence,' he said.

'None taken,' said the woman. 'Would you like some stew we found behind the tiffin room?'

'No, I'm dieting,' said Hari. He drew the line somewhat flexibly where it suited him, although on the far side, definitely, was eating garbage. He hadn't done that since childhood. 'Would you happen to have any clothing to lend me?'

They gave him a jute garbage bag, recyclable and eco-friendly, and she offered him her T-shirt, and then they left him alone.

The unspoken rule was that whoever got to a dumpster first had rights to it.

Hari wore the garbage bag as a lungi on his lower body and pulled on the *No Problem* T-shirt, and tried to convince himself that his problems were over.

Then suddenly there was the barking of street dogs. Before he knew it, Underdog, Hari's pet mongrel, was licking his face between bouts of frenetic yapping. Dogs were barking all around the dumpster. It was Hari's own pack of strays that had come to look for him … his only true friends had tracked him down.

Hari patted the excitable mutant creep. 'Great work, Undies. I've missed you, too.'

A few seconds later, the DCO at Mr Majestic OK & Co: Proper Investigations (Confidential) peeked into the dumpster. Triplex – he had come, too! – now said, 'Ready to go back to office, Majestic?'

'How is he?' came Doc's anxious voice.

'Lazing around as usual, pretending to be sick, dreaming of girls,' Gaadi growled.

Hari sat up in the dumpster and looked down at his friends who had armed themselves with bamboo sticks and long swords made from sharpened strips of a car chassis. He was amazed. And happy to see them. It was almost like a pleasant surprise party. If it hadn't been for his body aching so badly. 'What are you people doing here?'

'What do you think?' said Triplex while Underdog merrily sniffed Hari's face, as if he was checking that it was really his master in the dumpster. 'Just doing our jobs, just doing our jobs.'

Hari wanted to point out how close they had all gotten to being pink-slipped. Though in a sense, he was glad Triplex had disregarded his command to stay away from Bengaluru. Therefore, he decided to be diplomatic about it. 'Agent codenamed Blue, you may come in from the cold.'

'Cold?'

'Well, Mysore then.'

'Actually Majestic, it was rather hot there,' said Triplex and it occurred to Hari that Mysore, located at a lower altitude than Bengaluru, naturally experienced a somewhat higher temperature.

They helped him climb out of the dumpster. He was aching all over, as if his body was one big bruise with legs and arms attached to it, but otherwise he was feeling surprisingly intact, skull, crossbones and all.

Triplex and Gaadi walked on either side of Hari, supporting him. The bazaar street tilted this way and that with each step as he hobbled with his arms across their steady shoulders.

'I spoke to somebody at the hospital who said you left, but I had doubts,' said Doc, waving a USB stick. 'So I went through the recordings to find out what you've been up to, Majestic.'

'Then he MMSed the clips to me for analysis,' Triplex added, 'and I think that next time you shoot a romantic video, you should arrange for better lighting. This one is not worth uploading. Nobody will pay-per-view. The ending sucks too. Anyway, it seemed obvious to me that you needed my help. So I jumped on the night bus from Mysore.'

'Once he got here,' said Gaadi grumpily, 'he woke me up and told me to get the dogs together. And some weapons.' He waved his long sword at one of the dogs that tried to bite him back.

Pixellated memories of his affair with Nurse Diamond flashed before Hari's eyes. It was all over now, but at least he'd have those recordings to remember his hour of dalliance by. 'Listen, men, let's make one thing clear. Some of those recordings have to go through censorship.'

'Why are you taking tension about it?' said Doc. 'We've already seen everything.'

'I always thought you wanted to be a film hero, Majestic, and this is like your debut – even if it sucks big time,' Triplex added.

'So I fell in love!' Hari blurted out, still in the grips of an inner turmoil. Emotional things were difficult to speak of. 'And what about it? Is it a sin?'

'Bad enough, swami. Is it that girl?' As if Hari would fall in love with an autorickshaw or anything else that never wore a sari. Gaadi growled, 'Write a poem to her and I'll kill you with my own hands. We're detectives, like in the movies; we don't fall in love with villains.'

Gaadi had a point. The four of them – Triplex, Doc, Gaadi and Underdog – eyed him as if he was guilty of high treason. Unmarried friends would inevitably feel betrayed if he got involved with a woman and that too one on the enemy side.

'What do we do now?' said Doc.

'Let's wrap up this case,' said Hari.

He borrowed Doc's mobile. It had been programmed with the same codenamed speed dialling system that everyone at Mr Majestic, OK & Co used. Hari selected the number filed as 'Wrong Number'. It was the direct line to Sub-Inspector Pushpa.

'Uh … tell me?' said a sleepy voice.

'Sorry to disturb, Aunty, but if Aunty would come straight away then this might prove to be a great victory for the police force and lead to a promotion, too,' said Hari and did his duty as a police informer.

While waiting, they had some coffee and vada sambar in a nearby Darshini. *How he had missed coffee!* He'd been close to losing his mind without his daily dose of chicory … no wonder everything that went on in the hospital had seemed so out of tune with reality.

'I have some arrack in my auto, shall we return to the office and have another party?' suggested Gaadi.

'Good idea,' said Triplex.

'Bad idea,' said Hari.

'You've become boring,' said Doc.

'I'm having an existential crisis and I must go back to have a word with the head nurse before they lock her up.'

They returned to the twin hospitals, one block down the winding bazaar. A raid was on. Sub-Inspector Pushpa was a career hungry woman, destined to go far, and this morning she had acted without delay. Two khaki-clad constables stood on the steps outside the GSSS Hospital, two more guarded the entrance to Mediclinix Resorz across from it, and more uniforms were inside both. Now and then a constable carried out a hard disk to the Hoysala jeeps out in front. Their red and blue Lumax lights flashed.

It all looked very dramatic and assorted morning-walkers gathered to gawk.

After fifteen minutes, Sub-Inspector Pushpa came out. She spotted Hari. 'You okay?'

'Totally fine now, Aunty,' he replied. 'Had your breakfast?'

She hadn't. Hari sent Gaadi back to the Darshini to get her a casserole of piping hot bisi bele baath while he started a detailed upload of what he had been through during the last couple of days, events that had resulted in the loss of one kidney and 70 per cent of his liver, and various other unfortunate tribulations such as attempted murder which accounted for why he was dressed in nothing but a recyclable jute trash bag and a tattered T-shirt. Hari went on to count out the various other provisions of the Indian Penal Code that Philipovich and Viral could be charged under. He told Sub-Inspector Pushpa that the Mediclinix Resorz grossly violated building plan bylaws as per the Karnataka Town Planning Act – for example too many floors on too small a built up area – and that the GSSS Hospital had broken the fire regulations by locking its emergency exits and that, in the name of public safety, an inspection ought to be conducted by Karnataka Fire & Emergency Services officials at the earliest opportunity. Initially she reacted with mild disbelief, but then he showed her the surgery report. She opened it and started to read, and then she looked skywards.

'Boy, when you get into trouble, it's never ordinary trouble. It is always a bit crazy, nah.'

'What's that supposed to mean?' But he knew that she was blasting him in public interest. It was part of their usual banter.

'I wish you'd start behaving like normal people who face normal problems for your own good, okay? To your credit I have to say I'm impressed you're alive after all you've been through.'

'Me too. But Aunty, I'm simply doing what any *concerned citizen* would do to protect the laws of the land,' argued Hari – and started pulling down the jute sack to reveal his abdominal cuts. 'If you would care to see the physical evidence for yourself.'

'Keep your clothes on in my jurisdiction, okay?' She was very strict.

Soon afterwards, the suspects were led out. First the doctors, who vehemently protested their innocence, then Kolaveri Didi who was subdued. She had surrendered of her own will. Being the nurse in charge of the hospital she had a lot to answer for. When she caught sight of Hari, she got a bit hysterical and claimed that Hari preyed on innocent girls and must be arrested. 'Constable, you're a woman. Do something.'.

'I'm a Sub-Inspector, not a constable,' said Pushpa and turned to Hari, accusingly. 'As a "concerned citizen", what do *you* think I should do?'

The stray dogs were barking at Kolaveri. They knew who the culprit was.

'It's a misunderstanding, Aunty, let me clarify it.' Supported by Triplex and Doc, he approached Kolaveri. He made sure to address her with respect, 'Madam ji, do you remember that night when I was admitted and how I told you that I don't have a birth certificate?'

'What's that got to do with anything?'

'It depends a little bit on what you were doing twenty-eight years ago, madam ji.'

'Me?' she said, aggressively, still not getting it. Or refusing to accept what should have been clear to anybody.

'Yes, do you like movies?'

'What if I do?' She was puzzled. 'Everybody loves a good film with a happy ending.'

'So do I … In fact, one can say that my current incarnation began like a movie. The probable date of my birth, twenty-eight years ago, was stamped on a train ticket issued at Khatpadi Junction, tucked inside my diapers. I was rescued from under the seats of a cinema hall by the cleaning lady. The cinema was called Majestic Talkies.'

Kolaveri's jaw dropped. 'You must be lying.'

'Sorry, madam, but that's the sacred truth.'

'Why would you make such a preposterous claim?'

'Preposterous or not, but that's the way it is.'

'But it is not possible.'

'Yet it isn't impossible either.'

'I refuse to believe you.'

'You do as you like.' He gave her his best smile, the one where every tooth, including the wisdom teeth, showed. 'The fact remains that despite my humble origin, I could have lived happily ever after, if I hadn't been admitted to your hospital.'

She didn't say anything to that. Perhaps she felt guilty.

'Will you at least look at your son?' he said. 'Mum ji?'

Kolaveri turned to Pushpa, 'Please, take me to jail, Sub-Inspector.'

She was led into one of the waiting police vehicles and didn't look back.

'Bye-bye and all the very best,' he called after her. He would have wished Kolaveri to know that he wasn't going to make any specific allegations against her. Forgive and forget, it was all within the family now. And if one's mum sold one's kidney then what to do?

'What was that all about?' asked Pushpa.

'Hard to explain, Aunty.'

'Then do me a favour and don't even try, okay? I'd say you've done enough good deeds for the day, okay,' Sub-Inspector Pushpa thought aloud.

Later in his office, Hari lay on the cot, busy recovering, but he kept hearing stories about what happened at the twin hospitals.

Plenty of journalists came to interview him and his status as a hero was re-established and grew exponentially until he appeared to be the greatest private investigator in town. Not that he made any money out of it.

He pointed out in all the interviews that he couldn't even afford to hire a secretary. One of the interviews was even headlined thus: 'The Boss without a Secy'. Another, a tabloid, had got it all wrong: 'Bluru's Liver-Less Hero misses Heroin'. Nevertheless, he hoped that the message would get through to the intended recipient. There was little else he could do.

The hospital was temporarily closed, pending investigation, and all the staff had been suspended – now and then he wondered if Diamond was still reading local newspapers about local detectives, or if she had left town … then he'd never experience happiness again. Triplex, Gaadi and Doc dropped in daily, making their best to cheer him up.

'We're real heroes now,' said Triplex who had scored some weed and was puffing away, letting his dreams run wild.

Gaadi had parcelled non-veg fare for Hari, because he felt one should eat meat to cure a meat wound. Doc was talking about the need to get better cameras for undercover surveillance work.

'This case was largely solved thanks to my equipment,' he claimed. 'One could even say that the camera footage saved your life, Majestic.'

Triplex said, 'I also saved his life. I've always said that I'd take a bullet for him. One day I'll do it, too, mark my words.'

'I saved him most,' said Gaadi. 'If I hadn't been there, the loser would have been lost in the drain in the first place and there would have been no case to solve.'

Hari suspected his colleagues may have had a few valid points between the three of them, but on the whole he felt they exaggerated their own importance – because as everybody knew, he was the biggest hero. Then again, he didn't want to argue, so he decided to agree that everybody was equally as much a hero and that they had solved the case together. Doc was eager to get a new case to sink his teeth into.

'We should start working again. How about cyber crime?' Doc thought aloud.

He, of course, didn't know that Hari had worked as an online scammer in the past, so to cover his tracks Hari quickly said, 'We don't have a branch in Nigeria yet.'

'Why are you so negative? You know, the weed dealer recognized me from a newspaper snap. He knows I'm a hero. Maybe we should go and arrest him. I'm sure it'll make him proud to meet you, too,' Triplex went on, stoned and on his own track.

But nothing they could say was sufficient to make Hari happy. And they all knew that he was depressed because he missed Diamond.

Of course, it wasn't just that. Hari foresaw a real problem, too. Being a hero didn't automatically mean that you had food on the table and coffee in your mug. The main outcome of Mr Majestic being in the news, was that people came and asked them to solve problems for free – look for escaped pets, stop corruption globally and so on. Pretending to be a hero had been a nice dream, but it was high time to wake up.

In the middle of Triplex's bragging about all the foreign yoga students that he had smoked pot with during his Mysore exile, there was a knock and a special guest appeared at his doorstep.

Gaadi swallowed a mouthful of beer into his windpipe. Triplex smiled a stoned smile. Doc nodded calculatingly, as if he had known all along that this day would come.

Diamond hesitated outside. Instead of her nurse's uniform, she was wearing faded jeans and a chequered blouse. She was fashionable.

'Diamond! What a surprise!' exclaimed Hari.

'May I come in?'

'Sure, would you like coffee?'

'I don't take beverages with caffeine.'

Hari told his friends that it was time for them to go. 'Duty calls.'

'And what's our duty then?' said Triplex, his voice blurry.

'No smoking indoors is duty number one,' said Hari.

'What about drinking?' said Gaadi and burped.

To make his point clear, Hari quoted Gaadi's favourite poet, Michael Jackson, 'Beat it.'

When they were alone, Diamond sat down and looked at him tenderly. He waited for her to declare that she had missed him. Instead she said, 'You dirty boy.'

'I'm sorry.'

He thought whether he should quickly go to the public convenience on the corner and take a bath, but then she said, 'I'm sorry too. How are you feeling?'

'Top class as always.' The mere sight of her was invigorating. Neither of them spoke for a while. He had thought so much about meeting her again and what he should say to her. Finally, he told her that he hadn't a clue about how to shut off the recording device, as many aspects of the investigation had been outside his control. Diamond went on to explain that she had gotten most upset, naturally, when she learnt from the newspapers that

Viral and Philipovich had chased Hari off the roof and left him for dead.

'So I'm the one who should be sorry. I shouldn't have deserted you when you needed me. I felt so bad. When I read about you in the papers, I realized that you're not the kind that gives up, ever. Other people would have compromised,' she said, 'but you – you risked everything to solve the case. Say, I also saw in the papers that you might have use for a secretary.'

'Yeah, I'm thinking business might pick up if I had one. There are quite a lot of applicants.' He did his best to sound cool.

'Would you mind if I gave it a shot? Even though I let you down last time.'

'You?' he exhaled.

She volunteered to see to it that he recovered without complications, give him massage therapy with medicated oils and feed him ghee mixed with Ayurvedic herbal tonics that her father couriered from Kerala and run his office.

It was a good deal, he thought. While she manned the desk, Hari went for the court hearings. One day, Dr Viral was making his statement and he promised that, if he walked free, his hospital would become a truly charitable institution and perform all organ replacement surgeries for free. He even pledged his own organs, saying that he was prepared to donate everything. One surplus kidney was available right there and then.

'I'm at the service of the people,' he said. 'I shall deliver good health care humbly and without complaints.'

At that, there was a stunned silence in the courtroom. Nobody knew what to say to such an audacious claim. But then a lone voice was heard. It was Hari, calling the bluff, 'Boss, I'll take that kidney.'

23

How to Get Back into Business

Happy days were around the corner. Diamond screened his phone calls. One particular caller was sorry. Diamond handed the phone to Hari.

'Oh god, I don't know what to say,' said Kolaveri. Being in charge of the administration at both the hospitals, she had become the main suspect in the racket and the prosecutor called for seven years of rigorous imprisonment. They let her make one phone call from jail. She dialled up her only relative – Hari.

'You want to talk to me?' he said, feeling jolly.

'Yes, in a manner of speaking. I've understood that Diamond has found a new job with you. That's what I wanted to talk to you about.' She straightaway brought up the real reason why she was calling and demanded that Hari do the honourable thing and marry Diamond.

'Oh … oho,' said Hari. 'How come?'

'You've already ruined her reputation.'

'Oho, is it so?'

'But she doesn't want to put any pressure on you. Feels guilty, poor thing, trusts you too much, thinks you'll marry her like that only. But I know you: half of your genes come from your father. I expect you to prove that you're not the wrong man for her, not like your lousy father was to me. Son, all the best, now I've got a jail term to serve.'

'Oho,' said Hari. 'Just one moment, Mum.'

'Be quick. I don't have time to waste.'

He felt that the way she did this, speaking to him over the phone, was too impersonal. 'Wait a nanosecond, Mum. I'll do it on one condition.'

'And what's that?' she said suspiciously.

'That I can come and visit you and we talk face to face.' He held his breath. While he waited for her reply, he started worrying that the call might get cut.

Then she finally spoke.

One word.

'Okay.'

She hung up. Hari turned to Diamond and stared at her for a moment. She raised her eyebrows and smiled at him.

'The head nurse offered me some leads to a mystery I must solve,' he said, slightly pompously. 'I'll be out of office for the rest of the day.'

He walked across to the bus station a block away and took one of the frequent and air-conditioned Volvo buses to Electronic City, a kind of new, gleaming addition attached to the lower parts of good old suburban Bengaluru, as if the town had suffered from a slight attack of appendicitis. The bus reached there after crossing numerous endless flyovers.

Maybe it was all a joke devised by some humoristic town planner, but it was admittedly more than a little bit ironic that these glass towers of the future, that trapped people with their promises of a rich lifestyle, stood practically across the road from Parappana Agrahara Central Jail.

'I went through some bad times.' She had been a nursing student in Vellore, a town in Tamil Nadu with renowned medical educational facilities. Until she got pregnant, that was. She couldn't bring herself to get an abortion, and gave birth to a healthy baby boy. There was a scandal. She upped and left one day back in the 1980s, took the train from the nearest railhead, Khatpadi Junction, to Bengaluru – where she got rid of the child by leaving it behind in a cinema hall.

Rather than looking him in the eye while speaking, she stared at a muddy patch on the concrete wall. She was dressed in a plain white cotton sari. He had asked her if she had had her lunch yet and she'd told him that ragi balls had been served at noon. He asked if the food had been tasty. She had answered that it was what she deserved. He asked if they gave her idli or vada for breakfast. She told him that it was flattened rice on most mornings, but they got veg pulao on Sundays. It took a while to get down to business.

He asked, 'But why did you have to dump me in the cheapest ticket class?' The cheapness of it had resulted in a somewhat low self-esteem.

'If I could afford it, don't you think I'd have kept you? You really don't have a birth certificate?'

'Just that ticket issued at Khatpadi Junction. My adoptive mother used to say that it was where I came from.'

'So you are my son then?'

'Yes, Mum ji, I suppose I must be.'

'You were born in Vellore on Monday in the week before I abandoned you. A Monday child, that's who you are, and I've thought of you every single Monday ever since and whenever I walked past that theatre.'

Thus she had lived her life, almost as if in penance within a few hundred yards of the Majestic Talkies, the scene of her sordid crime.

'It was such a relief when they tore that cinema down. Then this business with … your kidney and liver. I've never done anything but bad to you. I must seem like the worst mother in the world. Oh, I find it hard to, hard to … you're so much like your father. I should have recognized you earlier, when you first came to the hospital. He was about your age when I got pregnant.'

'Oho. Who was he?'

'The wrong man.'

She didn't want to elaborate, but told him how she, after the sad and unfortunate events of her early life, worked for more than a quarter of a century at the Sickly Hospital before it was sold off. She had, of course, been sceptical about the foreign doctor and his globalized schemes, but there was little she could do about it but adjust. She had, with time, become an expert at that. 'They were the owners of the hospital.'

But they didn't own you, Hari thought and couldn't stop himself from rubbing in more guilt, 'You've been abetting them and what did you get for it?'

'A ₹500 bonus above the pay cheque.'

'Was that all?'

'Once they gave me an electric blow-drier.'

'But, Mum, you and I have the same hairstyle and I'm fine without one,' he argued, thinking about the unruly curly wave that always stood out from his head and hers.

'Perish the thought,' she said, remaining partially in denial.

'Show me the drier some time. I'd like to see what my organs were worth in the end.'

'It broke. And no warranty. Smuggled from China.'

'Oho! I nearly died for you to get a broken blow-drier?'

'Accidents happen,' his Mum admitted with a deep sigh. 'I should have known that this would be the result, considering how you grew up without parental guidance.'

He had heard that one before. He tried a smile. 'But now you're here, Mummy ji.'

Hari felt close to her. Only wire mesh separated them. She took a look around herself in the hall, where other prisoners were sitting and talking with their relatives, watched over by gloomy prison guards. 'Yes, now I'm here.'

'What did Didi want?' said Diamond when he reached the office. Climbing the steps was still cumbersome, although he was getting quite used to moving around with the walker.

Once he had caught his breath, he decided to drop the two bombshells, 'The strangest things. You won't believe, but she wanted to tell me that she's my mother and that I must marry you or else.'

'Really?' said Diamond, and he suspected that she had known it for some time.

'There's no doubt and she said it must happen pretty much without delay,' he persisted.

Diamond didn't get shell-shocked at all, but told him to hold his horses while she went through his appointment book, which was the blank side of a paper napkin from Suleiman's Veg Non-Veg Friendly Mess next door. 'But when to find the time for a wedding? You have lots of people wishing to see you. *Deccan*

Herald is featuring you as the hero of the year in their Diwali special, *Crime & Detective* wants to do a pin-up shoot with you in the famous sari get-up, *Times of India* is asking about the names of your favourite cafes and then while you were away speaking to Didi there was a call from one…'

'I'm an important man. They can't always expect to speak to me in person about everything.'

'…Mister Bhascar who wants to see you urgently,' she continued.

'Oho, about what?'

'He'll tell in person. I gave him an appointment for tomorrow, just before lunchtime. Then that woman patient wants to speak to you. The one from the hospital, if you remember.'

'Tell them all I am frightfully busy all of this year.'

'I've told her you'll give her half an hour.'

'Shit.'

'Dirty boy.'

Alice Frankenheimer stepped in, reminding him of the sad fact that he'd be forever deprived of a kidney.

'Hello Harry, so this is where you live?' she said and peered around, nearsighted, as if she was visiting a distant cousin in a strange country.

He liked it that the foreigner had remembered his name. In a manner of speaking, now there were blood ties between the two of them.

'Work,' Hari corrected her. 'It is an honour for my office to have you visit it, madam Alice. Had coffee?'

'Yes, well, some sort of herbal tea, curry-flavoured.'

'Masala chai maybe?'

'Oh, yes, that's what it was. Anyhow, so you're a private investigator. I've never met a real one before. You managed to have the clinic raided and shut down. And I had to check into a hotel for the duration of the court proceedings.' She looked around his office, which had pictures on the walls of practically every movie star and god that mattered in Bengaluru.

'I'm too sorry, madam,' he said. 'Merit or lack thereof from past births often create nuisance in the present.'

'That so?'

'Surprisingly often. So how is our kidney doing?'

'I'm an outpatient at one of the bigger hospitals. They're very good. The kidney keeps sending out these merry signals to me, that it is happy now.' She described an elite hospital that sounded like heaven.

If Hari had checked into such a place to start with, none of this mess would have happened. But in the event, the world had room for both good and bad, he thought, and then he further thought that it was such a deep thought that he should make a mental note of it, and perhaps one day put together a self-help book, a how-to bestseller, and get rich.

'I'm happy to hear that. I was worried that it might feel orphaned.'

'Anyhow I've had time to think about our conversation.' Luckily, she wasn't angry with him and so he didn't have to defend his actions. As a get-well gift she had bought him a foldable wheelchair, with the seat and backrest made of canvas. She opened it up proudly. The two side pieces sprung away from each other, then she checked that all the little hooks snapped in place and locked. She had also carried her scrapbook of photographs. 'Do you remember that place I had asked you about? From the photograph?'

The cogwheels began whirring. 'My bureau and its personnel are at the service of our clients twenty-four-slash-seven, round the year and forever,' he said then because he wasn't the one to refuse possible business. 'Or until the case is closed, whichever happens first.'

'So listen, Harry. I've had a new dream and I'd like you to interpret it.' She sat down on the rickety chair by his desk while he drove around his office in the posh wheelchair.

'But wouldn't a psychiatrist be more appropriate?' he stopped to ask.

'I don't want psychobabble, get enough of that from my own therapist back home in the States, and he doesn't believe in reincarnation anyway, so how can he help me, know what I'm saying?'

'I was just double-checking. Tell me more.'

'Did you or did you not recognize that place in the photo?'

'I have a gut feeling.'

'That's exactly what I hoped to hear. See, I had a most vivid dream, I can't recall when I dreamt such a … like a vision, you know? After the surgery, I've been having these intense nightly out-of-body experiences. The way I look at it is that I have your kidney in me, so I'm part Indian now, part you in fact, know what I'm saying? And therefore I would have to trust you to help me find out the truth about my Indian past, if we are one and the same, isn't it?'

'Provided that you dare to trust yourself to begin with, yes, absolutely.'

'Don't you think that dreams are messages from another dimension?'

Hari's view, based on knowledge gathered from the Internet and other equally trustworthy sources, was that dreams were like reruns of old TV shows, not worth taping because they'd anyway return to haunt you on some other channel. But he wasn't going to disagree with a client. He did the sideways head roll, which could be a yes, no or a maybe, depending on exactly how it was done, but which foreigners generally took to mean whatever they wanted it to mean.

'I'm glad you agree,' Alice said.

'Great minds think alike,' Hari said. 'And then?'

'In my dream, I saw a place I'd never seen before. It was a smaller town; there was a huge Maharajah's palace in its centre, broad avenues and statues at the intersections of the roads. There, near the palace, I saw a vegetable market where women in beautiful saris were shopping for hot curry powder and ripe juicy mangoes. There was a strong emotion within me, as if I belonged to that place – and that's where the photo must have been taken.'

'And then?'

'And that's what I want to know: can you find that place? You're the detective, aren't you?'

'I will have to investigate, but first I need to know if there was any other data that struck you as relevant, website URLs, email ids, phone numbers, license plates?'

'There was this man who was begging, next to a goat.'

'That narrows it down, definitely. Let me see that photo again.'

He drove up to his desk and as he leafed through the scrapbook, she stared out the door at the broken brick wall of the building opposite, a ramshackle hostelry with a bar called Deluxe on its ground floor. With some luck, she'd be too nearsighted to make out what a rundown and dingy address Hari operated from.

The place she was looking for could be almost anywhere, but as Hari thought for a beat or two, it did occur to him that the foreigner had given a more or less accurate description of Mysore, the town neighbouring Bengaluru, where there was a palace that Hari, earlier in his scamming days, used to sell off via eBay to foreigners looking to buy luxury properties in India. Near the palace, there was a traditional marketplace which was frequently featured on TV in exotic food shows by *National Geographic* – and it looked much like what was before him in the photograph. In her dream, Alice had added an erotic touch to it: hot spices, ripe mangoes. It could pass off for the same place, he thought.

'Don't worry madam, I've solved your mystery and I think that based on the clues in your dream, we can pinpoint the location of your previous incarnation to Mysore.'

'You know I had no idea,' she said, dreamily repeating the name of the city, 'My … sore … what strange place names you have in India.'

'It's named after the demon Mahishasura. Nothing strange about that.'

'Is my hometown named after a monster?' she said.

Hari smiled his broadest smile, 'Not to get panic attack, it's just a demon.'

'What's the difference?'

'Demons are not necessarily evil,' explained Hari and ladled it on, 'they're symbols of ignorance and bad mentality. That demon was stomped out long ago by a feminist goddess and has never returned. That is why taking rebirth once in a while in Mysore is so auspicious.'

'You don't say?'

'I do. Ever since Mahishasura was put out of circulation, we celebrate pujas in October to keep demons away, just like we've done last month. And hence, India is completely demon-free right now. Perfect timing for you.'

'How's that?'

'The mystical, seasonal powers will cleanse you after you make your sacrifice.'

'What sacrifice?'

'Don't worry, a sacrifice can be symbolic. Hand over a bearer's cheque to that beggar with the goat, for example.'

'I see … and the beggar with the goat is?'

Hari thought about it for no longer than 0.48 seconds. 'He's connected to your previous life.'

'Do you think so?'

'I never think, I know. Such a dream usually tells us that the man is your very own Daddy. Now he is waiting for your return, to patch up, so to speak, whatever it was that went wrong between the two of you.'

'And what do you think that was?'

'That we shall know when we meet him,' said Hari.

She got excited, 'No kidding! Dad's been dead for ages. But in India, he's alive?'

'To know that for sure, we simply need to go find Daddy and ask him. It is also the easiest thing to do.'

'Easiest, how?'

'Instead of sitting around here trying to second guess, we go to the railway station and take the train to Mysore. I'll come with you because he's unlikely to speak fluent English and I presume you haven't picked up enough Kannada although you've been here for many weeks?' said Hari, sensing that this would give him a good excuse to be out of office when Bhascar came the day after to chop his other leg off. Or whatever punishment it was that his ex-client had planned for him.

'You don't know how grateful I am.'

Hari knew – as usual he had hit the right note there. Most westerners had troubled relations with their daddies and therefore had to go through expensive Freudian counselling. The plan was clear in his mind, he'd get Triplex to go ahead to Mysore, procure a goat or at least some mutton biriyani and dress up as a beggar at the market. But aloud he just said, 'No mention.'

'So when can we go?'

'Tomorrow, first thing.'

'How much do you charge?'

'Hari…' said Diamond, reproachfully.

'A nominal ₹25,000 per day. First three days to be paid in advance. Miss Diamond, would you be kind enough to cancel my appointments for tomorrow?'

'But I've booked…'

Hari waggled his head. Diamond would learn, in due time, that money made the world go round. Hari wanted to be able to offer her a decent salary and pay for a grand wedding. 'Yes, too bad, but I'll be frightfully busy all day I'm afraid. I know, there was that businessman who had called – Bhascar something – I just can *not* see him tomorrow. Or the day after, for that matter, so kindly refer him to Total Safety Security Agents & Services which is a reputable firm in Rajaji Nagar on the far side of the railway lines.'

The next day, Hari left office early to be on the safe side and picked Alice up after she was done with her daily check-up at the hospital. It was one of the modern hospitals in town, a sound looking structure, and Hari thought that next time he broke a leg he'd go there. He'd just have to take out that health insurance first. And everything would be fine.

24

How to Achieve an Even Happier End

This time it was as if his eyes were filming everything that went on, no spy camera wired to his earlobes. Love was an emotion confirmed by itself, Hari thought philosophically, and needn't be documented, perverted or tattooed onto one's body.

The long celebratory season between the October pujas and Diwali in November was totally auspicious for something like a wedding party. Kolaveri was out on parole since Hari refused to testify against her. She had walked straight into his life, set up the date for the wedding and arm-twisted Pandit Pundit, Hari's astrologer, to second her decisions with indecipherable horoscope charts.

Earlier that week, she made several trips with Diamond to Commercial Street, a shopping area crammed with everything you needed from waterproof socks to bridal garments. They bought an exquisite sari and got a tailor to stitch a tight choli of raw silk and lace that hugged her … her … frontal body parts.

Diamond was ravishing when she alighted from AC Gaadi's autorickshaw outside the magistrate's office. Overcome by an uncharacteristically romantic mood, Gaadi had nicked a red carpet from some MG Road hotel so that she wouldn't have to step onto the potholey road. A flotilla of rickshaws stood dead still, every driver saluting and Hari's eyes zoomed.

And zoomed.

For various reasons, Hari was unable to pinpoint his own religion since his mother was reluctant to talk about his father. She herself was a Hindu. Diamond was, of course, a Nagaland style Christian from her father's side, while her mother was a proper Mappilah Muslim. So already three world religions had entered the picture.

To save money and time and to simplify things, Hari had toyed with the idea of getting his uncle to forge a marriage certificate, but it occurred to him that this was one time he should rather not fake it. Therefore, it was decided that they'd have a civil marriage and sign the documents before a magistrate. The only homemade document was the birth certificate. After all, one can't present a used train ticket from Khatpadi Junction before a magistrate.

There were not many 'I do' declarations or trick questions or existential problems at a secular wedding, just a legal statement to be read out and a paper to be signed, so to be on the safe side they went in a cortege of rickshaws to visit temples, churches, sacred banyan trees and Sufi dargahs to seek the relevant blessings, and then, finally properly wedded, they held a small reception, with coffee being served in the alley behind the office.

Of all people, Hari was most surprised to see Bhascar there and his instinct told him to run. The coffee miller's face and throat were scarred in the telltale pattern of Underdog's incisors. Then Hari relaxed when he saw that Bhascar had brought Apsara and his daughter along, dressed up in nice synthetics in radioactive colours.

'I'm sorry about what happened,' Bhascar said. 'The broken leg and all. I overreacted and I'm too much sorry for all the inconvenience I have caused you.'

'Yes boss,' said Hari. 'There's been lots of misunderstandings hereabouts lately.'

'Thanks for everything, Majestic.'

'Like what?'

'Let me tell you, on this auspicious occasion, that marriage should be built on trust. All was great until I became suspicious. Only myself to blame.'

Hari waited for the 'but'. But there was none. He was shell-shocked, as if two bombs had exploded on either side of his skull, for he had never ever before heard a man admit that he had been wrong. Something remarkable had happened in Bhascar's head. Then Bhascar grinned, 'It's going to be a boy.'

'Oho, that's too lovely,' said Hari who suddenly understood.

Of course, ultrasound solved every problem. Bhascar whispered, 'She told me she was already pregnant when she met that man at the hotel. She only went for the magic session to ensure that it was going to be a boy.'

One had to admit that Apsara was smart. Women often were smarter than men. Then Bhascar handed over an envelope. 'For your honeymoon.' He shook Hari's hand. 'May you be the father of thousands of sons.'

'Thanks boss, but one gent will be enough,' said Hari. 'And one lady.'

The envelope contained a voucher for a week's stay at a coffee plantation in the nearby hills – almost like the Himalayas but 23,500 feet lower – and tickets for the air-conditioned Volvo bus that was due to depart at midnight. Bhascar had arranged through his brother in the coffee growing business for Hari and Diamond to spend their honeymoon in a planter's bungalow-turned-guest house. Bhascar added, 'You might want to take the Volvo bus tonight itself. My dear friend Deadlyappa happened to hear about your auspicious moment and even though I told him to forget and forgive, he says he has to follow the rules of conduct.'

'Oho, and those are?' said Hari, although he was fluent in goonda talk.

'He has to bash your other kneecap with a cricket bat. But to show his goodwill, he agreed to wait until after your wedding night.'

'I see,' said Hari.

Diamond's parents had defied their taboos and taken an overnight video bus from Kerala – still afraid of the train. Hari's uncle, OK Mamool, sat like a wilted cactus in the wheelchair that Hari had handed down to him as a welcome-home gift. Hari himself had started walking with an elegant rosewood cane. The ceremonies at the reception were marked by a great deal of creative improvisation, as Kolaveri and Pandit Pundit colluded to fashion a set of rituals such as cutting a birthday cake with candles for all the birthdays Hari had spent without a mother.

Diamond threw her bridal bouquet over her shoulder and it hit Triplex who shrieked 'No way!' and chucked it on until it got stuck on the thumb of Sub-Inspector Pushpa who gave off a scream too, 'I'd rather burn in hell than remarry', and waved her arm until Doc got it in the eye – he had been eyeballing one of Diamond's nursing school batchmates and this was taken to be a sign of something.

To add to his joy, Hari noticed, while sitting on a cushion before Pundit who was reading out sacred formulas in the chaos, that his Mum had polished her nails. She was wearing a rather showy gown straight out of a time warp, last having been fashionable in the 1980s when her life had been put on hold. She had also removed her spectacles and the curl in her hair was extra curly, as if she'd put it in curlers the evening before.

But mostly, Hari's eyes were filming Diamond. Under a light pink pallu veiling her eyes, she was smiling so hard that her chipped front tooth showed. Her golden nose stud had a bigger diamond in it, dazzling in the sunlight, bought by Hari from one of the gem dealers in Basavanna Temple Street, one of Anchepete's best bazaars for jewellery shopping, where Hari had pawned his Enfield Bullet. He loved her more than he loved his motorcycle. He had also promised her a modular kitchen as a wedding gift, once his economy was in order. God willing.

Gradually a chant spread through the crowd of guests: 'Kiss the bride!'

Hari felt awkward but Diamond didn't – she practically sucked the lower half of his face off. For some reason, Hari had expected the whole experience to dissolve, like in films, when the lips were about to meet, and the screen faded into a song-and-dance sequence or an intermission. But none of that happened.

After the kiss everybody cheered and Sub-Inspector Pushpa remarked casually, 'Won't arrest you for public indecency this time.'

Unlike during the disastrous launch of the detective agency, this time there were strict prohibitory orders under Section 144 clamped on the CD Road area immediately surrounding the Puncherwallah Complex and so no free hooch. Sub-Inspector Pushpa had heard that Uncle Mamool was coming out of rehab and she didn't want any riots or damage to public property. Uncle behaved. As a precaution, he had been handcuffed to the wheelchair.

Everything was under control for the first time during Hari Majestic's current reincarnation.

Later, and since the family was such a new constellation, it was decided that they all – Hari and Diamond, Mamool and Kolaveri, and Hari's in-laws Amor and Gracie, born Begum Halwali – get to know each other over supper at Status Family Restaurant & Bar. It was an old Karwar style eatery on 1st Cross Road and one of the poshest messes hereabouts. This was where Uncle Mamool used to bring Hari and his adoptive mother in the good old days, thus making it the nicest restaurant Hari could think of.

In the background, a popular film song played, 'Please don't mistake me…' They hogged nicely. But Diamond's parents missed the foods of Kerala. Much fresher fish. Hari should come. Hog the famous mussels, fruits of the rocks. They'd feed him plump.

'Only one family member missing,' said Amor, who was getting more and more talkative.

'Who's that?' asked Diamond sharply.

'Your father-in-law,' he said.

Instantly, the conversation died. Kolaveri stood up from the table to pay the bill. They dispersed, Diamond's parents were taking the bus back to Kerala, unwilling to spend a night in their city of dread, and Gaadi drove them to the private bus company office near Tank Bund Road. Diamond went to her paying guest room to pack.

In the CD Road office, Kolaveri administered sleeping pills to Mamool so that he wouldn't freak out while he slept alone on the office cot. Hari helped her stuff the pills in. He couldn't stop himself from bringing up the inauspicious topic, now that the mood anyway had been ruined. He understood her view – he pointed out – for after all, life is a forward movement and if you always looked backwards you'd walk into a lamp post.

'But what about Papa?'

She shrugged: it was a shrug Hari had seen in the mirror when he spoke to himself.

'Mummy, I think we need to talk.' He wanted her to stop regretting everything. The hardest part for Hari was to deal with a top-heavy mum who materialized out of nowhere to perform all the maternal duties she had shunned since he was one week old, making up for lost time with twenty-eight years' worth of soap opera compressed into a single telecast. But generations clash, that's in their nature.

Kolaveri twiddled a button on her time warp gown. Even now she believed that the bad genes of Hari's father lived on in the son.

He pronounced, 'Pride's a character trait that ought to be neither nourished nor cherished.' It was one of Pandit Pundit's wisdom mantras that Hari did his best to follow, not always successfully. Bravely, he went on, 'It takes two to tango, but only one to do the bharatanatyam.'

'It's a long story,' she started.

'I'd love to hear it nevertheless. There's time before my Volvo. What happened?'

'Nothing.'

'Something must have been there or I wouldn't be here.'

She cried for the next ten minutes or so, the mascara running down her cheeks, while words tumbled out. 'He was a handsome popcorn seller. He was good at cutting a funny joke. Imitated big film stars. Always made me giggle. I told him my dream was to afford tickets to a movie now and then. One day, he borrowed a scooter and we went to Khatpadi Junction where nobody recognized us, to watch a film. I remember he told me about his plan to become famous. I guess you don't take so much after him when I think about it.'

Hari patted down the wavy curl on top of his head, self-consciously.

'I missed the hostel curfew. So I had nowhere to go. He offered to share his bed with me and one thing led to another. That's that.'

'Oho, simply he dumped you?'

'No, he left money for the abortion before he jumped on the bus.'

Just to confirm, Hari said, 'But you didn't get an abortion?'

'I hoped until the ninth month that he'd come back. But when he didn't, could I have stayed there? And I couldn't go home to Dakshinapathapalli – it would have ruined my parents' reputation. So I bought a one-way ticket to Bengaluru. Although this was a modern city, I couldn't apply for jobs and tell them I was a single mother … and you'd have starved. So while I was watching a film, I decided that since I myself enjoyed it so much, I'll leave you there, and then somebody like me, who loves happy endings, would find you and care for you. It was the only decent thing to do. Often I wondered what had happened to you, if you had become a superstar, so I watched lots of films looking out for somebody who bore a resemblance to … your father.'

'Hmm,' said Hari who had been cleaned out along with the other garbage left under the cinema seats.

'Listen Hari … so strange that you have a name, I never gave you one … you're young and your life is uncomplicated – but when you grow older you'll understand that there are impossibilities. We face them daily.'

'But where's Daddy now?'

Kolaveri sobbed as she rummaged in her handbag – 1980s' model – and pulled out a lacquer box with a tiny lock on it. 'Since memories can be so painful I threw away the key. But I never got rid of the box. I thought … that if I ever met you and you turned out to be a civilized boy, I'll give it to you.'

'What's inside?'

'I don't remember. I think beard shavings left in the sink, bits of nail cuttings from one time when I did pedicure for him. I had this idea ... it's silly, you'll laugh, but I believed that if I lock parts of him into the box, he'd return to me as if by magic. I used to be such a fool.'

'Don't, Mummy,' he said with a doglike stare. It gave him such pleasure to call her 'Mummy' and declare his love. 'At least there is one person who cares for you.'

Kolaveri's deluge of tears switched itself off as abruptly as a monsoon shower. 'Has Pundit said anything to that effect?'

Hari put together the clues – it had all been in plain sight, nail polish, curlers and Pundit's obliging efforts at getting him married – and then he said the only thing possible:

'It is possible.'

Everybody deserved a second chance.

•

Although Hari, by and large, had fun on his wedding day, he had been eager for it to get over and for the honeyweek to begin.

There was the Volvo waiting to take them away on a 260 kilometre journey to the Western Ghat hills. He packed fast – he didn't own many material objects apart from his new Nokia Asha phones, one red, one golden – but from his shelf of leftover touting equipment he dug out, to be on the safe side, seven 'Do Not Disturb' signs in case the guest house didn't provide any. They'd have a lot of quality time to kill.

They reached the following morning. It was the smallest and quaintest hill station and it overlooked a mountain range with coffee plantations in every direction.

The air tasted funny until Hari figured it was the unadulterated flavour of oxygen. The plantation bungalow guest house was at the outskirts and they had a room with a double bed. Hari put up a 'Do Not Disturb' sign on the door. Unused to being married, he couldn't rest after the journey but watched Diamond's face, a bit crumpled up because she was chewing the pillow, but oh-so-sweet in the light that seeped in through the sun film.

In the day, they sat on the veranda. He drank freshly ground filter coffee, she had locally made passion fruit juice.

During the night they heard frogs, cicadas and elephants. When the next dawn broke, they saw a valley with light creeping across jungly ridges and down craggy gorges, the morning sun dispersing the clouds that had run aground.

The following day, they ventured out to catch the sunset at a park where the Maharajah traditionally used to sit in a pavilion and enjoy the view while his enemies were being thrown off the cliff, or multitasking as it is called nowadays. Tourists were offloaded there from buses to clap when the disco fountain erupted with water splashing in colours and Hari dreamt that he and Diamond could retire to a town like this, offer services to visitors, sell treks and conduct coffee plantation walks.

The sunset was spectacular. Each time the fountain erupted in a rainbow to a booming disco beat, Diamond and Hari cheered until their voices got hoarse. They bought puffed rice with chillies from a vendor with a pushcart. Diamond asked for extra spice. She was too cute. A small schoolboy was lugging his satchel full of textbooks back from evening tutorials and when he saw them, the tourists, he called out, 'Good evening Uncle and Aunty! Have you finished your coffees?'

Hari and Diamond smiled at each other in bewilderment and then burst out laughing. Hari said, 'Home in Bengaluru they just ask "had coffee". Blunt, huh?'

After sunset, Diamond enjoyed herself thoroughly in the Main Bazaar. Small shops, run by balding men with ear-to-ear moustaches, sold homemade rice wines, organic honey, coffee powder – without chicory if one asked nicely – and the first time Hari smelt the fresh coffee from Sridevi Coffee Mill, he got such a caffeine rush that he spent nights without sleep.

They also found a shop where everything was forty rupees. Diamond had cashed in her last salary cheque and so she purchased household items, plastic buckets and mugs for their bathroom, coffee glasses and handy things; they also picked up gifts for the agency staff, a set of tiny screwdrivers for Doc, a vanity mirror for Triplex and a switchblade for Gaadi.

For their last supper, they ate mutton balls in a canteen that had a nice view and Diamond sipped on a brandy mixed with hot water and cloves, while Hari ordered his usual fresh lime soda, sweety-salty, with a drop of gin. An extra small drop of gin, to keep his liver sober. A micro-peg you might say. They toasted.

For a while Diamond was engrossed in a detective novel she had found in a second-hand bookshelf, it was called *The Iron Bra*, while Hari read his emails on his phone. It was slow going with the weak signal and tiny screen.

'So ... Majestic,' she suddenly said. 'Have you been here before?'

'No.'

She studied him with those lie detector eyes of hers. Her hands still had the henna patterns from the wedding, they were only darker now. 'But you know this town pretty well – what to shop, where to eat ... how are you so familiar with everything, then?'

He couldn't help bragging. 'Wikitravel, sweetmeats, memorized all entries.'

'Are you making that up?' She didn't trust him.

He worked out a quick defence strategy. 'Honey, you're going to get three correct answers before I ever think of lying again. The answer to your first question is: No. Next question?'

'So you never took a girlfriend here?'

'No.'

'Will you lie to me after you've answered my last question?'

She caught him there with a trick question. Hari knew from Triplex that girls sooner or later always wanted to know what they ideally shouldn't; it was in the nature of things. Many of Triplex's affairs had ended that way.

'Are you uncomfortable?' she said after a few seconds.

'No, I'm fully impressed. Nobody could hide anything from you.'

'I should be a detective, no?' She smiled and showed her chipped tooth, the one that always made his heart race.

'Yes, honey, absolutely.'

'Women today can do everything that men can do plus more – there are business women, police women, women soldiers, female lawyers, Lady Gaga and Mata Hari, and then we also give birth.'

He presumed it was the brandy talking. Refreshing her drink should soften her. 'Another small peg, honey?'

'Don't sound so patronizing. Women make much better detectives, if you think about it. We have intuition, we're careful, we observe people because we're interested in them and notice more.' She shut her eyes. He had been focusing on the mutton balls so when she popped the question it was too late. 'What's the colour of my eyes?'

When he looked up his gaze was met by her tightly shut eyelids. Knowing that 97 per cent of all Indians had brown eyes, Hari said, 'They are brown, of course.'

'Dark or light brown?'

'Coffee-coloured?'

'*Ha!* You have no clue. Are you aware that in China secretaries have to master martial arts and almost any Chinese woman can kill with her bare hands? Do you know that in New Delhi alone there are half a dozen detective agencies exclusively staffed by women? *Right*, people don't expect a woman to be sent out to spy on them, perfect cover, no, they believe us to be motherly so they are more likely to confide their secrets. A woman can talk a man into doing almost anything. It is a natural gift we have,' she said in that melodious, honeyed, sugary, jaggery-coated voice of hers.

He absorbed it. 'And then what? Some men are born stupid.'

'That's true Hari, and you think for example that you proposed marriage to me, didn't you? But what you didn't know was that I had already, long before that, decided my answer. Do you think I didn't first check you out? If you don't hire more women to work as field agents and undercover operatives, I predict your agency is going to collapse within a month. Look at your staff, maniacs the whole bunch.'

His resistance was lame. 'I would worry about your safety if you worked in the field.'

Outside the restaurant windows, the chilly hill air was filled with stars. She said, 'You know, hubby, I'd love to kick in a few doors.'

'Yes, honey,' he said without hesitation, because he knew then that he'd lose every fight against her, 'you could be our company health officer.'

His best offer.

'I'm disappointed. I'll tell you what I'm going to be: Deputy Director of Diamond Majestic Investigations,' she said. The diamond stud in her nose gleamed in the night. 'With annual increments, bonuses for especially dangerous and impossible assignments, and a view to a promotion within the initial contract period, and make that brandy a double.'

'Honey, you deserve nothing less.' He knew who the boss was. 'Anything else, sweety?'

'How about an expense account?'

The End?

Acknowledgements

No humans or animals were harmed during the writing of this book. However, fiction and fact is often mixed up and, by gullible readers, sometimes even believed to be one and the same; so let me point out that this novel is a work of the imagination and therefore it goes without saying that all the bad characters and shady locations in it are more or less totally made up. No doubt about it. If any real life character bears any likeness to the nefarious bad characters described on these pages, one sincerely hopes that they mend their ways before the police comes to arrest them under the relevant sections of the penal code. Also, please do not attempt any of the crazy stunts described in this book – none of it will work in real life.

I sometimes doubt I could write very much at all without my supporters, consisting of people who offer their valuable time and advice. Thanks to Anjum Hasan, always my first reader; also thanks to Shruti Debi at Aitken Alexander Associates Literary Agency, Pranav Kumar Singh and Sushmita Chatterjee at Pan Macmillan India and Pelle Andersson at Ordfront Publishing

House (Stockholm) for believing in Hari Majestic. I'd also like to thank *Crime & Detective Magazine* (New Delhi) in general for being such a great source of literary inspiration. Furthermore, Hari and I owe thanks to Nandita Aggarwal, Petter Lidbeck, Dr Kavery Nambisan, Naresh Narasimhan, Srinath Perur, Jan-Erik Pettersson, Pradeep Sebastian, Nat Sobel, Eshwar Sundaresan, Vinayak Varma and Stellan Wahlström for various suggestions on how to make things better, and the Shanghai Writers' Association for putting me up as a Writer-in-Residence one autumn in China, during the writing of a first draft of this novel. Then, of course, last but not least, I'd like to thank all of you who read and enjoy good books.